Books by Kasey Michaels

The Passion of an Angel
The Secrets of the Heart
The Illusion of Love
A Masquerade in the Moonlight
The Bride of the Unicorn
The Legacy of the Rose

Published by POCKET BOOKS

KASEY MICHAELS

The PASSION of AN ANGEL

POCKET STAR BOOKS

New York London Toronto Sydney Tokyo Singapore

This book is a work of fiction. Names, characters, places and incidents are products of the author's imagination or are used fictitiously. Any resemblance to actual events or locales or persons, living or dead, is entirely coincidental.

An *Original* Publication of POCKET BOOKS

 A Pocket Star Book published by POCKET BOOKS, a division of Simon & Schuster Inc. 1230 Avenue of the Americas, New York, NY 10020

ISBN: 0-671-79342-X

First Pocket Books printing October 1995

10 9 8 7 6 5 4 3 2

Cover art by Karen Kluglein

Printed in the U.S.A.

To CZ—My Personal Angel

Oh woman! lovely woman! Nature made thee
To temper man: we had been brutes without you;
Angels are painted fair, to look like you;
There's in you all that we believe of heav'n,
Amazing brightness, purity, and truth,
Eternal joy, and everlasting love.

Thomas Otway

PROLOGUE

COVENANT

There was a sound of revelry by night,
And Belgium's capital had gather'd then
Her beauty and her chivalry, and bright
The lamps shone o'er fair women and brave men.
A thousand hearts beat happily; and when
Music arose with its voluptuous swell,
Soft eyes look'd love to eyes which spake again,
And all went merry as a marriage bell.
But hush! hark! a deep sound strikes
like a rising knell!

George Noel Gordon,
Lord Byron

Never promise more than you can perform.

Publilius Syrus

Look at that one, would you, Daventry? Think she's ripe for the plucking? Ready to lie down in the soft grass outside and give comfort and solace to a soldier about to face the French horde? Or am I totally bosky, and seeing willing beauty in anything in skirts?"

Banning Talbot, Marquess of Daventry, who was more than two parts drunk himself, leaned forward to look in the direction of Colonel Henry MacAfee's rudely pointing finger. "Harriet Mercer? God's teeth, man, make your move. Steal a kiss, or more, with my blessings." Even as he spoke, Miss Mercer could be seen deserting the dance with her red-coated escort, the two of them making for the doorway, and the darkened garden beyond. "Whoops! Yoicks, and away! Pick another one, old man. Lord knows this great barn of a place is packed to the rafters with willing females."

MacAfee settled his shoulder against the pillar the two men were sharing, having strategically propped themselves alongside the dance floor more than a hour earlier, within good ogling distance of the young ladies going down the dance, and directly in the path the servants had to traverse between the pouring of drinks and the serving of those same libations to Lady Richmond's thirsty guests. The choice had been a sterling one, as there had been no dearth of either shapely ankles or chilled wine glasses orbiting their small outpost in the midst of what appeared to be a grand celebration of idiots.

Daventry drained his glass, deftly depositing it on a passing tray and scooping up a full one all in one fluid motion. "You know something, MacAfee," he commented to his friend—if their casual acquaintance of the past three days, combined with their bond of doing their best to drink themselves under the table together, could be considered a basis for friendship, "I've been thinking."

"Never a good thing, thinking," MacAfee said, sighing in a sorrowful way. "Try not to do it myself. Not with Boney running riot just outside our doors."

The Marquess smiled, running a hand through the thick, startling silver-on-black mane of hair that looked so out of place above his sparkling green eyes and youthful, unlined face. "But that's who I've been thinking of, MacAfee. Boney. I believe I've just now stumbled upon a way to defeat him. We'll just gather up this lot of sots here, our beloved Iron Duke included, and collectively *breathe* on the man. Brandy. Port. Wine. Canary. Why, the fumes will be enough to evaporate the man and his entire Old Guard!"

Colonel MacAfee giggled into his wineglass, an action that caused him to inhale a bit of its contents, then snort them out his nose, a trick Daventry considered top-drawer, which only proved he was perhaps a bit too well-to-go for his own good.

Not that he didn't have good reason to be seeking solace in the bottom of a glass. There was a battle coming, and coming soon. A possible apocalypse, if the rumors running rampant through the ranks were to be believed, with the evil Bonaparte being sent down to ignominious defeat at the hands of the Duke of Wellington, Blücher, and the rest of the allies.

And it would be Wellington, Blücher, and the allies who would take all the credit, garner all the glory, while the foot soldiers, the cavalry, and the junior officers did all the fighting, all the dying. Daventry was heartily sick of war, weary of the bloodshed, the screams, the sacrifice of individual lives in the name of the common good.

If only Bonaparte had been kept on his island. Had it been so bloody difficult to act the jailer to one defeated emperor? Apparently so, or else the man would still be penning wildly abridged histories in his journal rather than mounting an army and marching, even now, on a hastily assembled resistance and its hangers-on of society misses and brainless fops who believed the proper preparation for battle was a whacking good full-dress ball.

"Petticoat alert!" MacAfee exclaimed, nudging Daventry in the ribs as he inclined his head toward a blonde vision just coming down the dance with the Duke of Brunswick. "Hold me back, good milor'. I feel an imminent seduction coming over me."

The Marquess felt the skin over his cheekbones tightening as he resisted the urge to dash the contents of his glass in the colonel's leering face, for MacAfee had inadvertently reminded Daventry of the other reason he was finding the wine so irresistible tonight. "The young lady is Miss Althea Broughton, and you will kindly remove your lascivious gaze from her person," he warned in crushing accents, painfully aware that the word "lascivious" had damn near knotted his tongue. "She is spoken for."

"But not by you, I'll wager," MacAfee said, affably transferring his good-natured leer to a rather lackluster little pudding of a debutante who giggled, then attempted a reproving frown, and lastly blushed to the roots of her tightly curled hair. "Do I sense a story? And more to the point, is it a depressing story? Don't think I want to hear it if it's going to bring me down. Low enough, thank you, what with worrying about m'sister."

"There's no story, MacAfee," the marquess said, bowing with exaggerated stiffness as Miss Broughton looked in his direction, then moved on. The beauteous Miss Broughton. The one great love of his life, Miss Broughton. The woman who had two years previously turned his proposal of marriage down flat, Miss Broughton. The woman betrothed these last nine months to a peer so wealthy it took two straining valets to heft his purse into his pocket, Miss Althea Broughton. "And why are you worrying about your sister?" he asked, eager to change the subject, when if the truth were told he couldn't have cared a fig if MacAfee's unknown sister was locked in a tower and besieged by fire-breathing dragons.

"Prudence?"

Daventry, who had been watching Miss Broughton's progress out of the corner of his eye, swiveled his head to the left and repeated, aghast, *"Prudence?* Would that be a name or an affliction?"

Henry MacAfee grinned—he had a really pleasant grin, actually—and shook his head. "Ghastly name, ain't it? But she's the light of my life, Daventry. My Pru. My Angel." His smile faded abruptly and he took another long drink of his wine. "Poor, innocent baby. It's criminal how she is forced to live, Daventry. Criminal!"

"I'm sure," the marquess agreed absently, for his attention was now on the Duke of Wellington, who seemed to be deep in conversation with a subaltern who had just entered the ballroom at a near run, holding his sword as it threatened to swing wide from his waist, which would most certainly have caused the nearby dancers to invent a few new steps to the country dance in progress.

"It's true, my friend. You have no idea, none at all," MacAfee continued as a wave of whispers washed across the ballroom. "We're orphans, you know, and forced to live on the charity of our grandfather, Shadwell MacAfee—and the damndest pinch-penny ever hatched. Not that he's my guardian, or Pru's either, now that I've reached my majority. Are you listening to me, Daventry? Devil a bit, what's going on?"

Daventry held up a hand, silencing the colonel. "Listen! Do you hear it? By God, I think the drums are beating to arms! Blücher must have failed!"

MacAfee threw down his glass, which shattered into a thousand pieces at his feet. "No! Not yet! I haven't come this far just to—Daventry. Daventry!" he repeated, grabbing hold of the marquess's arm. "Listen

7

to me! If you're right, if we're to fight tomorrow, you have to promise me something tonight."

Daventry watched as the circle of uniforms around Wellington deepened and a few of the ladies, those closest to the Duke, cried out in alarm, two of them swooning into nearby arms. "Not now, MacAfee," he warned, shaking off the man's hand as he willed himself back to sobriety. "We have to get to the Place Royale, remember? That's where all the men have been warned to assemble at the first word of Bonaparte's march."

"I said, *not yet!*" MacAfee nearly shouted, so that Daventry turned to look at the man more closely, seeing the nearly feverish sparkle in the man's eyes, the ashen gray of his cheeks.

"What is it?" the marquess asked, wondering if the younger man was going to be sick, or break out in tears. After all, he barely knew the fellow. He had laughed with him these past few days, drunk with him, but he didn't know him. Not really. "Come on, man, you've seen battle before this. Think of your men."

MacAfee shook his head. "I can't help it, Daventry," he said, lifting a shaking hand to his forehead. "And I'm not a coward, I swear it. But I have had a dream, a premonition if you will. I'm going to die in this battle, my lord. I have already seen my death."

"You've seen the bottom of too many wineglasses, you mean," Daventry chided, trying to raise the man's mood while the musicians attempted to strike up another tune even as the ballroom turned from a small island of enjoyment to a morass of confusion and high emotions. "We're all afraid."

"No, no. This is more than fear," MacAfee said

8

fiercely, reaching into his uniform jacket and extracting a folded paper. "I'm going to die. I've even accepted it, save that I didn't get to bed any of these willing creatures tonight. My only regret is my sister, my little Angel. Leaving a sweet child like her alone with our grandfather? How can I do that and die in peace? And so I have come up with a solution."

Daventry eyed the unfolded paper with a wary eye. "I'm beginning not to like this, Colonel," he said quietly, knowing he was honor-bound to listen to the man. That would teach him to drink with near strangers!

"I've been watching you these past weeks, Daventry," MacAfee continued in a rush. "You're a responsible sort, if a bit stiff—at least until tonight. Make a tolerably pleasant drunk you do, too, not that I haven't had to help you along a bit, tipping the servants to be sure your glass stayed full as I dangled Miss Broughton under your lovelorn nose. You'll be a perfect guardian for my Angel. Take the sweet little love under your wing, so to speak. See that she's financially freed of Shadwell, given a season years from now, when the time is right—all that drivel that's so important to a female. And she won't give you a moment's trouble, I swear it."

If Daventry hadn't been sobered by the prospect of the coming battle, MacAfee's words served to push away the last of the wine-induced fog that blurred his senses. "Allow me a moment to reflect, if you will, MacAfee? You have *investigated* me these past weeks? You have deliberately sought me out in the last few days, ingratiated yourself to me—and all so that I might take your young sister as my ward if something were to happen to you? And that paper you're holding? That would be some sort of legal transference of guardianship?"

"Already signed by the Iron Duke himself," the colonel said, his grin now appearing much more calculating than friendly. "Old Arthur seemed very affected by my concern for my dear little Angel. He also said that you're the best of men, and plump enough in the pocket since that rich-as-Croesus aunt of yours stuck her spoon in the wall, so that you could take on a half-dozen wards without putting even a small dent in your fortune."

"I could kill you for this, MacAfee," Daventry drawled as he took the paper and read it, "except that any such personally satisfying action would definitely saddle me with your unfortunate sibling. And if I don't agree to sign, I'd be sending a distraught man into battle, wouldn't I—or at least that's what Wellington will believe. You're a singularly vile, clever bastard, Colonel, and I believe I detest you almost as much as I do myself for having fallen prey to your scheme. What's your sister's name again? Patience?"

"Prudence," MacAfee corrected him as he nearly succeeded in pushing Daventry into hysterical laughter by extracting both a pen and a small ink pot from his pocket. "My little Angel. You'll adore the little mite, truly. And as I said, she won't give you a moment's worry. Sweet, biddable, amenable—trust me in this, a true Angel. Just make sure she has an allowance to keep her fed until she's grown, that's all I ask. You don't even have to see her until she's ready for her season. Just leave her in Sussex for now. Honestly! Then," he added, pushing the quill at the marquess, "I can die in peace, having served king and country with the last drop of my soldier blood."

"Oh, cut line, you shameless bastard. And don't worry your head about dying, MacAfee," the marquess said, using the colonel's back as a makeshift desk as he scribbled his name and title at the bottom of the paper. "I don't intend to let you out of my sight until the battle is over—at which point I shall personally blacken both your eyes and rid you of several of those lying, conniving teeth!"

BOOK ONE

COMMITMENT

Tis true, your budding Miss is very charming,
But shy and awkward at first coming out,
So much alarm'd, that she is quite alarming,
All Giggle, Blush; half Pertness and half Pout;
And glancing at Mamma, for fear there's harm in
What you, she, it, or they, may be about,
The nursery still leaps out in all they utter —
Besides, they always smell of bread and butter.

George Noel Gordon,
Lord Byron

CHAPTER 1

Might shake the saintship of an anchorite.
George Noel Gordon,
Lord Byron

Prudence MacAfee, Prudence MacAfee," the Marquess of Daventry grumbled beneath his breath as he reined his mount to a halt on the crest of a small hill that overlooked the MacAfee farm. "Was there ever a more pru-dish, miss-ish name, or a more reluctant guardian?"

He lifted his curly brimmed beaver to swipe at the sweat caused by the noon heat of this early April day, exposing his silvered black hair to the sun, then turned in the saddle to squint back down the roadway. His traveling coach, containing both his valet, Rexford, and his sister's borrowed companion, the redoubtable Miss Honoria Prentice, was still not in sight, and he debated whether he should await their arrival or proceed on his own.

Not that either person would be of much use to him. Rexford was an old woman at thirty, too concerned with the condition of his lily-white rump as it was bounced over the spring-rain rutted roads to be a supporting prop to his reluctant-guardian employer. And Miss Prentice, whose pinched-lips countenance could send a delicate child like Prudence MacAfee into a spasm, was probably best not seen until arrangements to transport the young female to London had been settled.

Damn Henry MacAfee for being right! And damn him for so blatantly maneuvering his only-cursory friend into this ridiculous guardianship! He'd heard of the colonel's bravery in battle, up until nearly the end, when his second horse had been shot out from under him and he had disappeared. If Daventry could have found Henry MacAfee's body among the heaps of nameless, faceless dead, he would have slapped the man back to life if that were possible. Anything to be shed of this unwanted responsibility.

What was he, Banning Talbot, four and thirty years of age and struggling with his bachelorhood, going to do with an innocent young female? He had asked precisely that question of his sister, Frederica, who had nearly choked on her sherry before imploring her brother to never, *ever* repeat any such volatile, provocative question in public.

It wasn't as if he hadn't already lived up to his commitment. Having been wounded himself at Waterloo, which delayed his return to London only in time to discover that Frederica, his only relative, was gravely ill, the marquess had still met with his solicitor to arrange for a generous allowance to be paid quarterly to one Miss Prudence MacAfee of MacAfee Farm. Contrary to what Henry MacAfee had said, he knew he should at least visit the child, but he buried that thought as he concentrated on taking care of his sister.

He had directed his solicitor to explain the impossibility of Daventry's presence at the Sussex holding for some time, and had then dragged out that time, beyond his own recovery, beyond any hint of danger remaining in his sister's condition. Past the Christmas holidays, and beyond.

He would still be in London, enjoying his first full season in two years, if it weren't that Frederica, who had always been able to draw her older brother firmly round her thumb, had put forth the notion that she would "above all things" adore having a young female in the house whom she could "educate in the ways of society and pamper and dress in pretty clothes."

Why, Frederica would even pop the girl off, when the time came to put up the child's hair and push her out into the marriage mart. Her brother, Frederica had promised, would have to do nothing more than host a single ball, present his ward at court, and, of course, foot the bills which "will probably be prodigious, dearest Banning, for I do so adore fripperies."

It all seemed most logical and personally untaxing, but Daventry still was the one left to beg Grandfather MacAfee to release his granddaughter, and he was the one who would have to face this young girl and explain why he had left this "rescue" of her so late if the grandfather was really the dead loss Henry MacAfee had described to him. But the colonel had said an allowance would be enough to get on with, so the marquess had chosen to ignore his *real* responsibility—until now.

Daventry jammed his hat back down onto his head, cursed a single time, and urged his mount forward and down the winding path to the run-down looking holding, wondering why he could not quite fight the feeling that he was riding into the jaws of, if not death, great personal danger.

No one came out into the stable yard after he had passed through the broken gate, or even after he had dismounted, leading his horse to a nearby water trough, giving himself time to look more closely at his surroundings, which were depressing as the tepid lemonade at Almack's.

Daventry already knew that Henry, born of good lineage, had not been all that deep in the pocket, but he had envisioned a small country holding: neat, clean, and genteelly shabby. This place, however, was a shambles, a mess, a totally inappropriate place for any gentle young soul who could earn the affectionate name of "Angel."

Beginning to feel better about his enforced good deed—rather like a heavenly benefactor about to do a favor for a grateful cherubim—the marquess raised a hand to his mouth and called out, "Hello! Anybody about?"

Several moments later he saw a head pop out from behind the stable door—a door that hung by only two of its three great hinges. The head, that of a remarkably dirty-looking urchin, was rapidly followed by the remainder of a fairly shapeless body clad in what looked to be bloody rags. As a matter of fact, the urchin's arms were blood-red to the elbows, as if he had been interrupted in the midst of slaughtering a hog.

"I suppose I should be grateful to learn this place is not deserted. I am Daventry," Banning Talbot said, wondering why he was bothering to introduce himself.

"Daventry, huh?" the youth repeated flatly, and

obviously not impressed. "And you're jolly pleased to be him, no doubt. Now get shed of that fancy jacket, roll up your sleeves, and follow me. Unless you'd rather stand put there, posing in the dirt, while Molly dies?"

The first shock to hit Banning was the bitingly superior tone of the urchin's voice. The next was its pitch—which was obviously female. Lastly, he was startled to hear the anguished cry of an animal in pain.

He knew in an instant exactly what was afoot.

Leaving sorting out the identity of the rude, inappropriately clad female to later—and while lifting a silent prayer that she couldn't possibly be who he was beginning to believe she might be, or as old as she looked to be—the marquess stripped off his riding jacket, throwing it over his saddle. "What is it—a breech?" he asked as he tossed his hat away, rolled up his sleeves, and began trotting toward the stable door.

Banning bred horses at Daventry Court, his seat near Leamington, and had long been a hands-on owner, raising the animals as much for his love of them as for any profit involved. The sound of the mare in pain was enough to turn a figurative knife in his gut.

"I've been trying to turn the foal," the female he hoped was not Prudence MacAfee told him as they entered the dark stable and headed for the last stall on the right. "Molly's already down, and has been for hours—too many hours—but if I hold her head, and talk to her, you should be able to do the trick. I'm Angel, by the way," she added, sticking out one blood-slick hand as if to give him a formal greeting,

19

then quickly seeming to think better of it. "You took a damned long time in remembering that I'm alive, Daventry, but at least now you might be of some use to me. Let's move!"

Silently cursing one Colonel Henry MacAfee, who had already gone to his heavenly reward and was probably perched on some silver-lined cloud right now, sipping nectar and laughing at him, Banning forcibly pushed his murderous thoughts to one side as he entered the stall and took in the sight of the obviously frightened, tortured mare. Molly's great brown eyes were rolling in her head, her belly distorted almost beyond belief, her razor-sharp hooves a danger to both Prudence and himself.

"She's beginning to give up. We don't have much time," he said tersely as he tore off his signet ring and threw it into a mound of straw. "Hold her head tight or we'll both be kicked to death."

"I know what to do," Prudence snapped back at him as she dropped to her knees beside the mare's head. "I'm just not strong enough to do it all myself, damn it all to blazes!"

And then her tone changed, and her small features softened. She leaned close against Molly's head, crooning to the mare in a low, singsong voice that had an instantly calming effect on the animal. She had the touch of a natural horsewoman, and Banning took a moment to be impressed before he, too, went to his knees, taking up his position directly behind those dangerous rear hooves.

There was no time to wash off his road dirt, and no need to worry about greasing his arms to make for an easier entry, for there was more than enough blood to make his skin slick as he took a steadying breath and plunged both hands deep inside the mare, almost immediately coming in contact with precisely the wrong end of the foal.

"Sweet Christ!" he exclaimed, pressing one side of his head up against the mare's rump, every muscle in his body straining as he struggled to turn the foal. His heart pounded, and his breathing grew short and ragged as the heat of the day and the heat and sickening sweet smell of Molly's blood combined to make him nearly giddy. He could hear Prudence MacAfee crooning to the mare, promising that everything was going to be all right, her voice seemingly coming to him from somewhere far away.

But it wasn't going to be all right.

Too much blood.

Too little time.

It wasn't going to work. It simply wasn't going to work. Not for the mare, who was already too weak to help herself. And if he didn't get the foal turned quickly, he would have been too late all round.

The thought of failure galvanized Banning, who had never been the sort to show grace in defeat. Redoubling his efforts, and nearly coming to grief when Molly gave out with a halfhearted kick of her left rear leg, he whispered a quick prayer and plunged his arms deeper inside the mare's twitching body.

"I've got him!" he shouted a moment later, relief singing through his body as he gave a mighty pull and watched as his arms reappeared, followed closely by the thin, wet face of the foal he held clasped by its front legs. Molly's body gave a long, shuddering heave, and the foal slipped completely free of her, landing heavily on Banning's chest as he fell back on the dirt floor of the stall.

He pushed the foal gently to one side and rose to his knees once more, stripping off his waistcoat and shirt so that he could wipe at the animal's wet face, urging it to breath. Swiftly, expertly, he did for the foal what Molly could not do, concentrating his efforts on the animal that still could be saved.

Long, heart-clutching moments later, as the new-born pushed itself erect on its spindly legs, he found himself nose to nose with the foal and looking into two big, unblinking brown eyes that were seeing the world for the first time.

Banning heard a sound, realized it was himself he heard, laughing, and he reached forward to give the animal a smacking great kiss squarely on the white blaze that tore a streak of lightning down the red foal's narrow face.

"Oh, Molly, you did it! You did it!" he heard Prudence exclaim, and he looked up to see Prudence, still kneeling beside the mare's head, tears streaming down her dirty cheeks as she smiled widely enough that he believed he could see her perfect molars. "Daventry, you aren't such a pig after all! My brother wrote that you were the best of his chums, and now I believe him again."

As praise, it was fairly backhanded, but Banning decided to accept it in the manner it was given, for he was feeling rather good about himself at the moment. He even spared a moment to feel good about Henry MacAfee, who had been thorough enough in his roguery to smooth the way for Prudence's new guardian.

This pleasant, charitable, all's well with the world sensation lasted only until the marquess took a good look at Molly, who seemed to be mutely asking his assistance even as Prudence continued to croon in her ear.

I know. I know. But, damn it, Molly, his brain begged silently, *don't look at me that way. Don't make me believe that you know, too.*

"Step away from her, Miss MacAfee," Banning intoned quietly as the foal, standing more firmly on his feet with every passing moment, nudged at his mother's flank with his velvety nose. "She has to get up. She has to get up now, or it will be too late."

Prudence pressed the back of one bloody hand to her mouth, her golden eyes wide in her grimy face. "No," she said softly, shaking her head with such vehemence that the cloth she had wrapped around her head came free, exposing a long tumble of thick, honey-dark gold hair. "Don't you say that! She'll get up. You'll see. She'll get up. Oh, please, Molly, please get up!"

Banning understood Prudence's pain, but he also knew that the mare was already past saving, what was left of her life oozing from her, turning the sweet golden hay she lay in a sticky red. He couldn't let Prudence, his new charge, fall into pieces now, not when she had been so brave until this point.

"Please leave the stall, Miss MacAfee," he ordered her quietly, but sternly, already retracing his steps to fetch the pistol from his saddle.

She chased after him, pounding on his back with her small fists, screaming invectives at him that would have done a foot soldier proud, her blows and her words having no impact on him other than to make him feel more weary, more heartsick than he had done when Molly had looked up at him with a single, pleading eye.

He took the long pistol from its specially made holster strapped to his saddle and turned to face his young ward. He didn't like losing the mare any more than she did, but he had to make her see reason. To do that, he went on the attack. "How old are you?" he asked sharply.

She paused in the act of delivering yet another punch to his person. "Eighteen. I'm eighteen!" she exclaimed after only a slight hesitation, her expression challenging him to treat her as a hysterical child. "Old enough to run this farm, old enough to live on my own, and old enough to decide what to do with my own mare!"

He held out the pistol, which she stared at as if he might shoot her with it. Yet she still stood her ground. He admired her for her courage, but he had to do something that would make her leave.

When he spoke again, it was with the conviction that what he said would serve to make her run away. "All right, Miss MacAfee. Prove it. The mare must be put down. She's hurting, and she's slowly bleeding to death, and she shouldn't be made to suffer any more than she already has. Show me the adult you claim to be. Put Molly out of her pain."

He didn't know anyone could cry such great, glistening tears as the ones now running down the girl's filthy cheeks. He hadn't known that the sight of a small, quivering chin could make his knees turn to mush even as his heart died inside him.

He found himself caught between wanting to push her to one side and go to the mare and pulling Prudence MacAfee hard against his chest and holding her while she sobbed.

"Oh Christ, I'll do it," he said at last, just as she surprised him by raising a shaky hand and trying to grasp the pistol. The sight of their two hands, stained with the blood of the dying mare, each of them clasping one end of the pistol, brought him back to his senses. "I never meant for you to do it. And I'm sorry it has to be done at all. I'm truly, truly sorry."

"Go to blazes, Daventry," she shot back, sniffling as she yanked the pistol from his hand and began slowly walking toward the stable, her step slow, her shoulders squared, her chin high. Dressed in her stained breeches, and without the evidence of her long hair to prove the image wrong, she could have been a young man going off to his first battle, terrified that he might show his terror.

"Prudence," he called after her. "Angel," he said when she failed to heed him. "You don't have to do this."

She kept walking, and he wondered why he didn't chase after her, wrest the pistol from her hand, and have done with it. But he couldn't move. He had put down his own horse when he was twelve, a mare he had raised from a foal, and he knew the pain, was familiar with the anguish of doing what was for the best and then living with the result of that fatal mercy. Molly was Prudence's horse. She was Prudence's pain.

The stable yard was silent for several minutes, so that when the report of the pistol blasted that silence, Banning flinched in the act of sluicing cold water from the pump over his face and head. His hands stilled as his head remained bowed, and then he went on with his rudimentary ablutions, keeping his head averted as Prudence MacAfee exited the stable, the pistol still in her hand. She returned the spent weapon to him, then placed his signet ring in his hand.

He felt uncomfortable in her presence—stripped to the waist and dripping wet—hardly the competent London gentleman who had come to rescue an innocent child from an uncaring grandparent. He felt useless, no more than an unwelcome intruder, a reluctant witness to a pain so real, so personal, that his intrusion on the scene could almost be considered criminal.

And, with her next words, Prudence MacAfee confirmed that she shared that opinion.

"If you'll assist me with settling the foal in a clean stall, I would appreciate it, as I can't seem to get it to move away from . . . from the body," she said stonily, and he noticed that her cheeks, although smudged, were now dry, and sadly pale. "And then, my lord Daventry, I would appreciate it even more if you would remount your horse and take yourself the bloody hell out of my life."

26

CHAPTER 2

A mere madness,
to live like a wretch and die rich.

Robert Burton

Banning sat beneath an ancient, half-dead tree, his waistcoat and jacket draped over his bare shoulders as he rested his straightened elbows on his bent knees, and watched his traveling coach pull into the stable yard.

The forbidding expression on his lordship's face gave pause to the driver who had seemed about to venture a comment on his employer's ramshackle appearance, so that it was left to the valet, Rexford, to exclaim, within a heartbeat of descending from the coach and rubbing at his afflicted posterior in a surreptitious way, "Milord! You are a shambles!"

"Noticed that, did you? You can't know how that comforts me, as I've always thought you a veritable master of the obvious," Banning said, remaining where he was as Miss Honoria Prentice joined Rexford in the dirt-packed stable yard, her purse-lipped countenance wordlessly condemning her surroundings and her mistress's brother, all in one dismissive sweep of her narrowed, watery blue eyes.

"Lady Wendover most distinctly promised me that you had sworn off strong drink since Waterloo, my lord," Miss Prentice intoned reprovingly as she touched the corners of her thin lips with her ever-present handkerchief. "I see now that she is not as conversant with your vices as she has supposed. Now, where is the child? Heaven help us if she has seen you in this state. Such a shock might scar an innocent infant for life, you know."

Banning, feeling evil, and more than a little justified in seeking a thimbleful of revenge on his sister's condemning companion, reached into his pocket, drew out a cheroot, and stuck it, unlit, between his even white teeth. "Miss MacAfee has retired to the house after our brief meeting, Miss Prentice. She rushed off without informing me of her intentions, but I am convinced she is even now ordering tea for her guests, fine young specimen of all the feminine virtues that she is. Why don't you just trot on up there and introduce yourself? I'd wager she'll fall on your neck, grateful to see another female."

"I should imagine so!" Her chin high, her skirts lifted precisely one inch above the dirt of the stable yard, Miss Prentice began the short, uphill trek toward the small, shabby manor house, leaving Rexford behind to hasten to his master's side, clucking his tongue like a mother hen berating her wandering chick.

"The coachman is even now unloading the valise holding your shirts, my lord, as well as my supply of toiletries. Good God! Is that blood on that rag which was once your second-best shirt? You've been fighting, my lord, have you not? I knew it. I just knew it! You were set upon by ruffians, weren't you? Oh, this vile countryside! If we return to London alive to tell of this horrific journey it will be a miracle!"

"If we can discover a way to travel back to London, dead, to relate our tale, I should be even more astonished, Rexford," Banning said as he allowed his valet to assist him to his feet and divest him of his waistcoat and jacket for, in truth, he wanted very much to stick his arms into a clean shirt.

"Now stop fussing, if you please," he ordered, "and restrict yourself to unearthing a clean shirt so that I can present myself at the front door of the house in time to watch our dear Miss Prunes and Prisms Prentice being tossed out on her pointed ear. At the moment, the thought of that scene is the only hope I have of recovering even a small portion of my usual good mood."

"Sir?" Rexford questioned him, looking up from the opened valise, a fresh neck cloth in his hands. "I don't understand."

"Give it a moment, my good man, and you will."

A few seconds later, as Banning allowed his valet to button his shirt for him, true to his prediction, Miss Honoria Prentice's tall, painfully thin figure abruptly reappeared on the narrow front porch of the manor house a heartbeat before the echoing slam of the house's front door reached their ears.

"Ah, dear me, yes," the marquess breathed almost happily, snatching the neck cloth from Rexford's hands and tying it haphazardly about his throat, "she's an angel, all right. Unfortunately, however, I believe she is also one of Lucifer's own. Come along, my long-suffering companion, we might as well get this over with all in the same afternoon. As I awaited your arrival, I thought I saw some hint of activity just beyond that stand of trees. Let us go and search out this grandfather, this Shadwell, and discover for ourselves what sort of fanciful lies the dear, dead Colonel MacAfee wove about this last member of his family."

"Over there? Into that stand of trees? With you?" Rexford, who prided himself in never having been farther from London than Richmond Park—and then only this once, and under duress—swallowed hard, his Adam's apple bobbing up and down above his tightly tied cravat. "There will be bugs, milord. Spiders. Possibly even bees. I do not at all care for insects, milord, as well you know. Better I should remain here, repacking the valise, and praying for a swift remove to the nearest inn."

Banning looked down his nose at the quivering, shivering valet. "You know, Rexford," he commented entirely without malice, the unlit cheroot still clamped between his teeth, "if you didn't possess such a fine hand with the pressing iron, and if the mere thought of finding a suitable replacement were not so fatiguing, I'd dismiss you right now and leave you here to discover your own way back to civilization."

"Coming right along behind you, milord!" Rexford exclaimed, skipping to catch up with his rapidly striding employer as the two crossed the yard and entered the stand of trees.

The marquess's eyes had just begun to become accustomed to the shade beneath the cooling canopy of leaves when he found himself stepping out into the sun once more, so that at first he disbelieved what he was seeing. It took Rexford, nearly fainting into his employer's arms, to convince Banning that his eyes were not deceiving him.

Not that he could be censured for wondering if he had succumbed to hallucination, for the sight that greeted them in the small, round clearing, an area completely encircled by trees, was enough to give any man pause.

There were two people inhabiting the clearing, one of them buried up to his chin in dirt, the other standing nearby, waving flies away from the first with an ancient, bedraggled fan of ostrich plumes. The latter man Banning dismissed as a servant, but the other—with his bald-pated, no-eyebrows, gargantuan, bulbous head resembling nothing more than a gigantic maggot with raisin-pudding eyes—commanded his full attention.

"Let me guess," he drawled, removing the cheroot from his mouth and taking a step closer, then retreating as a vile stench reached his nostrils. "You'd be Mister Shadwell MacAfee, wouldn't you? And you're a disciple of dirt baths, I presume—a practice of which I've heard, but never before witnessed. Water is an anathema to those who indulge, as I recall, and as my sense of smell verifies. First the Angel who is nothing of the sort, and now the grandfather who is more than described. I'm beginning to believe Colonel Henry MacAfee had a pleasant release, dying in battle."

"Eh? What? Did someone speak? Hatcher! I told you not to pile the dirt so high. It's in m'ears, damn your hide, so that now I'm hearing things." Shadwell MacAfee twisted his large, hairless head from side to side, using his chin to plow a furrow into the dirt in front of him, then looked up at Banning, who grinned and waved down at him. "By God! I'm not hearing things after all. Hatcher! Dig me out! We've got company."

"Hold a moment, Hatcher, if you please," Banning suggested quickly. "If your employer is as naked under that dirt as I believe him to be, I would consider it a boon if you were to leave him where he is for the nonce. Although we all might consider it a small mercy if you could wave that horsefly away from his nose."

MacAfee's cackling laugh brought into evidence the sight of three rotting teeth, all the man seemed to have left in his mouth, and the marquess nodded his silent approval as Rexford moaned a request to vacate the area before he became physically ill, "if it please you that I cast up my accounts elsewhere, milord."

"You'd be Daventry, wouldn't you, boy?" MacAfee bellowed in a deep, booming voice once he had done with chortling. "Have to be, seeing as how nobody ever comes here unless they're forced. Been waiting on you for nearly a year now, you know. Damned decent of you to send that allowance, not that Pru would have known what to do with a groat of it, which is why she hasn't seen any. Only waste it on what she calls 'improvements,' anyways. Bank's the only place for money, I keep telling her. Put it somewheres where it can grow. Pride m'self on not having spent more'an hundred pounds a year these past two score and more years. So, you thinking of taking my Pru away?"

Banning believed he could hear the beginnings of a painful ringing in his ears, and he was suddenly thirsty for what would be his first drink of anything more potent than the odd snifter of brandy since Waterloo.

"I'd just as soon leave her," he answered honestly, brutally banishing the memory of those huge, heart-tugging tears he'd witnessed not two hours previously, "but I have promised your late grandson that I would do my possible to care for his sister. As *my* sister, Lady Wendover, has agreed to give the child a roof over her head until it is time for her Come-out, I have come to collect her, not knowing that she is already grown, and must therefore be whipped into some sort of shape to partake in this particular season. Would you care to give me odds on my sister's chances of success?"

MacAfee laughed again, and Banning turned his head, reluctant to take another peek into the black cavern of the man's mouth. MacAfee continued, "I'd as soon place odds on her chances of turning Hatcher here into a coach and four. My wife had the gel to herself for a half-dozen or so years before she kicked off, teachin' her how to talk and act and the like, but the child's gone wild since then. Now, go away, Daventry. Been standing in this pit long enough, I have, and it's time for my man to dig me out. Wouldn't want any worms taking a fancy to m'bare arse, now would we?"

"Not I, sir," Banning answered coldly, turning on his heel, already planning to mount a frontal assault on the manor house, believing that, of the two unusual creatures he had encountered in the past hours, Prudence MacAfee seemed far and away the more reasonable of the pair. "After all, being a bit of an angler, I hold some faint affection for earthworms. Good-day, sir."

Prudence was a mass of conflicting emotions. Sorrow over Molly. Anger over the injustice of it all. Fear caused by the appearance of the man Henry had named as her guardian. Outrage over her childish displays of sorrow, anger, and fear.

How dare the man arrive in the midst of tragedy? How dare he offer his assistance, then utter the damning words that had forced her into taking up that pistol, walking back into Molly's stall, and . . .

Who had asked him, anyway? She certainly didn't want him here, at MacAfee Farm, or anywhere else vaguely connected with her life.

All right, so Henry had picked the man. Picked him with some care, if she had read between the lines of her brother's explanatory letter to her correctly. Well, wasn't that above all things wonderful? And she was just supposed to go along with this unexpected change in plans, place herself in this Marquess of Daventry's "sober, responsible, money-heavy hands?"

When Hell froze and the devil strapped on ice skates! Prudence shouted silently as she stuck her head out the kitchen door—checking to make sure Lizard-woman wasn't hovering somewhere about and ready to spit at her with her forked tongue again—then bounded across the herb garden, on her way to the stable yard once more.

She had bathed in her room, shivering as she stood in a small hip bath and sponged herself with harsh soap and cold water before changing into a clean facsimile of the shirt and breeches she had worn earlier, but she hadn't done so in order to impress the high-and-mighty Marquess of Daventry.

Indeed, no. She had only done it to remove the sickly sweet stench of Molly's blood from her person before tending to her mare's foal. She didn't care for spit what the marquess thought of her. Some responsible man he was, not so much as sending her a bent penny to live on, and then showing up here at MacAfee Farm, which was the last thing she had ever supposed he would do. Oh yes, Henry had picked himself a sure winner this time, he had. And pigs regularly spun their tails and flew to the moon!

Prudence slipped into the stable, keeping a careful eye on the two men standing beside a traveling coach not twenty yards in the distance, wondering if either one of them had the sense they were born with, to leave the horses in traces like that, and headed for the foal's stall, armed with a make-shift teat she had loaded with her brother's recipe for mother's milk.

"Hello again, Miss MacAfee," the Marquess of Daventry said from a darkened corner of the stall, and Prudence nearly jumped out of her skin before rounding on the man, a string of curses—more natural to her than any forced pleasantry—issuing, almost unthinkingly, from between her stiff lips.

"Please endeavor to curb this tendency toward profanity, Miss MacAfee," Banning crooned, pushing himself away from the rough wall of the stall, "allowing me instead to continue to labor under the sweet delusion that you are but an unpolished gem. I had first thought to join you at the house, but quickly decided you would be more likely to show up here. How comforting to know that I am beginning to understand you, if only a little. Now, seeing that I am to be denied any offer of refreshment or other hospitality, perhaps you will favor me with some hint of your agenda? For instance, when will you be ready to depart this lovely oasis of refinement for the barbarity of London?"

Prudence felt her jaw drop, but recovered quickly,

brushing past the man to offer the teat to the foal who, thankfully, began feeding greedily. "You actually intend to take me to London?" she asked, looking over her shoulder at the marquess, and wondering how on earth a man with silver hair could look so young. It had to be the eyes. Yes, that was it. Those laughing, mocking green eyes.

"I'd much rather leave you and all memory of this place behind me, but I have given my word to act as your guardian, even though it was wrenched from me under duress. Therefore, Miss MacAfee, yes, I intend for you to remove with me to London, preferably before I have to endure more than one additional interlude with dearest Shadwell."

Prudence grinned in momentary amusement. "Met m'grandfather, did you? I'd have given my best whip to see that. Was he already in the dirt, or were you unlucky enough to catch him in the buff? He's a wonder to see, you know. Especially in this last year, once he decided to pluck out all his hair in some new purification ritual he read about somewhere. He's bald as a shaved peach. Not a single hair left anywhere on his body. No eyebrows, nothing on his brick-thick head, nor on his—"

"You will find, Miss MacAfee," the marquess broke in just as she was about to do her best to shock him into a fit of apoplexy, "that I do not permit infants the luxury of attempting, however weakly, to make a May game of me. Now if you don't wish to be turned over my knee, I suggest you dislodge that chip of resentment from your shoulder and give your full attention to impressing me with your finer attributes. I shall give you a moment, so that you may cudgel your brain into discovering at least one redeeming quality about yourself that I might employ to soothe my sister once she recovers from the swoon she will surely suffer the first time you open your mouth in her presence."

"My brother told me you were a high-stickler," Prudence grumbled, scratching at an itch on her stomach that could not be denied. "Very well, my lord, I'll behave. But I won't like it. I won't like it above half."

"Which, you might notice, is neither here nor there to me, Miss MacAfee. Now, when will you be ready to leave? I don't believe it will take Miss Prentice long to pack up your things, if your current attire is representative of your wardrobe. Freddie will enjoy dressing you from the skin out, or so she told me. I do hope she has sufficient stamina, for she can have no idea of the height and breadth of the consequences of her impulsive commitment."

"I liked you worlds better when you were helping me with Molly," Prudence said, pushing her lower lip out in a pout. "Now you sound like some stern, impossibly stuffy schoolmaster, if my brother's letters from school about his teachers are to be used as a measure of puffed-up consequence. And I go nowhere unless this foal goes with me—and until Molly is taken care of."

"And what, exactly, do you propose to do with Molly?" the marquess asked, pulling a cheroot from his pocket and sticking it in between his teeth, exactly the way she was wont to jam a juicy bit of straw between hers. He looked very much the London gentleman again, as he had when first she'd seen him, and if he made so much as a single move to put a light to the end of the cheroot while they stood inside the stable, she'd toss a bucket of dirty water all over his urban sophistication.

"I intend to bury her, my lord," Prudence declared flatly, praying her voice wouldn't break as she fought back another explosion of tears, "and I shall do so, if it takes me a week to dig the grave."

"A burial?" Banning Talbot's grin, when it came, was so unexpected and so downright inspired, that Prudence felt herself hard put to maintain her dislike for him. "Ah, dear Angel, I believe I know precisely the spot, and with our work already about half done for us."

It didn't take more than a second for Prudence to deduce his meaning. "Shadwell's pit?" Her large golden eyes widened appreciably as she contemplated this sacrilege. "He used it today, which means he won't avail himself of it again until Friday, but—oh, no, it's a lovely, marvelously naughty thought, and Molly would be sure to like it there, among the trees . . . but no. I can't."

"I've been sending you a quarterly allowance since I returned from the continent, Miss MacAfee. A very generous allowance meant to soothe my conscience for not having leapt immediately into a full guardianship. An allowance I understand you have yet to see?"

Prudence breathed deeply a time or two, remembering having to say goodbye to their only household servant save the totally useless Hatcher six months earlier because she could not pay her wages, remembering the leaks in the roof, the "small economies" her grandfather employed that invariably included large sacrifices on her part. Why if she could have afforded to send for the local blacksmith to assist her when Molly had first gone down, the mare might be standing here now, with her foal.

"I saw two men standing beside your traveling coach," she said, reaching for the shovel she used to muck out the stalls. "If we all dig together, we can have the grave completed by nightfall."

CHAPTER 3

*Diogenes struck the father
when the son swore.*

Robert Burton

The Marquis of Daventry would have racked up at a country inn if there had been one in the vicinity, but as the single hostelry near MacAfee Farm had burned to the ground some two months previously, and because the marquess had no intention of remaining in the area above a single night, he had dragged a quivering, weeping Rexford into the chamber allotted them by Shadwell MacAfee once the old man had waddled back to the manor house, his huge body swathed in what looked to be a Roman toga.

The chamber could have been worse, Banning supposed—if it had been located in the bowels of a volcano, for instance. Or if the bed had been of nails, rather than the ages-old, rock-hard mattress he had poked at with his fingertips, then sniffed at with his nose before ordering Rexford to take the coach and ride into the village to procure fresh bedding to replace the gray tatters that once, long ago, may have been sheets.

Banning then positioned a chair against the door, as there was no lock and he knew he might be prompted to violence if Miss Prentice barged in during his bath to continue her litany of complaints concerning her own bedchamber, a small box room in the attics, last inhabited by three generations of field mice.

Stripped to the buff, the marquess stood in front of the ancient dressing table, scrubbing himself free of the grime and stench associated with first digging a large pit, then employing an old field gate hitched to his coach horses as a funeral barge for the deceased Molly.

Rexford had, of course, cried off from the actual digging of the grave, citing his frail constitution, his propensity to sneeze when near straw, and his firm declaration that returning to the vicinity of MacAfee's dirt bath would doubtless reduce him to another debilitating bout of intestinal distress.

That had left Banning, the coachman, Hatcher (who had been bribed into silence and compliance with a single gold piece), and—although he did his best to dissuade her—Miss Prudence MacAfee to act as both grave diggers and witnesses to Molly's rather ignoble "roll" into the pit and subsequent interment.

Prudence hadn't shed a single tear, nor spoken a single word, until the last shovelful of dirt had been tamped down, but worked quietly, and rather competently, side by side with the men. Only when Banning had been about to turn away, exhausted by his exertions and badly craving a private interlude with some soap and water, did she falter.

"I'm going to miss you so much, Molly," he heard her whisper brokenly. "You were my only friend, after my brother. I'll take good care of your baby, I promise, and I'll tell him all about you. One day we'll ride the fields together, and I'll show him all our favorite places . . . and let him drink from that fresh stream you liked so well . . . and . . . and . . . oh, Molly, I love you!"

Banning was so affected by this simple speech, this acknowledgment that a horse had been Prudence's only friend since her brother had died, that he forgot himself to the point of placing an avuncular, comforting arm around the young woman's shoulders, murmuring, "There, there," or some such drivel articulate men of the world such as he were invariably reduced to when presented with a weeping female.

The memory of the fact that this sympathetic gesture had earned him a swift punch in the stomach before Prudence ran off across the fields did nothing to improve Banning's mood as he dressed himself in the clothes Rexford had laid out for him, pushed the chair to one side, and exited his chamber, intent on locating some sort of late supper and his ward, not necessarily in that order.

He walked down the hallway, past the faded, peeling wallpaper, skirting a small collection of pots sitting beneath a damp patch on the ceiling above them, and was just at the stairs when he espied a sliver of light beneath a door just to his left. Already knowing the location of MacAfee's chamber, Banning deduced that his ward was secreted behind this particular door, probably plotting some way to make his life even more miserable than it was at this moment—if such a feat were actually possible, for the Marquess of Daventry was *not* a happy man.

His knock ignored, he impatiently counted to ten,

then pushed open the door that lacked not only a lock, but a handle as well. He cautiously stepped into the room, on his guard against flying knickknacks, and espied Prudence MacAfee sitting, her back to him, at a small desk pushed up against the single window in the small chamber.

"Love notes from some local swain, I sincerely hope not?" he inquired as he approached the desk to see that she was reading a letter, a fairly thick stack of folded letters at her left elbow. "Freddie has visions of someday making you a spectacular, society-tweaking match with one of the finest families in England. But then, my sister was always one for dreaming."

Prudence swiftly folded the single page she was reading and slipped it back inside the blue ribbon that held the rest of the letters. "Knocking is then not a part of proper social behavior, my lord?" she asked, turning to him with a sneer marring her rather lovely, golden features. "My late Grandmother MacAfee, who all but beat the social graces into my head until the day she died, would have most vigorously disagreed."

"I did knock, Miss MacAfee," he corrected her with a smile, then added, "but as *my* tutor's teachings of etiquette did not extend to dealing with bad-tempered, rude termagants foisted upon one by conniving, opportunistic brothers, I then just pushed on, guided more by my inclinations than any notions of what is polite. Now, tell me, if you please. Does anyone in this household *eat?*"

Prudence opened the top drawer of the small writing desk and slid the packet of letters inside before turning back to Banning, a mischievous grin he had already learned to distrust lighting her features.

"Grandfather eats nothing but goat milk pudding and mutton, my lord. If you are interested, I am sure Hatcher can serve you in the kitchens. As you may have noticed as you barged into the house, there is no longer any furniture in either the drawing or dining rooms. For myself, I have no appetite tonight, having just buried my horse."

"You're enjoying yourself immensely at my expense, aren't you, Miss MacAfee?" Banning asked, not really needing her to answer. "Perhaps another visit from the redoubtable Miss Prentice is in order. She is most anxious to mount a inspection of your wardrobe before we depart for London in the morning."

"Let her in here again and I'll probably shoot her. Besides, I'm not going," Prudence stated flatly, turning her back on him once more.

Resisting the impulse to grab hold of the young woman by her shoulders and shake her until her teeth rattled, Banning restrained himself enough to utter through his own tightly clenched teeth, "Then, Miss MacAfee, may I presume we may number lying among your other vices? Or was I incorrect in assuming that when you gave me your word you would leave with me after Molly was settled, you were intending to keep true to that word?"

She jumped up from her chair, still most distressingly, disturbingly dressed in a man's shirt and a patched pair of breeches that clung much too closely to her hips, and rounded on him in a fury.

"You ignorant jackanapes!" she exploded. "Do you really believe I would *want* to stay here? That anyone with more brains than a doorstop would want to stay here? My God, man, I *detest* the place! This damned pile is falling down around my ears, I haven't a penny for repairs to either the house or the land, my grandfather is a mean, miserly, to-let-in-the-attic nincompoop who hasn't bathed since the day I was able to lock him outside in the rain two years ago. He picks his teeth with a penknife, sleeps on a mattress stuffed with receipts from his deposits in London banks, saves the clippings from his fingers and toes for luck, and bays at full moons. My brother swore he'd get me out of here since the day we first arrived after our parents' funeral—get us both out of here—and by damn, Daventry, I would have to be a candidate for Bedlam myself to refuse to go. But I can't. Not yet."

Banning sat himself down in the chair Prudence had just vacated, pressed his elbows onto the desktop while making a steeple of his fingers, and looked out over the run-down grounds of MacAfee Farm, giving out with an occasional self-depreciating, close-mouthed chuckle as he considered all that his new ward had just said.

"It's the foal, isn't it, Angel?" he remarked at last, slowly swiveling on the chair to look up at Prudence, who was still standing close beside him, her fists jammed onto her hips, her wild tangle of honey-dark blond hair giving her the appearance of a lioness with her fur ruffled. "You won't leave without Molly's foal."

"Well, you can think! And here I was beginning to believe you were slow, as well as arrogant and supercilious and domineering and—"

"Yes, yes," Banning interrupted, "I believe we both know how you view me. But remember. I am also your brother's choice of savior. Thinking back on that evening, I begin to see why he would have traveled to such lengths to insure your future. You and Henry might have been your grandfather's only heirs, but the scoundrel might live for years and years yet, a prospect Henry—and in his place, I myself—could not look to with much forbearance."

"My brother escaped to the war," Prudence told him, her voice soft as she spoke of Henry MacAfee. "He stole the money to buy his commission, sneaking the profit from the sale of the dining room furniture out from under Shadwell's nose before he could ship it off to the banks. He is going to—*was* going to send for me once Boney was locked up again. Life here wasn't easy for either of us, but it was especially difficult for my brother, who was a dozen years older and had known another life more so than had I, for I was still fairly steeped in the nursery when Mama and Papa died in that carriage accident."

Beginning once more to feel as if he was not quite so put-upon, as if he had actually been selected to do what could only be considered a very good deed, Banning decided there and then that a week—no more—spent at MacAfee Farm couldn't be considered too great a sacrifice, especially when he thought how he had heartlessly left poor little Prudence MacAfee to suffer here for the better part of a year longer than necessary.

He could make do on the farm for seven short days, long enough for the foal to gain strength and make arrangements for its transport to his stable in Mayfair. Why, he might even enjoy being in the Sussex countryside, as he had been confined to London since returning to England, recovering from his wounds, hovering over his ill sister—and then dancing the night away, gaming with his friends, attending the theater and other such indulgences for several months, he remembered with another fleeting pang of guilt.

Slapping his hands down hard onto his thighs, he rose to his feet, saying, "It's settled then. I think a week in the country would do both Rexford and Miss Prentice a world of good."

"I won't let that lizard near me, you know, so you can ship her off any time it suits you," Prudence pronounced, preceding Banning to the door. "She slithered in here earlier, to pack for me she said, and left with a flea in her ear after I listened to her going on and on about the fact that I don't have any gowns. As if I'd be mucking stables in lace and satin! And she's fair and far out if she thinks I'm going to put up my hair, or let her touch me with those cold white hands as she spits out something about clipping my nails and—"

Banning stopped just inside the doorway, putting out his hands to apply the brakes to Prudence's tirade before she could grab the bit more firmly between her teeth. "Did you say you don't own any gowns? Not even one in which to travel to Freddie's? You've *nothing* but breeches?"

"Oh, close your mouth, Daventry, unless you've always longed to catch flies with your tongue. Of course I don't have any gowns. I was only a child when I came here, and once Grandmother MacAfee was gone, Shadwell decided that my brother's castoffs were more than sufficient for a growing female. And it's not as if I go tripping off to church of a Sunday or receive visitors here at MacAfee's Madhouse, which is what the locals have dubbed the place."

Banning took a long, assessing look at Prudence as she stood in front of him in the dim candlelight. He had already noticed that her honey-dark hair was thick and lustrous, even if it did look as if she'd trimmed it with a sickle and combed it with a rake. Her huge, tip-tilted eyes, also more honey gold than everyday brown, were far and away her most appealing feature, although her complexion, also golden, and without so much as a single mole or freckle, was not to be scoffed at.

Of average height for a female, with an oval face, small skull, straight white teeth, and pleasantly even features, she might just clean up to advantage. If London held enough soap and water, he added, wishing she didn't smell quite so much of horse and hay.

There wasn't much he could tell about her figure beneath the large shirt, although he had already become aware that her lower limbs were straight, her derriere nicely rounded.

"You know something, Angel?" he announced at last, draping a companionable arm around her as they headed for the staircase, just as if she was one of his chums. "I think we'll go easy on any efforts to coax you out of your cocoon until we're safely in Mayfair. I wouldn't want Shadwell to start thinking he'd be giving up an asset he could use to line his pockets."

"I don't understand," Prudence admitted, frowning up at him. "Shadwell's always said I am worthless."

"Not on the marriage mart, you're not," Banning

told her. "Now if we've cried friends, perhaps you could find a way to ferret out some food for me and my reluctant entourage before we all fade away, leaving you here alone to face Shadwell's wrath on Friday when he discovers his dirt bath already occupied."

"Oh Christ!" Prudence exclaimed, proving yet again that it would take more than a bit of silk and lace to make her close to presentable. "Bugger me if I didn't forget that. We'll have to clear out before Friday, won't we?"

As they reached the bottom of the staircase, Prudence took her guardian's hand, dragging him toward the kitchen and, he was soon to find out, her secret cache of country ham. "I suppose we could still leave tomorrow, if you find some way to bring Lightning with us."

"Lightning being Molly's foal," Banning said, wondering if he had been born brilliant or had just grown into it. "I suppose it could be managed. My, my, how plans can change in a twinkling. I imagine I shall simply have to endure Rexford's grateful weeping as we make our way back to London."

There were only a few things Banning wished to do before he departed for London, chief among them taking a torch to the bed he had tossed and turned in all night, unable to find a spot that did not possess a lump with a talent for digging into his back, but he decided to limit himself to indulging in only one small bit of personally satisfying revenge. He would inform MacAfee that his money supply had been turned off.

Dressed with care by a grumbling but always punctilious Rexford, and with his stomach pleasantly full thanks to Prudence's offer to share a breakfast of fresh eggs and more country ham out of sight of her grandfather, the marquess took up his cane and set out to locate one Shadwell MacAfee.

Resisting the notion that all he would have to do was to "follow his nose," Banning inquired his employer's whereabouts of Hatcher, who was lounging against one peeled-paint post on the porch of the manor house, then set out in the direction the servant had indicated.

He discovered Shadwell sitting cross-legged beneath a tree some thirty yards behind the stable, his lower body draped by a yellowed sheet, his hairless upper body—a mass of folded layers of fat that convinced Banning he would never look at suet pudding in the same way again—exposed to the air. His eyes were closed as he held three oak leaves between his folded-in-prayer hands, and he was mumbling something that, in Banning's opinion, was most thankfully unintelligible.

"A jewel stuck in your navel might add to the cachet of this little scene, although I doubt you'd spring for the expense, eh Shadwell?" Banning quipped, causing MacAfee to open his black-currant eyes.

"Come to say goodbye, have you, Daventry?" MacAfee asked, beginning to fan himself with the oak leaves. "But not before you poke fun at me, like the rest of them. I'll outlive them all—you too. Have myself the last laugh. You'll see. Purification is the answer, the only answer. Dirt baths, meditation, weekly purges. That's the ticket! I'll die all right, but not for years and years. And I'll be rich as Golden Ball while I'm at it. Have everything I own in banks and with the four percenters. Yes, yes. It'll be me who laughs in the end."

Banning raised his cane, resting its length on his shoulder. "Dear me, yes, I can see how gratified you are. And all it cost you was the life of your grandson and the affection of your granddaughter. Henry went to war and to his death, to escape you, and Prudence can't wait to see the back of you as she leaves this place. You've a fine legacy, MacAfee. I can see why you must be proud. And what a comfort all that money will be to you in your old age. Or are you planning to have your coffin lined with it?"

"Henry was a wastrel and a dreamer, like his father before him, and gels ain't worth hen spit on a farm," MacAfee stated calmly, moving from side to side, readjusting his layers of fat. "This land is no good any more, Daventry, any fool can see that, even you. And a house is nothing more than a house. It is a man's body that is his main domicile, his castle. Why, in the teachings of—"

"She's been allowed to run wild," Banning interrupted, not wishing to hear a treatise on dirt baths or purgatives. "She's grown up no more than a hoyden, although at least your wife was with her long enough to give her something of a vocabulary and a sense of what is proper, for which I am grateful—even if the girl delights in her attempts to shock me. She's lonely, bitter, mildly profane, purposely and most outrageously uncouth—and I lay the blame for all of it at your doorstep, Shadwell."

"She's one thing more, Daventry," MacAfee said, smiling his near-toothless grin. "She's yours. Now, go

51

away. Hatcher will be arriving shortly with my purgative. I prefer to evacuate any lower intestinal poisons out of doors, you understand."

Longing to beat the man heavily about the head and shoulders, but adverse to touching him even with his cane, Banning turned on his heel to go, saying only, "I hope you've had joy of Prudence's allowance, for you'll not see another groat from me."

"And that's where you're wrong, my boy. I will see it every quarter, like clockwork, if you hope for Prudence to inherit any of my considerable wealth," MacAfee warned, causing Banning to halt in his tracks. "Ah, that stung, didn't it, Daventry? So upright. So honest. So much the responsible guardian. But you hadn't thought of that, had you? All that lovely money. It's up to you now. I'm to cock up my toes someday, as we all must, and worthless little Prudence is now my only heir. Do I leave my lovely blunt, my security, to the chit, or do I give it all over to the Study for Purgative Restoration?"

His grin widened to disgusting dimensions. "What to do, Daventry, what to do?"

"I'll want your solemn word as a gentleman," Banning said, hating himself for bowing to the man's demands but unable to cut Prudence off from funds that rightfully should be hers. "Now, this morning, before I take my leave of this hell hole."

"Of course, Daventry. You have it," MacAfee said soothingly as Hatcher appeared, carrying a large jug of some vile-smelling elixir and a single glass. "A small quarterly pittance now against a fortune in the future. It seems fair. Care for a sip? 'Course, I'd recommend unbuttoning your breeches first, as it works quickly."

Unable to resist impulse any longer, Banning

snatched the pitcher from the servant's hand and dumped its contents over MacAfee's plucked pate.

Three hours later, her pitifully small satchel of personal belongings tucked up with the luggage, Prudence, wearing her best pair of breeches, climbed into Banning's traveling coach behind a pinch-lipped Miss Prentice, without so much as turning about for one last look at her childhood home.

CHAPTER 4

Ah! happy years!
Once more who would not be a boy?

George Noel Gordon,
Lord Byron

Prudence heard the knock on her door, but ignored it, as she had a half hour earlier; just as she was prepared to ignore it for the remainder of the day.

How could anyone ask her to rise when she was so bloody comfortable? She could not recall ever feeling so clean, or lying against sheets so soft and sweet smelling. How long had it been since she had listened to a gentle rain hitting the windowpane without worrying that the roof might this time cave in on her? At least not since she had been a very young girl.

There was a small fire still burning in the grate across the room, her appetite was still comfortably soothed by the roast beef and pudding she had downed last night when first they had arrived at the inn, and if she felt a niggling urge to avail herself of the chamber pot, well, that could wait as well.

Giving out a soft, satisfied moan, she turned her face more firmly into the pillows and settled down for at least another hour's sleep, a small smile curving her lips as her naked body sank deeper into the soft mattress. . . .

"Rise and shine, slugabed! The sun's shining, the air smells fresh as last night's rain, and I'm in the mood for a picnic. It's either that or I'll have to hide out in the common room, away from Rexford's incessant groaning now that I've told him we don't travel again until tomorrow."

Prudence sat bolt upright in the bed, clutching the sheets to her breasts, her eyes wide, her ears ringing from the slam of the door against the wall inside her room. "Daventry!" she exclaimed, pushing her badly tangled hair from her eyes and glaring impotently at the idiot who dared barge in on her just as if he were her brother Henry, come to tease her into a morning of adventure. "Are you daft, man? Go away!"

Banning turned around—not before taking just a smidgen more than a cursory peek at her bare back and shoulders, she noticed—and said, a chuckle evident in his voice, "Sleep in the buff, do you? Is this a natural inclination, or wouldn't Shadwell spring for night rails, either? I suppose I should be grateful you have boots."

"You're a pig, Daventry," Prudence spat out, tugging at the bedspread, pulling its length up and over the sheets in order to drape it around her shoulders. "And consider yourself fortunate I didn't sleep with my pistol under my pillow, or you'd be spilling your claret all over the carpet now rather than making jokes at my expense." And then her anger flew away as she leaned forward slightly, asking, "Did you say something about a picnic?"

Still with his back to her, he nodded, saying, "As long as we're forced to make our progress to London in stages, taking time to find you some proper clothes and allowing Lightning to gather strength, I thought it might be amusing to indulge in a small round of local sight-seeing. I haven't picnicked since I was little more than a boy, but for some reason I awoke this morning with the nearly irresistible urge to indulge in some simple, bucolic pleasures. However, if you'd rather play the layabout . . ."

"Give me ten minutes!" Prudence exclaimed, her feet already touching the floor as, the bedspread still around her, she lunged for her breeches. "I'll meet you downstairs, and we can be off."

"Agreed," Banning said, heading for the door. "Only remember to tie back your hair and wear that atrocious straw hat you insisted upon bringing with you, or otherwise we'll be forced to drag Miss Prentice along as chaperone, a prospect that leaves me unmoved. Dressed as a boy, you and I can tramp the countryside quite unencumbered, perhaps even dabble our bare feet in some cool stream while we lie on our backs and search out faces in the clouds. There will be time enough tomorrow to begin your metamorphosis."

"There are moments I really could like that man," Prudence told herself as she searched in her small valise for fresh underclothes. "Of course, he is still arrogant and overbearing, deucedly bossy, and takes this guardian business entirely too seriously," she added, remembering that he had all but broken into her bedchamber. "Oh well, Angel. Think of it this way. It won't be for all that long, and he has promised to buy you some gowns."

"According to the guidebook, and I dare to quote," Banning told Prudence in a comically pompous tone some two hours later as she perched on a low pile of rubble, contemplating the ruin before her, " 'Cowdray House was erected in approximately 1530 by the Earl of Southampton.' "

"The earl wasn't much of a housekeeper, was he?" Prudence asked facetiously as she pulled a length of sweet grass from between her teeth, looking up at the roofless structure, half its walls tumbled down, its windowpanes gone, the stone turrets that remained blackened and thick with moss.

They had already visited a stream and wriggled their toes in the water, had discovered a chariot and two white horses in a cloud formation, and she was feeling very much in charity with the world, and with the man who stood close by, reading to her from the guidebook he'd purchased at the inn. "Makes MacAfee Farm, although worlds smaller, seem almost comfortable."

"Hush, Angel." Banning scolded in his best imitation of a schoolmaster. "This is vastly educational and adds a modicum of moral tone to our outing. Let's see, where was I? Oh yes, with the Earl of Southampton. Oh dear. It seems he left the picture in time for one Lord Montagu to take up residence. Lord Montagu? Isn't he the fellow who drowned somewhere in Germany? Yes, yes, here it is. Montagu drowned only a week after Cowdray House mysteriously burned down in 1793. And all because of an ancient curse."

"Rotten run of luck, I'd say," Prudence put in, for

she was not one to believe in curses, ancient or otherwise. "Go on, please. Are there ghosties and ghoulies here as well? Should I be making signs against the evil eye, or can we just spread out that blanket now and have our picnic? My belly's thinking my throat's been sliced."

"Gowns, shoes, discovering a lotion that will remove the stain of manure from your fingernails, some ribbons for your hair—and intense lessons in speech and deportment," Banning said pleasantly, sitting down beside her. "Freddie will certainly be able to keep herself busy. I can't decide if I am the best or worst of brothers to have discovered for her such a challenging project."

"Oh stubble it, Daventry," Prudence groused goodhumoredly, then hopped down from her perch, as the marquess was suddenly entirely too close for her comfort. Why couldn't she keep thinking of him as her guardian, instead of seeing him as a man? "Tell me more about the curse while I unpack the basket."

She kept her back to him while she worked, painfully aware of his proximity, and the fact that the two of them were distinctly isolated here among the ruins.

What was the matter with her? She couldn't care less about the man, who was older than God, even if his face gave the lie to his silvered hair. Perhaps he dyed it? No. That was a ridiculous notion. Who would purposely dye more than half their hair a bright, glistening white, leaving the back of it still deeply black, with only a few silver threads layering the top of it, like sweet cream icing dribbling down over the sides of a dark plum pudding?

And would he *stop* staring at her? She could feel his

eyes boring into her back, so that she deliberately sat down on her haunches, aware for the first time that her breeches fit her nearly like a second skin.

"Daventry?" she prompted when the only sound she could hear was the buzzing of some nearby bees. "If you're still reading, your lips have stopped moving. You were going to tell me more about the curse."

"Hum? Oh! Oh yes. The curse. Well, it says here that the curse was put upon the family by a monk."

Prudence swiveled around to look up at him, her hands deep in the basket as she went about unearthing the roasted chicken the marquess had promised her she would find there. "That doesn't seem very Christian."

"Neither does Henry VIII's edict dissolving the monasteries, but that's what it says here. It seems the monk, who was driven out of Battle Abbey, was ejected quite personally by the first owner of Cowdray House. Obviously the monk wasn't about to simply forgive the man and turn the other cheek. It took a few centuries, but the curse finally worked."

"Well, I think that's stupid," Prudence declared, undaintily but effectively ripping the legs off the roasted chicken and placing one on each of the two plates she had spread on the blanket. "More than two hundred years passed between the laying on of the curse and the destruction of this place. That would be the same as blaming the discovery of the American continent for the war that eventually severed the colonists' ties with England."

"Logic, from an infant. Angel, I am impressed." Daventry came to join her on the blanket, kneeling beside her—too close beside her, for she could once again smell the cologne he wore, its scent tickling her nose and doing something extraordinarily strange to her insides.

"Have a chicken leg," she ordered, picking up his plate and nearly jamming it against his nose. Damn her short-sighted brother! Didn't he know he'd picked her a rutting old man for a guardian? And how could he have forgotten that she was no longer a child, but a woman, a woman who had seen precious little of handsome, charming men? Why couldn't her brother have given her over to Wellington or some sympathetic peeress? But no. He had to pick the Marquess of Daventry. A worldly, witty, at times bitingly sarcastic, yards too self-assured man with entirely too-intriguing green eyes and a boyish smile that turned her knees to water . . .

First he shows up almost nine months too late to be of any help at all, and now he makes noises like he can barely abide me half the time, while he is not only being nice to me but is also near to drooling over me the other half of the time. Let him buy me gowns? Oh yes. But first I want a night rail—one that covers my toes and buttons all the way to my ears!

"Shall I continue to read as we eat?" Banning asked, removing himself and his plate to the far side of the blanket, his expression telling her that he was questioning why he had knelt down beside her in the first place. "I could tell you about the sadly mutilated carving of the arms of King Henry—who actually visited on this spot in 1538—that is still visible above the entrance arch of the hall porch. Or perhaps we could do as is advised on this page, and stroll down to Benbow Pond after our meal—there, to the east, along that footpath—and indulge in partaking of the delightful views visible across the valley of the Rother."

"I'd *rother* not, thank you," Prudence told him cheekily, pleased to see that he, too, was disconcerted by the events of the past few minutes—if she wasn't totally overreacting to what she believed to be his very un-guardian-like behavior. "I'd much prefer to sit here and listen to you tell me how long it will be before we reach London. Lightning is in no danger now that your man has found a mare to feed him, so I figure on three or four days and nights on the road, as the poor little thing still can't be confined to the wagon for too many hours a day."

"That's about right, three days and two nights. We'll pass the nights in Milford and Epsom, and arrive at Freddie's by nightfall of the third day. It will be a slow progress, but we'll get there eventually."

"Each mile that takes me farther from MacAfee Farm is cause for rejoicing. Goodness, I'm thirsty!" She was feeling slightly more in control of herself now that the marquess was not so close, but watching him eat, delighting in gnawing at the chicken leg as if he were a schoolboy on holiday, was not making her attempts at general conversation easier.

Banning set down the chicken leg, wiped his greasy fingers on a linen serviette, and reached inside the basket for the bottle of wine she had seen there, nestled beside a small jug of lemonade she supposed he expected her to drink. She watched him struggle to uncork the bottle, then she quickly held out both glasses, daring him to deny her what he was taking for himself.

"You are too young for anything save watered

wine," he said, holding the bottle upright. "Or are you now going to tell me that Shadwell refused to clothe you yet kept you in strong spirits?"

"I drank what was to hand," Prudence told him, feeling herself growing angry, and thankful for the feeling because it seemed easier to deal with the marquess from the position of adversary. "Ale, wine, port, brandy, even gin. Although I heartily dislike port, and too much ale makes my teeth numb and my nose itch. Still and all, plenty were the times it was safer than the water from the well. Come on, Daventry, pour me a glass. I won't disgrace you by falling into my cups so that you have to fling me over your shoulder like a sack and haul me back to the inn. Besides, you've already broken one rule of guardianship by bringing me out here without a chaperone. What's a little wine after that?"

Banning tipped his head to one side, his green eyes twinkling in a way that made her wonder if, perhaps, somewhere deep inside himself, he was as young as she. "Very well, Angel, if you promise to breathe most heavily directly in Miss Prentice's face once we get back to the inn. I believe I'd rather enjoy watching her blanch."

Prudence held out the glasses again, stubbornly keeping them there until he'd filled both of them to the brim. "Blanch, is it?" she said, giggling. "And how do you suppose we could tell? She's already as sickly white as the underbelly of a fish. How does your sister abide such a dedicated pain in the rump? I'd have tossed the woman out dog's years ago if she were mine."

"You'd have to know my sister to understand. If there ever was a woman who should be called 'angel,' it's Freddie. Rodney, Freddie's late husband, had employed Miss Prentice as housekeeper before the wedding, and when Rodney died Miss Prentice saw the chance to move herself up a notch, to become Freddie's companion. She doesn't like the woman, and never did, but if Rodney chose her, then Freddie doesn't believe she can get rid of her. My sister is sweet and loving and gentle—but if she were to develop a bit of a backbone, I wouldn't complain."

Prudence took a deep, satisfying sip of the still cool wine. "Put some starch in her spine? I'll take care of it," she said in all sincerity, believing she should offer something in return for her rescue from Shadwell. "It's the least I can do, seeing as how your sister offered to take me in. And," she added, feeling daring, "in return, you can take me to St. Bartholomew's Fair. My brother says—said it's magnificent, and would suit me to a cow's thumb."

"If you like crowds, the smell of unwashed flesh, gaudy trinkets, fakers, pickpockets, and rancid kidney pies, I suppose it is magnificent," Banning said before sinking his white teeth into the glistening red flesh of an apple he'd pulled from the basket. "However," he continued moments later, speaking around a mouthful of the fruit, "as your time is going to be filled with dancing lessons, fittings, morning visits, and the like, I believe we shall both simply have to forgo partaking of this particular delight. As your guardian, although I will not be in your company more than I have to be once I deliver you into Freddie's hands, I cannot approve. Sorry."

And with that single statement, Prudence felt all her enjoyment of the morning disappear.

"No, you're not in the least bit sorry, so don't lie to

me! Leave it to a man to ruin everything—as men always do! Just when you start feeling comfortable, they take themselves off!" Prudence shot back at him, scrambling to her feet and giving the picnic basket a quick kick. She tossed off the remainder of her wine, just daring him to say something cutting about her manners, and ordered him to repack the basket, as she was anxious to get back to see if Lightning was faring well under the coachman's care.

She had taken no more than three steps when she felt Daventry's hands come down on her shoulders, halting her where she stood. "Let me go, my lord, before I do you an injury," she warned, unshed tears stinging her eyes because she had begun to like him, just a little bit, and now he had gone and turned their picnic into yet another disappointment. Couldn't wait to be shed of her, could he? Well, she was just as eager to see him walk out of her life!

He released her, saying, "In any other young woman, I would consider that to be an idle threat. In your case, however—"

"Oh, cut line!" she shouted, rounding on him, just to have him plop her wide-brimmed straw hat down hard on her head, nearly to her eyes, keeping his hand on top of her skull and her body at arm's length.

"Can't take the chance of freckles popping up on that pert nose, now can we?" he said by way of explanation, although she knew he was only saying that because he needed an excuse to keep her at a distance, which was probably a good thing because she would otherwise have sharply lifted her knee into his groin, as her brother had taught her to do after that leering traveling tinker had dared to corner her behind the stables four years ago.

"Why'd you have to ruin things by treating me like your unwanted ward again, instead of continuing on as the friends we were this morning, tramping here from the inn with the picnic basket swinging between us?" she asked him, her emotions a sudden jumble she did not wish to examine. "You gave a little, allowing me some wine, not saying a word when I deliberately ripped the chicken with my fingers, and I gave a little, promising to be a help to your sister. And then you took it all back, reminding me that you are dealing with me only because you have to, because my brother asked you to and you could find no way to wriggle out of your promise."

Banning turned back to begin repacking the picnic basket. "That's it, no more wine for the infant," he said as if to himself. "And to think I'd worried that I'd find some simpering milk-and-water puss when I traveled to MacAfee Farm. Ha! What I would give now for a simple-headed die-away miss, rather than this bundle of contradictions I am saddled with. One moment the hoyden, a born temptress the next—but beneath it all the ragamuffin with the temper of a prodded ox!"

"I did *not* tempt you to anything!" Prudence corrected him heatedly. "I did not invite you into my bedchamber, you lascivious ogler, nor did I ask you to take me on this picnic, sans chaperone. But I came along with you, believing we could cry friends, putting myself on my excruciatingly best behavior, hoping that you might begin to believe that Henry's request had not made you the most put-upon, persecuted person on earth. Hah! Fat lot of hope in any of that, is there, Daventry? You're nothing more than a rutting old dog—as if I'd have you!"

He stopped in the midst of repacking the basket, one hand on the lid as he looked her up and down dismissively. "You wouldn't know what to do with me," he said coldly, "just as I haven't the foggiest notion of what to do with you. Which, my dear Miss MacAfee, is precisely where I do believe we should both leave the matter."

CHAPTER 5

Every man, as the saying is,
can tame a shrew but he that hath her.

Robert Burton

Stand still, Miss MacAfee. And you are to remember that you are now a young lady and stop swearing at once, if you please."

"The bloody hell I will, you prune-faced old biddy. You stick me with one more pin and I'll have your liver on a skewer!"

Banning took a moment to smile as he stood peeking around the slightly ajar door, then entered the room without knocking, feeling it best to intervene before Prudence, looking hot and flustered in a morning gown definitely designed with a much different female in mind, made good on her threat.

"Learning to rub along together fairly well, are you Miss Prentice, Miss MacAfee?" He inquired brightly, unable to hold back a satisfied grin at the sight of his ward in a temper. "How above everything wonderful, truly. I'm convinced of it—you'll be bosom chums by tomorrow night, when we arrive in Park Lane to meet with my sister. I think this little stop in Epsom was just the ticket, although I can't say, Miss Prentice, that I'm overfond of our 'angel' in that particular shade of pink."

"It's downright ugly, isn't it," Prudence declared, almost seeming in charity with him for the first time in days as she spread her hands and glared down at the gown Miss Prentice was still trying without notable success to pin more snugly around her left wrist. "All my life, I've been dreaming of beautiful gowns, of cutting a dash in society with my stylish wardrobe—and this is what that paperskulled ninny brings me. *Pink!*"

Banning hid a rather nasty smile as he bent his head and pretended an interest in adjusting his shirt cuffs. He had found, much to his amazement—considering the fact that he believed himself a gentleman—that he truly enjoyed baiting the child.

"I was speaking of your complexion, Miss MacAfee," he then explained, hoping his expression was sober and very guardian-like, "which has a tendency to go nearly puce with temper, an unfortunately too common occurrence, considering the fact that you fly into the boughs almost hourly. As for the gown Miss Prentice purchased for you on my orders, it is passable enough, I believe."

"How amusing you are, Daventry," Prudence retorted, pulling her wrist free of Miss Prentice's grasping fingers. "I'll wager you launch yourself into hysterics three or more times a day, just reflecting on your own comic brilliance. Now, if you're not going to be of any help to me—go away. Find yourself a monkey and a tambourine, and go perform downstairs in the common room, where there are doubtless enough drunken farmers eager to giggle at your cutting wit. I want to get back into my breeches, and I intend to do so in the next ten seconds. That's *ten . . . nine . . . eight . . .*"

Miss Prentice walked to a corner of the room, picking up her almost always present glass of water and taking a sip before saying, "Lady Wendover has not sufficiently recovered her strength after her ordeal of last year, my lord, and should not be forced to deal with such an ill-mannered child. I beg that you rethink the matter, then go about discovering a suitable school for at least a year. I personally have heard of such an establishment in the north, somewhere near Edinburgh, I believe. Backboards, firmly administered corporal punishments for insubordination, thrice daily prayers—"

"Oh stubble it, Prentice. You've interrupted my counting. Besides, I know very well how a lady behaves—probably better than you, as a matter of fact. My grandmother was very particular that I should understand what it takes to be a lady. I just don't like you, that's all, and don't give a fig what you think of me," Prudence explained, turning her back on the woman.

"I'm not too taken with you, either, my lord Daventry," she continued, smiling. "But you don't have to worry about your sister. I know which side of my bread is buttered, and I'll be good when I have to be. Now, where was I? Oh yes. Eight. Eight . . . seven . . . *six . . .*"

Banning inclined his head slightly in her direction. "How you soothe my troubled mind, Miss MacAfee," he drawled, addressing her formally, as he had since entering the bedchamber here at the Cross and Battle, as he had done since their stormy interlude at

69

the ruin—not that he had seen her above twice since then, as he had secreted himself in the private dining room at the inn just outside Milford and rode ahead of the coach during the day. "Just remember as you count down the numbers, and as you are playing the proper young miss around my sister, that *I* am the one footing the bill for your coming excursion into London society."

"Don't blame me for the promises you made, Daventry. Counting time is over, I fear. Don't say I didn't give you fair warning," Prudence shot back, grinning as she began unbuttoning the unsuitable pink gown, starting with the buttons that seemed to climb halfway up the front of her slim throat. "Oh, look at me! The country bumpkin stripping down in front of the London gentleman. Quickly, Miss Prentice! Scream! Faint!"

"Angel, please," Banning whispered in warning, unwilling to look away. Unable to look away. Good God! What was wrong with him, that he could not look away? How had he come to be so eager for the sight of a few inches of Prudence MacAfee's sun-kissed skin, when he had just to walk into any ballroom in Mayfair to see yards and yards of bare, supple, creamy white female shoulders and bosoms.

Three more buttons were pushed free of their moorings, exposing several more inches of flawless, golden skin. *"Please,* my lord Daventry? Please what? Please stop? Please continue? Better run away, my lord, run away quickly—or else take another look, as your first one the other morning seemed to interest you so much."

"His—your . . . your *first,* my lord?" Miss Prentice asked, her watery blue eyes rounded in question, in anticipated horror. "My lord, I fear I must insist you explain."

"The bloody hell I will!" Banning exploded and bolted for the door, ushered on his way by the lilting trill of Angel MacAfee's delighted laughter.

It was dark in the private dining room that adjoined his bedchamber at the Cross and Battle, but the Marquess of Daventry made no move to light more than one of the tapers stuck into the small branch of candles sitting at his elbow on the table.

After all, if he lit the remainder of the candles it would then be possible to see his reflection in the nearby windowpane, and he had seen more than enough of the man he was in the past two hours to wish to look himself in the eye just now.

It was depressing, believing himself to have turned, almost overnight, from a sober, upstanding man of the world, into a lech. A lusting, dirty-minded lech.

Yet here he was, a reasonably intelligent man of nearly five and thirty, reduced to drooling over a green goose of an eighteen-year-old woman-child with the come-hither body of a siren, the all-knowing eyes of a vixen, and the brash language and devil-take-the-hindmost attitude of a young buck first out on the town.

She had no shame, no wiles, no carefully cultivated airs, and no compunction about saying what she thought, doing what she wished, flaunting convention —not because she was being deliberately difficult, but just because she was Angel MacAfee, and Angel MacAfee didn't give a flying pasty what anyone thought.

Flying pasty! Christ on a crutch, now he was being

reduced to thieves' cant, taken back to his own fairly rackety salad days—corrupted by a female barely old enough to be out of her leading strings!

Ah, what imp of mischief had entered Henry MacAfee's mind that he would christen his sister with such a misnomer as *Angel*? Banning knew he would say that she had all the makings of a wanton, baiting him the way she had, except that he also knew she had acted more from anger that he would dare to look at her as a woman than she did from any longing to crawl into the nearest bed with him.

She had dared him with her lush, golden young body, successfully pushed him away by the simple tactic of pretending to draw him closer, made him embarrassed to be a man, ashamed to feel what could only be considered normal male desires, wants, needs.

Not that her daring warning had been necessary. He was certainly not about to do anything about his absurd attraction to her, save for possibly attempting to drown it tonight, and forever.

"Damn her for having seen the last thing I wanted her to see, the last thing I wanted to acknowledge, even to myself," he grumbled aloud, reaching yet again for the wine bottle he had ordered sent up from the common room. It was his second bottle of the evening, and he might just order a third if this one didn't do the trick.

Lusting, longing . . . and now a descent into spirits, a headfirst dive into a bottle. And all because of Angel MacAfee. It was lowering, distinctly lowering, and he filled his glass to the brim, just thinking about it, and ignoring the slight squeak of the door to the hallway as someone, probably Rexford, pushed it open.

"The lizard said you gave up drinking more than

the occasional glass of wine ever since you got yourself so bosky you couldn't think clearly enough to conjure up a way of slipping free of my brother's request that you be my guardian. As far as I can see, the next time that woman's right will be the first time, eh, Daventry?"

Banning swallowed the wine all at once, tossing it back as he would have done a stronger spirit, then glared at Prudence, who was still in the doorway, grinning at him across the darkness. "That large wooden contraption you are leaning against is called a door, Miss MacAfee. It is employed by civilized people as a method of ensuring privacy. It is also used to knock on, if a person of manners and breeding desires admittance to that place of privacy. Kindly close it behind you as you leave."

"Certainly, my lord Grumpus," Prudence said affably, leaving the door open as she crossed to the table plunking her shirt- and breeches-clad self down in the chair facing his, her forearms resting on the thick oaken arms, her legs splayed out in front of her in the way of a young buck settling in for a night of gaming and drinking. "But seeing as how I'm not planning on going anywhere just yet, maybe you'll remind me again when I do leave. I've got the breeding, or so my brother assured me over and over, but my manners might still need a little work."

"I suppose this unexpected visit to my private dining room means you no longer believe I have any designs on your virtue?" he asked, thankful his voice sounded light, teasing, and just a little condescending.

"Ah, Daventry," she cooed, pushing the thick curtain of her hair up and away from her neck as she winked at him. "I'd be a damned fool to think an old

73

man like you capable of even planning a seduction, let alone executing one. I was just trying to get your goat, that's all, and I wanted to let you know I knew you'd been looking. Guess it worked, huh?"

"You do enjoy baiting people, don't you?" Banning asked, watching as she leaned forward and poured herself a glass of wine, then crossed her booted ankles in front of her on the table top, tipping her chair back slightly on its hind legs. "Or is it just that you take great pleasure in—you believe—shocking people with your uncouth behavior?"

She looked at him over the brim of her wineglass, then sighed in patently false impatience. "I've already demonstrated to you that I have a fine vocabulary, Daventry. I've already promised you that I will be a patterncard of all the finest and most stultifyingly boring virtues whenever I am with your sister. In truth," she added, her smile as wide and innocent as a child's, "I am by and large a most agreeable, friendly sort of person, really I am. But I'm afraid you probably will have to indulge me as I go about exacting a small spot of revenge aimed at punishing you for leaving me with Shadwell months longer than necessary. You cut it a slice too fine, so that I'll have to rush myself into the season. Remembering that fact, I'm still fairly angry with you, but it's a feeling that's slowly wearing off as we draw closer to London. As to the lizard? Well, she just plain *begs* to be shocked."

"All right," Banning said, raising his glass as if in a toast, "I suppose I can withstand the slings and arrows of your childish tantrums for another day. As long as, in turn, you understand why I barely slow the coach as I deposit you at my sister's doorstep."

Prudence's laugh was full-throated, not the simpering giggle of most society misses, and he found himself joining her in her amusement, feeling better than he had in several hours, several days.

"Just be sure to toss the lizard out first, so I can have the pleasure of landing on her. She wouldn't be a soft cushion, God knows, but I have developed a nearly overwhelming longing to knock some of the bile out of her. I'm not used to having enemies, you know, and she has threatened to tell your sister that I'm incorrigible and past saving. The interfering bitch," she ended quietly, taking a deep drink of her wine.

Banning sighed, wondering how he could be sitting here, fairly calmly, sharing the night with Prudence as if she were a young chum of his, listening to her swear, watching her drink, laughing with her. He was rather proud of himself and felt slightly foolish for his earlier thoughts, his earlier fears. It was remarkable. He felt no desire for her now, no longing to kiss her, run his hands along the tightly outlined sweep of her hips, press her body close against his own . . . molding her . . . shaping her . . . taking her . . . breathing in her fire, her vitality, her lust for life. . . .

He sat forward and poured himself another drink, wondering whether the wine would be of any real benefit to him in merely sliding down his throat as he swallowed the lie he was trying to tell his better self, or if he would be better served to dash the contents of the glass in his slowly heating face, shocking his system back under some semblance of control, of sanity.

"This patterncard of all the finest virtues soon to be delivered on my sister's doorstep," he said after a moment's internal battle, having reminded himself that he really didn't have a single thing in common with Prudence MacAfee. "Will she likewise treat *me* with the respect and consideration owed one's legal guardian? Or should I be watching my shins, on the lookout for childish kicks, whenever my sister isn't in the room? Not that I'm worried, mind you. I just would appreciate having the rules laid out, so that we both know where we stand."

Prudence unfolded her long legs and dropped her booted feet hard against the floor, tipping the chair to an upright position once more as she plunked the empty wineglass on the table, all in a single masculine, yet deceptively feminine, graceful moment.

Leaning forward so that she ended with her elbows propped on her knees, close enough now that, just for a moment, Banning thought he could see the devil peeking out from behind her golden eyes, she said, "I really bother you, don't I, Daventry? You can't figure out who I am, what I am—or what I want."

She sat back against the wooden slats of the chair and began counting off on her fingers as she spoke. "Well, let me set your mind at rest. One: who am I? That should be obvious enough. I'm an innocent, hapless, helpless, penniless orphan, a sweet young bud doing her best to bloom in a cold, cruel, uncaring world."

"I could argue with you on the *helpless* part of that statement," Banning said, beginning to relax once more. She was a child. A precocious, faintly amusing child. "As for being *sweet,* well, I won't even bother to refute such an obvious crammer. Please, go on."

She nodded solemnly, her only acknowledgment that he had spoken, then went on, as if doing him a personal favor by speaking, "Two: what am I? Ah, the answer now becomes more involved, more difficult, as you perhaps have already figured out on your own, much to your chagrin. Care to count along with me this time?"

She needs a good spanking, that's what she needs, Banning decided, finding himself caught up in her brashness, while feeling himself fascinated with her brutal honesty, her bald admonition that she was not in the least ordinary or even acceptable.

When he didn't answer her facetious questions she shrugged, then held up four fingers, touching them one at a time as she spoke. "I am, my Lord Daventry, the sum total of all my parts. Part child of long-forgotten doting parents, part product of a stern and socially conscious grandmother, part victim of a half-crazed grandfather who values money and his pathetic rituals more than he does his own flesh and blood, and part sister of a devoted but frequently absent, much older brother who loved me enough to see that I'd be taken care of, but not enough to make the effort of taking care of me himself."

Her regal demeanor evaporated even as he watched, and all at once she looked very young, and very insecure. "And, now, lastly—what do I want? I don't know, Daventry!" she exclaimed after a moment, grinning brightly again. "Not yet. But when I do, I'll let you know. All right?" That said, she slapped her palms against the arms of the chair, then stood, obviously ready to leave the room.

Stung by her honesty, and once more feeling sorry for her and the bizarre, almost unnatural life she had led, he called out toward her retreating back: "I convinced your grandfather to make me a solemn promise before we left him to wallow in his purgatives. I agreed to continue paying him the quarterly allowance I'd been sending to you, and he gave his solemn word that he would will you his fortune. You'll be a rich orphan one day—one day soon, if Shadwell also ambles about in that toga of his in mid-winter."

His words stopped her just as she got to the door, and she turned to look at him intently, her hand frozen on the tarnished brass door latch.

Compassion hastily shoved to one side and delight at his good deed forgotten, he suddenly realized the full import of what he had accomplished in his gentleman's agreement with Shadwell MacAfee. No wonder Prudence couldn't think of a thing to say. He had her now. She was in his debt now, just as he was bound to the promise he had made to be her guardian.

They were, finally, on an even footing. His guilt over leaving her in the country, locked away at that hellhole of a farm, and his second, worse guilt—that of coveting her, seeing her as a woman to be desired rather than a responsibility to be discharged—was no more.

It had been just this moment replaced by the sure knowledge that he had rescued her from that hellhole, and was about to launch her into society—into, he hoped, a quick, advantageous marriage with the promise of a fortune as an added fillip to the dowry he would bestow on her.

He had no reason to drink, to chastise himself. The scales he had been seeing in his mind, scales so recently tipped in favor of this comely ragamuffin, had just evened out, balanced by his maturity, his sense of duty, his intelligent, measured approach to what could, if he had let it, have disintegrated into a never-ending battle of wills.

He was, at last, established as her guardian. She was, at last, firmly in the position of grateful ward.

Though perhaps, as Prudence's next words, dipped in vitriol and delivered in sharp, staccato jabs, those scales were still sadly out of kilter.

"You know, Daventry," she said, shaking her head, "just when I thought you and I had come to some sort of agreement, just when I thought I could begin to be open with you, explain myself to you, prepare you, you went and proved to me that you have no understanding at all. None. But then, that's why my brother picked you, isn't it? You're just the sort of honest, responsible, upstanding, *gullible* gentleman who believes in the value of promises, aren't you? And I hate you for making me feel sorry for you!"

And with that, the enigma, the chameleon that was Angel MacAfee was gone, the door left open behind her, not because she had forgotten to close it, Banning was sure, but because he had asked her to shut it, and she wasn't about to do anything he asked of her, required of her. Not, at least, without a fight.

Mostly, she wasn't going to leave his mind. Not when he could close his eyes and still see her as she roused, warm, tousled, and eminently touchable, from her bed.

Not when the memory of the way she had walked toward him, taunting him with her eyes as she slid open the buttons of her gown, still caused his throat to grow dry, proving to him that he was not above lusting after her, even while knowing that she was too young, too innocent, too unsuitable, too alien to the image of the woman he would choose as his wife.

Not when, even with his eyes open and his head reasonably clear, he could still see her sitting in this room, drinking and lounging with the assured nonchalance of an equal, yet never letting him forget that she was an exciting, vibrant, desirable, unconquerable creature of unending contradictions.

Lastly, he would never forget, waking or sleeping, that she was his ward, his sworn responsibility, and therefore totally beyond his reach.

She pitied him. Even as she teased him, deliberately tormented him, she still pitied him, as if she were the adult and he the child. Perhaps she even despised him, believing him to be simple beyond belief in having put credence into Shadwell's assurances as to the disposition of his wealth.

With the clear eyes of youth, she seemed to see all the vices, lies, and cynicism of the ages, making him the young one, the naive one. Still he wondered to himself why he seemed so lamentably unknowing to her when he was accustomed to believing himself a mature man of the world.

Perhaps she's right, Banning thought, pushing the cork back into the wine bottle. All right. It didn't seem that far-fetched. Perhaps Shadwell wasn't going to live up to his side of their agreement. Prudence must know her grandfather better than he did, having lived with him, witnessed his crushing economies in the name of fortune firsthand.

The man was an abomination, a miserable excuse for a human being, consumed by his eccentric rituals and a mad desire to amass wealth at the expense of his estate, his grandchildren, his own creature comforts.

But Shadwell had promised, and Banning knew that he had given his promise in return. And that, in Prudence's mind, had branded him as a irredeemable fool.

What had she said to him earlier, flinging the words

at him? Oh yes. He remembered now. *Don't blame me for the promises you made.*

And he had been making a plethora of promises in recent years.

He had promised her brother that he would care for his "angel."

He had promised his sister he would fetch that same unwanted ward to Mayfair where she could mold her into a simpering, giggling, die-away debutante.

He had promised Shadwell MacAfee a quarterly allowance against the fortune Prudence deserved.

He had promised his father that he would put away the silliness of youth when it came time to take on the family title, and would behave with the circumspection and sobriety befitting that title.

He had promised a multitude of things to people he could neither contact nor refuse.

But the real trick of the thing, the promise he would find most difficult to keep, was the one he made now to himself late on this quiet night in Epsom—his personal vow to stay as removed from the life of Prudence MacAfee as possible. To banish the image of this obstinate, headstrong, willful, profane, smudged-face "angel" from his mind, and—if he was very, very lucky—from even the fringes of his heart. . . .

CHAPTER 6

I stood
Among them, but not of them; in a shroud
Of thoughts which were not their thoughts.

George Noel Gordon,
Lord Byron

It was just coming on to dusk when Daventry's coach entered the city, Miss Prentice snoring rather loudly in the shadows after being pushed into a corner by Rexford, who had squealed in disgust when the slumbering woman's angular body had listed in his direction, her wide-brimmed purple bonnet slamming into the bridge of his nose.

Prudence, who had been sitting squarely in the center of the facing seat ever since reentering the coach at the last posting inn—stubbornly refusing to move to one side to allow Miss Prentice to sit beside her as she had done since leaving Epsom that morning —scooted to one of the windows and dropped the leather curtain, eager for her first sight of the metropolis.

"Do not look, Miss MacAfee," Rexford warned unexpectedly, raising a snowy white handkerchief to his nose. "And, whatever you do, do not drop the window. We will be past this unfortunate area shortly, and into more civilized territory."

Rexford's warning was all Prudence needed. Where she had been interested in seeing London, she was now avid to take it all its sights and sounds and even its smells. "I have lived with a man who bathes in dirt," she said, reaching for the latches that would lower the glass. "I doubt that I—*oh my God!*" She slammed the glass back to its closed position, turning to Rexford to exclaim in disgust, "Do they use the streets for latrines?"

"Among other things," the valet told her, reaching into his pocket and withdrawing a small bottle of scent. He then pulled out the stopper and handed the perfume to a grateful Prudence, who quickly waved it beneath her nostrils. "As Prentice is a dead loss," he went on, his rather high-pitched voice holding the tone of an indulgent, wiser adult speaking to a child, "and as Lady Wendover, although a lovely creature, is not known for her mental profundity, I suggest you listen carefully to what I have to say as we near the end of our journey."

Prudence grinned, for the man had barely opened his mouth all the way from MacAfee Farm, unless it was to bemoan his fate at having been sent into the country in the first place.

"Feeling more the thing now that you're closer to home, are you, Rexford?" she asked, passing the scent bottle back to him and watching as he dripped some of its contents on his handkerchief then breathed in deeply. "I didn't think Daventry would keep you if whining and retching were your only fortes. And I must say, I do admire the way you dress his lordship.

He is a credit to your art. Please, anything you might say that could be helpful in easing my way into Lady Wendover's world would be most appreciated by this country bumpkin."

Rexford inclined his head to her, the ghost of a smile visible behind the handkerchief, and Prudence knew she had made her first conquest. Finally. She had begun to believe she had lost her touch! Not that her brother had said she was all that lovable. It was, according to him, just her wide, golden eyes and "innocent angel" expression that had everyone from dairy maid to Squire tripping all over themselves to help her, to confide in her, to—simply—*like* her.

"We don't have much time," Rexford pointed out, "and I won't be seeing you on a regular basis, I imagine, but I believe you would be best served by keeping your mouth firmly shut when you are un-sure of yourself, restrain the impulse to scratch at any covered areas of your body, imitate Lady Wendover's manners at table and in the drawing room, and lastly, find some way to get yourself shed of—as I have noticed you have so aptly dubbed her—the *lizard.*"

"Rexford! How naughty of you!" Prudence exclaimed, liking the valet more with each passing moment. "I am ashamed to admit to not paying attention to you these last days. I now know that it is entirely my loss."

"Yes, it is," Rexford said matter-of-factly, slipping his handkerchief back into his pocket. The coach accelerated slightly as it ran over smoother cobbles, hinting that they were leaving both the congestion and rough streets of the poorer district behind them. "But I have been observing you, Miss MacAfee, and I believe you have some promise. Now, listen closely. With your coloring—those strangely pleasing dark golden tones—you are not to wear white. Never. Not at all."

Prudence was confused as well as fascinated. "But white is the color of debutantes, isn't it, Rexford? You wouldn't be trying to coax me into making a cake of myself, would you? That wouldn't be nice, you know."

His eloquent shrug was barely perceptible inside the rapidly darkening coach. "There are shades of white, Miss MacAfee. Try for materials with a slight sheen to them for evening, muslins for daytime. You may wear ivory—if it has a golden cast. Ecru. Any shade that has either a golden or beige cast to it—even a hint of peach, which would, now that I think on it, be a particularly outstanding choice."

"Rather the shade of aged linen?" Prudence offered, remembering her sheets at MacAfee Farm.

"Exactly. You may also, in your day dresses, spencers, riding habits, cloaks, and the like, gravitate to carefully chosen shades of faded green, lightest yellow —more of a soft gold, actually—dusky rose, and even the most delicate lilac. No pinks, Miss MacAfee, as I believe you have already discovered. No clear colors, no whites, and nothing that could be considered in the least bit bright. Select nothing that is not muted, subdued, almost colorless—and always be sure the color has a hint of drabness to it, of beige. This is most important, for your complexion must be made to be a part of your ensemble. I want you to appear all of a piece, a vision of honey and cream. My, I am becoming almost poetic. It has been a long journey, hasn't it?"

Prudence bit her lip, trying not to giggle even as she longed to reach across the space that separated them and give the valet a hug. "Rexford, you amaze me. Truly."

"Yes, well, I do have my master to consider, now don't I? It wouldn't do, wouldn't do at all, for his ward to be an embarrassment to him—to *us*. I have hopes that Lady Wendover will have some sense when it comes to the dressing of you, but as she has this most lamentable tendency to bow to the wishes of the person closest to her, and as I have already been a reluctant witness to Miss Prentice's notion of fashion, I felt it my duty to step in. Besides, impossible as this might seem, I believe you just might be beautiful in an odd, as yet unfashionable way. If you behave yourself, smooth your rougher edges without losing any of your fire and wit—well, with care, we could create a sensation, a true Original. Now, as to the cut of your gowns—"

Prudence did kiss him then for, if truth be told, she had been worried that she was totally friendless as she embarked upon her new life. Daventry barely tolerated her when he wasn't sneaking looks at her, Rexford had been silent and staring, and Miss Prentice—well, it wasn't as if the lizard counted one way or another, really.

But Prudence liked people, truly enjoyed them, thrilled in making them happy, and longed to make new friends. Before Shadwell's descent into the most outrageous of his rituals, when he had been regarded by their near neighbors as merely eccentric, Prudence and her grandmother had been welcome everywhere.

It was only after her grandmother's death, as Shadwell had begun dirt baths and purgatives, and serving goat's milk puddings to visitors, that her friends had distanced themselves from her on orders from their elders.

Or, she had sometimes wondered, had it been more than that? For the near shunning of her had also coincided with the summer her body had blossomed rather alarmingly beneath her shirts and breeches, the same summer that Squire Barrington's oldest son, James, had brought her a fistful of wild flowers, and asked to touch her. No longer in her girlish gowns, she may have been seen as a threat—and who in their right mind would want to see their son married to the wild granddaughter of that madman, Shadwell MacAfee?

But none of that mattered now, as she leaned forward and kissed Rexford's cheek, delighting in his horrified, yet pleased expression.

"Miss MacAfee!" the valet exclaimed as Prudence sat back against the velvet squabs once more, grinning as she rubbed the sleeve of her horrible pink gown across her tear-filled eyes. "That is *not* done!"

"I will attempt to restrain myself in future, my new friend," she promised, "if you will help me find some way of having you by my side as, together, we assemble the wardrobe that will captivate the *ton.*"

"And my lord Daventry?" Rexford questioned her, his knowing tone hinting that he had seen her looking at the marquess as he rode out of the inn yard each morning.

"I couldn't care less what that high-nosed stickler thinks of me!" she countered, bristling even as her smile froze on her lips.

Rexford wagged a finger at her. "If we are to rub along together with any ease, Miss MacAfee, I suggest you be honest with me. You are interested in his lordship, and he is intrigued by you. Not wishing to expend my energies in assaulting my eyes with visions of trees, or grass-chewing animals with a propensity for doing entirely private things very much in the public eye, I have concentrated my attention on both of you these past days. He will fight the inevitable, and you will doubtless exasperate him mightily until you come to a compromise, but I can see my future when I look at the two of you. And I will not allow my employer's marchioness to become an embarrassment to me. I do have my reputation to consider, after all."

"Me? Daventry's marchioness? You haven't been chewing on any of the local plants, have you, Rexford? A rather darkish green one out near Shadwell's dirt bath, perhaps, a tall grass with little white flowers? I saw one of the goats doing that last spring, and he acted silly for days," she replied teasingly, doing her best to cover her sudden embarrassment. Rexford was deep, deeper than he gave any indication of being as he strutted around like a hen in stubble, fussing over his accommodations, or all but weeping as he complained about the food he was served, or loudly lamenting over the occasional drift of horsy scent that wafted his way as he stood balanced on a flat stone in a muddy stable yard, waiting for the coach that was, in all too lengthy stages, bearing him back to London and civilization.

"*And,* Miss MacAfee," he continued, rolling his eyes at her last statement as the coach slowed to a stop, "you must promise to never, *never* drag the marquess or his most loyal servant to any location within fifteen miles of Shadwell MacAfee or his farm. Do we have a deal, Miss MacAfee?"

"About the gowns, yes, we do," Prudence told him quickly, straining to peek out the coach window, but not able to see much more than the brightly lit flambeaux on either side of a wide white door. "But you're wrong about the marquess, my friend and kind co-conspirator. He barely tolerates me, and I find him dull and disappointingly unintelligent. And he's old. I'll find my own husband, if you don't mind—for that is supposedly why I am here—and he won't be anyone who thinks he *owes* me anything."

With that, and hoping she hadn't said too much, Prudence smiled to the coachman who had opened the door and pulled down the stairs, holding her ugly pink skirts out of her way as she descended to the flagway. She then took a deep breath as Daventry, who had chosen to ride his horse into London just ahead of the coach, appeared beside her to stiffly offer her his arm, and she took her first steps into her new, devious life.

Number ninety-six Park Lane, home of the widowed Lady Wendover, was set back from the street in a way not considered especially fashionable, although Prudence couldn't know this as she stood, delighted, looking up at the beautiful four-story structure.

As the coach pulled away, she turned and could see the outline of a high brick wall on the opposite side of the street, a wall, Daventry told her, that enclosed Hyde Park and should, in his opinion, be replaced by iron railings or some such improvement that would afford those in Park Lane a view of the park.

"Freddie would sell tomorrow," he told her as she did her best to keep her mouth from dropping to half-mast at the sight of all this grandeur, "except that

I have assured her that soon hers will be one of the most sought after addresses in London. Somerset has already bought here, and Breadalbane is just a short distance away. Having one's town home set back from the curb is a modern notion I much admire, and I am willing to believe those houses now having their entrances facing Norfolk Street will soon be constructing new entrances facing Park Lane."

"So you're thinking of your sister's happiness," Prudence asked at last, wishing to begin the necessary distancing of herself from her guardian now that she was safely in London, "and the thought of any monies to be gained when this land becomes more valuable is of little concern? Why do I doubt that, my lord?"

"You doubt it because you are a rude, underbred, malicious, ungrateful little beast, I should imagine," Banning returned quite evenly, obviously refusing to be baited by her now that he was so near to being shed of her. "Now, if you've spent your budget of nastiness at my expense, perhaps you can dredge up some of those marvelous manners you've promised me you possess so that we can go inside and meet my sister. She's probably waiting to welcome you with open arms, and if you do anything to disabuse her of the notion that she is taking a sweet, simple country miss under her protection I shall most probably boil you in oil."

Prudence held tightly to his arm and deliberately gifted him with her most amenable smile. "La, sir, how you do go on. I vow, you must be the most droll creature on earth," she trilled, simpering in a way that her brother Henry had said debutantes on the lookout for rich husbands mastered in their cradles. Of course, as Henry had added that such obviously false effusions inevitably had the power to set his teeth on edge as he looked for a way out of the room, she was pleased to feel the muscles of Lord Daventry's arm turn to steel beneath her clinging fingers.

The large white door opened before they could ascend to the topmost step and the wide half-circle of porch punctuated by thick Ionic pillars on either side, and Prudence was immediately dazzled by the sight of an enormous crystal chandelier ablaze with more candles than she would think to burn in a month. There was light spilling from everywhere, warmth and welcome permeated the very air as she stepped into the black and white marble tiled foyer, and Prudence knew that if she did not control herself she just might burst into tears.

"Good evening, my lord," a tall, thin, aristocratically handsome man of some forty or more years said, bowing his blond head respectfully as he received Daventry's hat, cloak, whip, and riding gloves, then passed them to a waiting footman before assisting Prudence with her cloak. "Lady Wendover is within, anxiously awaiting your arrival."

"Anxiously, Quimby? That isn't good. I sent a message saying I would be detained in the country longer than first anticipated," Banning said, motioning for Prudence to follow as he headed toward an archway to their left. "Didn't she receive it?"

"Indeed, sir, she did, and you explained everything so that it was easily understood," the butler responded, deftly moving in front of the marquess in order to open the double doors recessed inside the archway. "But if I may say so, sir, it still remained difficult for her to tamp down her anticipation of your arrival. And yours as well and most especially, Miss, of course," he added, inclining his head in Prudence's direction.

"Thank you, Quimby," Prudence said, hating that her voice trembled with nervousness. "Then I suppose," she added, smiling brightly, "we might as well end all this anticipation, as I, too, have been nearly sick with it, unable to believe my good fortune in having Lady Wendover agree to bring me into her household."

"Well done, imp," Banning whispered out of the corner of his mouth as Quimby bent to open the doors, then stepped inside to announce them. "Just don't lay it on too thick and rare, or Quimby will catch you out. He is fiercely protective of my sister."

"As well he should be, with a grumble-guts like you haunting her house," Prudence shot back just as quietly, stepping past him and into the most beautiful room she had ever seen.

Once again, all was light, with candles burning in dozens of holders and reflected in a multitude of gilded mirrors hung on every wall. The room was as large as it was magnificent, with couches and chairs and fragile rosewood tables scattered about like flower petals randomly settled there by a gentle breeze. And in the center of it all, reclining on a chaise covered in a garden-scene tapestry, was one Frederica Davidson, Lady Wendover.

She looked like a painting, an artist's loving rendition of Refined Womanhood. Hair as dark as night clouded around a faintly square face of remarkable beauty. A complexion as fair as a summer's day and as unblemished as a infant's, wide blue eyes as innocent as they were appealing, and a slim, long body clad in a dressing gown of virginal white completed a vision that both inspired Prudence's admiration, and at the same time made her wish herself a thousand miles away.

"Banning!" the beautiful creature cried out in easily read joy, aiming her teacup at a nearby low table and not sparing a moment to look at it as it missed its mark and fell to the floor, milky tea instantly soaking into the carpet that must have cost more money than Prudence had seen in her lifetime. "Oh, darling, you're back! How was your trip? Did you have a good time, I hope?"

"Back, and bearing gifts, my love. As for my trip? I imagine you could say I was tolerably well amused," the marquess said, deserting Prudence where she stood in order to go to his sister, who embraced him warmly, kissed him on both cheeks, then embraced him yet again. "Have you been good? No late nights? No skimping on your rest?"

Prudence might as well have been on the far side of the moon for all the attention either of them paid to her. That's the way it had been between Henry and herself. With no one else in their lives, they had clung to each other. The lump in Prudence's throat grew to the size of a boulder.

"Oh Banning, don't fuss," Lady Wendover said at last, giving him a loving tap on the cheek with her slender fingertips before drawing away from him. "I am as healthy as a horse now, with all that silliness behind me. Goodness, between you and Quimby, it's a marvel I'm allowed out of bed. Now—step away, if you please, and let me see our little Angel. I have her chamber all prepared and have only to make my final selection on hiring just the perfect nurse for her and—*oh, my!*"

Prudence twisted her hands together at her waist, feeling suddenly as if her feet, her hands, and perhaps even her nose were all miles too big, her hair was inhabited by snakes, and her face, never pleasing to her own eyes, resembled that of some gorgon in a pennypress novel. "Hello," she squeaked, then quickly cleared her throat, curtsied, and added lamely, "my lady."

"Hello yourself, Angel," Lady Wendover said in obvious surprise and delight, smiling indulgently even as she motioned Prudence to come closer, telling her she was short-sighted and wanted to see her better. "Banning, you incorrigible scamp. You didn't tell me Angel was ready for her Come-out. I was expecting a child of eight or ten, but she's seventeen if she's a day."

"Eighteen, my lady, nearly nineteen," Prudence corrected, taking two more steps into the room, wishing she had a pistol with her, so she could shoot the Marquess of Daventry with it. If he'd had time to pen his sister a note saying he'd be delayed in the country, couldn't he have squeezed in a line or two about his ward, listing her age at the very least? Or had he done this on purpose, knowing she would be put off her stride by his sweet sister, confident his recalcitrant ward would lose a lot of her bluster as she tried to find a way to apologize for being a woman grown?

"If the thought of bringing out Prudence is too much for you, Freddie, I'll see about removing her to one of my rental properties and hiring a chaperone for her or something," Banning offered, and Prudence felt her hopes hitting her toes.

She didn't want to leave this house of lights, leave this friendly woman. And she most certainly didn't want someone like Miss Honoria Prentice brought in to ride herd on her. Not when she could already see that Lady Wendover, who might be older and more worldly than Prudence but who certainly had never developed a single questioning bone in her body, would be putty in her hands.

"Don't frown, Angel, as Banning is just being his usual, worrying self," Lady Wendover said as Prudence sank into a chair, having resisted the impulse to pick up the fallen teacup and use one of the serviettes to sop up the spilled tea, an action which doubtless would have led to Daventry saying something cutting about her auditioning for the role of maid rather than that of debutante.

"I was most depressingly ill for some months last year," her ladyship explained, "and Banning refuses to believe I have recovered. But I have, I assure you, and now that I'm out of mourning for my husband, having someone young and vital running about the house is just what I need to brighten my days."

"Allow me to extend my deepest sympathies on your sad loss. I'm so sorry for intruding into your household at such a time," Prudence said stiffly, wishing she didn't already like Lady Wendover so well.

"Oh no, no! Don't be sorry. Rodney was called to his fathers more than eighteen months ago. It was a marriage of convenience, you understand, forged when all Banning and I had to our names were our names, eh, Banning? Rodney was sweet enough, and impotent into the bargain, which could only be conceived of as a blessing, but then he was also dead old, for all he was on Wellington's staff. Now, bless him, he's simply dead."

"Freddie," Banning said softly, "I don't think there's any need to tell Prudence all of that."

"Nonsense, Banning. If she's to live here, she'll hear everything, eventually. Lord knows I've been simply dying to talk with someone other than that depressing Honoria Prentice. The woman gives me the fidgets with her thin lips and cold stares, and if Rodney hadn't been the one to hire her, and died before I could convince him to dismiss her, she'd have been replaced long since."

Prudence swiftly lifted a hand to her mouth, pretending a cough to cover what had come dangerously close to an appreciative giggle at Lady Wendover's honest admission. Couldn't even bring herself to dismiss a servant she didn't like? Oh, yes, taking the reins in this household would be mere child's play.

"I'm the dowager countess now," Lady Wendover went on artlessly as her brother rose to pour himself a glass of wine, "but as there was no issue from our marriage, the title and lands have all gone to one of Rodney's depressing cousins and his equally depressing wife. Not that I miss Wendover House, for I don't. It's located deep in Buckinghamshire, you understand, and there is no more boring place on earth. I never go there even to visit the dower house, for Rodney's relatives all remind me of a stuffy clutch of pigeons, continually posing and puffing out their chests. Yes, indeed. Wendover—which is known only for pillow lace and the manufacture of straw-plait, whatever that is—is in the back of beyond, with the nearest community of any note being Stoke-Mandeville, and if you have heard of that town I shall be amazed, for no one has."

"And you won't mind taking such a sad specimen as myself under your wing?" Prudence asked, having decided not to enter into a discussion as to which of the two of them had suffered more living in the country. After all, comparing Wendover House to MacAfee Farm would be much like comparing a castle to a pig sty, if the Park Lane mansion could be used as a yardstick. "As your brother pointed out to me already, I am very green, and will require your assistance and tutelage if I am to know anything— although my new guardian has been most kind and gentle and endlessly helpful," she added, smiling broadly as Banning choked on his wine.

"Oh, aren't you the sweetest thing! And so well-bred and polite! It's settled then, brother dear. I simply have to rearrange my plans slightly." Lady Wendover frowned, looking to the marquess. "Banning, dear, do you suppose you could find some way to have those dolls and toys removed from the house and delivered to an orphanage? I doubt Angel—Prudence—will have any need for them."

"Please, Lady Wendover," Prudence said, relaxing now that she felt certain she wasn't about to be banished from Park Lane. "I'd much rather you called me Angel, if that's all right with you. My brother called me Angel, and I have missed hearing it."

"Oh, how sweet! Isn't that just so *sweet,* Banning?" Lady Wendover asked her brother who, Prudence noticed, seemed to have a slight tic working in his left cheek. Not trust her to know how to act, would he? Ha! She could give him lessons!

Her ladyship turned back to Prudence. "And you

must call me Freddie. Ah, to have a child in the house would have been lovely. But this is above all things wonderful! We shall be merry as crickets as we rub along together—outfitting you, launching you, giggling together like young girls over all the silly gentlemen who will be dangling at your shoestrings. Banning? Is she dowered? She must be dowered."

"I'd give half my fortune to have her off my hands, if that answers your question, darling," Banning said, bending to kiss his sister's cheek. "I do not think I was cut out to be guardian to anyone other than you, dear sister. And now, I shall be off. Rexford is pining for his own bed, and if I don't get him there soon I may have to put down a mutiny. Good evening, Prudence."

"Angel," Lady Wendover reminded him. "Your ward wishes to be addressed as Angel, remember?"

"Very well, Freddie," Banning answered, moving toward the hallway. "As long as you take care to remember that it is just a name, and not a description."

"Muckworm," Prudence muttered beneath her breath, then turned to smile brightly at Lady Wendover, feeling she had cleared her first hurdle rather well, and wondering why she suddenly felt so alone when she had been telling herself she had wanted nothing more than to see the back of Lord Daventry since first she had laid eyes on the man.

CHAPTER 7

*It is a truth universally acknowledged,
that a single man in possession of a good fortune,
must be in want of a wife.*

Jane Austen

Morning came hours too soon after a long night spent mostly tossing and turning in bed, so that Banning listened with little more than half an ear as Rexford dressed him comfortably in shirt, pantaloons, and dressing gown after his bath and then disappeared, having rapidly gushed out something about Park Lane, and ecru satin, and, if he had heard correctly, pink lizards.

Not that the marquess minded being on his own, as he usually preferred a solitary breakfast in his chamber, and Rexford possessed an annoying habit of dancing about the room, fluffing pillows, mouthing the latest gossip from the taproom where many of the premier valets gathered in the evening, and clucking over a mud stain on a boot toe or a snag in a new pair of buckskins.

Although Banning had delighted in being in the country—with the exception of the single night spent at MacAfee Farm—after nearly a year spent in town, and had not minded roughing it in a succession of inns as they made their way back to London, it was nice to be in his own house in Chesterfield Street again, sitting at his own table, enjoying the breakfast sent up by his own chef, and reading his own morning newspaper as he reclined in his own soft leather chair.

Here, in the solitude of his bedchamber, he could forget for a moment that he was now guardian to one of the devil's own spawn, a maddening young woman whose golden eyes had invaded his dreams, seeing into corners of his mind best left private. Not that he still desired her, of course. He had nearly succumbed to a bit of madness, probably having something to do with a lingering pity he'd felt for the child after the loss of her mare and something to do with the intriguing sight of a smooth, bared shoulder when he hadn't been expecting to see one.

Why, he didn't even *like* Prudence MacAfee.

She was rude, unkempt, blatantly disrespectful of both his age and his position, and had all the makings of a Piccadilly bubbler—a chameleon with the ability to alter her behavior to suit her surroundings, or her desires.

Although she was not totally without appeal.

Little monkey, he thought, remembering Prudence's shenanigans of the previous evening, recalling how she had played the sweet young miss so seamlessly for the benefit of his sister, who would never believe "Angel" MacAfee capable of rattling off a string of swear words that would bore a hole in an iron pot.

And unfortunately for his own peace of mind, it was better that his gentle sister remain ignorant of Angel's less than desirable talents. If the girl proved good to her word, she would behave while she was beneath Freddie's roof, and they would find a way to foist her onto some unsuspecting young dandy before the season was half begun, freeing Banning of his unwanted guardianship.

Or at least he hoped it would work out that way.

Banning picked up the newspaper even as he raised his cup to his lips, determinedly pushing thoughts of Prudence out of his head as he began reading, wishing to catch up on the news he had missed while out of the city.

He had just begun perusing a story relating to growing unrest in the Midlands due to another factory closing when the door to his bedchamber flew open and his friend Marmaduke Kester, Earl of Preston, exploded into the room, nearly coming to grief as he skidded to a stop on a small carpet.

"There you are!" the earl exclaimed, his unruly shock of mud-brown hair standing nearly straight up on his head, as if he had just endured a sudden shock. "Gone for more than a week, and he's sitting here calm as can be, reading his newspaper, when his friends are longing to hear all about his adventure. Still wish we'd all gone, but I hate the country, and Dewey sneezes when we ride in the park. Did you find MacAfee's baby sister? How did you find her? She wasn't starving, or anything, was she? Dewey and I have been worrying about that, seeing as how you left her on her own for so long. Bloody irresponsible, you know, especially for such a upright man as you're so hellbent on making yourself. Ain't that right, Dewey? Dewey? Now where did he go?"

The Honorable Dewey Norton, a good eight inches

shorter than the tall, bony earl and nearly a third more rounded, entered the chamber almost suspiciously, his eyes darting from side to side as if he expected wild Indians to spring out from behind the velvet drapes and attack what little hair he had left on his head.

"You left me to pay off the hack again, Duke," he said, his tenor voice taking on its usual whine. "I gave him what I had, which wasn't much. I think he spit at me as I mounted the curb." He turned his back to the two men, trying to look over his own shoulder as he asked them to look at his coat, just to see if there was any spittle on it.

"I want my own coach," he said morosely after they assured him his coat was bone-dry and he walked toward a chair, still trying to peek over his shoulder. "This being the eldest, and the only son, is not all it's touted to be. Not when we still have to pop off two more girls. Four of 'em gone, and still not a penny to spare for me, the heir, and if m'father sticks his spoon in the wall before Harriet and Agnes are bracketed it'll all fall to me."

He collapsed into the chair, sticking his rather short, plump legs straight out in front of him as he balanced himself on the base of his spine. "God, how I hate hacks! Mornin', Banning. Good to see you again, and all that. Montgomery sent us on up, seeing as how we've been running tame here in Chesterfield Street for ages. Good man, Montgomery. Checked my back for me, too. I'd have a butler myself, if I didn't have so many sisters."

"Good morning, Dewey," Banning responded, waving Marmaduke to a chair, then hiding a smile as the earl moved to sit himself down, but not before nearly tipping over a china figurine on the table beside it, falling into the seat jerkily juggling the delicate statue before nervously clasping it to his chest.

"I hope the both of you are well?" Banning added as he uncovered two extra cups a maid had thoughtfully placed on his tray and Marmaduke and Dewey went about pouring themselves coffee.

The three had been friends since their school days, and if they had grown apart in some ways, the emotional bond between them remained strong enough to withstand Dewey's constant complaints and insecurities, Marmaduke's clumsiness, and Banning's recent depressing descent into maturity and determined sobriety.

Many were the larks they had indulged in over the years, the signposts they had changed while out on a midnight spree, the rigs they had run on unsuspecting souls, all in the pursuit of adventure, excitement, and the chance for a giggle or two.

"Get yourself drunk yet?" Marmaduke asked, as he did nearly each time they met, heaping sugar into his cup while Dewey drank his sans either sugar or cream, hating the taste, but determined to rid himself of the growing bulge around his middle. "Been nearly a year, you know, but we think it's time. Dewey got himself drunk as a lord while you were gone, didn't you, Dewey? Opera dancer threw him over for a deep-in-the-pockets baron."

"Didn't want her anyway, Duke, and why don't you just drop it? You've been going on and on about it all week, all but walking up to strangers in the street to tell them how she tossed me aside, and I slopped up canary all night until you had to carry me home," Dewey said, pouting. "Now why don't you button your lip a minute and let Banning tell us about his little ward. In case you haven't noticed, and you never do, he didn't answer when you asked him about her. So? What's up, friend? Did the little terror bite you? Agnes used to bite. Gwendolyn pulled my hair."

"Explaining your sad lack of it now," Banning teased, reluctant to tell his friends about Prudence. "My ward is fine, however, and nicely settled in with my sister. You'll see her soon enough, when Freddie has her dressed up like a Christmas pudding and parades her all over town to scrape up a match for her. I'd be obliged if you each danced with her a time or two, just to get her established."

Marmaduke sat forward all at once, sloshing coffee onto his sleeve. "What's that! You went and got yourself a debutante? God's hangnail, Banning, what did you go and do something like that for?"

"Yes, Banning," Dewey put in, shaking his head. "Cost you the earth to clothe her, feed her, buy her all the gewgaws and furbelows that chits seem to think they need. And then there's the dowry, and the wedding, and Christening gifts when she starts hatching out babies. 'Course, that would have happened sooner or later in any case, with a girl. Bad move, in my opinion. You should have found yourself a boy ward, if you were so hot to be someone's guardian."

Banning put down his fork, his appetite gone. "I wasn't hot to be *anyone's* guardian, if you'll recall. I was tricked into it."

"That's true enough," Marmaduke concurred, nodding his head so fiercely that his shock of mud-brown hair trembled like a cock's comb as the animal prepared to crow the dawn. "He was tricked into it, Dewey. Getting slow in his old age, not able to scent a rig when it's about to be run on him. Shame MacAfee had to die, though. High price to pay for a trick, don't you think?"

"When they meet his sister, they might think he had himself a happy release," Banning murmured under his breath, but not softly enough, for Dewey overheard him.

"What is it? The girl's an antidote? She has a squint? How about her teeth? M'sister Mary Louise had this gap between her two front teeth. This wide," he said, demonstrating by pulling up his top lip and laying his index finger against his own teeth. "Should have seen her trying to eat an apple. Looked like she was a farmer, plowing furrows for a spring planting. Has three girls of her own now, each one of them cursed with teeth just like hers or worse. I'd shoot m'self if I had to try to marry those three off, I tell you."

"Angel has good teeth," Banning said, wishing he could find a way to change the subject before he found himself explaining a lot of things he'd rather left unsaid. "Tell me, have I missed anything while I was away? You two arrived before I could do more than read the first page of my newspaper."

Marmaduke and Dewey exchanged quick, rather amused looks. "He doesn't know," the earl said, grinning.

"She won't like that he's got a ward. At least not one this old," Dewey Norton answered, frowning. "But if she's homely, then that's probably all right. Besides, she's not exactly new goods any more, now is she? Can't be particular any more."

Banning waved at them from across the low table. "Pardon me, gentlemen—hullo! Would it be possible for me to join this conversation? Although first, I suppose, one of you two loobies might have to explain just *what the devil you're talking about!*"

Dewey wet his lips as he screwed up his face, deep furrows appearing across his forehead beneath his receding hairline, obviously belatedly struck by the seriousness of his information. "It's the Broughton, Banning. Althea. *Your* Althea. And you know, it's the damndest thing. Brace yourself, man, for this is a shocker. Seems the wedding's off. Was eating breakfast as I first read about it. Damned near choked on my kippers. Um . . ." Dewey dissolved into a short giggle. "Didn't you hear?"

"That's not funny, you two," Banning told his friends, his breathing suddenly painful.

"That's what you think, Banning, or you would if you weren't working so hard on becoming a prig," Marmaduke said, looking to Dewey, who nodded.

So it *was* true. Althea Broughton was no longer engaged. The woman he'd loved and lost was back on the marriage mart? Banning waited for a wave of elation to wash over him, but it didn't happen. Maybe he needed to hear more, so that he could believe his good luck. "She was to be married next month, as I remember it, having to delay the wedding while she went into mourning for her cousin after Waterloo. And now the wedding's been called off completely? Duke? You want to tell me what happened?"

The earl sniffed a time or two, wiggling his nose with each twitching snort, as if he too had to marshal his courage to tell Banning what everyone else already knew. "It was Wexford. Seems he forgot to mention eloping to Gretna with his mother's maid some three years ago. Tried to get shed of her quietly once Althea accepted his offer, buy her off or some such thing, but it all came out last week at Lady Wexford's soiree in honor of her son's upcoming nuptials, when the little missus came barging into the music room, Wexford's brat in her arms."

Dewey quickly took up the story when Marmaduke stopped talking to take a sip of his coffee. "Lady Wexford screamed like a stuck pig and then swooned, Althea popped Wexford smack in the face with a candlestick, and those that were there have been dining out on the story all week. Wish I could have been there to see it, but I wasn't invited. Never am, unless you're in town. That's what happens when you're only an Honorable."

"And Althea hasn't retired to the country? She's still in London, still going about in society?" Banning was surprised that Miss Broughton hadn't taken to her heels, embarrassed to the depths of her soul.

"Why should she go anywhere?" Marmaduke asked, rising, as he had never been able to remain in one spot above five minutes, a failing that had saved his life at Quatre Bras, when he had volunteered to take information to Wellington and therefore barely missed being blown to pieces by the French artillery that had exploded precisely where he had been standing a few heartbeats earlier.

"Wasn't as if she was the one caught out with a wife and child in the woodpile," the earl continued bluntly. "She's on the town every night, smiling and dancing and telling everyone she's much relieved, as she never liked Wexford above half in the first place. It was her father who pushed the match, looking to marry her to a fortune. As you should know."

"Money," Dewey spat, shaking his head. "It all

comes back to that, doesn't it, Banning? But now that you've got buckets of it, thanks to that dead aunt of yours, Althea's papa would probably fall on your neck, weeping, if you was to ask for her again."

"If the ward's ugly, maybe," Marmaduke slipped in, already heading for the door. "Won't be best pleased if you're squiring a little beauty around Mayfair, putting Althea in the shade, and keeping the tongues wagging about how young you are to be anyone's keeper. Good thing about the gray hair, Banning, or else the tongues would be flapping nineteen to the dozen from here to John O'Groats."

Banning closed his eyes for a moment, remembering how Angel had looked that morning at the inn, when he had discovered her with her hair down, her cheeks flushed with sleep, her usual mulish expression softened. He shook his head, replacing that vision with the one of Angel as he had last seen her, rigged out in that juvenile gown, spouting miss-ish, simpering drivel, and looking, if not plain, extremely ordinary. Almost drab.

Which had been the truth? The lush body in the bed or the boring milk-and-water debutante in his sister's drawing room? Or, when either surface was scratched, was the true Prudence MacAfee revealed—a hoydenish, profane, breeches-clad termagant totally unsuited to society?

He *had* to get her married, had to get her out of his life, out of his mind. And the easiest way to do that now stared him straight in the face: Althea Broughton.

Althea would know what to do with Angel. Between Freddie and Althea, they would have Prudence MacAfee safely wed to some half-pay officer within a month, and Banning didn't care what it cost him by way of a dowry—even an outright bribe, if it came to that.

In the meantime, he would concentrate on Althea, the woman he had loved two years ago and might love again, if he still felt as he had the last time he'd seen her, going down the dance on the eve of Waterloo, before her cousin's death, and her nearly year-long removal from society.

"Leaving so soon, Duke?" Banning asked as he came out of his short reverie, suddenly feeling like taking himself on a brisk walk, maybe even going so far as to drop in at his sister's, just to see how she and Angel were rubbing along together.

"He's trying to break in his new boots," Dewey explained, also rising. "Told him to go to my man, but he wouldn't listen. We'll walk a couple of blocks, then end up in another damned hack. Which I'm not paying for, Duke!" he shouted toward the door before turning back to Banning. "See you at Almack's? Have to get your ward a voucher in a hurry, won't you? Try Sally Jersey. She's usually good for one at the last minute."

He shook his head. "Wouldn't be you for thousands, Banning, old friend. You won't like being a guardian. I only help out with the girls when m'father screams at me, and I can't stand it."

"And here I'd hoped my friends would offer themselves as supporting props as I struggle through the season," Banning said facetiously, laughing as Marmaduke, looking at his friends as he headed for the hallway, walked straight into the door jamb.

"Tell you what," Marmaduke offered, briskly rubbing his bruised forehead as if it might somehow help him in coming up with a solution to Banning's problems. "We'll dance with the chit like you asked, talk her up in the clubs as your ward. Your sister has a good heart and will do all her possible, but we know she's not up to bear-leading a chit through a whole season. So, as I see it, you have only two ways to go. Marry Althea quick, while she'd be grateful to you for whisking her away from the gossips, then have her pop off the ward. Or marry the ward herself and have done with the thing all in one fell swoop. Time and more you were setting up your nursery, you know. My mother's after me day and night to do the same."

Dewey pursed his lips, nodding. "Sounds reasonable enough, Banning, even if it is Duke who thought of it," he said, following his friend to the door. "Quick, clean. Think on it, Banning, why don't you? Either way, the important thing is that you have it all settled before we leave for Newmarket. Then there's that business about heading up to Scotland . . ."

The door closed behind the two men and Banning sat back in his chair, wondering if being cursed with a ward was aging him, for suddenly his two friends seemed very much like rackety loose screws, while he was burdened with a whole new world of responsibilities.

Marriage to his ward, just to stop the gossip or, as Dewey said, to be shed of his problems before the races at Newmarket?

Ridiculous!

Marriage to Althea so that she could help him get shed of Prudence MacAfee? Banning had thought of that solution even before Marmaduke mentioned it. He had wanted to marry Althea Broughton two years ago, had thought his life was over when she had turned him down.

Now he was rich, which made him acceptable to Althea's father.

He was also burdened with a ward. Even if his sister had agreed to present her, house her, it was he who was ultimately responsible for her. He had worried the moment he'd first realized that Angel was of a marriageable age that tongues would wag from one end of Mayfair to another as soon it was learned that the Marquess of Daventry, a bachelor, was in possession of a female ward.

That fact had bothered him, but not to any great degree—until now. Until he had heard his friends confirm his apprehensions, and the person of an eligible Althea Broughton had been added to the mix.

Banning stripped off his dressing gown and headed for his dressing room, wondering, in a small corner of his mind, why he was heading off to see Angel rather than racing to Grosvenor Square to make a morning call on the woman he would make his wife.

CHAPTER 8

*It is not only fine feathers
that make fine birds.*

Aesop

The dress shop was located in a distinctly unfashionable section of the city, but Prudence didn't know that, and if she had, it wouldn't have mattered anyway, as she was entirely too well pleased to be out and about to concern herself with such a meaningless thing as being "proper."

Rexford had shown up in Park Lane before nine of the clock, hours too early to expect Lady Wendover to be awake and thinking like a responsible guardian, but hours after Prudence, used to country hours, had been up and about, clad in her shirt and breeches, snagging herself a hearty breakfast in the kitchen with the cook, following the maids about as they began a day of dusting and scrubbing, and even finding time to chat with Quimby who, as she informed the man, was "not nearly as starchy" as he looked.

She was like a child set loose in a toy shop, eager for adventure, hot to learn everything about her new surroundings, and as willing to like everyone she met as a puppy making friends through the sheer exuberance and love of life that she exuded without even trying.

Indeed, Prudence was so filled with youthful energy, so naively inquisitive, that she actually followed the dowager countess's maid, Isobel, as that woman tiptoed into milady's bedchamber to place some fresh towels near the tub, and woke her unsuspecting hostess by giggling aloud when she espied the woman sleeping in, of all things, a white satin eyemask.

"Sure could have used one of those the day Shadwell's toga slipped on the way back from his dirt bath," Prudence had exclaimed, dissolving into giggles once more, a statement that sent both her ladyship and her maid into hysterics, as they had already been privy to a few of Prudence's stories of both Shadwell MacAfee's eccentric behavior and his less than handsome appearance.

Which probably led to the kindly Lady Wendover's reluctant but smiling approval of Rexford's plan a few minutes later to "take Miss MacAfee in hand— sartorially speaking, that is—so that she should not be an embarrassment to either the marquess or yourself, my lady. I thought of it last night, and am still wondering why it took so long for inspiration to strike me. Both his lordship and myself are concerned that the exertion necessary to complete Miss MacAfee's wardrobe would be entirely too taxing for you, and as Miss Prentice is, if you'll pardon me saying so, a dead loss, this seemed the logical solution. And we must be rid of these breeches!"

There had been only one slight hitch in Rexford's plans. He had not realized that while Prudence's attachment to her breeches ran deep, it did not even approach her hatred of the infamous pink gown. It was only after a short, heated debate that a triumphant Prudence, still in her breeches, was all but stuffed into the marquess's town coach and the pair were on their way to the unfashionable address of the valet's dearest friend, David Wallace.

"Your friend is one of those fancy French dressmakers?" Prudence asked as she hesitated a moment before stepping inside the small shop bearing the painted words *La Belle Friponne* in the bottom-most right corner of its equally small window.

"You are to forget this information within the time it takes me to convey it to you, Miss MacAfee, but *La Belle Friponne* translates, rather rudely, into *The Beautiful Hussy*. David is the most talented, creative creature on this earth, but for the moment he is reduced to dressing only well-kept *courtesans*. You, my dear, are going to bring him into fashion."

"I am?" Prudence asked nervously, looking around the shop as she slowly eased herself further into the front room, racking her brain for the definition of the word *courtesan*, for her education had not included a formal study of the French language. "Oh, my stars!" she exclaimed when her wildly grabbing mind latched on to an answer.

"You're going to dress me like a high flyer, a light-skirt, a doxy, a—a *whore*? Well, that ought to please his lordship straight down to his toes. Oh yes. I can hear him now. He'll fly straight up into the boughs—and stay there for at least five minutes, at which point he'll climb back down to fire you and beat me into flinders. I thought you said we could be friends!"

"David does not dress *whores,* Miss MacAfee," Rexford explained tightly as he picked up a small reticule decorated with delicate beading. "But we all must begin somewhere, mustn't we? And with you," he said, looking her up and down, then shuddering, as if her appearance gave him the shivers, "I believe any less discerning designer would throw up her hands, crying off from the challenge. Now do be quiet, if you please. David must have heard the bell as we entered, and will join us shortly."

Prudence did as she was told, partly because she had no desire to anger Rexford, and partly because she was so overwhelmed by the sheer amount of haphazardly piled fabrics spilling from the floor to ceiling shelves, the mounds of delicate lace, the rolls upon rolls of colored ribbon, and even the dozens of shoes—none of them with a mate to be seen anywhere—all of which made walking through the room not only an adventure but a challenge.

She was just reaching for a long, poufy feather dyed a glorious deep red when there was the "swoosh" of a curtain being pulled back and a short, slightly-built man burst into the room, his arms held out in front of him as he fairly flew toward Rexford.

"Darling man," David Wallace exclaimed, taking hold of Rexford's shoulders, then kissing the valet soundly on both cheeks, an affectionate greeting Rexford quickly returned. "Thank God you've survived your enforced sojourn into the wilds of Sussex! I received your note late last night, and have been on tenterhooks since then, knowing I was soon to see you again."

He released Rexford and cast his quick, nervous gaze around the room, barely hesitating when he espied Prudence, who was fairly well occupied doing her best to hide behind the red feather boa.

"Where is she, Jonathan?" he asked. "Where is this incredibly unique angel who is going to catapult me to the forefront of London's *modistes?* All I see is this pretty young man mauling a very expensive plume."

"Miss MacAfee," Rexford ordered sharply, "take off that ridiculous hat, if you please. And, as I said, you will remember *nothing* of your visit here—except to tell all who admire your gowns that your *modiste* will be locating in Bond Street within the month—as soon as the marquess pays all the bills you will run up for him and the funds necessary to rent such a costly establishment become available."

He smiled kindly at Prudence, even as he patted David's hand. "That last part will, of course, also remain our little secret."

Prudence grinned at the valet. "Oh, you're a regular slyboots, Rexford," she said, laying down the feather boa and pulling her hat from her head, allowing her honey-dark hair to spill down past her shoulders, "and I take my hat off to you. There. Is this better?"

David left Rexford where he stood and approached Prudence, a finger to his lips, staring at her for a long time with his head cocked to one side, then walking fully around her, speaking only to tell her to kindly stand up straight and not try to twist her head in a full circle in order to watch him.

"Jonny," he said at last, with the air of one making a long-awaited pronouncement, "go into the sewing room and fetch a shift, then take her to a room where she can change. I'll need to see her as nature made her in order to take my full measure of her potential. But I think you've done it. You have brought me my ticket to the ladies of Mayfair. Hurry! I can feel the ideas beginning to form!"

"Hold it right there, Rexford!" Prudence exclaimed, clutching her hat to her breasts as if she had somehow already been stripped of her clothing. "If either of you thinks I'm going to go peeling myself to the buff while you two parade around me, *umm-ing* and *a-ha-ing*—well, I'll be damned for a tinker if I'm going to do it, that's all!"

Rexford sighed deeply, shaking his head. "You are nothing to either David or me save a mannequin and a means to an end, Miss MacAfee. We have no designs on your modesty or your person."

Prudence threw back her head and laughed in genuine amusement. "Well, bloody hell, Rexford, what do you take me for—a complete looby? I've already figured *that* one out! But we've cried friends, remember? I want to be a part of this, not just stand around, having pins stuck in me while everyone else decides what I should wear. And to start, *I* will be the one to pick out my own shift. Agreed?"

Rexford and David exchanged looks, then David shrugged, spreading his hands. "I suppose it's only fair. As long as she doesn't covet that red feather boa, Jonny," he said, looking to Prudence, who grimaced and shook her head. "All right. Let us begin!"

Banning's man of business detained him for the better part of two hours, insisting he sign documents that had been awaiting his return from MacAfee Farm, thus delaying his departure for his sister's until noon, when the memory of his chef's outstanding success with a fillet of beef postponed his visit to Park Lane by yet another hour.

The weather was quite fine, and thinking to walk off some of his substantial lunch, Banning waved away Montgomery's suggestion that he have the curricle brought round and started off on foot, still wondering why he hadn't raced hot-foot to Grosvenor Square to express his condolences to Miss Althea Broughton—and perhaps sniff out the lay of the land concerning both his remembered affection for the lady and her opinion of his now deep pockets.

For it was time he set up his nursery, more than time. The title was one thing, but his inheritance—although it had come too late to press his initial suit with Althea—also carried with it a responsibility to wed and procreate and thus complete his determination to become a solid, sober, upstanding citizen of his rarefied world. The war was at last completely over, his grasstime was decidedly behind him, even his hair was gray, for pity's sake, and—with one notable lapse into silliness that had prompted that ill-fated picnic with Prudence—it was time, more than time, that he and Marmaduke and even Dewey realized that they were not children any more.

What a pity that it all seemed so deadly dull.

He made the turn off Park Lane and into his sister's drive, taking time to admire what would be her marvelous view of the park if ever anyone had the sense to knock down that ridiculous wall, skipped lightly up the steps to the front door, and gave a few quick, hard raps of the ornate brass knocker.

"Good afternoon, my lord," Quimby said as he opened the door and ushered the marquess inside, relieving him of hat and cane before Banning could be sure he saw a faint hint of apprehension in the man's usually noncommittal eyes. "You will find Lady Wendover resting in the drawing room, as is her custom these past months. I have personally opened all the doors to the garden, for the beneficial air, you understand. Shall I have a tray brought in?"

"You take very great care of my sister, Quimby, and I am endlessly in your debt," Banning said in all sincerity, heading for the drawing room. "I'll assume that Miss MacAfee is with her, the two of them gossiping and exchanging girlish stories?"

"You could assume that, sir," Quimby said in a strange, almost strangled tone that caused Banning to turn back to him in question. Warning bells began clanging inside his head, although he didn't want to know why he felt suddenly on edge. "But unfortunately Miss MacAfee is out, and you have missed her. That tray, my lord? I believe cook has prepared strawberry tarts for tea. They are your favorite, as I remember?"

"Out?" Banning felt his hackles beginning to rise, then quickly calmed himself. What was the matter with him? It wasn't as if he would be devastated if Prudence wasn't at home. He had come to see his sister. Prudence MacAfee just happened to reside here at the moment, that's all. Nothing more. "Oh, I see. She and Miss Prentice must be shopping. Lord knows I've seen enough of that pink gown to last me. That's it, isn't it? Where have they gone? Madame Burgaud's? That would have been my choice."

"I really couldn't say, my lord," Quimby responded stiffly, setting a distance between the two men that hadn't existed in the months they had, together, nursed Lady Wendover back to health, spending many a long, torturous night pacing the same drawing room floor, worrying that each night might be her last.

"But," he added, relenting and seeming more the old, friendly Quimby, "if you were to conclude your interview with Lady Wendover and be left with any remaining questions, I believe I might be of some small service to you. My lord," he ended, bowing.

Giving the butler a last, questioning look, Banning headed for the drawing room, eager to talk to his sister about her house guest.

"Banning!" Lady Wendover exclaimed as he entered the room, her tone more accusatory than welcoming. "Whatever are you doing here? I hadn't thought you'd show your face in Park Lane until I summoned you, threatening all sorts of mayhem if you didn't act more the competent guardian. Oh Banning, how very bad of you!"

"And a cheery good afternoon to you as well, my dear sister," he said, bending to kiss her cheek, the warning bells inside his head now setting up a tremendous pealing. "I see our little Angel has yet to burn down the house around your shoulders or haul a spittoon into the drawing room, which I suppose must be considered a gift from the gods. Where is she? Quimby says she and Miss Prentice didn't go to Madame Burgaud's."

Lady Wendover gave his cheek a playful tap. "You're such a tease, Banning, as is Angel. We talked long into the night, you know, and the girl tells some shocking rappers—mostly about her grandfather, Shadwell. To hear her tell it, she should have grown up half wild, which of course she didn't for she did have her grandmother—at least for a while. She is quite the loveliest, most *genuine* creature, and very well behaved, although a trifle naive and perhaps untutored in her manners. Besides, I haven't been so diverted in years, so I allowed her to believe I believed her."

Banning looked closely at his sister, who seemed to be having some difficulty in meeting his eyes. "Prudence's winning ways to one side for the moment, Freddie—where did she and Miss Prentice go today?"

"Would you care for some strawberry tarts, Banning? Cook made some lovely ones this morning, and Angel brought me one while it was still warm. Yes, yes. A sweet, lovely child. Shall I ring for Quimby?"

Banning sat himself down in a straight back chair he'd pulled up to the chaise where his sister was sitting stiffly, not looking in the least comfortable. "You know," he ventured, trying to keep his tone light, "if one more person tries to fob me off with an offer of strawberry tarts, I might just begin believing you have done away with my paragon of a ward and even now your servants are busily burying the body in the cellars."

"Burying the body? Don't be silly, Banning!" Lady Wendover declared, laughing just a little too long to make her mirth seem genuine and just long enough for her brother to decide that, when he at last pried the truth from his sister, he wasn't going to like it. He wasn't going to like it one bit.

"Freddie?" he inquired sternly, unknowingly giving a very good impression of their late father at his most intense and disapproving. His sister had always been so malleable, so easily brought to follow where others led. Prudence, his ward of the many faces and even more wiles, had probably wrapped the poor, impressionable thing firmly around her thumb within a half hour of his departure last night.

Why hadn't he realized that? This must be what was meant by that melodramatic saying about having nurtured a snake at one's bosom. In short, the girl was a menace! "What's going on?" he pushed when his sister sat mumchance, looking increasingly guilty. "Where did Prudence and Miss Prentice go? And if the words 'Bartholomew Fair' dribble off your lips, I'll—"

"Oh bother!" Lady Wendover exploded at last, falling back against the cushions, rolling her curiously childlike blue eyes. "Here it comes. The riot and rumpus I wished to avoid, and would have if you'd stayed away, which is what Rexford promised you'd do when he came to visit with Angel this morning."

"Rexford? What has my valet to do with any of this?" Banning leaned forward, intrigued.

"Rexford? Why, he's got her, of course," Lady Wendover said, pouting. "I worried at first, but then when I got a close look at that *atrocious* gown, and the lizard—Angel calls Miss Prentice that, you know, which I find highly original and diverting—well, when the lizard said the pink was just *exactly* the sort of gown Angel should wear, and I knew it was all wrong but even the *thought* of shopping fatigued me past bearing, and seeing how Rexford appeared with a *brilliant* solution, and his promise that you would approve, and even Quimby agreed, and when I realized that I've been quite moped to death until Angel miraculously appeared and reminded me of what it's like to be young and impulsive and daring—."

She took a deep breath, then added sprightly: "So,

did you hear that Althea Broughton is on the lookout for a title again? You were one of her suitors a few years ago, as I recall. Have you thought about making her an offer? She'd probably kiss your boots, grateful to get herself settled and the gossip behind her."

Banning slowly rose to his full height, so that he towered over his sister, and pronounced slowly: "Where did Rexford take Angel? If she found some way to snare him into taking her to Bartholomew Fair, I'll—"

"Bartholomew Fair, Bartholomew Fair! You do go on, don't you, Banning? Just like Papa when he'd gotten the bit between his teeth. Now don't go putting yourself into a taking, if you please, for it's very disturbing to see you this way," she said, holding out her hands as if to ward off an imminent attack.

"Furthermore," she continued, doing a fair impression of a filly who'd taken the bit between her *own* teeth, "raging at me will only make me mulish, as well you know. Honestly, Banning, I liked you worlds better when you were gaming and wenching and racing all over town with Marmaduke and Dewey. Now you're depressingly like Papa, which I must tell you I cannot consider a good thing. Honestly, give a man a title, follow it with a little money, and *presto!* he goes one of two ways, either straight to the devil, or up into his altitudes, turning all stuffy and stodgy and *mean.*"

Banning was doing his level best to remain calm, but he was fighting a losing battle, and he knew it. If his sister did not give him answers, and give them soon, he was going to shake her! "Would you please stop throwing my past in my teeth and, worse yet, comparing the ramshackle youth I was with the man I am trying to become, praising the former and condemning the latter? You act as if growing up, recognizing that I have certain responsibilities, is a disaster. Now, where is she?"

"I don't know precisely where they are are, Banning," Lady Wendover admitted, concentrating her gaze on the open doors to the garden. "Rexford promised he could make Angel into an Original. Ask Quimby. He knows."

Banning was already halfway to the foyer, having belatedly remembered that the butler had hinted that he could be applied to for information, when Lady Wendover called after him: "Don't you hurt her, Banning!"

He stopped, turning to glare at his sister. "Hurt her, Freddie? You underestimate the depth of my anger. I'd kill her if I were to have any option at all—throttle her with my own two hands—but I doubt it would answer the purpose."

CHAPTER 9

No rule is so general,
which admits not some exception.

Robert Burton

Prudence kissed David Wallace on both cheeks, then kissed Rexford just as enthusiastically, not caring a fig if it was proper or not, as she had never been so happy in her entire life. Well, perhaps she had been once, long ago when her parents were alive, but as she could no longer remember those years very well, this morning's adventure into the world of fashion would be enough for her to go on with at the moment.

"But there isn't *anything* I can wear back to Park Lane, David?" she asked, pouting without really being upset that she was once more clad in her shirt and breeches, as she felt more *real* in her comfortable old clothes than she believed she ever would when she was clad in silk from head to toe and staring into a mirror at the rather appealing stranger who frowned back at her.

"David will have a bare minimum of gowns to you by the end of the week, as promised, Miss MacAfee," Rexford said with a tired sigh, for Prudence had certainly put both he and the dressmaker through hoops these past three hours and the valet was nearing the point of exhaustion. "But we cannot take the chance that a beautiful young lady of fashion will be seen leaving this place with me, as I am highly recognizable as the marquess's valet. No one will notice you dressed as you are. Do you understand now, Miss MacAfee?"

"Yes, Rexford, I understand completely. I am beneath notice, a nothing, a cipher, and will remain so until David's gowns and your direction transforms me into the Toast of Mayfair," Prudence said, winking at David. "I understood before, but I do so love it when you cut up stiff and put on airs. Are you really so important?"

"Jonny is a premier valet, Miss MacAfee," David said in all seriousness as he patted Rexford's shoulder. "Although the marquess is a fine figure of a man, he sometimes does not show to advantage because of his penchant for dressing himself on the odd occasion, which may have put you off. But Jonathan is highly prized for his expertise in knowing precisely what is right and proper—even more so than for his talent with the pressing iron. Isn't that right, Jonny?"

"I have heard that I have that reputation," Rexford agreed, tilting up his chin so that to Prudence it looked as if he might be examining the ceiling for cobwebs. "Lord knows the Prince of Wales was quite actively courting me at one time. As if I should deign to dress that dissipated, corpulent frame. I do have my reputation to consider, after all."

"And yet you have seen fit to take me under your wing," Prudence said, giving into impulse and kissing the man yet again. "If it weren't for the fact that you're doing it mostly to shove David into the *ton's* face, I'd be extremely humbled. As it is, I'm starving. Do you think we can find something to eat before we go back to Park Lane? I'd adore seeing the inside of a London tavern, and a tall glass of beer wouldn't go amiss either, now that I think of it. This dress-fitting business is thirsty work."

"You *have* promised to work with her on her manners and deportment, haven't you, Jonny?" David asked, nervously chewing on his thumbnail. "I wouldn't wish to see any of my greatest creations parading about on entirely the wrong end of Bond Street. Beer, indeed! Only lowbred barbarians and the Irish drink beer."

"Snob!" Prudence declared laughingly, winking at Rexford as she pushed open the door of the shop. "I'll leave you two to chat while I stand stock-still on the flagway, behaving myself just as I would if I'd just landed smack in the middle of Almack's. All right?"

Rexford looked to David, then through the window-pane to the fairly deserted street and the marquess's coach that had returned as ordered a good twenty minutes ago. "Five minutes, Miss MacAfee," he said firmly. "For David and I do have some business to discuss. And the ivory satin with the pearl and crystal-line appliques will never see the interior of your wardrobe cabinet if you take so much as a single small step away from the other side of that door. Do you understand me?"

"You're a hard man, Jonathan Rexford," she said as sternly as was possible when her lips kept curling into a smile, then she slipped out the door, eager to see if anything interesting was occurring anywhere on the street.

She looked down the street to her right, and there was nothing—only a single, shuffling individual as ugly as a mud fence and twice as dirty, ambling along as if he had all the time in the world to get where he was going and no destination in mind.

She shrugged, turning away in the hope that the view would be more interesting to her left. And it was. Just four or five doors away, at the corner, a man was selling meat pies, holding up one of his greasy offerings while the remainder sat in a large tray hung around his neck.

Prudence reached into her pocket for the purse holding all the money she had managed to pilfer from Shadwell over the years, extracting the coins needed to make up the price the pie man was shouting to all who could hear, then shoved the purse deep into her pocket again.

With only a quick look through the windowpane to be sure David and Rexford had removed to the sewing room, and another quick look, this time to the coach-man who was nodding off up on his box, she began sidling her way down the block, her stomach growling even as her heart leapt at this small bid for excitement.

Pushing her chin down into her chest, and her voice into her stomach, she held out the coins and growled, "One pie, bucko. And it'd better be *real* meat or Oi'll be eatin' yer liver fer m'dinner. No dog, y'hear?"

"Ooh! 'ot-'eaded little bugger, ain't yer?" the pie man crowed, snatching up the coins just as fast as Prudence could snaggle the pie, the even exchange pleasing both of them. "Now 'op the twig, kiddy. Iffen yer wuz ta fall down dead at the first bite, it'd ruin m'business all 'ollow iffen yer wuz still 'ere, yer ken?"

Prudence shot the man a wide smile, for she had just had her first conversation with a *real* Londoner, and made to set off back down the street, with Rexford none the wiser that she had been gone from her assigned spot. She was about to turn sharply on her heels when she felt a slight tug at her pocket.

The meat pie slammed onto the flagway as she spun around in a full circle, ending by roughly grabbing onto the nearly rotted sleeve of the man she had seen earlier, ambling down the street. "Got ya, you slimy, cow-handed bastard! You were making a try for my purse!" she exclaimed, giving the man a shake.

"Yer purse?" The man shook his head, looking at Prudence as if she had gone mad. "Oh, no, sir. Not me. Oi didn'na do nothin' loik that. 'Onest!"

"And you're a bleeding bad liar into the bargain," Prudence yelled, although she didn't know she was yelling. She didn't know anything save for the fact that this vile-smelling creature had attempted to rob her of every penny she had in this world. She grabbed his other arm, freeing her right hand. "You miserable, thieving bye-blow of a cross-eyed whore. You're not even a good buzman, clumsy as a drunken lord in a pig sty. Now don't you move a hair until I've checked my pocket. You hear me!"

"Yer're dicked in the nob, boyo," the would-be thief protested, trying to pull away, a move that only served to increase Prudence's tight grip on his sleeve. "Oi wuz jist walkin' down this 'ere street—"

"And you'll be walking down it again," Prudence told him, her grip easing slightly in relief when she felt the comforting weight of her purse still sitting snugly in the bottom of her deep pocket. "Only don't be walking down it when I'm here—you *ken,* boyo?" she ended, giving him a mighty shove, which was all the pickpocket needed to send him on his way.

Prudence watched him go, feeling strangely proud of herself for standing her ground. It wasn't so very difficult here in London. People were people. You just had to know how to handle them, that's all. And she had handled this particular situation quite well, despite the loss of her pie—or at least she thought she had until she turned back toward the shop and saw the Marquess of Daventry standing on the flagway, his hands on his hips, his face a thundercloud.

"Oh, gloomy hour!" she said. Sparing only a moment to look down at her ruined meat pie—and she hadn't so much as gotten a single good bite of the thing, blast it!—she started walking down the street, dragging her feet and muttering under her breath. "I should have known old surly boots would sniff me out, and he's mad as fire, too. Brace yourself, Angel. This is *not* going to be pretty!"

She reached the front of *La Belle Friponne* at precisely the same time that Rexford stepped outside, the three of them coming together in a suffocatingly small area of the narrow flagway.

"What are you doing here, Daventry?" she asked accusingly, deciding to go on the attack rather than just stand there like some sorry truant and have him read a lecture over her. Besides, if she could make him angry enough, he might forget that Rexford was on the scene, saving that man a similar dressing-down. "Come to check up on me, have you? And here I thought you couldn't wait to be shed of me, or that's how it looked when you ran out of Lady Wendover's last night, near to skipping with your glee to be freed of your responsibility."

"I am here because you are my ward and I cannot in good conscience shirk my duty," he replied through clenched teeth, obviously doing his best to hang on to any shreds of his temper left to him.

"Hoo! That's rich! After nearly a year of pretending I didn't exist? Have any more crammers you want me to swallow?"

"My lord!"

"Rexford, you will please me by staying out of this. Besides, you're dismissed. Fired. Let go, if you need any further explanation."

"Oh, cut line, Daventry. Rexford couldn't know I never do as I ought to do when I want to do what I want. You're the only one who knows that."

"You could have been killed."

"Ha! By that bundle of rags? Hardly. He's running for cover so fast and hard he'll probably end back in his mother's belly."

"Bundle of rags? Killed? Miss MacAfee, what is—"

"He could have had a knife."

"He could have been dragging a bleeding cannon around with him, too. But he wasn't."

"You shouldn't have touched him."

"He tried to nip off with my purse!"

"Oh bother! You moved, didn't you, Miss MacAfee? And here I thought you prized the ivory gown above all the others."

"A purse which he wouldn't have tried to steal if you weren't running around like a skip-brained ninny in the first place. Rexford? You're still here? I thought I dismissed you."

"I . . . um . . ."

"Well, if that isn't above everything stupid! He's only trying to help you. Very well. You dismiss him, and *I'll* hire him. You don't deserve the man."

"You can't have him. If I had an ounce of control in the matter, I wouldn't give you a crust of bread, you ungrateful little monster!"

"I'm ungrateful? When Rexford has gone to such lengths, put himself and his sterling reputation into jeopardy to make sure I'll be all the crack and cut a dash in society—just so that *you'll* look good? Oh, for shame, Daventry. *You* are the one who is ungrateful. And you're a great whacking looby into the bargain!"

"I see you have Lady Wendover's coach, my lord. I'll just toddle off now in yours, and leave the two of you to sort this out."

"Looby? You dare to call me names? Why you abominable little brat!"

"Paphead!"

"Oh dear. Miss MacAfee, do you really think this wise? But I was just going, wasn't I? Yes, that's what I'll do. I'll take the coach and—"

"You're impertinent!"

"And you're a selfish, prudish, stick-in-the-mud, mutton-witted *prig!*"

"That ends it! You will never learn to hold that tongue long enough to make your way in any civilized society. Angel? *Ha!* You are nothing more than a little demon, a pernicious—"

"Cork-head—"

"Deceitful—"

"Odious—"

"Underbred—"

"Lech!"

"Bitch."

132

"Oh, foul. Foul!" Prudence whispered, unexpectedly hurt to the quick as Banning lowered his voice to growl out his last, damning denouncement of his unwanted ward.

The next thing she knew, Prudence was sitting inside Lady Wendover's coach and Banning was pulling up the shades, locking them in place even as the coachman gave the horses the office to be off.

Would his lordship allow her to say her goodbyes to Lady Wendover and Quimby and Cook and Isobel, and all the other servants in Park Lane, or would he simply order the coachman to make for the main road to Sussex, summarily dumping her back in her grandfather's lap and then riding out of her life?

She'd ask him, but she didn't trust her voice. She didn't trust her bottom lip not to quiver if she said so much as a word, couldn't rely on her eyes not to tear if she dared to blink. Where had her anger gone? Why was she unable to look away from the Marquess of Daventry as he sat, stonefaced, on the facing seat? And why, oh why, was she suddenly so crushed to know once and for all time that he thought badly of her—when the last thing she wanted, needed, was for him to like her?

If she wasn't going to talk, and as she certainly refused to cry or beg, Prudence was left with nothing to do but slouch ungracefully on the seat, her chin tilted at a belligerent angle, her hands clenched into fists at her sides, her eyes narrowed, her chest heaving as she slowly willed herself to breathe normally.

"You're not in the least penitent, are you?" Banning asked at last, the ghost of a smile dancing at the corners of his mouth. "As a matter of fact, you don't even see that you've done anything wrong."

She rolled her eyes. "Oh, hang you, Daventry, *of course* I know I was wrong," she said, sitting up straight and dragging the hat from her hair, revealing her thick, thoroughly mussed mane. "I saw something I wanted and just went wandering off without thinking. I should have stayed where Rexford put me."

"You shouldn't have gone with Rexford in the first place," he said, then sighed. "But Freddie allowed it, didn't she, and I can't reasonably expect you to know more than my own scatterbrained sister—although I'm willing to wager you played that deuced little trick with your eyes and she couldn't refuse you."

"Trick with my eyes?" Prudence asked, truly confused. "I don't play tricks with my eyes. Do I?"

Banning looked at her for several moments, several long, disturbing moments, before looking away. "Never mind. If you knew what you were doing none of us would be safe. Now, tell me what you and Rexford purchased. Am I to be buried in bills?"

He wasn't going to banish her! He was going to let her stay! Prudence sat up even straighter, wriggling in her seat as she grinned at him. "Up to your earlobes, Daventry!" she exclaimed happily, her heart suddenly feeling at least two stone lighter than it had a moment earlier. "I don't wish to sponge on you, truly, but Rexford was adamant that I do you proud. And David is a genius, really. Everything he picked for me is slap up to the mark, or so Rexford assured me. You should see the one—the ivory I was going to wear to Almack's until I wandered away from the shop. It's the eel's eyebrows!"

"Really? The eel's eyebrows. Well, I suppose I should be grateful for that." Banning was still, thankfully, looking amused. "And this David person? He would be your new dressmaker? Although Rexford has always held my highest esteem when it comes to knowing what is right and proper, I must say I harbored a few misgivings when Quimby gave me the name and direction of *La Belle Friponne.*"

"Oh, *that,*" Prudence said, dismissing both the shop's name and unfashionable address with a single sniff and a wave of her hand. "Nobody's going to know *that.* David will be moving to a new shop, on Bond Street, the moment you pay your bills. Only then will I be allowed to tell anyone the name of my dressmaker. But you weren't supposed to know that either, I think. Well, it's enough that David will have a good address."

"How you ease my mind, Angel," Banning countered, laying his hat, which he had been holding on his lap, beside him on the seat. "And Rexford? How did he come to know this man, this redoubtable David?"

Prudence was so relieved that she wasn't going to be banished, and so very relaxed now that the marquess no longer seemed angry, but merely amused, that she answered freely, "They're lovers, of course. It's really rather sweet, the way they——"

The atmosphere inside the coach chilled a good twenty degrees in an instant as Banning snarled coldly, "Oh, good. Good. It wanted only that, didn't it? I can see you now, Miss MacAfee, chatting with the patroness at Almack's, delighting them with news of your new dressmaker and his affection for my valet!"

Prudence frowned, not quite understanding. "You disapprove of David and Rexford?"

Banning shook his head, clearly exasperated with her. "It is not for me to approve or disapprove. It is, frankly, none of my business. However, if you had even the smallest notion of what is and is not expected of an innocent young debutante, you would realize that you are not to know such things, much less speak about them."

The tension was back, the electrically charged atmosphere that was an almost palpable thing between them. Angering her. Exciting her. "Oh, my dear Lord Daventry," she said, almost eager to shock him further. "Do you mean I must pretend that I am not only civilized, but ignorant into the bargain if I plan to go into society? What a bother! How could I grow up at MacAfee Farm without learning anything? There were more than a few Davids and Rexfords among the stock over the years. I remember Wilbert, one of the goats. He had this most fascinating relationship with one of the other—"

"Shut up!"

Prudence's eyes grew wide, her grin even wider. "I do adore shocking you, Daventry, although it is lamentably easy. Freddie says you used to be a lot of fun, before that gray hair and your new fortune turned you into such a dull stick. I saw you come close to laughing earlier, before you squashed it down and went all stiff and sober on me. Now, come on—admit it. You aren't shocked by me. Not really. You're envious. Yes, that's it! You're envious that I can do what I want and not care a fig for anybody's opinion of me, while all you can think about is being a good little marquess—which I find deadly dull, if you want to know the truth of it. And I think you're wrong. I will do just fine in society. Rexford says so. He says I'm going to be an Original."

"You can't be an Original, Prudence," Banning shot back at her. "London has already had its Great Fire, so disaster is nothing new to this city. You'll just be another one."

"How droll, my lord," Prudence drawled in her best imitation of him, her upper lip curled into a sneer. "And do you think Miss Althea Broughton will giggle when you relate your latest stick-in-the-mud witticism to her while you're on bended knee, begging for her hand again now that you're rich enough for her, and not just the owner of a stuffy old title? Will her heart go pitter-pat as she throws herself into your arms, overcome by your charm, your wit—your deep pockets? Ah, what a pair you will be!"

"Freddie!" Banning growled, slamming his fist into his hand. "And you!" he continued, glaring at Prudence in a way that told her that, at last, she had gone too far, teased too hard, dared too much.

"You can make all the promises in the world, attempt to dazzle me with your aping of good manners and your snatches of cultivated speech," he went on tightly, "but at the bottom of it you're nothing but a crude, foul-mouthed guttersnipe. You may have been able to charm my sister into allowing you your head, and Rexford may be using you for his own ends, but that does not make you any sort of a lady. Do you know—do you have any idea of what will happen to you if you talk so freely in society? If you act the trollop, teasing anyone else as you do me? Let me tell you what will happen. Even better! I'll *show* you!"

Before she could move, mount any sort of verbal or physical defense, Banning had pulled her from her seat and onto his lap, his lips searing hers as his hands roughly assaulted her body, humiliating her with the intimacy of their touch.

She remained still beneath his kiss, shocked into

137

that stillness by his unlooked-for attack, his passion. Yes, his passion. His kiss was violent, his touch equally punishing. He was kissing her as if he hated her, desired her. . . . was torn between some strange need of her and an equally strong determination to somehow exorcise her from his mind. . . . quench that desire by taking all that he could, until he'd had his fill and could be done with her forever.

And she didn't care! Did not care why he was kissing her . . . as long as he didn't stop. Did not mind that he thought he hated her . . . for she knew in her heart that she could not risk his affection. Did not flinch as his roughness hurt her . . . because she deserved to be punished . . . because she was guilty. Guilty . . . guilty . . . guilty.

"Christ!"

Prudence blinked rapidly as Banning abruptly pushed her away, so that she found herself once more sprawled inelegantly on the facing seat, her mouth still tingling from his attack, her body on fire wherever he had touched her. He looked dazed, as if he couldn't believe what had just happened between them.

"Banning, I'm sor—" she began, then broke off just as she impulsively began to apologize to him, for she knew it had been dangerous as well as wrong to have teased him beyond his endurance, to have fairly begged for him to lose control if just for a moment, to react with something more than the anger of a responsible guardian; to want him to respond to her as a man, to recognize her as a woman.

"Don't dare apologize, Angel," he warned, his tone terse, his breathing harsh and slightly labored. "This was my fault, not yours. And for God's sake, stop crying. I feel bad enough as it is without having to look at those godawful great tears of yours."

She rubbed at her cheeks with the back of her hand, devastated to find them wet. "I never cry, Daventry. Never!" She fairly hurled the words at him as the coach finally drew to a halt and the entire vehicle lurched slightly as the driver climbed down from the box. "Only with Molly . . . only with *you!*"

"I know," he said quietly, nodding. "God help me, I know. But now you must listen to me. We're back at Freddie's. I won't come in, but you can tell my sister I'll return her coach later this afternoon. I promise you won't have to see me again until next Wednesday, when we go to Almack's. And I shall be sure that you have the ivory gown, I promise. Angel—" he hesitated, frowning as he continued to stare at her. "Angel, I—"

"No! Don't say anything else. If anyone asks, I'll tell them you read me an ear-scorching lecture on my ramshackle ways, reducing me to a puddle of repentant tears. Nobody is ever to know what really happened. Especially me, for I shall forget everything the moment you are out of my sight."

She picked up her hat, stuffing it down over her hair until it nearly reached her eyebrows, then moved forward to brace her arms on either side of the now open door of the coach. She wanted to leave Banning there without another word, his apology choking him just as hers was sticking in her own throat, but she had to look back, had to see him one more time as he sat there with his innermost thoughts exposed to her, unwillingly laying bare his dismay, his self-disgust, his lingering desire.

He stared at her for a long time, his gaze so intent it was as if he was attempting to memorize the way she looked in her man's shirt and too-tight breeches, her ridiculous hat crammed onto her head. As if, for some reason she did not wish to understand, he wanted to remember the outlandish creature he had found at MacAfee Farm. As if he worried that he would never see that creature again. Or see himself that way again—young, uninhibited, perhaps even slightly wanton.

At last, Banning turned his head away from her in dismissal, so that she had no choice but to exit the coach and stand alone, watching it drive away.

BOOK TWO

COMPROMISE

Her angel's face
As the great eye of heaven shined bright,
and made a shunshine in the shady place;
Did neer mortal eye behold such heavenly grace.

Edmund Spenser

CHAPTER 10

Man, being reasonable, must get drunk;
the best of life is but intoxication.

George Noel Gordon,
Lord Byron

The banging of the Marquess of Daventry's bed-chamber door as it slammed back against the wall—its sound reverberating painfully inside his drink-abused skull—heralded the arrival of Marmaduke Kester, Earl of Preston.

"Whoa! What is this?" the earl exclaimed, his voice just slightly less abusive than having all the bells of every church in all of London rung, at precisely the same time, directly beside Banning's ear. "Still abed, old fellow? Thought you'd be slopping up eggs, at the very least. Pity. I'm still hungry, myself."

"Duke, where are you? Rexford says we're not to go barging in and—uh-oh! Too late. Morning, Banning, and all that. Still in bed? Late night, I suppose. You're looking . . . no, that wouldn't be polite, would it?" Dewey Norton turned on the earl, waving his arms as if attempting to become airborne, so that he could more easily box his friend's ears. "Duke, you're such a skip-brain, always bursting in on people without so much as knocking."

"Skip-brain? Me?" Marmaduke returned with a quick, jolting movement of his head, just as if he had been physically struck. "And you're the one to tell me that? Who was it spent nearly all of the past five days whining and moaning that Banning here must be dying, or else he'd have been at the clubs, or the theater—or *anywhere?* Who nearly had the man underground, hmm? Not me. *You're* the loose-noodle!"

"Lard head!"

"Please! Please!" Banning called out painfully, using his legs to push himself free of the covers. "No name-calling. It'll end badly, I promise you." He sat up, reaching for his dressing gown. "Would one of you please open the door for Rexford. He's probably hovering just outside in the hall, waiting to bring me some strong tea. Or to kiss the hem of my dressing gown," he ended beneath his breath, for the remorseful valet had been all but tripping over himself these past days, trying to wedge himself back into his employer's good books.

"You're looking in queer stirrups, Banning. As a matter of fact, if I didn't know you'd sworn off, I'd say you were cup shot," Marmaduke remarked a few minutes later as they sat together at a small table in a corner of the large bedchamber, Rexford having gone about his duties with an efficiency that was almost awe-inspiring before bowing himself out of the room. "You haven't been drinking, have you, Banning?"

"You're dead as a house, Duke," Norton said, lifting his handkerchief to his nostrils. "Of course he's been drinking. I can smell it all the way over here. Do you have troubles, Banning? I'd rather you didn't, you know, as I'm your friend and have to listen to you if you do, which I'd rather not, as other people's troubles are always so upsetting. I would sleep nights, you understand. If you had any consideration, you would have thought of that before diving into a bottle."

"Althea must have turned him down flat yet again," the earl said, wincing as he sipped his tea, then putting it down so that he could shovel several spoonfuls of sugar into the cup.

"Or someone died," Norton suggested, looking hopeful. "Last time that happened, Banning landed in the deepest gravy boat in all London. Get yourself another fortune, old friend? Pretty shabby of you to go celebrating without first calling on us, you know."

"No, he don't look happy," the earl pointed out, shaking his shaggy head. "My vote goes to the Broughton. Heard Ramsden's back in town. He was hot after her, too, remember. Is that it, Banning? Did the villainous viscount cut you out?"

Banning put down his cup and rose, heading for his dressing room with the intention of cleaning his teeth—or drowning himself in his shaving basin, which seemed a viable option. "Feel free to discuss me between yourselves, gentlemen. I'll rejoin you shortly."

Rexford was already in the dressing room, hot water and towels at the ready, unnerving Banning with his solicitous administrations even as he was grateful for the man's assistance.

"More than time I came up from the depths, isn't it, Rexford?" he asked, allowing himself to be stripped of his dressing gown and then heading for the basin, and his tooth powder.

"It is not my place to comment, my lord," Rexford

replied, draping a large white towel around his master's throat before turning for the shaving soap.

Banning gave out a crack of laughter, which wasn't precisely intelligent, for his head began to pound once more. "A little late for you to be learning your place, isn't it, Rexford? But no. We've settled that, haven't we? Have you made progress in finding your friend a more suitable address? If Miss MacAfee is to be the sartorial sensation of all Mayfair as you promise, I wouldn't want anyone sniffing out the damning knowledge that she has been outfitted by a dressmaker most recently associated with a clientele best known for the roundness of their heels."

"Mr. Wallace is moving into his new shop on Bond Street even as we speak, my lord," Rexford assured him, then most politely inquired if it would be possible for his lordship to please raise his chin just slightly, "so that you shouldn't suffer a nick, my lord."

"And Miss MacAfee?" Banning asked, avoiding the valet's eyes. "She is in receipt of the first few gowns? She is not the sort to suffer confinement gracefully, I believe, and she cannot be seen outside my sister's house again in those damnable breeches."

"Again, sir, everything progresses beautifully. Mr. Wallace has outdone himself, working 'round the clock, all his seamstresses devoted only to the wardrobe of your ward. The materials—outstanding. The bead work on the ivory gown—well, Mr. Wallace wept, he was so overcome by its beauty. I saw him. I also have seen the voucher for Almack's, and I daresay you will have every reason to be proud of your ward as you introduce her to the patronesses tomorrow evening."

"Tomorrow night?" Banning moved his head sharply, earning himself a small nick just below his left ear. "My God, man—that soon? Is she ready?"

Rexford whipped the towel from his lordship's throat and motioned for him to rise, using a sweep of his arm to encourage Banning to rinse off his face in the basin. "All has been taken care of, sir," he said, wiping his hands on the towel before discarding it and picking up another, which he handed to his now dripping-wet employer. "Knowing you did not wish for your sister to overtax her energies, my lord, and aware that you were otherwise occupied in more important matters—"

"Which had a lot to do with hiding myself in my study for four days then, with nothing else to occupy my mind except the fact that I'm a total ass, drinking myself senseless last night," Banning put in wryly. "But don't let me interrupt. Please, tell me more."

"Miss MacAfee has already had three extremely productive sessions with the best dancing master I could find, a milliner has been, a glove maker visited just yesterday, Lady Wendover has made great strides in explaining all the proper protocol, and her hair has been cut."

Banning paused in the act of roughly rubbing his face and neck with the towel to glare at his valet. "Her hair? Damn it, Rexford! It had better not be short! Who gave you permission to cut Angel's hair?"

"Not Miss MacAfee, my lord," the valet said, his smile seeming to say he knew something the marquess had yet to learn. "In the end, and only after coaxing poor Monsieur Thebault out from behind Lady Wendover's skirts, a compromise of sorts was reached. I believe your lordship will be well pleased with the result."

"Pleasing me has nothing to do with it. I just want the girl presentable—and then gone." Banning tossed the towel in Rexford's direction even as he picked up his dressing gown once more, jamming his arms into it and tying the sash with more energy than finesse. "Have my bath ready in an hour, if you please," he ended, striding back into his bedchamber once more, feeling cleaner but not necessarily better.

"Oh well, that's an improvement," Norton proclaimed as Banning seated himself once more. "Of course, dragging a comb through that mass of silver couldn't have come amiss, but you'll do. Now—tell us if we're right. We've been discussing and discussing, and have decided that Althea isn't the problem. It's this business of taking on MacAfee's sister, ain't it? Been everywhere these last days, looking to see her but she's nowhere to be found. Still hiding her out with your sister, aren't you? She's totally unsuitable, and you're stuck with her."

"Give her a whopping dowry," the earl said from somewhere behind Banning, the man having given up his chair in favor of pacing the carpet. "We'll bruit it about that she's up to her ears in your money, and you'll have every fortune hunter and second son in the city breaking down your door, no matter how ugly she is."

"She's not ugly, Duke," Banning said, pouring himself another cup of tea. "She is rather unique, but she is certainly not ugly."

"Then what is it? She's not a bluestocking, is she?" Norton asked, leaning forward, a strange expression on his face. "No, that's not it. Duke! I think I have it! Banning here is taken with the chit. That's it, isn't it? Why, you sly old dog, you!" He cupped a hand to his ear. "Duke—do you hear that? I think it's wedding bells."

The earl shrugged, and when the earl shrugged, his entire tall, thin frame shook all the way down to his toes. "So? Didn't we say he could marry her? Her or Althea. Makes no never mind. All the same, women. Now hunting dogs—there's where you have real differences. Some of them smart and hot on the scent straight off the mark, some of them thick as wood, running in all directions, chasing their own tails—"

"Would you two please stop!" Banning exploded, wishing he'd had the good sense to find himself some friends with a modicum of sense inside their heads rather than picking them only because he happened to like them. "I'm years too old for Angel, and her guardian into the bargain, if you'll recall. I doubt marrying his sister off to a man nearly twice her age was what Henry MacAfee had in mind when he handed Prudence into my custody." *And she hates me,* he added silently, remembering the anguished expression on Angel's face as she had exited the coach after his impulsive attack.

"Tricked you into taking her, you mean," Marmaduke slid in even as he collapsed his long, angular frame into his seat once more.

"But I'm still right. He wants her all the same," Norton said, showing the first bit of insight in his entire self-absorbed life. "Oh, Banning. You *are* in a pickle, aren't you?"

His friends had been gone for over an hour when Rexford, having assisted his master with his bath and helping him into fresh clothing, scratched at the door to Banning's private study, then stuck his head in to announce, smiling, that her ladyship, the Dowager Countess of Wendover desired an audience with her brother.

Banning looked up from the communication from his steward at Daventry Manor that he had been reading without really assimilating, and asked, "My sister? Here? Is she alone?"

"Her maid is in having tea with the housekeeper, sir, but Miss MacAfee is not with her, sir, if that is what you are asking," the valet told him, already stepping back to allow her ladyship entry to the room Banning had always considered sacrosanct and beyond the reach of females who had no understanding of the pleasures of leather chairs, warmed brandy, and the sharp bite of good tobacco. Although Angel might be an exception . . .

"I don't recall asking you about Miss MacAfee, Rexford," Banning bit out, rising. "My ward can be in Jericho for all I care."

"Is that so?" Lady Wendover asked, stripping off her gloves as she swept into the room on a cloud of her favorite scent. "If you intend to be disobliging, which you have been these last days, not deigning to answer any of my notes or show your face in Park Lane, then I doubt we have anything more to say to each other. Good day to you, brother." And with that, she turned on her heels, hesitating just long enough for Banning, who knew what she was about, to call after her, asking her to please stay.

"That's better," she said, smiling, looking very young, very happy, and in better health than he would have ever believed possible six months earlier, when she had nearly faded away before his eyes. "Will you now go so far as to ask me to sit down?"

He went to her and kissed her cheek. "I'll go even further, my love, and ask why you are here. You look exceedingly fetching in that bonnet, but I sense an air of determination about you. Have you come to beg for more money for my ward? If true, you have *carte blanche,* as well you know. I must do all my possible to assure Rexford's friend a decent living, you understand."

Lady Wendover accepted the chair her brother offered, arranging her brilliantly blue skirts as she sat down, then looked up at him, watching him entirely too closely as he returned to his own seat behind the desk. "You have been kindness itself, Banning, to both Rexford and Prudence. You have done all that is required of a guardian, which demonstrates the solid worth of your character. You have not, however, done anything more than that. Opening your pocketbook is laudable, but I believe there is a wont of personal involvement, almost as if you are avoiding us. Angel feels it too, although she is too sweet, too polite, to complain."

"Sweet? There's that word again. And polite as well? A real patterncard of all the finest virtues, I'm sure," Banning said, picking up his letter opener and moving it between his fingers. "I had begun to relax, believing my ward in competent hands, but now I find myself suffering some serious qualms. You cannot possibly believe Prudence is simply another debutante, can you? She's good, I'll warrant you, but the façade of civilization slips from time to time. You have noticed, haven't you?"

"I've noticed that she's not happy, Banning," the countess said, eying him sternly, "and she hasn't been since the day you snatched her from Rexford's care and kept her with you for nearly an hour, only to send her back to me, dissolved in tears."

Banning put down the letter opener, having nearly drawn blood by pushing its pointed end into his palm. "I see."

"No, Banning, I doubt that you do—and don't go pulling a Friday face at me. We still giggle like children together, Angel and I, enjoying our association immensely. If you could have seen her all but tree that silly French hairdresser with his own scissors, you would have been delighted! She is quick to learn, aping my manners like an adorable little monkey, eager to please, and a nearly endless joy to me. It is only when your name is brought into any conversation that she goes all silent and sad. And that's why I have come here today, brother dear. Something happened between the two of you, I am sure of it, and I want it resolved before we go to Almack's tomorrow evening."

"She's said nothing to you, Freddie?"

Lady Wendover waved away whatever explanation Prudence had given her, sniffing. "You rang a peal over her head, stripped some hide off her, delivered a blistering setdown concerning proper behavior—all that rot. As if Angel could be cowed by you. You do look prodigiously like papa when you're being stern, and I admit to not liking it a bit, but Angel isn't the sort to fall to pieces over a verbal reprimand."

She leaned forward, her eyes narrowed. "You didn't hit her, did you, Banning?"

Banning heard himself give out with a long, deep sigh, which surprised him, for he hadn't thought he was the sort for melodrama. "No, Freddie, I didn't hit her," he said, picking up the letter opener once more, wondering if it might be chivalrous to slit his throat with the thing, thus taking his shame with him to the grave and not inflicting knowledge of his unforgivable behavior on his sweet sister. "In point of fact, I kissed her."

"Oh dear," Lady Wendover breathed quietly, beginning to fan herself with her gloves. "Oh dear, oh dear."

Banning felt himself bristling. "It's not as if it's the end of the world, Freddie," he said, pushing back his chair and rising to turn his face to the window.

"Are you going to offer for her?" his sister asked after a moment. "Of course, as you'd have to apply to yourself for permission, that could be slightly awkward, couldn't it?"

Banning spun around to face his sister. "Offer for her? Because of a single kiss that was meant more to punish, to educate, than for any other reason? I found her walking the streets, alone, and wanted to show her how little she could defend herself. I only kissed her because I *couldn't* hit her. Offer for her?" he repeated, shaking his head. "My God, Freddie, what would I do with her once I'd got her? She's a child. Why, I bedded my first woman before the chit was even born!"

"Banning!" Lady Wendover exclaimed, clearly shocked. "You are but four and thirty this past January. Angel is eighteen, nearer to nineteen. That would have made you about—oh, Banning! That's *obscene!*"

"Hardly, Freddie," Banning replied, smiling as he remembered a hot summer afternoon, a fragrant haystack, and a willing young barmaid whose name he had long ago forgotten. "But it was highly educational, I'll grant you that."

"What a rakehelly youth you were, Banning," Lady Wendover said, beginning to giggle. "Why, when I told Angel some of your exploits, we were both nearly overcome with hilarity."

Banning's own humor faded. "Was there really any need for that?" he asked.

"Why yes, I suppose there was," she answered, frowning. "You've become such a stickler this past year that I have to keep reminding myself that you were once so much younger, so very carefree." Her frown deepened. "You know what, Banning? It think it is longer than a year, and closer to two. It's ever since Althea Broughton turned you down flat."

"Nonsense."

"No. No, it's not!" Lady Wendover exclaimed, beginning to fidget in her chair. "Papa died, which started you on this boring road to respectability, then Althea turned you down, and then Auntie died, leaving you all that lovely money—why, you've been in a downward spiral for more than two years, haven't you, Banning? Goodness, if sobriety and maturity ever attempted to enter *my* life, I should just bolt the door and ask Quimby to tell them both to kindly be on their way!"

"You're forgetting Waterloo, my love, and my fear of almost losing you," Banning put in quietly, wishing there were some way to change the subject. But as Frederica would probably just return to that of Angel and why he had kissed her, he didn't push.

"Oh bother! Don't try shoveling the blame onto me and my weak chest, for it won't fadge, brother dear. I lay the blame most firmly at Papa's door, if you want the truth. He made you promise to live up to what he always considered our good name, didn't he? A death-bed promise. How utterly like him, and totally gothic! Why, that's probably why you offered for Althea in the first place, as she is certainly an upstanding young woman, with an impeccable lineage. Boring as watching the lizard embroider hour after hour on that wretched tapestry of hers, but quite unexceptional. I imagine you figured she'd drain any remaining spunk out of you within a year. And now she's back on the market."

Lady Wendover sighed, looking to Banning pleadingly. "Are you quite sure you didn't kiss Angel because you're attracted to her? I'd much rather you married Angel, you know. Althea could put a damper on anything, even worse than Papa."

"Marriage! Why all this sudden interest in marriage?" Banning asked, running a hand through his hair. "Duke, Dewey—and now you. It's Prudence we're trying to settle, remember? I like my life as it is, thank you. Peaceful, pleasant, uneventful. Or at least it was, until Henry MacAfee tricked me into becoming his sister's guardian. The sooner we have her settled, the happier I'll be."

"Of course, Banning dearest," his sister said soothingly, rising to kiss his cheek. "Well, I must be going. Angel and Miss Prentice are rubbing along together beautifully, with the lizard being almost eerily agreeable, but I still don't like leaving them alone together for too long. You will be nice to Angel tomorrow night, won't you, Banning?"

"I shall act in the role of guardian, Freddie," he promised her, returning her kiss and offering her his arm so that he could walk her to her coach. "I will even go so far as to put myself out in requesting her first waltz. Beyond that, however, I will not go."

"Yes, Banning, you will go beyond that," Lady Wendover said, looking stern for the first time in his memory. "You will apologize to Angel for having frightened her. A kiss as punishment! No wonder she loses her smile whenever your name is mentioned. The poor child is probably dreading having to see you again, afraid of what you might attempt next in an effort to cow her into behaving herself as you see fit. I've never heard of anything so thoroughly cork-brained. Why, only the most complete paphead would—"

Banning's smile was rueful as he kissed his sister yet again, then handed her over to her maid. "I see that Angel has been broadening your vocabulary, sister dear. I can only hope this sharing of education has been a two-way street. Otherwise, tomorrow night's excursion into society will not only be Prudence's first, it will be her last."

Lady Wendover smiled, tapping Banning's cheek, just a little too sharply to be considered a purely affectionate gesture. "Just you worry about bending that stiff spine of yours a little, brother dear, and let me fret about Angel. And right now, I only worry that I will become fatigued in beating away her suitors with a pointed stick!"

"She is that improved?" Banning asked, wondering why he wasn't overjoyed to hear his sister's assessment of Prudence's possible success in society.

"Ah, a flush hit! You do care about her!" Lady Wendover's smile turned coy, so that she looked like the young girl he so loved, almost as if her unwanted marriage to a man decades older than herself had never happened. "We'll meet you at Almack's, and you can then decide for yourself. And don't let your mouth fall to half-cock when you see her, my dear. Papa and Althea wouldn't approve."

Banning watched his sister leave, cheered by her quick, light step, then allowed Montgomery to step forward and close the door as he returned to his study, wondering just how long it would be until he went stark, staring mad . . .

CHAPTER 11

Like watermen,
that row one way and look another.

Robert Burton

Prudence slipped into the mews, tiptoeing past a sleeping groom who sat on an overturned bucket, his head propped against the open stable door, and then ran to the end of the alleyway, launching herself at the figure waiting for her there in the predawn darkness.

"Oh Lord, Enby, but I've missed you!" she exclaimed in a fierce whisper, greedily showering his face with kisses, rubbing her cheek against his full beard. Then, disengaging herself from his embrace, she hauled off and delivered a solid punch to his mid-section, almost doubling him over. "Rotter! Sneak! No-good!" She pulled back her arm and took careful aim, planning to hit him once more as soon as he righted himself.

"Angel, please," her victim pleaded, grabbing her wrist before she could do any more damage. "Not the stomach. I had a glass or six too many last night to celebrate my return to England, and the results could be disastrous." He smiled, his straight white teeth visible in the dim light. "So, how are you faring thus far in your new life? You certainly look well enough."

"If I look good to you it's only because the sun isn't yet up, you miserable hound, you. I've aged twenty years since last you saw me. And you had it planned all along, didn't you, without so much as even asking me if I'd agree until it was already too late? I hate this. I absolutely *hate* this! Deception may come easy to you, but lying isn't my strongest suit."

"Maybe not, but it's necessary. Just another three months, Angel, I promise. And then we'll be free as two birds, our nests well-feathered, and the world ours for the asking."

"But they trust me, Enby. They even *like* me. Well, at least most of them do. And I like them." She shook her head, her shorter hair slipping out from beneath her straw hat. "It wasn't so bad, waiting, not really. Maybe I should simply go back and—"

"Go back to what? More of the same? No, we're committed. Daventry will continue to do right by you in the meantime. He's that kind."

"Really? You think you're so smart, but you don't know anything, do you? What would you say if I told you he has brought me to London with some notion of popping me off long before the next three months have passed? What would you say if I told you he kissed me? Touched me? And not because he has any great love for me, let me tell you. I think he hates me."

"Pop you off, is it? And I suppose he's going to give you a fat dowry as well? You're not a very good liar, are you? I don't believe that whisker for a minute. You're just saying that to make me feel guilty, but it won't work." He grabbed her shoulders, shaking her gently. "As for the rest of it—you must have asked for it. Daventry's a gentleman, not the sort to maul women, or the sort who would have to, come to think of it. You've gone and been provoking, haven't you? I thought I could count on you to behave yourself, but you're still such a obnoxious little beast at times, even at your most appealing. What did you do to him, Angel?"

"What did *I* do to *him?*" Prudence shook herself free. "Lord, you men are all the same—totally insufferable! Daventry isn't blameless. Why do you think it was all *my* fault?"

He laughed, a soft, throaty sound that warmed her heart in spite of herself, for she loved him very much and could forgive him almost anything, had already forgiven him nearly everything. "Why? Because I know you better than anyone, precious Angel, remember? You'd try the patience of a saint without even trying. It's either kiss you or throttle you, I suppose, or at least Daventry must have thought so. Now, what did you do?"

"Never mind. You're right, damn you. It was all my fault, but I can promise you it won't happen again." She looked at him longingly, knowing their time together was limited and not wishing to waste any more of it talking about the maddening Marquess of Daventry. "Where are you staying? Can I come to you?"

He shook his head. "Much as I want to say yes, it wouldn't be safe. Just enjoy yourself, Angel. That is what this is all about, remember? I have to know that you're safe and happy."

"I was happy enough before, with you. It was you

who wasn't happy, Enby, remember? It was you who needed to be free, to see the world—"

"As we'll soon be doing together. Three more months, Angel," he said, pulling her close once more. "My plan is working so far, but I need to know that you're safe. Just don't you go marrying one of the hundreds who'll be chasing after you. We have plans, you and I, remember?"

"I remember, Enby," she said, hugging him, and then he was gone, slipping back into the shadows.

It seemed as if she was forever watching a man walk out of her life.

Banning knew he had sunk to the very depths when he realized he was counting on the Earl of Preston and Dewey Norton to act as supporting props to him as he braved the portals of Almack's, to act the responsible guardian for his ward's first appearance in polite society.

"I hate this place worse than my mother's drawing room," Norton said, handing his cloak to one of the footmen only after looking the fellow up and down and making him promise he wouldn't lose the thing. "Hot, stuffy, and crammed to the rafters with women. All that's missing are Mama's elephant-feet tables."

The earl, whose skinny shanks never looked at their best in the breeches and stockings the patroness had declared *de rigueur,* stepped to the entrance of the ballroom, struck up a pose with one hand pressed to his chest, and recited from one of Henry Luttrell's scribblings: "'All on that magic *list* depends; fame, fortune, fashion, lovers, friends: 'tis that which gratifies or vexes all ranks, all ages, and both sexes. If once to Almack's you belong, like monarchs, you can do no wrong; but banished thence on Wednesday night, by Jove, you can do nothing right.'"

"Oh, goodness, how very droll," a young miss dressed all in anemic white from her feathers to her satin-clad toes gushed, waving her fan beneath her nose with enough force to ruffle the lace on the earl's cravat. "My lord Preston, are you by chance attempting to flirt with me?"

The earl shook himself all over like a terrier just exiting a pond, then quickly stepped behind Banning, who was doing his best to hold his countenance. "Make her go away," the earl whispered into Banning's ear.

Before Banning could tamp down his amusement and summon up anything to say, Norton, who admired women as much as they inexplicably admired Marmaduke, stepped forward and bowed over the young lady's hand. "Dewey Norton, Miss, and your devoted servant. The earl does not dance, more's the pity. I, however, have long been a devotee of that delightful convention. Would you care to have me scribble my name on your dance card?"

The debutante looked Norton up and down before pronouncing: "I'd rather die, sirrah!" She then turned on her heels to head back to her chaperone, who probably had her hands full with this one, Banning thought, already scanning the room for some sight of Prudence, his own personal charge, his own personal headache.

"I didn't really want her, you know. Just trying to help," Norton said, taking out his handkerchief to wipe at the perspiration beginning to gather just ahead of his receding hairline. "See your ward yet, Banning? If I'm not insulted at least once every ten minutes, I won't feel like I'm at Almack's. Duke? You going to hide behind Banning the whole night long?"

The earl stepped out from behind Banning, brushing at his coat sleeves as if he had just climbed out from a dusty hidey-hole, and grinning sheepishly. "It's a gift, you understand. M'father had it, and his father before him. Females tripping over us whether we want them or not. I'm going to have to pick one soon. My heart can't take this. I only hope your ward isn't like the rest of 'em, Banning. Wouldn't want to break her hopeful heart, seeing as how she's yours— well, not exactly yours, not precisely, but you know what I mean."

Banning rolled his eyes at his friend's admission-*cum*-complaint, wishing he could understand the attraction, but silently hoping Prudence wouldn't be one of those young ladies who found the earl irresistible. Poor Duke wouldn't have a chance if Angel took a dead set at him. Besides, when she married, he hoped it would be to some country gentlemen who was in town just for the season, and would then retire to somewhere conveniently distant, like Wales, so that she'd be out of his sight, gone from his mind.

"Spot her yet?" Norton asked as they began strolling the perimeter of the dance floor. "I don't think you told us. Or maybe you did. Whatever. Tell us again. What color's her hair? Isn't red, is it? Too bad if it's red. You'll have enough trouble popping her off it it's yellow, seeing as how dark hair is all the vogue this season. Had that from m'mother just today. Dark hair. And tall. Can't say as why, but you know how it is. As well hunt for mare's nests as look for logic in fashion."

"Prudence's hair is brownish—light, and somewhat golden, I suppose. And she's not too tall," Banning said absently, trying to look for his ward without appearing as if he was searching for her. He was late, thanks mostly to his own reluctance to be here this evening, and his sister was probably sitting somewhere in a corner, seething, but he was here now and wanted nothing more than to see Prudence, introduce her to the patronesses, secure her permission to waltz, take her on a turn around the room, and then skulk back to his study, most probably on the lookout for his store of brandy.

"Golden brown, and she's short into the bargain? That's too bad, really. Up the ante on her dowry then, Banning, that's the ticket," Norton advised, snagging a glass of lemonade from one of the passing waiters, then making a face as he took a sip. "Warm as piss. Breeches, no ice, gambling only for tame stakes, insipid chits on the hunt for a fortune. Why do we come here, Duke, do you know?"

"To dance with the MacAfee, remember? Lend her our consequence—and talk up her dowry, of course," the earl answered, then crashed into Banning, who stood frozen to the spot, staring across the room. "I say, old fellow, I don't mean to complain, but you could warn a person if you're—what's the matter? You're looking dashed queer all of a sudden, stap me if you aren't."

Six days. Had it only been six days? How long did it take for a caterpillar to turn into a butterfly? Surely longer than that?

But there she was, standing quite alone within a

wide circle of male admirers. Poised. Self-assured. Glorious. Incandescent. Intoxicatingly beautiful.

Prudence MacAfee. Butterfly.

"Angel." The word was a whisper, a near benediction, a plea.

"God's teeth, Banning!" the earl exclaimed, looking across the room, following the marquess' open-mouthed stare. "That's *her?*"

"Where? Where?" Norton asked, chin stretched, fretfully hopping up and down like a small child stuck in the second row at a street parade and trying to see what everyone else saw.

Prudence was dressed in white, yet not in white, but more of a golden ivory, the heavy silk gown all but sleeveless, its modestly scooped bodice encrusted with pearls and some sort of small, sparkling disks that captured and reflected every bit of golden fire from every chandelier in the ballroom, so that she appeared to be surrounded by a halo of soft, sun-drenched light.

The skirt of the gown, which began just beneath her perfect breasts—and he knew they were perfect, to his everlasting damnation—was barely more than straight, skimming lovingly over her hips with only the faintest hint of gathering running across the flat of her stomach and ending at the base of her spine, where it was caught up in a wide flat bow.

Her arms were covered almost to her shoulders in soft kid gloves—arms he had first seen bathed in the blood of a dying mare—leaving only a glimpse of softly glowing skin to tantalize the dozens of young bucks eagerly soliciting her attention.

Three tight strands of perfectly matched pearls—making up the necklace he had nearly beggared himself to give to his sister on her twenty-first birthday—encircled her long, slim throat, more pearls dangling from her ears to tickle at her jawbone as she tipped her head to listen to one of her admirers, then laugh in genuine delight.

Her hair, piled high on her head and utterly unadorned by feathers or ribbons, was less curled than shaped, with only a few shoulder-length tendrils looking as if they had escaped their pins only for the privilege of kissing the nape of her neck. And her face—that perfect oval he had seen so clearly beneath her horrible straw hat—was more womanly, more flawlessly beautiful, than that of any heavenly angel.

If she were to turn her back to him, and he then saw glittering angel wings fluttering gracefully in the breeze, he would not have blinked.

She was, indeed, an angel.

But not *his* angel . . .

"Good evening, brother dear," the dowager countess said, coming up beside Banning, startling him as she slipped her arm around his elbow. "Come to do your duty by your ward?"

Banning blinked, bringing himself back to his senses, and bent to kiss his sister's cheek. "You're lucky we English no longer burn witches, my love," he said quietly. "And you must be a witch. How else could you turn a country mouse into the belle of the season?"

"I claim no credit, Banning," she answered, presenting her hand to both the earl and Norton, who both perfunctorily kissed the air above her fingertips before once more turning to stare at Prudence MacAfee. "Rexford and Mr. Wallace are the talented conjurers who performed such supremely satisfying magic. Not that Angel wasn't already quite presentable, or else no amount of hopeful incantations could have wrought such a satisfying change."

She raised her hand slightly, waving to Prudence and motioning for the young woman to join them. "Sally Jersey is waiting for you to ask permission for Angel to waltz, my dear. Do you think you can manage to be civil long enough to take her on a few turns around the room? Not that it's all that necessary. Except for this first waltz, Angel's card is already full. Even Ramsden is down for a Scottish reel, if you can believe that. Not that he isn't hot after the Broughton, having escorted her here tonight, along with her mother, of course. The Broughton wouldn't do anything that isn't socially correct, although being seen with Ramsden can't be considered entirely prudent. Has the air of the desperate about her, I'm beginning to think. Pity."

Banning felt a nudge in his ribs, and turned to Norton, who was shaking his head. "Strangest thing about your ward, old friend. I've looked and looked, and each time I do, I'm reminded of my love of honey drizzled over warm scones. Does that mean I'm besotted—or just hungry?"

The earl adjusted his collar, his ridiculously high, starched shirt-points having already turned his neck a fiery red. "You are going to introduce us, aren't you, Banning? You said you'd introduce us, remember? Uh-oh. Quiet! Here she comes!"

"Good evening, your lordship," Prudence said, extending her right hand even as she dropped into a flawless curtsy, not so shallow as to be presumptive or so deep as to be overdone, but just right, and graceful into the bargain. "How condescending of you to attend me this evening, lending me the consequence of your presence."

She wants to murder me, Banning thought, keeping his hand steady until she rose from her curtsy, then avoiding her gaze as he bowed over her hand, longing to turn it so that he could kiss the soft inside of her wrist where a single pearl button held the glove in place.

"It is my honor and my pleasure, Miss MacAfee," he answered stonily before performing the introductions between his ward and his two friends, both of whom nearly made complete cakes of themselves, falling over each other in their zeal to be the first to kiss her hand.

"Yes, well, now that everyone has done the civil," Lady Wendover trilled, obviously preening. "Banning, Sally Jersey is just there, across the room. Do your duty, if you please, as I'm quite sure a waltz is next on the program. You wouldn't wish to be stuck here another two hours, waiting to take your ward onto the floor."

"Indeed, no, my lady," Prudence said, placing her hand on Banning's forearm, branding him, her heat searing deep into his flesh, his bone. "His lordship has already been much too kind, having gifted me with invaluable lessons in deportment and proper conduct. I should dislike above all things inconveniencing him further."

"Duke?"

The earl bobbed his head several times in understanding, saying, "It will be my pleasure to return

Lady Wendover to her chair. Dewey, haven't you finished that lemonade yet? Put it down somewhere, and help me escort the countess back to the dowagers."

Norton looked to his left hand as if surprised to see the glass still there. "What do I do with it? Isn't that just the way it always is? You get it easily enough, but you can't get rid of it. No tables in sight, or waiters either, now that I'm looking. And it's not like I wanted it in the first place, you know."

"I agree, Mr. Norton," Prudence said, winking at the man. "It's atrocious, isn't it, and yet more than a half dozen gentlemen have brought me glasses of the horrid stuff. I'd ask for wine, but I wouldn't want to blot my copybook my first evening. However, if you were to be fortunate enough to snag a glass of anything stronger sometime soon, just signal me, and I'll meet you on one of the balconies and we can share it in secret, as I'm about to perish from thirst."

As Banning slowly counted to ten, and Lady Wendover's smile froze to her face, the earl and Norton exchanged looks before exploding into delighted laughter.

"Banning! You didn't tell me Miss MacAfee was a wit," Norton exclaimed, obviously taking Prudence's statement as a joke.

"What a card!" the earl seconded, still laughing. "About time I heard a gel talk like a real person, I say. She drinks wine, does she? Do you hunt, Miss MacAfee? If you do, I'll marry you myself, and save Banning here the trouble of popping you off."

"La, my lord, thank you," Prudence answered, smiling up at the earl. "My first proposal. And so nicely done. I'm flattered, truly. But I do believe I should have at least one giddy, girlish waltz before thinking of anything so serious, don't you?"

Banning, sparing only a moment to shake his head at his two friends who, together, obviously didn't have the brains of a single flea, mumbled something unintelligible and drew Prudence off toward Lady Jersey.

"I like your friends, Daventry," Prudence said as they walked along, Banning glaring at three young men within the space of ten seconds, silently warning them away. "Mr. Norton reminds me of a cuddly brown bear I once saw at a local fair, and the earl is so nervous his nose actually *quivers*. Tell me, what on earth do either of them see in you?"

"More than you do, obviously," Banning said, smiling and nodding to a purple-turbaned dowager whose name escaped him at the moment. "Are you having fun, dazzling all the young bucks with your beauty and confounding them with your mix of manners and blunt speech?"

"I'm beautiful, Banning?" she asked in return, passing over his veiled insult. "It's not simply David's wonderful gown?"

"I saw no lack of unlicked cubs vying for your attention when I came in," Banning said quietly. "I cannot believe none of them told you that you are beautiful. If not, Miss MacAfee, allow me to be the first."

"You'd be the twelfth, actually, but I accept the compliment," Prudence told him just as quietly, adding, "although I'd rather hear your apology. Freddie said you would, and I think we'd best get it over with as quickly as possible, so that we can put the whole business behind us once and for all. And then you can explain to me why you'd be so cork-brained as to tell your sister what you did, because it was thoroughly stupid, you know. She's hatching a romance between us even as I speak, a hope that is certainly doomed to disappointment."

Banning noticed Sally Jersey turn away from the group of ladies she was standing with, raising one eyebrow as she saw he and Prudence approach. "Very well. I'm sorry, I couldn't see any way to avoid it, and Freddie has known disappointment before this. There, now be on your best behavior and let's get this over with."

Five very uncomfortable minutes later, Banning found himself leading Prudence onto the floor for her first waltz, feeling as if the eyes of the entire world were on the two of them. He slipped his hand onto the flat plane just above the sweep of her hip, felt her rest her hand lightly on his shoulder, held out his right hand for her to complete their politely distanced joining, and whirled her into the first turn of the dance.

She immediately stepped on his foot.

"Damn and blast!" she gritted out from between clenched teeth, trying to recover herself. "Why am I so bloody nervous?"

At last, Banning relaxed. Prudence was young, she was beautiful, and she was still the Angel he was beginning to believe he knew so well. His sister may have coached her in the ways of society, Rexford and his dressmaker friend might have given her all the outward trappings of a proper young lady, but she remained, at the bottom of it, the same Prudence MacAfee who had burst into his life, into his consciousness, and refused to go away again.

"You have that wrong, my dear," he said, guiding her more firmly with his right hand, so that she could follow his lead more easily. "I believe you should have said, blushing girlishly as you did so: 'I beg your pardon, my lord.' To which I would have quickly responded, 'No, no, Miss MacAfee. It was my fault entirely.'"

"Oh, go to the devil, Daventry," Prudence told him without heat, then smiled. "And I do like your friends. Are they ancient, like you? Which one is Dewey—which is a very amusing name, by the way—and which is the duke? I was so nervous that I've already forgotten that, I'm afraid."

"Mr. Norton is Dewey, and the earl is Duke," Banning said, being deliberately vague, just to confound her.

"The earl is a duke, or is the duke an earl? And stop grinning like a bear. I've met so many titles tonight I'm getting dizzy!"

"The earl is Marmaduke, a name he loathes and one his parents would have reconsidered if they had known it would cause so much trouble," Banning explained, wishing he could be unaware that his sister was standing at the edge of the dance floor, smiling as if she had just now been granted her dearest wish. The waltz ended then, and not a moment too soon. "Prudence," he said quickly, wishing the world would disappear, if only for a moment, "I am sorry, you know. More sorry than I can tell you."

Her golden eyes glistened with unshed tears before she blinked rapidly, then smiled up at him. "You made up for everything quite nicely by sending Lightning to me in Park Lane. We won't speak of it again, all right? Besides, it was my fault entirely, Daventry."

"Banning," he said, squeezing her hand even as the fist that had been crushing his heart these last six days finally eased its painful grip. "Angel."

"Daventry?" a deep male voice inquired politely, if forcefully. "If you would be so kind, I believe this next dance is mine."

Banning turned slowly, having already recognized the distinctive voice of Leslie Orford, Viscount Ramsden, an outstandingly handsome, well-born, and therefore still acceptable rake who had spent the last year or two in Italy, fleeing there after killing his man in a duel over a Covent Garden opera dancer. "Ramsden," he said, barely inclining his head in greeting as he reluctantly gave Prudence over to the tall, blond man and retired to the side of the ballroom, deliberately keeping his back to the dancers.

"You shouldn't have allowed that, you know," a female voice said from behind him, and Banning turned to see that Miss Althea Broughton, the beautiful and once more eligible Miss Althea Broughton, was standing there, smiling at him just as if they had last spoken yesterday, and not almost two years ago— and then only to say goodbye.

"You are her guardian, aren't you, Banning?" she continued, holding out her hand to him in her usual graceful, slightly imperial way. "I found the news highly diverting when first I heard it, but you must be feeling horribly oppressed, poor man. The child appears to be a bit of a handful."

"I am merely her guardian, Althea," Banning said, motioning with a slight nod of his head that he would like to join the dancers, a silent suggestion to which she readily complied. "Freddie is bringing her out."

"Freddie? Oh, dear me, then you *will* need my help, won't you? With Freddie as her only guide, she'll end tumbled on her back in some garden before the week is out, if that look in Ramsden's eye is to be trusted." Althea smiled, and he was struck, not for the first time, by her patrician good looks, her sleekly drawn back blonde hair—wasn't blond hair out of fashion? his mind prompted evilly.

They were separated by the moves of the dance for a few seconds, Banning asking as they came together once more: "Are you volunteering your services, Althea?"

"I would be delighted, Banning," she answered sweetly. "You know I have always held you in high esteem. Shall we meet tomorrow, to discuss your ward's behavior? She is already committed to driving out tomorrow with Leslie, you know—Leslie told me himself, his eyes gleaming with mischief—and that cannot be considered good."

Banning sliced a look across the dance floor, only to see Prudence laughing at something the witty viscount was whispering into her ear. "The promenade, Althea? I shall be honored to take you up in my carriage just before five, if that suits you?"

"It suits me perfectly, Banning. Perfectly."

CHAPTER 12

*As clear and as manifest
as the nose on a man's face.*

Robert Burton

There was a lot to be said for becoming, overnight as it were, London's newest Sensation, not the least of it being awakened to the delighted laughter of one of the dearest, purest ladies in all the world as she danced into Prudence's bedchamber, waving a sheaf of invitations as if they were the first prize in some sort of competition.

"Freddie, stop," Prudence warned lovingly as she watched Lady Wendover pirouette daintily just at the edge of a fringed carpet. "You're going to trip and fall if you're not careful. And then Daventry would blame me, and I really don't think I'm up to a scolding this morning. What time did we finally stop chattering like magpies and come up to bed? Three? Four?"

"Half-past four, to be precise about the thing," Lady Wendover said, collapsing onto the bottom of the bed. "But, as it's nearly noon now, I think it's time you were up and about. Poor Quimby has already had to turn away at least a dozen hopeful suitors, all of them bearing flowers, I might add. The drawing room is stuffed full of them, and the scent—ah, it's delicious! The lizard, of course, is sneezing fit to blow her ears off, which only makes it all the more delicious, don't you think?"

"Miss Prentice isn't all that bad, Freddie," Prudence said, smiling to her maid as that young woman helped her into her dressing gown. "Thank you, Geranium," she said, then crawled back onto the bed, to sit cross-legged on the covers and pick up several of the pressed cardboard invitations. "It's merely a matter of knowing how to handle her."

"Which you do very well. I, on the other hand, have been comforting myself with the knowledge that—when the day comes that she is finally done with that horrid tapestry she is forever working on—I shall inform her that she cannot hang it in my house. But even that small notion of revenge has lost its pleasure for me, with her being so amenable and all. As a matter of fact, Miss Prentice has been a near paragon almost from the moment you came to Park Lane. I only wish you'd tell me how you managed it."

Prudence watched as Geranium moved off toward the dressing room, out of earshot, then leaned forward to say confidentially, "You know that glass of water the lizard keeps constantly at her side?"

Lady Wendover nodded. "She has it with her all the day long. I always thought it odd, but once we'd begun calling her a lizard, I'd decided she needs it to keep her scales moist. What about it?"

"It's gin," Prudence confided, her eyes dancing, *"that's* what's about it, Freddie. Straight gin. The second day I was here I was thirsty and picked up her glass, thinking to take a sip until I could get up the courage to ring for a servant, because it was always so much easier at the farm, where I could just go to the pump and stick my mouth under it, without disturbing an entire household of people. First Quimby comes to ask what I want, then he summons a maid, then—"

"Gin!" Lady Wendover exclaimed, having moved her lips for several seconds without being able to produce the word. "I don't believe it!"

Prudence's grin was downright evil, and she was enjoying herself immensely. She had come to love Frederica Davidson as the sister she'd never had, and if she could make the beautiful, yet somehow sad woman laugh, bring some light into her life, she could feel better about her small—or not so small— deception.

"Believe it, Freddie," she went on earnestly. "But this has to remain our little secret, all right? I promised the lizard I wouldn't tell as long as she behaved herself. And even you have admitted that she's being quite good, although I can tell it's killing her."

"Gin," Lady Wendover repeated softly, shaking her head, and then she frowned. "And just how would you know it was gin, Angel? Surely *you've* never before tasted the vile stuff?"

Prudence was about to inform her friend that, not only had she tasted that particular vile stuff, but she had tasted, and enjoyed, worse. But as the dowager countess had not believed any of her other true but admittedly bizarre stories about life on MacAfee Farm, she had no great hope, or worries, that she would believe her now.

And so, as she so often did these days, Prudence lied. "Heavens, no, Freddie. I only knew it wasn't water, and that it tasted like medicine. Worried that the lizard was sick, I straightaway took the glass to Quimby, and he identified its contents for me."

Lady Wendover sighed, patting Prudence's hand. "And you've been holding your terrible knowledge over Miss Prentice's head ever since. How very devious, yet inspired. I'm proud of you, Angel, truly I am."

"I only wanted to make your life easier, Freddie, as she doesn't bother me," Prudence said truthfully. "Poor woman. She hasn't had an easy life, you know. When I confronted her with the glass, she burst into tears, telling me all about how she was to marry some vicar's son some two dozen years ago, but he heartlessly jilted her for the baker's daughter, leaving her no choice but to flee her village in shame and seek employment in London."

Prudence wrinkled her nose at the melodramatic story, which she hadn't truly believed when Miss Prentice had told it to her, and believed even less now. "Which, of course," she ended brightly, "doesn't excuse her for being a lizard, but it does explain it, I suppose."

"I suppose," Lady Wendover said thoughtfully, slipping from the bed to call to the maid: "Rose? Have you rung down for Miss MacAfee's chocolate as yet? If not, please do it now, for we have a busy day planned."

"Her name is Geranium, Freddie," Prudence corrected, smiling as she laid back against the pillows, enjoying both her physical comfort and the fact that she was, yet again, about to be waited on and fussed over as if she were royalty, or some such thing. "Her mother named her after the flower because of that shocking red hair, remember?"

Lady Wendover shrugged. "Geranium, Rose—I'll never get the straight of it, I don't think. But no matter. Tell me about Banning. You refused to say a word against him last night when I teased you about him, but he must have done something terrible again. I mean, he only danced with you the once—and then with the Broughton, which I believe to be entirely stupid—and then he left, looking like a bear with a sore paw."

"I think he might have been put out that the Earl of Preston and Mr. Norton refused to leave with him because they wished to remain with me," Prudence said, carefully keeping her gaze on the stack of invitations, sorting them according to size on the bedspread. "They're both very sweet, don't you think—although the earl hums when he walks, which can be slightly unnerving, and Mr. Norton is very much taken with worrying about the silliest things."

What Prudence didn't say to the dowager countess was that, as her dance card had been full, she'd allowed Daventry's two friends to escort her down to dinner—if that uninspired buffet could have been so described—and had spent the entire time deftly squeezing information about the marquess from them. Or perhaps not so deftly, as the two men seemed eager to talk.

Daventry, they had told her, although they appeared to be speaking between themselves, almost as she weren't there to listen and absorb everything they said, was:

"... the best of good fellows—"

179

". . . or at least he was before his father died and the Broughton refused his suit, turning him down flat because he had a title but no money—is that Hartley? Gad, where did he find that waistcoat?—which is precisely why poor Freddie had to do what her father said all those years ago and marry that rich old goat, Wendover, which *really* upset poor Banning all the way back then, as I remember the thing—"

". . . and then he went and inherited a fortune, and Wendover obligingly met up with that French sniper when he went to relieve himself in some bushes, but it was too late by then to get the Broughton, who wasn't married in the end after all thanks to Wexley's elopement with his mother's maid, so that she's smacked herself right back into the thick of the marriage mart—"

". . . which is a good thing—blast, if this wine ain't corked! worse than the lemonade!—because Banning needs to set up his nursery, or at least I think he thinks he does, and if he's so hell-bent on becoming a stickler for propriety he could do no better than the Broughton, seeing as how she is impeccably bred, dashed deep in the pocket, and dull as ditchwater, not to mention that Miss MacAfee here is years too young for him, to hear Banning tell it—"

". . . and, besides, she can help pop off Banning's ward, which is also a good thing because he just hasn't been the same since he became a guardian, even going so far as to drink himself under the table, which he hasn't done since the eve of Waterloo, when Henry MacAfee plied him with drink and started talking about dying and all and forced him into taking on a ward in the first place—"

". . . and does Miss MacAfee know that Banning

and Viscount Ramsden really don't like each other very much—I've always distrusted the fellow, he's too handsome by half—even before Banning began trying his hand at being a stickler for propriety, because Ramsden always was a thorough-paced rake out to bed as many women as he could before somebody's husband shot him—"

". . . so maybe it wouldn't be a good idea for Miss MacAfee to go out driving with the rotter, which is sure to set Banning's back up, and that can't be a good thing because it looks to me as if his back already is up quite far enough—"

". . . oh yes, quite far enough. I say, Miss MacAfee, have we been neglecting you?"

Still smiling at the memory of that strange conversation, although her heart had been troubled ever since—something she refused to admit, even to herself—Prudence turned to Lady Wendover and asked what that lady thought she should wear for a drive in the park. Because she was most definitely going out driving with Viscount Ramsden, especially now that she knew her guardian wouldn't like it above half.

"Oh yes, that," Lady Wendover replied, tapping a finger against her only slightly rouged lips. "Banning sent round a note this morning, my dear, advising me that it was against his better judgment to have his ward to be seen in the park with Viscount Ramsden. According to Banning, Althea Broughton agreed with him thoroughly, which I imagine he thought would help influence me because I never know just what to do, but I am aware that Althea knows the straight of everything."

"Well, Christ on a crutch, Freddie!" Prudence exploded, not knowing which she hated most—Banning's distrust of her own good sense or this damning information that her life, it would seem, was to be dictated to her by Althea Broughton. The marquess might disapprove all he wanted, but she certainly wasn't going to let him issue orders to her! "What does he think the man's going to do to me—throw me willy-nilly to the ground and ravish me on the lawn, taking out time to tip his hat to Prinny as he rides by?"

"Angel, your language, please," the dowager countess warned quietly, nodding her head toward Geranium, who was standing in a corner, grinning broadly at her mistress's outburst. "Although I must say I do agree with you, Angel. Nothing untoward could happen in the park. Leslie is a lovely man, even if he has acquired a bit of a reputation—and then there was this sad business of a duel. I am not quite clear on the particulars, as I was still in mourning for poor Rodney at the time, and then I was ill for so long. However, Banning did not forbid it—I read the note twice, just to be sure. He only said it would be against his better judgment. Angel? Your face is rather flushed. You're not going to cry or anything, are you?"

Cry? Certainly not! Prudence had always wondered how it felt to have one's blood boil, as bubbling anger had been described in the novels Henry had brought her, and now she knew. It felt wonderful!

"Ha!" she exclaimed, waving her hands as if attempting to clear the air of some horrible stench. "Then we've got him, don't we, Freddie? Miserable rotter! All he cares about is how he'll look as my guardian. How dare he pretend to be concerned for me? The only mauling I've ever had was from my so-proper guardian, if you'll remember. If I were to compare the two, I would say that Daventry is the rake, and the viscount is a perfect gentlemen. At least he isn't a wolf in sheep's clothing. I *know* what to expect from him. That being said, and in the firm belief that Althea Broughton should go hang herself—Freddie, brace yourself, and try to be brave, because I'm *going!*"

He knew she'd be here, of course. He'd known it last night when he asked Althea to drive out with him, he'd known it this morning when he penned the note to his sister, and he'd known it even as he steered his curricle into the park to immediately begin looking for Viscount Ramsden's distinctive yellow-wheeled phaeton.

"Banning? You haven't said above two words to me since we left Grosvenor Square. You aren't still put out with me for having to turn down your suit in favor of Wexley's, are you? You know it was all Papa's idea. And he did mean well, wishing to see me settled comfortably. Besides, that is all in the past, isn't it? We are civilized people; we can adjust our memories in order to look to our expectations."

Banning peeked down at his sleeve, to the place where Althea had rested her gloved hand on his forearm, remembering a time when this small, personal gesture would have sent his heart to pounding and his hopes to soaring. But he felt nothing, not even disgust. Yes, Althea would make him the perfect wife, even better now than when he had believed himself in love with her cool English beauty.

Whatever traces of youthful willfulness and love of excitement still left in him would be snuffed out within a week of their marriage and then, having dutifully wed his fortune to another fortune, he would be free to go about the business of being a proper English gentleman—seeing to his various estates, producing the next marquess and another son for insurance, giving the occasional meaningless speech in the lords, hunting with similarly bored and boring cronies, and setting up a mistress on the fringes of Mayfair.

This was what was expected of him, what his grandfather before him had done, what endless generations of Englishmen had aspired to even as they dreaded it. Or was he the only one who dreaded it? No matter. He had seen what could happen when these rules were bent in any way. His father had married for love—for what he'd thought was love—and had quickly lived to regret not having married for the right reason. Money. And what had his reckless disregard of the rules gotten the man? A penniless son who could not make a decent match, and a daughter sold off to the highest bidder.

The latter rankled more than the former. Banning still remembered how he had watched his sister be sold in order to feed the Daventry coffers. But he had learned. The rules were the rules, and breaking them could only end in unhappiness. As in marrying someone as unsuitable as Prudence MacAfee. Too young. Too vibrant. Too prone to make him forget that life was earnest and his carefree days must be forever put behind him.

Not that he would force his ward to marry for financial gain. A large part of him still believed that his sister had nearly wasted away from guilt, so happy to have Rodney underground and be free once more, yet so ashamed to be left with the fortune he had bestowed on her.

And yet. And yet?

Would marriage to Prudence be a betrayal of his promise to his dying father? Would marrying a near child, someone who had just barely begun to live, be so very unfair to her? If he loved her, no.

Did he love her? There were times . . .

But she made him so angry! Distracted him from his purpose in life; with her youth and beauty and outrageous behavior, made him long to be young and reckless and even frivolous. And alive. So very, very alive.

". . . and so I told his lordship, if you will persist in speaking of mills and fisticuffs in my presence, I shall have nothing whatsoever to say to you, sir. Well, that silenced him, I daresay! Banning. Banning? Did you hear what I just said?"

Banning snapped himself back to attention. "Of course, my dear," he told her, still looking for Ramsden's phaeton even as his lips lifted in a slight smile, knowing that Prudence would not have been put out by any discussion of a mill. She probably would have sat, eyes wide, drinking in every snippet of information she could glean, delighting in the telling. His smile faded. Would he spend the remainder of his life considering how Prudence would react to things, setting up scenes in his head that showed her to be both wonderful and unsuitable?

"Papa asked if you would come to dinner Saturday evening, Banning," Althea said, unfurling her parasol now that the sun had crept out from behind the clouds, for her complexion was milky white and she wouldn't dare allow a freckle to mar it. "I know it is short notice, but he is extremely anxious to speak with you."

Her smile was coy, and as close to flirtatious as he'd ever seen her. "I think you might know why."

Banning's collar suddenly seemed too tight, as if he could feel a noose slipping over his head and being pulled taut. "Saturday night? Yes, I believe I'm free in the earlier hours. Far be it from me to turn down an invitation from your father, Althea. And then we might go to the theater, I suppose."

"Dear Banning! I knew you'd understand!" Her hand was on his sleeve once more, this time squeezing him through the cloth of his jacket. Losing Wexley must have shaken her more than her calm exterior would suggest, the whispers of the *ton* about her recent disgrace must have reached her ears, for she was almost pitiful in her zeal to make clear to Banning that she was not only available once more, but even embarrassingly willing. Eager. Perhaps even desperate. "It's as if the past never existed, isn't it? We will have such fun settling your little ward, Banning."

And that, he was to remember later—too much later—was when he should have put a halt to Althea Broughton's hopeful aspirations, for he had just espied Ramsden's phaeton out of the corner of his eye and felt his heart leap when he saw Prudence sitting up beside the rake, looking as if all the sunshine in the world had come to warm itself in her softly glowing presence.

To hell with respectability, his rapidly pounding heart told him, and the devil with all he knew and believed and had done his level best to ascribe to these past two years. Prudence MacAfee was summer and freedom and laughter and loving—and he was not going to settle for anything less than anything she might be willing to give him! He was older than she? Nothing! He was her legal guardian? A mere trifle! She didn't love him? A temporary inconvenience!

He wasn't any other Englishman. He wasn't his ancestors and he wasn't his father. And he damn well wasn't going to be, either! He was Banning Talbot, Marquess of Daventry, and he liked the man he was, even if that man had been hiding behind a graying head and another's man's vision of who he should be for two long, frustrating years.

"Althea," he said, doing his best to be polite when all he wanted was to pitch the beautiful blond creature headfirst from the curricle and take off in Prudence's direction, "I do believe I see my ward sitting up beside Viscount Ramsden. Do you mind if we ride over that way, so that I might have a word with her?"

"Only one word, Banning?" Althea questioned him, sniffing. "I should think you'd wish to deliver more than a single admonition, considering the fact that she is, if my eyes are not playing tricks with me, tooling Ramsden's grays while that ramshackle fool sits there grinning like an ape, allowing it."

"Yes," Banning said, feeling his own mouth spreading into a wide smile, "and she is quite good at it, isn't she? Light hands. A firm grip. Slap up to the echo, I believe Angel would say."

CHAPTER 13

This, no tomorrow hath,
nor yesterday. . . .

John Donne

Angel,

Saw you flying high in the park yesterday with Ramsden. Naughty girl. You are to drop him at once!

Less than three months now, my love, and the world is ours.

If you have a few pennies to spare, send them to me through the posie post.

Enby

Prudence quickly folded the note and slipped it into her gown pocket as Lady Wendover entered the drawing room, her smile rather beatific. As a matter of fact, the dowager countess was smiling almost constantly these past days, although she refused to comment on her very obvious happiness, protesting that Prudence was years too young for such confidences.

"What? I'm not tripping over drooling young men?" Lady Wendover questioned Prudence teasingly as she nodded to Miss Prentice, who was propped in her usual corner, a glass at her elbow, silently working her tapestry. "This room was chock full of languishing swains an hour ago. Did you send them all off with sadly broken hearts, Angel, to do their utmost to find solace with some other, lesser debutante?"

"They're all nice enough, Freddie," Prudence answered honestly, "but they are also all so very young. I believe I was too old for any of them years before I allowed you to put up my hair."

"Hoo! Did you hear that, Miss Prentice?" Lady Wendover exclaimed, gracefully seating herself on the chaise, her long legs modestly covered by her muslin skirts. "Methuselah, here, is too old for her gentlemen callers. Viscount Ramsden wouldn't have anything to do with this sudden revelation, would he? He's a year or two longer in the tooth even than Banning. Driving in the park with the pretty fellow yesterday afternoon, having him all but stuck to your side last night at Lady Hertford's party? I've never seen him so attentive, but then reformed rakes are touted to make the most constant husbands. However, Banning wouldn't approve."

"That's two," Prudence said beneath her breath, moving her hand to cover the note in her pocket, adding, for Lady Wendover's benefit, "I don't feel that way about the viscount, Freddie. He's pleasant and extremely charming, but no more than a friend."

"A friend. And *he* knows that? I think not!" Lady Wendover replied, smiling up at Quimby as she accepted the glass of sherry he'd brought her, as he did each afternoon at three. "Thank you, Quimby. Angel, Leslie doesn't have female friends. He has *conquests.*"

"He has a *reputation,* Freddie," Prudence said, shaking her head as Quimby pointed to Lady Wendover's glass and silently indicated that he would secure her one also, if she cared to request it. "A reputation he assures me is unearned."

"Ha! And Boney didn't really want to conquer the world!" Quimby exclaimed, then quickly cleared his throat, nodded in Lady Wendover's direction, and bowed himself out of the room as that lady dissolved in mirth.

Prudence felt her cheeks grow warm. "Oh, all right, so he was once a rake, a devoted out-and-outer, and is still fairly proud of it into the bargain," she admitted pettishly. "But he let me tool the reins, which few others would do, and he's not at all starchy, like one other I could mention in particular."

"Meaning Banning," her ladyship interrupted, giggling. "Did you ever notice, Miss Prentice, that each time our Angel opens her mouth, sooner or later she comes around to speaking of my naughty brother? But please, Angel, don't let me interrupt. Tell me more of Leslie—this acknowledged wolf in his brand-new sheep's clothing."

Prudence bit her tongue, mentally chastising herself for doing just as Lady Wendover had said, then pushed on doggedly: "I would be delighted. I thought my sides would split last night, as Lord Ramsden pointed out some of Lady Hertford's guests, telling me all sorts of silly little stories about them. Did you know that the Earl of Fawkham can touch the tip of his nose with his tongue? He can do it most easily—and will perform for anyone who springs for a drink in the clubs. And Lady Uphill stuffs cotton in her bodice because she's flat as Prinny's seat cushion when he rises from his chair."

"Poor Lady Uphill. I can imagine how dear Leslie came by that last piece of information," the Marquess of Daventry drawled as he strode into the room, shaking Prudence's composure down to her toes. "Did he fail to mention that Lady Uphill's sister, the redoubtable Miss Granton, can't see more than three feet in front of her nose but refuses to wear spectacles, so that she walked straight into the Serpentine last month when she strayed from her keeper?"

"No! Oh Banning, that is delicious!" Lady Wendover said, girlishly giggling into her sherry. "But what are you doing here? I had thought you'd quite forgotten your way to Park Lane."

So had I, Prudence thought nervously, her hand once more straying to her pocket and the note Enby had sent to her via Geranium. What if he had arrived a half hour earlier, just as Geranium had brought the note to her, here in the drawing room, with Miss Prentice leering from her corner, torn between wanting to learn the contents of the note and knowing that her damning glass of gin sat just at her elbow?

Would Banning have been rude enough to inquire as to the contents of the note? Would the lizard have been daring enough to have jeopardized her position in Park Lane for the chance of a reward from the marquess for having exposed his ward as the perfidious creature she knew her to be?

Most importantly—why had he come here this afternoon? And did he have to look so achingly handsome, his silver hair so thick, so adorably mussed, his green eyes sparkling with what looked to be mischief? Since the beginning, since that first sad, sad day with Molly, the image of the Marquess of Daventry in shirt-sleeves, his eyes so eloquent and sympathetic, had been burned into her brain and—from the first moment of their unexpected interlude inside Lady Wendover's coach—her soul.

His teasing ways, his maddening bouts of arrogance, his lapses into foolery such as on the day of their picnic at Cowdray House, his blatant determination to keep her out of his life one moment and his too-obvious pursuit of her the next—all of it had combined to make thinking of Banning Talbot and the memories of their every meeting as much a part of her life as breathing.

She seemed to live for her next sight of this impossible, infuriating man, then only wanted him gone each time he deigned to walk into her life. Didn't he know how he confused her, confounded her—frightened her?

He was a complication she had not counted on, a problem impossible to solve, a temporary means to an end she had contemplated with only minor misgivings not quite a year ago but now had learned to dread because accomplishing that end would mean losing any small affection he held for her—and saying a last goodbye to what she now could believe might have been her one great happiness in life.

"I've come to take my ward out driving with me, Freddie." Prudence roused from her private sulk, her solitary reverie, to hear Banning's announcement to his sister, his back turned to his ward as if her opinion in the matter was of no real importance.

So, today it was going to be "maddening arrogance," was it?

Prudence was about to point out to the man that she really couldn't wish to so much as cross the street with him, when he turned about, showing her a smile that seemed, if not completely apprehensive, at least a smidgen less self-assured than she would have thought, and her anger melted away. "I've just taken delivery of a pair of matched bays I picked up at Tattersall's two days ago, and thought I'd give them a run into the country, test their mettle, as it were. Interested, Angel?"

Interested? It had been wonderful to have the reins in her hands in the park, but to sit up beside Banning, a noted whip, as he put a prime pair through their paces on the open road? Ah, that was a treat not to be missed!

And they'd be alone, just the two of them, isolated in the countryside. They could talk, and maybe laugh, and perhaps he would stop the equipage at some point and . . . but, no. She wouldn't think of that. Couldn't think of that. She had already mortgaged her future to Enby, made him her solemn promise, and had nothing to give Banning that he would not throw back at her when he finally, inevitably, learned the truth.

"I suppose," Prudence answered dully, shrugging to show that it didn't matter one way or the other to her whether she drove out with him or not. After all, she reminded herself, she was still fairly well put out with the man for having ridden past her yesterday, the Broughton at his side, without doing more than grinning like the village idiot and tipping his hat in her direction.

She had expected a through dressing-down, a public scolding from her stern guardian for having disobeyed his "better judgment," but he had disappointed her, making her feel as if he didn't care enough about her to do more than protest her behavior by letter, then go on his merry way with the cool, blonde beauty.

She had to keep that anger firmly in mind, and forget that he had come to see her today, come to ask her to drive out with him today, be alone with him today. Forget that she knew today, as she would for all the long, lonely days of her life, that he held her heart, damn him!

"Good, then it's settled," Banning said, looking once more to his sister. "My groom will accompany us, of course, and we shall have dinner at an inn I know just past Richmond, returning here by early evening."

"As I believe that was a statement of intention, dear brother, and not a request, I suppose there is nothing else for it other than for me to remind Angel to take a wrap, as the day may turn cool. Angel?"

"I'll just nip upstairs and ask Geranium to help me find something suitable. David has pinned notes to all my clothing, to help her know what goes with what, but as she can't read, it really hasn't been much of a success," Prudence volunteered quickly, thinking to slip Enby's note inside the ribbon tied around her other letters.

"Ring for your maid, Angel, and place your faith in her judgment," Lady Wendover said kindly, shaking her head. "You'll have the poor dear frightened for her position if you persist in acting as your own servant. Honestly, Banning, if I have a single complaint to register about your ward, it is that she is entirely too reticent about having anyone do for her. Why, if it were left to Angel, Violet would do little save sit in a corner, munching grapes, while she watched her mistress preparing her own tub."

"That's *Geranium,* Freddie," Prudence corrected with a smile, moving to the middle of the room after giving a tug on the bell pull, knowing it would only serve to summon Quimby, who would relate her request to a downstairs maid, who would tell it to the tweeny, who would dash upstairs to convey it to Geranium—just to have the entire process repeated in reverse before her cloak would appear in the foyer, folded over Quimby's arm as he awaited Miss MacAfee's appearance.

"Not Violet," Prudence continued, "not Rose, nor any of the other flowers you might list in your extensive vocabulary. I can't imagine why everyone seems to have this problem with Geranium's name. Although I will tell you that she is endlessly flattered that you persist in attempting to get it right. Daventry? Shall we be off now? I'll admit I'm champing at the bit to see your new cattle. I saw the pair you had yesterday, and they were prime tits."

"You mean, my dear, outspoken ward, that you're above all things delighted to have the opportunity to view my latest purchase—or at least that's what any other young debutante would say, then confine their comments to the beauty of the animals, not saying a word about the quality of their withers or the deepness of their chests," Banning corrected with a broad, indulgent smile as he waved Prudence ahead of him, then bent to kiss his sister goodbye.

"There are horse-mad debutantes, you know, Banning," Lady Wendover reminded him, giving his cravat a playful tug. "However, as those young ladies are also most invariably horse-faced, I suppose such plain speech is only more obvious to you when it is our sweet Angel who is so knowledgeable and so adorably blunt. Be good to her, brother—be very, very good to her—or I shall have Quimby take a whip to you."

Prudence hurried into the hallway, Lady Wendover's caution to Banning burning her ears, for she was quite sure she wasn't meant to have overheard it. She looked to Quimby who, as she had thought, was already holding out her cloak to her, and—to her immediate consternation—grinning like an ape.

"I don't like the man, he's probably only taking me out because of some misguided sense of duty, he'll probably spend the entire time telling me everything I already know about Ramsden, and when we get to the inn he'll make me eat in a private dining room while he takes another for himself," she said, her eyes narrowed as she snatched the cloak from the butler and laid it over her own arm.

"Anything you say, Miss MacAfee," Quimby replied quietly, turning about to lift the marquess's hat and driving gloves from a nearby table. "And may I be so bold, Miss MacAfee, as to convey to you the firm opinion of both her ladyship and myself that you shall make a fine marchioness. Top drawer, actually."

"Quimby, you see entirely too much, yet not nearly enough," Prudence countered, looking over her shoulder to be sure that Banning was still in the drawing room. "He's after the Broughton, not me. As for myself—well, I'll be gone soon enough, and then it won't matter to anyone how I feel in the matter, will it?"

"I think it will matter very much to you, Angel," the

butler replied, his tone low and fervent as Banning's approaching footsteps could be heard on the foyer tiles, Quimby's smile now replaced by the blank expression of the perfect servant. "When the heart is involved, it matters very much indeed."

She was his Angel of the smudged face again.

Not that she wasn't lovely almost beyond comprehension, dressed in a most lovely pale peach gown that flattered her golden complexion, her honey-hued hair all but hidden beneath a straw bonnet as unlike her battered straw hat as chalk is to cheese. Indeed, it had taken everything that was in him to keep him from dropping to one knee the moment he had entered his sister's drawing room, declaring his love to her for Freddie and even the lizard to hear.

It still amazed him that he could have fallen in love so quickly, so very deeply, caring nothing for conventions and even less for any ideas he'd once harbored as to his direction in life. Yet here he was, driving along a country lane, needing his full concentration to keep the lively bays under his firm control, and so delightfully aware of the woman by his side that he could barely keep himself from laughing out loud.

He was young again, after trying much too hard to be old. He felt vibrant again, eager for each new day to dawn, delighted by everything he had begun to take for granted. He was in love, for the first time in his life. Really, truly, deeply in love.

It was amazing, that's what it was!

For the past hour he and Prudence had spoken of the perfection of his new bays, of Lightning, Freddie, Marmaduke, and Dewey—even that rakehell, Ramsden—so thoroughly in harmony with each other that one regularly completed a thought the other had begun, the pair of them laughing and joking, and—just the once—inducing the unfortunate groom who clung to the bar at the rear of the vehicle to a spasm of hilarity that had nearly ended with the poor fellow losing his grip and tumbling into the dirt.

But now, as they turned onto the long, gently rising drive that would end in the courtyard of the Star and Garter Inn at the very top of Richmond Hill, Banning couldn't think of a thing to say.

Prudence had gone similarly silent, he'd noticed, and he wondered if she could feel the tension emanating from him or if she had simply grown tired of doing her best to entertain her aged guardian, doing him a favor in being on her best behavior in order that she could have had the pleasure of riding behind his new bays.

Good God! Had it come to this? Was he to be reduced to the role of nervous swain, tongue-tied by a pair of golden eyes, rendered stupid by the thought of baring his heart, frightened witless over the chance that she might turn him down flat—or worse yet, laugh at him?

"Hungry, Angel?" he asked as he drew the horses to a halt inside the courtyard, waiting for the groom to jump down and run to their heads. "The inn is known for its country ham, ham such as that we shared in secret at MacAfee Farm, as I remember."

"I'll be the judge of that, Banning," Prudence said teasingly, his Christian name sounding different, more intimate, on her tongue than he had ever heard it before. "As I've heard that stolen sweets are always best, this ham would have to be extremely tasty."

Banning hopped down from the seat, holding out

his arms to assist her to the ground. "Are you telling me that I ate pilfered ham?" he asked, his fingers burning as they made contact with her slim waist, so that he drew back sharply, stepping away from her.

"Sad to say, yes," she said, patting one of the bays on its rump before walking toward the door to the inn, Banning falling into step beside her. "There is only so much goat's milk pudding a person can endure before she is at last reduced to thievery. Besides, I believe the Squire might have owed it to me, and it was only a small pig. Have I shocked you yet again?"

He took her arm, assisting her over the threshold. "The only way you could shock me, Angel," he told her honestly as the innkeeper came toward them, wiping his hands on his apron, "would be if you were to stop shocking me. Ah, Innkeeper! A private dining room for two, if you please, and your bill of fare."

"Right this way, milord," the innkeeper gushed, bowing them toward the stairs and one of the private rooms Banning already knew existed on either side of the long, narrow hallway. "Betts? Betts! Where are you, gel? Look alive up there! See to his lordship and his lady!"

His lady. Banning liked the sound of that. He liked it very much.

"Oh, this is much nicer than the dining room in Epsom," Prudence declared, untying the strings of her bonnet and placing it on the table, then walking to the window that looked out over the stable yard. "Banning, come look. Your groom appears to have his hands full with your bays. I don't think they approve of their temporary quarters. I adore an animal with spirit, don't you?"

Banning quickly ordered a bottle of wine, two

199

glasses, and a simple supper of ham, bread, and cheese, dismissing the barmaid with the admonition to hurry and there would be a guinea in it for her. He wanted the food on the table and the prospect of an uninterrupted hour alone with Prudence as quickly as possible. The door had barely closed behind Betts when he had stripped off his gloves, tossing them and his hat on a chair in the corner of the low-ceilinged room, and crossed to the window, slipping an arm around Prudence's slim waist.

She didn't pull away. Her body did not stiffen in either anger or surprise. If anything, she seemed to lean toward him slightly as she said, "Oh, you're too late. An ostler came to the rescue and the bays have been moved inside."

"Am I too late all round, Angel?" he asked, keeping his eyes firmly on the horizon.

She turned toward him slightly, the sunlight pouring through the window setting small golden flames to dancing in her hair. "I don't understand. Banning?"

He withdrew his arm as the barmaid reentered the room, breathless and faintly staggering under the heavily laden tray she balanced on her shoulder. He stood silent, watching as a crusty loaf, a plate piled high with thick pink slices of ham and another holding a half-round of cheese joined the wine bottle and glasses on the table, then inclined his head slightly as Betts bobbed a curtsy and exited the room, closing the door firmly behind her.

"I was too late in coming to you in Sussex," he said as he held out a chair for Prudence and watched as she daintily spread a serviette in her lap—seeing in his mind's eye a flash of the breeches-clad Prudence who had tipped back her chair at another inn, plopping her booted feet on the table. "Unlike Freddie and Rexford, and even Marmaduke and Dewey—who sing your praises to me constantly—I was too late in recognizing your innocence, your good heart, your beauty that goes worlds deeper than your extremely appealing exterior."

"Banning, I—"

"No, Angel, don't interrupt, please. Allow me my moment of sackcloth and ashes, for I deserve it. I was a pig-headed fool, a paphead, if you will, and I've made your entry into society more difficult because of it. I do, however, have a reason."

Prudence refolded her serviette, placing the edges together with a preciseness that betrayed her own nervousness, then stood, turning to Banning, her eyes playing that tear-wet trick that, from the very beginning, had held the power to destroy his ability to think.

"Freddie told me, Banning. And the earl and Mr. Norton, too, although I doubt they realized it. I know all about your father, and why Freddie married Lord Wendover, and what the Broughton did to you—all of it. You've been carrying so many problems and promises for so long. It wasn't fair that my brother handed you another batch."

Banning felt a corner of his mouth lifting slightly in a self-depreciating smile. This was it. His single moment. Time for him to lay it all on the line, put it all out there for her, and watch as she either turned from him in disgust, or picked up his aching heart and made it her own.

"You forgot to mention my most glaring failure, Angel. I'm a lech, remember? If I was horrible to you, and I was, much of my animosity stemmed from the fact that, for all my sins, for all my skewed beliefs in what my life should be, I have wanted you since the first day I saw you. Fool that I am, I didn't know it was love. Not until yesterday. *Yesterday!* When I listened to Althea planning my life the way my father had done. Yesterday, when I saw you riding in the park with Ramsden. I want you to marry me, Angel. Marry me, and love me, and keep me young and sane and human. Now, Angel, tell me. Am I too late again?"

She reached out a hand to him, her fingertips touching lightly on his cravat, relieving him of his ability to breathe. Tears as large as sweet summer peas spilled onto her cheeks. "Yesterday was almost a year too late, Banning," she said quietly, her hand dropping to her side. "Please, could we return to Park Lane now?"

"Of course," Banning said quickly, and rather too loudly, he believed, reaching in his pocket for a handful of coins he threw onto the table without bothering to count them out. "And please accept my apology, Miss MacAfee. I hadn't thought your affections to be engaged, as you had assured me they had not been at the time of our first meeting. If he is suitable, I, as your guardian, shall of course entertain his petition for your hand. Even if he isn't," he added tightly, snatching up his hat and gloves.

Prudence picked up her bonnet, pausing in the act of retying the ribbons just beneath her left ear, her mouth opening and closing several times before she looked back at the crowded tabletop and said—and they were the very last words she uttered until he had deposited her back in Park Lane, "I believe I have forever lost my taste for country ham."

It was only after she had hopped, unassisted, to the

drive and run into the house, the handkerchief she had pulled from her gown to dry her tears still pressed to her lips, that Banning discovered the small, creased note that must have fallen out of her pocket and somehow become wedged between them.

He picked it up, thinking to call after her, then decided not to distress her further. After all, it was probably no more than a list of ribbons and other feminine fripperies she wished to purchase. Jamming the note into the pocket of his bottle-green jacket, he flicked the reins, setting the bays on their way back to Chesterfield Street, feeling once more a very old man at the tender age of four and thirty.

CHAPTER 14

I am ashes where once I was fire.

George Noel Gordon,
Lord Byron

Y our ward seems to return to me in tears each and every time she has been with you, Banning. I do not appreciate it."

Banning, who had been sitting slumped at his desk, a cup of very cold coffee at his elbow, opened one eye to look up at his sister forbiddingly, then deliberately turned his chair, and his back, to her. "Go away, Freddie," he grumbled, for grumbling was better than shouting when it came to dealing with sisters. "I'm in no mood to be teased."

"Well, that's just capital with me, Banning," Lady Wendover pronounced tersely, standing in front of the desk, her palms pressed hard against the wood as she leaned across it at her brother, "because I am not in a teasing mood. I'm angry! More angry than I would have ever believed possible. So angry, that I don't care a hoot that you looked exactly like Papa just now, and sounded just like him, too, now that I've had a moment to refine on it. In fact, I'm so overwhelmingly

204

angry that Quimby drove me here himself, probably thinking he might save me from committing mayhem, which I most certainly might do if you don't stop staring out the window and *look at me!*"

Banning turned to the desk once more, dropped his forehead into his hands for a moment to hide a small smile at his sister's vehemence, running his fingers through his silver mane, then slowly got to his feet.

"All right, Freddie," he said, breathing deeply through his nose, doing his best to clear his head enough to talk to her. "I imagine you do deserve an explanation, and Angel obviously has been no more forthcoming with you than she was with me. But let's get out of this room. I think the walls are beginning to close in on me."

"Angel's harboring secrets?" Lady Wendover asked as Banning steered her toward the hallway, and another smaller hallway leading to the small enclosed garden just outside a pair of French doors. "I find that difficult to believe. She is an extremely open and honest child."

"All right, Freddie," Banning said as his sister bent to sniff at a particularly lovely red rose. "If she's so honest and aboveboard, so open, perhaps she has told you about Enby?"

Lady Wendover stood up straight, sucking at her thumb where she had inadvertently pierced the skin when she had taken hold of the thorny stem. "Enby?" she repeated, examining her injured thumb. "Well, congratulations, Banning. You have both deflected my anger and confused me. What's an Enby?"

"Enby, for your information, is the man Angel loves, has loved and, I believe, plans to marry—or something less laudable—in less than three months. We can never be sure of Angel's devotion to the rules governing polite society, now can we?" He reached into his pocket, pulling out the note he had discovered then read, much to the detriment of his already depressed spirits.

Lady Wendover took the note, one delicately constructed eyebrow raised as if to ask how and where her brother had come to be in possession of the thing, then began reading, mostly to herself, but commenting occasionally as she deciphered the masculine scrawl. " 'You are to drop him at once.' Well, that's sensible, if a tad autocratic. Although Leslie has been on his best behavior. '. . . the world is ours, my *love?'* Oh dear. That doesn't sound good, does it? And what's this about a posie post? It is posie, isn't it—and not *penny* post? No, that makes no sense. No sense at all. He means the penny post."

She folded the note along its original creases and passed it back to Banning. "So. Enby is not a what, but a who? Or is that *whom?* I never could get the straight of that, not that it matters, does it? And why hasn't Angel told me about him? I've told her all my little secrets—all my bigger secrets as well. Why, I believe she knows every secret of every person residing with us in Park Lane. It's so easy to talk to her, you understand."

"With one notable exception. *I* can't seem to communicate with her at all. We talk at each other, we have screamed at each other, we have even—well, never mind." Banning shoved the note back into his pocket, where the damning thing had been residing all morning after spending the night on his desk, the marquess himself sitting behind that desk, staring at the message until he'd nearly bored a hole in the paper.

"I have formulated a few theories on this Enby person," he said after a moment, motioning for his sister to be seated on a small wrought-iron bench at the side of the narrow brick path. "She is not in London long enough to have formed any permanent attachment, so this Enby must be someone from her past, someone from Sussex. Not that I found that deduction difficult, because Angel as good as admitted that she has been involved with someone for at least a year. He's in need of money, so he is probably not in society at the moment unless he's dining out on his good looks or wit. And he brags about seeing the world—which makes him young, stupid, and most probably a rascal."

"I'd like to see the world, Banning," Lady Wendover said, pouting. "And I am not stupid or a rascal."

"Yes, but you're not talking of dragging a young girl along with you on your travels. But why three months? The season will be over in a little more than two, so perhaps he'll come asking for Angel's hand after that, thinking I'll gladly pass over my still-unwed ward and her dowry just to be rid of her. Which would explain why she's being so friendly with Ramsden. She knows he won't be mucking up the works by asking me for her hand. Although her paramour seems to object."

"Paramour! Banning, don't you think you're jumping—fairly *leaping*—to conclusions? The lizard has been hinting that Angel is more than she seems—although she has not come forward and said anything outright nasty, which she wouldn't, not when Angel knows what she knows, but the lizard doesn't know that I already know what Angel knows and still haven't dismissed the horrid woman. No, Banning, don't ask, for it is a private matter. I just know that the lizard does not hold Angel in affection, no matter how well she's been behaving, sewing on her tapestry and sipping her *water*. However, it's not at all like *you* to be so hasty to judge anyone. Why, if I didn't know better, I'd think you're acting like some lovesick puppy yourself, and—oh, my. That's what's got you so sunk in the glooms, isn't it? It's what I've been hoping for ever since you brought her to me. You sly dog—you're in love with Angel!"

Shoving down the juvenile impulse to shout, "I am not!" Banning gave in to the inevitable, saying, "I asked her to marry me yesterday and she turned me down flat. I see no point in attempting to hide the fact, as you'll never rest until you wheedle it out of me. She refused me, saying someone had a previous claim on her affections, or something to that effect. I really didn't hear much of anything once she started to cry those damn huge tears. No one in this wide world weeps to better effect than Prudence MacAfee, as I am sure you already are aware. No sobs, no sniffling—not a sound. Just those great, huge, heartbreaking tears."

"Oh, poor, poor brother! You really *are* in love this time, aren't you? Not the way it was with the Broughton, who was no more than a disappointment to your pride, no matter what anyone says. I've never seen you so low—or so very *human!*"

Lady Wendover jumped up from the bench, to hug him close, patting him on the back as if she were the elder, not he. Then, just when he—only mildly berating himself for being so weak—was beginning to enjoy being the object of her pity, she placed her hands against his shoulders, sharply pushing him away from her. "You're the better man, Banning. I can't believe you'd give up so easily, not if you really love her. *Fight* for her!"

He raised her hand to his lips, then smiled and shook his head. "It's passing strange, Freddie, and the thought has kept me up all night long, but I have found that the last thing I would do is interfere—not as her guardian, nor as the man who wishes to marry her. I love Angel and, loving her, I want her to be happy. I'm heartily sick of being the reason behind her tears. If this Enby fellow makes her happy, then who am I to object?"

The hand he had just kissed balled into a fist and found its way into his mid-section, once again demonstrating to Banning that Prudence's sojourn in Park Lane was proving to be an educational experience for his sister, who was supposed to be instructing his ward in the manners of a lady, not taking lessons in hoydenism.

"You are her guardian, you dolt! You have every right, indeed, every *responsibility,* to object. Stop feeling so wretchedly sorry for yourself and think! The man is too cowardly to present himself to you, he jeopardizes Angel's good name by sending her notes behind both our backs—and he has the unmitigated gall to ask her for money! Object? Why, you should take your whip to him!"

Banning laughed, although without much mirth. "First I'd have to find him, you know, Freddie," he pointed out, ushering her back into the house. "Because you're right. I don't want to give up so easily, even if it is the gentlemanly thing to do. Because I've been deciding something these last, sleepless hours. I damn well don't like always playing the gentleman! Angel took me off guard yesterday, I suppose, and instead of pushing her to explain, I tucked my tail between my legs and left the field. I *should* get to know this Enby, and discover just what in blazes is going on between the two of them."

He patted his pocket. "And I think I know how to go about it."

"The note! Of course! It's obvious, isn't it, once you think about it? Where there's one, there are bound to be more. Angel is forever reading from a packet of letters she keeps locked in her desk. Whenever I come into the room she puts them away, which didn't really offend me, as everyone should be allowed some privacy, but—"

She frowned, then smiled broadly. "Her maid! Angel has everyone in Park Lane wrapped 'round her thumb, but Quimby would never allow something as clandestine as note-passing. It would have to be someone Quimby does not control. Not a footman, nor any of the kitchen servants. Yes, definitely. It's Angel's own maid. Petunia! There must be an address for the penny post—pity this one is without its outside sheet—so all we'd have to do is wait for Angel to send another note and then intercept it, which will doubtless send the dear child into the treetops with anger when Petunia tells her about it. That could prove sticky, couldn't it? Do you think we can swear the maid to secrecy? She's terribly loyal to Angel, Petunia is."

Banning shook his head. "Not Petunia, Freddie. Geranium. Angel's right, you do have trouble remembering the creature's name."

And then he felt his blood begin to stir as, finally, at least some of the note became clear to his formerly love-thick mind. He grabbed his sister's elbows and gave her a smacking kiss on the cheek. "Why didn't I see it before now? Maybe you aren't the only one who can't remember her name. Perhaps Enby suffers from the same problem—or perhaps he possesses a trace of humor. That would explain the 'posie post,' and the absence of an outside sheet. It isn't penny post at all! It's posie post, and Geranium makes her deliveries in person, so that we have nothing to do but follow her whenever she goes out—with Angel none the wiser. Well, thank you, Freddie. That does simplify things."

"I do so love intrigue, don't you?" Lady Wendover hugged herself, obviously delighted to have been so brilliant. "So, we simply have someone follow Pe-*Geranium,* and *voilá,* we'll have found our man. Enby. Very odd name. Are you sure it couldn't be some sort of pet name, Banning? You know—a variation of something like Edward, or Entwhistle?"

"Or Emory, or Esterby—or any of a thousand names," Banning agreed. "We'll know soon enough, won't we? You said Quimby brought you here today? I think I'll have a small talk with him, if you don't mind. He could be of enormous help, I believe."

"Oh, Quimby is always an enormous help, Banning," Lady Wendover said, her cheeks turning a rather lovely pale pink. "I value him more each day."

Banning tipped his head to one side, something in his sister's manner, her suddenly softer tone of voice, telling him that he should be paying attention to this last statement, but he was too involved with his own affairs at the moment to allow anything to interfere with his mission to discover the identity of Prudence's correspondent.

He had been acting the fool, been on the verge of going into a miss-ish decline, all because he had opened his heart to a young woman who had not immediately returned his affection. And that, he thought as he closed the door on Quimby and his sister a few minutes later, was dressing the thing up in fine linen.

What he had really been was a first-rate ass!

Where had all the fire in him disappeared to since that moment in the park when he had realized that he was in love with Prudence MacAfee? This wasn't the Banning Talbot of five years ago, ten years ago. This was the Banning Talbot who'd been dismissed because of his lack of fortune, the Banning Talbot who had for the past two years been making such pains to be civilized and gentlemanly and self-contained.

Well, the devil with that Banning Talbot! That Banning Talbot was a bloody fool.

He would find this Enby, this man who passed notes, scribbled endearments, and then asked for money. He'd find him, meet with him, and judge for himself whether or not Prudence would be throwing herself away on the man.

If he was basically a good man, if Prudence truly loved him—well, then, that would be the end of it. Banning would have no other choice than to be mature. He would be gracious, and he would bow out.

But if this Enby was a rotter, a conniver?

After all, Angel had cried yesterday when she turned him down. She'd sat up beside him all the way back from Richmond, her hands squeezed tightly together in her lap around her sadly crushed handkerchief, tears streaming down her cheeks. A woman didn't cry unless she felt some small affection, did she?

He remembered that Althea Broughton hadn't cried when she'd told him that her father had refused his suit. She had just gone on, smiling her way through the season in the same determined manner she had been smiling her way through this one after the Wexley debacle, ready to become engaged to the very next man who proposed—the very next rich man, that was. It had rankled him, hurt him very badly at the time, but he had understood.

But Angel had cried. He should have seen hope in those tears, not defeat. And maybe he would have done so sooner, if he weren't so hopelessly in love with the little demon.

Banning began to whistle as he climbed the stairs of his Chesterfield Street house two at a time, suddenly eager for his bath and a hearty luncheon.

Because Banning Talbot, Marquess of Daventry— the man he had been until two years ago, and the man he had become again only a few days ago—refused to go down to defeat without a damn good fight!

Prudence sat very still on the floor in the middle of the basement-level laundry, surrounded by towering piles of gowns and shifts and night rails and even wrinkled bedding, a single silk stocking hanging drunkenly from her left shoulder. She said nothing, just stuck out her bottom lip and blew upwards, shooing away a lock of honey-brown hair that had dropped down over her forehead.

"I told you there weren't no note, Missy," the downstairs maid said kindly, beginning to rummage through the mess that had only a half hour earlier been sorted into neat piles in preparation of the weekly chore of washing the laundry belonging to the Park Lane household. "I'm that sorry, but there just isn't. Quimby taught me long ago to always check pockets and the like before I dumped anything into the tub, seeing as how someone once forgot to, and her ladyship lost a favorite gewgaw she'd stuck to her shift and then forgot. Was it so very important?"

Prudence smiled up at the maid. "No, Harriet, it wasn't important. Really." *Just a trifle, only a small, damning piece of evidence that, because of the signature at the bottom alone, could end with Enby and myself going to prison—or worse,* she lamented silently, believing that having to face Banning's rightful wrath and disappointment just might be even more terrible than any legal punishment she could name.

Nothing had gone right for Prudence from the moment Enby had involved her in his scheme.

If only Banning could have been a more usual sort of guardian; caring for her financially as was his duty, but not personally involving himself in her life.

If only dear Freddie hadn't wanted a plaything to ease her boredom, causing Banning to make his announcement that she, his ward, was to move to London.

If only Enby hadn't credited Shadwell with enough scruples to turn her allowance over to her so that she had been angry enough at her grandfather to consider coming to Park Lane with Banning in the first place when he'd unexpectedly arrived in Sussex, and then revengeful enough to bury her poor, dear Molly in Shadwell's dirt bath—a rash act that had forever precluded her remaining within "beating" distance of her grandfather.

If only Banning was not so handsome, so adorably confused about his place in life, so willing to argue, so considerate of both her needs and her foibles, so heavenly to touch and be touched by . . . so impossible to have.

If only.

And if it weren't for all those complicating "if only's," Prudence knew she would still be at MacAfee Farm, still fairly miserable, but with enough money to care for herself—and still heart-whole—patiently waiting for the time to be right, waiting for Enby to come for her.

"You musta dropped that note somewheres yesterday," Harriet said at last, when Prudence remained on the floor, staring into the middle distance. "Here you go," she added bracingly, holding out a hand so that Prudence could avail herself of it as she scrambled to her feet. "That's what happened, all right. Dropped it somewheres whilst you was out. Doubt anyone'll ever find it."

"Thank you, Harriet," Prudence said, smiling at the maid. "Please excuse the mess I've made. I would stay and clean it up with you, except that I have to haul my sorry self upstairs now for my bath, as I've been invited to the theater tonight by no less than two gentlemen, if you can believe it. The Earl of Preston and Mister Dewey Norton are to be my escorts. But I'll hold that comforting thought close as I go off to play the debutante and at the same time do my best to remember exactly what was in that damned note. Thank God no one knows who Enby is!"

CHAPTER 15

Quickly, bring me a beaker of wine,
so that I may wet my mind
and say something clever.

Aristophanes

See that fellow over there, Miss MacAfee?" Dewey Norton asked, pointing none too subtly to a rather ferretfaced young man dressed all in pink and ridiculously high shirt points. "This ought to tickle you. Badly dipped from gaming, he is, viscount or not, so he's rigged himself up like he's rich as Golden Ball and gone out trolling for a fortune. Heard he's considering a coal merchant's daughter this week, but that's not who's with him now, of course. Got a warbler on his arm, a high-priced one, too. I know I couldn't afford her."

"Dewey, you're dead as a house, you know that?" the Earl of Preston complained as he rapidly and none too gracefully ushered Prudence through the crowd and along the broad hallway that led to his mother's box, which she had allowed him to use for the evening. "Miss MacAfee is not interested in gossip, and she certainly doesn't know what a warbler is. Do you, Miss MacAfee?"

216

"Me?" Prudence asked, pressing a hand to her bodice, completely unaware that her magnificently cut peach peau de soie gown was causing a considerable amount of envious teeth-gnashing among less elegantly attired ladies in the crush of people.

How she delighted in these two very different, yet equally wonderful gentlemen. And how she delighted in teasing them, saying now: "I should say not, good sirs! I have no knowledge of cant or other low-bred slang. So, my lord, Mister Norton—what are we to call this money-mad, title-peddling, pink atrocity? A Peep-O-Day boy? A chicken-livered, fortune-trolling twit? A greedy little shrimp who heard the coins jingling in his mother's purse before he was born? A seed-selling, lie-telling, groat-grubbing—"

"Miss MacAfee!" Dewey interrupted nervously, coloring to the roots of his thinning hair. "Please, don't go on. I know you're only poking fun, because you're the best of great guns, but Banning will murder all three of us if he hears you."

Prudence's amusement vanished in the time it took for her to look to her left and see Banning, the coolly beautiful blonde Broughton dangling from his arm.

Well, he certainly seems to have recovered from any disappointment without much trouble, she thought meanly, not realizing that she wasn't exactly hiding in her own bedchamber, still overcome by the grief she'd so stupidly shown when turning down his offer of marriage.

If there was one thing love could do to a person of Prudence MacAfee's temperament, it was that it could make her daring—and possibly foolhardy.

217

"Yoo-hoo!" she called out loudly, waving her hand in the air. "Banning! Over here, my lord, if you please!"

She watched from between slightly compressed eyelids as Banning turned his head in her direction. Then she grinned widely, as if delighted to see him, and called to him again, leaving him no choice but to either give his ward the cut direct or come to her as if he were on a chain she could pull with impunity.

Being the dutiful, rule-obeying gentleman he tried so desperately to be—Prudence noticed with a smile that was beginning to hurt her cheeks—Banning allowed the tug on his leash.

Perhaps foolhardy was too tame a word to use on a young woman of Prudence's temperament, for she felt an immediate leap of happiness in her tastefully decorated bosom.

"Good evening, my lord guardian," she piped up gaily once Banning and the Broughton were standing in front of her, Banning looking pained and the clinging Broughton appearing bored.

Prudence immediately decided that the woman would have to pay a price for her "clinging" ways. The marquess would also "pay," for being seen with the woman in the first place, but that could wait. Reminding the Broughton that she was the object of gossip thanks to her broken engagement, however, could not.

"And Miss Broughton as well," Prudence went on doggedly. "Oh yes, although we have not been formally introduced, I'd be a silly widgeon indeed if I did not know who *you* are. My goodness, but I've heard so *very* much about you. Haven't I, Lord Preston, Mister Norton? She's quite the talk of the town!"

"Angel—" Banning said quietly, warningly.

"And all of it good. *Good!*" the earl interjected

218

quickly, his entire body quivering as he nodded vigorously. "All of it good. Splendid! Nice seeing you, Banning. We'll be off now. I think there's a draft here in the hallway. Got to keep moving. That's what I always say, don't I always say that, Dewey?"

"You say a lot of things, Duke, but you don't say anything important," Dewey countered, obviously intent only on his own concerns and oblivious to the tension hanging above the heads of the small group. "Had a whacking great piece of parsley stuck between my front teeth the other day the whole time we were talking to Miss Sinclair, and you didn't tell me about it. Could have set me up for life, getting myself leg-shackled to her. But now that's over—done with! —and she'll never look at me again without seeing that parsley. Right here!" he exclaimed loudly, jabbing his forefinger against his two front teeth. "Big as life—right here! And you knew it all along."

Dewey dropped his hands to his sides and sighed deeply, seemingly suffering the slings and arrows of his social defeat yet again, then glared up at the earl. "So, no, Duke. You don't say anything important."

Prudence looked to Banning, whose eyes seemed to laugh with her at Dewey's sad tale even as his expression remained remote and faintly cold. "Lovely gown, Miss Broughton," Prudence said, figuring she'd better demonstrate at least one "ladylike" talent so that Freddie couldn't be faulted as a poor mentor; that of showing she was able to carry on a polite conversation with someone she had already proved she could not like. After all, wasn't that the true mark of the Quality—an ability to pretend?

The Broughton now held Banning's arm with both hands, attached to him rather in the way of a barnacle to a hull, Prudence thought, longing to tear the woman's sleekly pulled-back hair out by its roots. "So, Banning," the woman trilled in the tone of one forced to confront a naughty nursery brat but unwilling to converse with it directly, "this is your little ward. We really shouldn't allow her to expose herself to the sun quite so much, should we? Or is her skin naturally that odd shade?"

"Oh no, Miss Broughton," Dewey piped up, clearly eager to defend Prudence who, as he had said earlier, was a "great gun." "Her skin's not odd at all. It's golden, that's what it is. Reminds me of honey and warm scones, I've decided. Golden sun and honey. And the color's becoming all the crack, you know. Why, it's even got m'sisters sunning themselves in the herb garden every afternoon, so hot they are to look like her. Not that it'll help. They're just getting red and spotty, and the younger one is beginning to shed her skin like a snake."

"Thank you for falling on your sword for me, Mister Norton," Prudence said, patting his sleeve as she managed to maintain her painfully bright, polite smile, "but it won't be necessary. Miss Broughton meant no harm." *Bloody hell, she didn't!* she thought as she dropped her hand to her side once more, drawing her fingers up into a tight fist.

"Harm? My dear child, whatever do you mean?" the Broughton countered, moving even closer to Banning, so that Prudence doubted a person could wedge a wafer thin slice of Spitalfields ham between them. *Ham?* She winced inwardly. *That was a bad choice, Angel,* she told herself.

The earl all but jumped between Prudence and the Broughton, pushing one long leg out in front of him and then jerkily drawing the rest of him along behind until he had stepped forward a good two feet. "Heard the farce tonight is going to be top-rate, Banning. You hear that? Delighted Miss MacAfee could join us. Delighted! Well, nice seeing you. We'll just toddle off now. Wouldn't want to miss anything, would we, Dewey? Miss MacAfee?"

"In a moment, my lord," Prudence said, peeking past the tall earl in order to take a closer look at her guardian, who had been standing stock-still and silent as a mummy throughout most of this odd exchange.

"Banning?" she asked, deliberately using his Christian name. "Would it be possible, at intermission perhaps, for you and I to have a private word? I seem to have a problem I do not wish to burden your sister with unless I have no other option. A matter of an offer made to me yesterday, to be frank about the thing." *Now, Banning, pretend you don't know what offer I'm talking about and I'll curl the ends of the Broughton's hair with a few home truths!*

"I believe that can be arranged, Prudence," Banning responded, his lips barely moving, although she was pleased to see a vein in his neck begin to throb in a most uncomfortable looking way. "I am sure the earl and Mister Norton will be happy to stay with Miss Broughton while we two converse. Until intermission?"

"Until intermission, Banning," Prudence agreed, belatedly wondering why on earth she had just instigated a private meeting with the man when the last thing she needed was to be alone with him, especially if her "lost" note had found its way "home" to him. But then Prudence saw the angry frown on the Broughton's face, the way she had gone even stiffer and straighter—removing her clinging hands from Banning's arm when she heard she was to be abandoned at intermission—and she remembered.

And when that intermission finally came? What then? Ah, then Prudence MacAfee, who deep down inside still knew she shouldn't do anything of the sort, would turn Alexander Pope's poetic words around and take a chance at playing the foolhardy Angel, rushing in where any rational angel would fear to tread . . .

"She's unflatteringly forward, Banning. Forward and cheeky and entirely too demanding. Calling out to us like some fishwife screeching to be heard in the marketplace. Really!"

Banning steadied the Broughton's chair as she took her seat, then sat down beside her, saying nothing.

Which did not, alas, stop the Broughton from speaking. "And then to ask you to interrupt our evening by meeting with her about some lovesick swain who has wrongly approached her, rather than you, with his suit? Well, that has never happened to me, I tell you. Gentlemen know to respect me. Even you had the good sense to petition my father, who then allowed me the courtesy of denying you."

She stopped speaking for a moment, frowning slightly at what she had said, then shrugged and continued: "But what can you expect from a country girl with no notion of what is right and proper? I knew Freddie would be a dead loss as chaperone, and I've been proven right tonight. First the child is seen not only riding with that notorious Ramsden, but giggling with him at a party that same evening as well—a totally nonsensical relaxation of all that is proper—

and then she wastes another entire evening and an outrageously expensive if unsuitable gown on two confirmed bachelors. Oh yes, Banning. It will be such a comfort to you when I have taken over management of her season. Agnes? My shawl, if you please," she said commandingly, addressing herself to the middle-aged chaperone who sat at the back of the box. "I feel a decided draft in here."

"Allow me, Althea," Banning said helpfully, rising to take the shawl from the older woman's hand and then fighting down the almost unconquerable urge to either stuff the soft woolen shawl down the Broughton's gullet or strangle her with it.

He had made it through dinner—having arrived in Grosvenor Square nearly fifteen minutes late because he had, frankly, forgotten making the commitment to join her and her family for the evening—and if he could only keep a firm grip on his temper for another two hours he could be shed of Althea Broughton once and for all time.

Dinner itself had been an ordeal of denial; refusing to follow up his lordship's leading questions with anything vaguely resembling an answer that could be misconstrued as an offer in form, avoiding her lady-ship's pointed talk of weddings and churches and trips to the Lake District so often being the norm for honeymooning couples, and, just the once, pretending not to notice that Althea's hand had somehow come into contact with his knee under cover of the table-cloth.

But Banning's patience, his belief in his gentleman-ly role, were both rapidly reaching their limits.

Angel might not want him, might not love him, but at least he could find some solace in the fact that she wouldn't accept him just to gain his fortune. Althea Broughton coveted his money, desired his name, couldn't care less if she loved *him* or not, and wouldn't have understood Angel's refusal if Banning himself explained it to her using props and charts like his old schoolmaster had done at Eton.

The first act had begun on the stage below them, which did not keep the Broughton from continuing her one-sided conversation in a normal, easily heard tone—which also, of course, didn't matter all that much to anyone save the actors, as voices could be heard coming from nearly every box in the theater.

The *ton* came to the theater to see and be seen, and whatever action was taking place on the stage was only secondary to its use as a social gathering place. Although Prudence, as Banning could see out of the corners of his eyes, was sitting forward between Marmaduke and Dewey in her box half a theater away, a rapt expression on her face, her wide eyes shining as she drank in every word of the ridiculously high-flown soliloquy.

Why had she called him over to her anyway? What did she want from him? That business about wanting to speak of his offer for her yesterday, and her veiled threat to run to Freddie if he wouldn't speak to her, was all a ruse, and he knew it. *She* knew he knew it.

It had to be about the note. She needed to know if he had it, if he'd read it, and what he was prepared to do about it. That was the only sane answer.

Except that, if he didn't have the note, she would be opening herself up to an interrogation when she admitted that there had been a note.

Not that common sense could be applied to Angel —who invariably did what she wasn't supposed to do.

He'd had that out of her own mouth, and she had even seemed pleased with herself at the admission.

"You never answered Papa when he asked if you wished to meet with him tomorrow, Banning," Althea said as the act came to an end and there was a smattering of desultory applause heard rippling through the audience, nearly overshadowed by the hoots and cat-calls raining down from the gentlemen and whores in the upper balconies. "I really think it is important that you do so, considering."

"Considering what, Althea?" Banning asked, smiling as he watched Prudence clapping with enough enthusiasm to prove she had no taste in theater—until the moment she stood and launched an orange into the pit, showing that she had been applauding the critics. *Little barbarian,* he thought, wishing himself beside her, and not stuck here with the chattering magpie who was his companion for the evening.

"Never mind, Banning," Althea said, drawing her shawl more closely about her bare shoulders as if to protect herself from the touch of his jacket before she leaned her upper body stiffly against his arm, her intent obvious, her technique painfully unromantic and cold. "It's all been settled anyway, after all. Papa promised."

At this figurative sound of a key being turned in a cell door, Banning decided that being a gentleman had nothing to do with handing himself over to the torture that would be a marriage to Althea Broughton.

In one second, he had hoisted the beautiful blonde to an upright position. In two, he was speaking, softly, but firmly.

"I will not be calling on your father tomorrow, Althea. I will not be visiting him Monday. Or Tuesday. Or the second Wednesday of next month. Have I made myself clear?"

"You're leaving the city for a space? In the first flush of the season? How odd. Why?" the Broughton inquired sweetly, whether because she was unbelievably obtuse or because she was desperate to be settled now that her marriage had been delayed by mourning and destroyed by contemplated bigamy—and she was now nearly three and twenty!—Banning did not care enough to discover. He only knew she was not going to go away quietly. "It's your ward, isn't it?"

Banning was momentarily deflected, and immediately protective of Prudence. That would be all he needed. Althea Broughton, feeling vengeful, could have a lovely time telling all who would listen—and everyone would listen—that the Marquess of Daventry was lusting after his young ward. "Angel? Certainly not. What does she have to do with anything?"

"Don't fly up into the treetops, Banning, as I certainly meant nothing indiscreet," the Broughton said, beginning to flutter her ivory-sticked fan beneath the sculpted curve of her jaw. "I can see that she is a sorely trying little beast. I had only thought perhaps you have planned to escape from her for a space, hoping Freddie will get her settled before your return. That would be just like a man, fleeing from any sort of entanglement with the necessary fuss of popping off a daughter, or a ward. Eight years ago Papa dragged a small hunting party into a three-month sojourn in Scotland, not returning home until Mama wrote saying that my sister Theodora had brought Rupert to the sticking point. Papa came back straight away, as Rupert could have had his pick of all the debutantes that season, and it was necessary to snap him up at once."

Banning couldn't resist. Besides, he thought he actually might deserve a bit of fun, considering the fact that he had wasted half an evening being subjected to the most obvious sort of matchmaking possible. "Rupert? Oh, Lord Dunbar, of course! Didn't he hang himself in his study about seven or so years ago? Couldn't have been over gaming debts, rich as he was. And so young, too. Pity."

"He broke his neck in a fall down the stairs at their country estate!" Althea exclaimed just a little too quickly, a little too defensively. "He and Theodora were stranded there for nearly a month that awful winter, just the two of them and their staff, all alone in Buckinghamshire, and one morning he was found, found . . ."

"At the bottom of the stairs?" Banning supplied tactfully, although he knew differently. Everyone knew differently, which might explain the fact that Althea's sister was still a widow and not once more a wife, even though she had been left with a fortune many would envy. Why had he never connected marriage to a Broughton with viewing suicide as a lucky escape? He certainly could see the correlation now, with the lovely Althea by his side.

"Yes, at the bottom of the stairs," Althea answered, the fan now folded in her lap, the subject of the unfortunate Rupert Dunbar now also closed, it would seem. "Delayed my Come-out a year, his death did. I always thought it prodigiously selfish of him to have attempted the stairs without a candle. But we are speaking of your ward, Banning, whom I already said I would take in hand, so you most certainly have my permission to abandon London, and her, for a space. I, like Mama, will summon you home when an acceptable suitor appears on the horizon."

Banning gave it up. What was the point? After all, a person could only slam his head against a stone wall for a measured amount of time before the exercise became both painful and obviously fruitless. Althea was going to remain obtuse if she had to clap her hands over her ears in order not to hear Banning say he was not going to marry her and, frankly, he had lost the interest in trying.

She could sit in her drawing room, her father could wait in his study—they could place a candle in the window to help guide him on his way—but he was not going to come within shouting distance of Grosvenor Square again. Sooner or later, they'd figure that out on their own.

"It will be intermission in a few minutes, Althea," he said, rising from his chair. "You'll be fine here with your chaperone until Marmaduke and Dewey can join you—I'll have them bring you lemonade if you'd like? But I must see to my ward. You understand, of course."

"I understand, Banning. I think we both understand," Althea said, looking almost relieved to see him go, which worried him only long enough for him to remember that Angel was most probably up to something, which—quite frankly—worried him even more.

CHAPTER 16

*Pleasure's a sin,
and sometimes sin's a pleasure.*

George Noel Gordon,
Lord Byron

She had the look of Satan's own angel in her bewitchingly lovely eyes as she turned in her chair to welcome him into the box. "Banning! Isn't the theater lovely? Isn't it the most banging good time you've ever had? Duke here bought me some oranges and let me throw them. They were nearly rotten and very soft, so they couldn't have hurt too much, don't you think? I hit that fellow down there smack on his silly, pomaded head—that one right there, the one dressed all in pink—the fortune hunter with the warbler. I think he cried!"

Dewey stood, rubbing at the back of his neck as he avoided Banning's eyes. "She clipped Lord Brookings on the ear with another one, and he looked up here with blood in his eye. Brookings has hands like anvils, Banning. *Anvils!* Everyone knows Duke is to let in his attic, so he'll come to me for satisfaction if he comes to anyone. She failed to mention that, you'll notice.

It's like riding herd on my sisters all over again, except that Duke here doesn't listen half so well. I tried to stop them but—" He raised his head and looked at Banning imploringly. "I like Angel—she said I could call her Angel—I really do. But you are going to take her away for a while now, aren't you?"

"Actually, Dewey, he's going to take me home, back to Park Lane, as I have a *crushing* headache," the wondrously healthy-looking Prudence piped up, already searching for her shawl, which had fallen behind the chair. "You'll be happy to provide that same service for the Broughton, I'm sure, especially as she would never be the sort to throw oranges." She looked up at Banning, her smile as warm as her eyes were now cold. "Ready, my lord?"

She was lying, of course. She no more had the headache than he, Banning, had a bumblebee perched on his nose buzzing out the tune of "God Save The King." She was up to something, had something to say to him that she could only say in private. But did he want to hear it? Was he strong enough, gentleman enough, "guardian-like" enough to behave himself once he got her to himself?

And why was he taking so long to make up his mind? It wasn't that difficult a decision. Remain at the theater and continue being bored with Althea's inane talk or be alone with Angel in his coach? Stay with the icy blonde or warm himself in the sunshine of Angel's golden presence? Spend the rest of his evening trying to keep his head out of Althea's matrimonial noose or a pleasant hour arguing with Angel? There was no need to call on the wisdom of Solomon in order to make up his mind.

"Althea would like some lemonade, Dewey," Banning said, draping Prudence's shawl around her smooth shoulders. "And take one for the chaperone as well, although I imagine Althea wouldn't notice if the woman dried up and turned to dust, sitting in the back of the box. Duke? You're frowning. Am I interrupting your pleasure? Perhaps you'd like to toss that last orange I see lying at your feet? I'm sure there are still several good targets moving about below us."

The earl looked down at the floor, shook himself all over as if a snake had just poked its forked tongue at him, then swiftly kicked the orange beneath his chair. "Freddie wanted for us to show Angel a good time," he said as if in explanation. "Said we were like uncles, or something. Chaperones, you understand. Took it very seriously, you know, given our responsibility."

"So, in your interpretation of what my sister might constitute showing Prudence a pleasant evening, you very *responsibly* handed her a pile of oranges and encouraged her to select a target." Banning nodded, doing his best to sound stern, as the Earl of Preston in a fidget was a pure delight to behold. "Completely understandable, Duke, really. You will, however, remind me not to allow you to escort my ward to a balloon ascension. I would not like to think of her floating high above the city, waving down at me as I take my afternoon stroll. Might put me off my dinner, you understand."

Dewey, who had been staying as far away from the rail, and the possibility that Lord Brookings might be looking up at the box, stepped forward, clearing his throat. "You know, Banning, Duke has a point. Freddie said we were Angel's chaperones this evening. How will it look if she goes off with you? Shabby? Wouldn't want the poor thing to get a reputation."

"I'm her guardian, Dewey," Banning responded, beginning to lose his humor. "No one will say a word against Prudence if I return her to Park Lane when she has so obviously taken ill." He shot a quick look to Angel, who immediately raised a hand to her brow and frowned, as if in excruciating pain. Little minx! If she withdrew a vinaigrette from her reticule and began waving it under her nose he just might throttle her.

After very politely thanking her escorts for their kindness, Prudence, her fingertips pressing rather painfully into Banning's forearm, steered him out of the box as if she were a ship hauling up anchor, and they were soon outside the theater, awaiting the arrival of his coach.

"You aren't actually considering getting yourself bracketed to that horrible female, are you, Banning?" she asked with her usual bluntness, so that he wasn't totally taken aback at her question. "She'd suck you bloodless in a fortnight."

"I don't believe that is any of your concern, Angel," he answered tightly, wishing his coachman would hurry. He wanted Prudence off the street and away from the interested eyes of a small group of fairly nasty looking men who stood just to the left of the theater, in the darkness beyond the flambeaux.

"Oh, Banning, but it is, because it's entirely my fault! I realized that the moment I saw you two together inside—the Broughton trying to attach herself to you like a sticking plaster," Prudence replied, all pretense of having the headache gone as she moved in front of him, as if physically halting him in his tracks before he could march down the aisle to Althea Broughton.

The coach arrived and the driver had barely put down the steps before Banning shoveled Prudence inside, hoping she would take a moment to realize that he really didn't want to hear anything else she might have to say.

Banning might as well have wished for the world to turn upside down so it could rain Chinamen, for all the good wishing was going to do him, as Prudence was already talking nineteen to the dozen, even as she was patting the velvet squabs next to her, indicating that she wished him to sit beside her.

"I turned you down yesterday, remember? Turned you down flat, which probably pleased you, because I'm not at all suitable and you know it. You had a momentary lapse, that's all, and it's over now. But it would be just like you to do something stupid after such a refusal. You're a wonderful man, Banning—funny and clever and with a very good heart—but sometimes you try entirely too hard to be all grown up, which is depressing as well as stupid. I can't let you throw yourself away on such a dry stick as the Broughton—even though you did ask for her once and not get her—just because you think it the *mature* thing to do. I'd never forgive myself!"

"Are you quite finished? Because if you are, I would like to suggest that you *shut up!*"

She gave him a playful tap on the hand. "That's it, Banning! Forget being a gentleman. Yell at me—scream at me if you want—but for pity's sake, don't be a gentleman the way you were yesterday. It's damned depressing, that's what it is, watching you give up without a fight."

Banning looked to his right for a moment, as if seeking enlightenment in his view of the shuttered window, then sliced another look to his left—at Prudence, who was sitting quite still, just staring at him.

"Let me see if I'm understanding you correctly, Angel, all right?" he said after opening and closing his mouth several times without being able to say anything. "You turned me down, and now you're complaining that I accepted your rebuff?"

She nodded vigorously, so that a few curls escaped her smooth upswept style, one lock falling just between her eyes, so that she hastily pushed it aside. "Exactly! I had a very good reason for turning you down, and couldn't possibly have said yes no matter how I felt in the matter, but you didn't even *try* to convince me that I would be making a mistake in not agreeing to marry you. Do you always just tuck your tail between your legs and go away, Banning? And isn't it injurious to your spleen or something— playing at the gentleman when you knew full well you wanted to kiss me into near insensibility, the way you kissed me that day in Freddie's coach?"

He should knock on the roof right now and direct his coachman to drive straight to St. Bethlehem's Hospital rather than Park Lane. He didn't know which of the two, he or Prudence, should be introduced to the first straight-waistcoat Bedlam had to offer, but he was certain at least one of them deserved to be locked up as a lunatic.

Banning poked his cane against the roof of the coach, the coachman's head appearing through the small door cut into the roof a moment later. "Just drive, James," Banning directed shortly. "I'll signal again when I wish you to take us to Park Lane."

"Right yer are, milor'," James replied, his toothy

grin very much in evidence until the door closed once more, leaving Banning to consider what to do next.

He decided to do his thinking out loud. Lord knew Prudence seemed to prefer the practice, saying just what came into her mind without any notion that what she said could possibly be interpreted in a way she might not have considered.

"Please agree to bear with me a moment, Angel, as I attempt to muddle through this," he said, turning to look at her closely. "You like me—if I may be so blunt about the thing—but you are dismayed, nay, *disgusted* by my belief that a gentleman should be just that, a gentleman. Am I correct so far?"

Her head bobbed again, just as vigorously, so that he could not help rolling his eyes at her so obvious enthusiasm for verbally dissecting him. She must have put a lot of thought into what she now believed, and it wasn't usual for someone to think all that much about someone who wasn't, in some way, important to that person. That could be seen as an encouraging sign, he supposed, beginning to feel, in earnest, the headache Prudence had feigned earlier. He waited, deciding that it might be better to stay silent, so that Prudence would talk.

"You're like two different people, Banning," she said at last, as if that explained anything. "You were wonderfully kind with Molly, masterful with Shadwell. You're the best of brothers to Freddie and a generous guardian. You didn't bite Rexford's head off or sack him, and you allowed me to misbehave like the most obnoxious of precocious infants until I had found my feet, as it were, with our new arrangement. You took me on that lovely picnic, made me laugh with your readings from the guide book, introduced me to your friends who are quite the most amusing idiots I've ever met. You couldn't have either Duke or Dewey within ten yards of you if you were such a stickler for propriety—not if you were as sober as you pretend to be."

"But?" Banning prompted, a part of his mind still reciting Prudence's earlier words to him: *"kiss me into near insensibility, the way you kissed me that day in Freddie's coach."*

"But," Prudence said, laying a heavy emphasis on the word, "you also ruthlessly bullied me into taking care of Molly when all I wanted to do was weep into your waistcoat, and although you probably did the right thing it certainly didn't seem so at the time. You took Shadwell at his word, which only a complete jackstraw or a blockhead of a *gentleman* would do. You make a whacking great too many promises to people who don't deserve them."

She had the bit firmly between her teeth now, and Banning knew he couldn't stop her from saying more even if he wanted to, which he didn't.

"Your new fortune weighs entirely too heavily around your neck," she went on after taking a deep breath, "making you believe you must be sober and upright and all those other boring things normal people are not. You are about to throw yourself away on the Broughton because she once said no to you and you want to prove to yourself that it's true, money does make a gentleman—and you are too thick-headed and stupid to see that I love you very much and it bloody near killed me to break your heart! You didn't even ask *why* I had to turn you down, for God's sake! You just assumed I loved someone else, and then went running after the Broughton, so ready to sacrifice yourself that you make me *sick!*"

She sat back on the squabs, that single errant lock of hair falling into her face once more, where she let it lie, and folded her arms across her lap. "Well, Banning, I do hope you're happy now, because I am completely ashamed of myself and will probably weep into my pillow all the night long like some noodleheaded, die-away ninny in one of Freddie's stupid novels. Tell James to drive to Park Lane now, if you please, unless you'd rather just continue to sit there in the shadows like some hulking great marble statue, gawking at me."

"Who is Enby, Angel?" Banning asked after a moment in which he somehow experienced both all the joys of heaven and the burning pains of hell, hearing that Prudence loved him, while not being able to forget that she had also, once more, turned him down—even before he could ask.

She wheeled about on the seat in a most unloverlike fury, plummeting his chest with her small fists. "You *rotter!* I knew it. I just *knew* it! You found Enby's note! How am I supposed to keep a secret with you poking about like some bloody spy? How *dare* you!"

Banning grabbed for her flailing hands, finally succeeding in taking hold of her wrists, pulling her chin to chin with him so that he could see the fury in her golden eyes. "You said you didn't want me to be a gentleman, Angel, remember? A gentleman might not have asked you, but I have had done with playing the gentleman. Now I'll ask you again. Who in bloody hell is Enby? What power does he have over you? If he's not your lover, what is he? Is he blackmailing you in some way?"

Her eyes shifted from side to side, as if seeking escape or a likely lie. "Yes, all right," she said after a moment, her hands still balled into fists. "He's blackmailing me. He-he wants money. Yes, that's it, money. To-to keep my secret."

"He wanted a few pennies, if you could spare them," Banning told her, sure she had been trying to remember the contents of the note he had found. "And you're a wretchedly poor liar, Angel. I think you can understand how I, in my new role of former gentleman, might be tempted to point that out. Now, try again. Who is Enby?"

"I told him I'm a terrible liar," Prudence said quietly, as if to herself. "But I truly thought I was getting better at it. This is very lowering, you know." She looked at Banning across the bare inches of space that separated them, her smile washing away all his anger and most of his curiosity. "Would you please kiss me, Banning? We can always sort all this out later, can't we? It's all I can think about, ever since that day in Freddie's coach. I'd really like it if you were to kiss me . . . hold me."

There was a time for talk, and a time for action. Banning wanted to know Enby's identity. But he didn't want to know that half as much as he wanted to know the touch of Prudence's mouth on his . . . the feel of her soft body crushed against him . . . the damning rapture of what her eyes promised . . . the reality of her already wandering fingers as they stroked his neck . . . even the limits of his endurance as he did his best to remember that he and Angel were inside a moving coach, driving through the darkened streets of London, and he was considering how difficult it might be to take her . . . take her here . . . take her now . . . and damn the consequences!

He looked deeply into her eyes, difficult as it was to see anything except the sparkle of her unshed tears, and gave up any argument his better, more sober, self might have attempted in order to discourage him.

"Angel, I ought to murder you now and put us both out of our misery," he admitted on a groan, then roughly pulled her into his arms, his mouth crushing hers as, together, they toppled sideways onto the velvet cushions, his right foot braced against the facing seat so that they didn't topple to the floor as the coach continued to rumble along the London streets.

The sleek, heavy fabric of her gown was recognized at once as superfluous to the moment, and in a moment it was gone, as was Banning's evening coat, which he somehow balled into a pillow and slipped beneath Angel's head.

She lay there on the velvet, only her shift, her silk stockings and one delicately made slipper covering her, watching him rise to his knees, struggling to rid himself of the remainder of his clothing, giggling as one of the coach wheels found a rut in the street and he fell on top of her, only one arm free of his shirt.

Banning laughed with her, then ripped off the shirt, so that he was bare to his waist, delighting in the way his skin burned everywhere Angel touched him.

And then, without conscious thought as to how he had accomplished the feat, all of their clothing was gone, and they were alone together, as nature had made them.

They were like children set loose in Eden, without shame, and aware only of the moment . . . eager for each new experience . . . giving themselves over completely to each other . . . learning their way together . . . delighting in each new discovery.

Her full, moist mouth was a lure he could not resist. Her perfect breasts were a delight to his senses of touch, of taste. The curve of her slim waist beckoned, her smooth flare of hip issued an invitation to wander.

And all the while he moved his hands over her, memorized her with the touch of his fingers and his mouth, she stroked his arms, his chest, and pressed kisses against his throat, his hair.

They didn't speak, for there was no time for words, for lies, for secrets. It was a time for taking, for giving, and for sharing.

How his hand came to be between her slightly spread legs he would never remember, any more than he would be able to recall more than the feeling of his manhood pressed against her thigh, the nearly overwhelming mix of passion and tenderness he felt for her at the moment, and would feel for the remainder of his life.

She was warm and wet and so ready for him that he was momentarily taken aback by her willingness to surrender herself to him here, inside his darkened coach, without a promise made or an explanation given.

She was offering him her love, the all of it and the nothingness of it, for her love was all she had offered. His love was less than nothing, for in what he was about to do he was taking away her future, her plans that did not include him, leaving her only her secrets.

Don't think, don't think, Banning told himself even as he could hear his blood rushing in his ears, feel the pounding of his heart like the beat of a thousand drums inside his chest. *Don't think.*

His fingers moved, almost without conscious thought, beginning to give to her, not take from her, even when she offered all. He felt her start to relax, then begin to tense as the man who had made love so many times *gave* love for the first time in his life.

He didn't stop, spreading her, taking the sweetness of her between his fingers, stroking, teasing, finding the very heart of her and then ministering to her until her legs fell completely open and the soft, breathless sigh that held his name slipped from her mouth and caressed his ear.

He could feel her opening to him more with each stroke of his fingers, sense her building tension. He reveled in her growing passion, knowing that she had no idea where he was leading her, no possible conception of what she would feel when the final moment came and her body could no longer resist its headlong ascent to ecstasy.

He wanted to be with her when it came, that heart-pounding explosion. He wanted to be deep inside her, filling her, allowing himself the same release he willed so very desperately for her to have.

But that was impossible. She wasn't his, even as she gave herself to him. He could make promises to her, but he couldn't make love out of the nothing that she offered him. He could only steal this moment, and then wait for her to leave him alone, with so many promises to others and so little of his own.

He would take this moment. He would give her this moment. He would give . . . and give . . . and give. . . .

"Banning."

His name was a terse whisper as it was issued from between Prudence's lips, a tightly phrased question, a declaration, a cry for help.

"Oh God, Banning. *Banning!*"

He held her as her release came to her, still stroking her as she moved toward ecstasy and beyond . . . until she arched herself against his hand, her body thrashing on the cushions, trying to fight her way closer, attempting to remove herself from the sensations that had to be frightening in their intensity.

"Hush, Angel, hush," he whispered at last, cradling her head against his chest, keeping his own body very still so that he could begin to control his own passion. His body was slick with perspiration beneath her frantically clasping hands, his stomach a knot of tension and a quick, painful nausea he hadn't felt since the long forgotten sexual frustration of his youth. "And lie still, for God's sake," he told her, almost pleaded. "If you feel anything for me at all, please don't move."

She immediately did as he asked, which would have amused him if he'd thought of it, for it was the first time she had ever obeyed him without question, but he was too occupied in locating his self control—and the breeches that would cover the evidence of his frustration.

They dressed in silence, Prudence helping him with his shirt cuffs and jacket, Banning playing ladies' maid as he clumsily fastened the buttons of her gown.

There still was no shame between them, but there was no longer any satisfaction either. Only the wall of Angel's reluctance to explain about Enby, and her refusal of Banning's marriage proposal.

"Angel—" he began as they once more sat side by side on the squabs, neither looking at the other one.

"Don't say anything, Banning, please," Prudence said quietly. "Only tell James to drive to Park Lane. I have to—to talk to someone before I can say anything else to you. I want to tell you everything, I truly do, but it is not only my secret."

She turned to him, lowering the invisible wall between them for just a moment as she ran the back of her hand down the side of his cheek. "But I do love you, Banning. I love you, and I always will, no matter how this all ends."

"And I love you, Angel," Banning told her, catching up her hand and pressing his lips against her palm. *What have I done? What am I doing? This is insane . . . insane!* his intellect screamed to him, even as his heart sang. "Is tomorrow too soon?"

He could feel the warmth of her smile in the darkness. "I had thought yesterday was too late, Banning, and I was wrong. But I do know that tomorrow is too soon. Monday. Come to me Monday, please. By then I'll know just what I can do and what I can't. That is why I will always be grateful for tonight. You see, it's not just my decision or Enby's. At the bottom of it, when you know what I know, the decision will be *yours.*"

CHAPTER 17

*Merely innocent flirtation,
not quite adultery, but adulteration*

George Noel Gordon,
Lord Byron

Sunday morning dawned bright and fair, although Prudence didn't get to see it, as she had stuck her head beneath the pillows when Geranium came in bearing hot chocolate and gone back to sleep until nearly noon.

She enjoyed her dreams most thoroughly, lying in her bed, halfway between waking and sleeping, reliving the previous evening, the pillow hiding her blushes, the soft feathers muffling her occasional giggles as her mind's eye remembered Banning half in and half out of his shirt, his expression caught between passion and dismay as the coach hit a rut and he toppled onto her.

He was so very young, for all his silver hair. So very innocent, for all his worldliness. So gentle and giving, for all his sometime bluster. So often the rash, impulsive rule breaker, for all he yearned to be sober and upright and proper.

So very much the man she loved, for all that he would mostly probably soon hate her. Before he had left her last night, returning her to Park Lane, he had kissed her a dozen times, promising to be on her doorstep by nine on Monday morning, "Or else you'll know I'm dead, my darling. At nine, and not a moment later."

"Damn you, Enby!" Prudence had exclaimed when at last the bad thoughts succeeded in crowding out all the good ones, and she pushed back the covers, reluctant but resigned to doing what she must do.

An hour later, after racing through her bath and then sitting down to a remarkably hearty breakfast for a young lady with so much on her mind, Prudence sat at the writing desk in her bedchamber, her simple ivory gown glowing almost golden in the puddle of sunlight streaming through the windows that looked onto Park Lane.

She had written a half dozen notes to Enby in the past fifteen minutes, all of them now squashed into balls and tossed in the general direction of the small wire basket Geranium had more than once decried as a totally useless contraption since her mistress had yet to master its function. "Couldn't hit the floor with her slippers" is how the maid had described Prudence's poor aim, and Prudence had not bothered to point out that, be it with a bullet or a brick, she rarely failed to miss what she aimed at—if she felt so inclined.

But writing to Enby since coming to London had never been an exercise she had looked forward to with unmitigated glee, so that she only wanted her discarded efforts gone from her desk, tossing them willy-nilly without a care for where they landed.

Prudence laid down the pen, noticing with a small wince that she had chewed its end like a chawbacon farmer's son munching a piece of hay, and looked out the window, trying to collect her thoughts.

She had to tell Enby what had happened—without *really* telling him, of course, or he'd straightaway challenge Banning to a duel, which wouldn't help anyone. She had to appeal to Enby's better self, his unselfish self—the side of him that had prompted this mad scheme in the first place. At the same time, she had to acknowledge that a change of plans would not only be a breach of his trust in her, but could also lead the two of them to the nearest guardhouse.

No, that wasn't true. Banning would never allow her to be taken to jail. He'd simply murder her—and Enby as well—and then be hanged for his crimes.

And then there was the very real danger that Banning, for all his promises to wait until Monday for her "answers," might take it into his head to follow Geranium when she took the note to Enby's lodgings. Men were like that. Sneaky. And nosier than any woman, although men didn't see it that way. They gave their curiosity nice little titles like "concern" and "interest" and even "my duty as a gentleman and protector of innocent females."

Hah!

But if she couldn't trust Banning not to follow Geranium—whom he must have by now deduced as the "postman" Prudence used to get word to Enby—what was the point of writing a note?

And it was not as if she could deliver the note herself, which would be ridiculous in any case because if she could get to Enby's lodgings without being detected, she might as well tell him in person and there would be no need of a note.

She almost wished she hadn't wheedled Enby's direction out of him and couldn't reach him at all!

"A more clever person would have set up a pigeon post or some such ingenious device if she was so bent on clandestine note-passing, although explaining away a pigeon coop on the roof might not have been easy," she said, absently rubbing her hand across her chin and depositing a blotch of ink on her skin. "Of course, a more clever person wouldn't be in this fix at all. She would have refused to come to London in the first place, which would have kept her from falling in love, and just waited out her time in Sussex like she was supposed to do. And *that,* at least in my mind, would be the greatest crime of all. Oh, what a bloody mess!"

Geranium, who had entered the room unannounced and unnoticed, halted in the process of picking up the discarded notes, asking, "Was you talking ta me, Miss?"

Prudence waved the maid to silence as she looked out the window, watching as a curricle pulled into the drive. "Hush, Geranium, please. I think—*yes!* Why didn't I think of it before?" She quickly picked up her pen, dipped it in the ink pot, scribbled a single line on a clean piece of paper, sanded it with more flair than aim, then folded it and stuck it in the pocket of her gown.

"Geranium?" she then asked, pushing back her chair and rising, her hands smoothing down the skirts of her gown. "Quickly—do I look all right?"

The maid tipped her head to one side, inspecting her mistress's appearance, then lifted up her apron, spit on a corner of it, and stepped forward to wipe at Prudence's chin. "This ink has ta go—hold still now and stop pulling that face on me! You're worse than a baby for fidgetin'. There! You're well enough, I suppose. What's goin' on, if I could ask? You look fair ta burst."

"I won't need you to go to the Spread Eagle today after all, Geranium," Prudence said, racing to her mirror just to check on her appearance, for appearances counted when one was making a request—especially if one had to do a small bit of "flirting" before asking for that boon and swearing someone to secrecy at the same time.

"Good!" Geranium answered, already stooping to pick up another discarded note. "Don't much like goin' there, you know. All those brutes, leerin' down from the balconies, like the only reason I was ta come by there is so that they can tell me how bleedin' red m'hair is or how good it would look spread out on their pillows. Gennulmen? I don't think so, Miss, not a one of 'em. Now where are you runnin' off ta in such a fine hurry?"

Prudence hesitated, her hand already on the door latch. "Where? Well, Geranium, if you were to listen very closely, you'd probably hear the knocker go any second now, heralding the arrival of my own personal pigeon. Isn't it wonderful how things work out sometimes?"

And then she pulled open the door, holding up her skirts as she dashed toward the stairs and tripped down them quickly until she pulled herself to a stop on the third step from the bottom and struck a pose, waiting for Quimby to answer the knocker.

The butler looked up at her, one brow raised in

question. "You're looking particularly eager, Miss MacAfee," he said, a hint of amusement in his voice. "Might I suggest you throw a net over the poor creature if you're so hot to have him, and just have done with it? It is an eligible gentleman I'll see on the other side of this door in a moment, isn't it? Does his lordship know about this? And a better question— *should* he know about any of this? Especially when I consider that you told me the marquess is the one who—if I remember your words correctly—*will forever hold my love, damn him anyway!"*

"Quimby," Prudence said, winking at him although she didn't move a single hair out of her purposely appealing pose—one hand on the rail, the other holding her skirt just a shade too high above her ankle to be considered maidenly. "I thought we'd agreed to keep each other's secrets. Why, you wouldn't go to the marquess with my secret any more than I would think to trouble him with yours—or Freddie's. Now, please, hurry and answer the knocker. I'll soon get a cramp in my foot from pointing my toe in ladylike elegance."

"I shouldn't drink, you know," Quimby said, shaking his head. "Not even when my wound pains me. Not a drop. You never know who you'll think to confide in when you're in your cups."

"You couldn't help yourself, Quimby, any more than Freddie could when she told me *her* secrets," Prudence said sympathetically, apologizing for her own generous nature. "People have always talked to me. My brother once said I have a trusting face, whatever that is. You cannot imagine the amount of other people's secrets I have locked up inside my very discreet brainbox. Even the gentleman whose Hessians you have deigned to keep cooling on the marble steps outside that door has shared a thought or two with me."

"Then perhaps I'll leave him where he is, Angel," the butler said, easing into the familiarity he and Prudence usually kept to the early morning hours when neither of them felt ready to seek their beds and sat together in the dark kitchens, talking of everything from Prudence's checkered youth to Quimby's well-hidden one. "I shouldn't think I'm being a party to the downfall of yet another of our fine English gentlemen. Park Lane is already crowded to the rafters with young bucks more than half in love with that 'trusting face' of yours."

"Quimby, I'm going to fall if you don't hurry!" Prudence warned, laughing, then held her young-maiden-surprised-in-the-act-of-descending-the-stairs pose a moment longer, as the butler opened the door, admitting London's most notorious, handsome, and eligible rake, Leslie Orford, Viscount Ramsden.

"Angel!" Ramsden exclaimed, tossing his hat and gloves in Quimby's general direction before approaching the staircase, his hand held out to assist her in descending to the tile foyer. He kissed her hand, but only perfunctorily, as he seemed distracted. "How lovely you look this afternoon, as always. Pick any other three compliments you might like hearing on your gown, your hair, or your melted gold eyes and consider them said. Quickly, send for the lizard, and we will stuff her in a corner to chaperone us while we whisper like schoolchildren. I have great news!"

Abandoning her pose, as it was not doing her much good and she was beginning to get a crick in her neck from keeping her head at a coquettish tilt, Prudence motioned to Quimby to send for Miss Prentice, then took Ramsden's hand and led him toward the drawing room.

"What is it?" she asked as soon as they were seated, eager for any news that could possibly make the handsome ne'er-do-well look like a satisfied cat with canary feathers sticking out of the corner of his mouth.

"I did it, Angel," he said, raising his hand to her cheek just as Miss Prentice entered the room, her tapestry bag in one hand, a glass of "water" in the other, her eyes narrowed at the sight of the viscount's familiarity. "Oh, Angel, you were right. You see before you the prodigal son, newly welcomed back into the fold of his family."

"And no sackcloth and ashes in evidence either," Prudence remarked happily. "I told you, Leslie, blood is thicker than port, or whatever the saying is. Your parents couldn't turn you away, no matter what terrible stories they may have heard about you."

The viscount grinned. "And all of them true, remember? The gambling, the wenching, the parties, the general carousing. But it was the duel that well and truly set my father against me. And do you know why?"

Prudence shook her head. "No, Leslie, I do not. You said he simply told the servants to refuse you admittance once you'd come home to England, even though he continued your allowance. It was that allowance, if you'll remember, that made me believe your father was not wholly committed to hating you."

"It was my mother," Ramsden said, sitting back against the cushions, his new happiness seemingly tempered by the mention of the woman. "It nearly killed her—my leaving the country, which I wouldn't have had to do if I hadn't dueled. She had only just begun to recover from that blow when I resurfaced, and Father didn't want her to have to suffer again, if I were to continue on in my rakehelly ways. That's why he denied me his house."

"But when you apologized, when you cornered him at his club as I begged you to do—and told him how you had seen the folly of your ways and wanted nothing but his forgiveness and his blessing before you emigrated to America forever, so as to not embarrass him again?"

"Then he put me through hell for the next two hours, actually," Ramsden said, lowering his voice as Miss Prentice pointedly cleared her throat at his plain speech. "Read me a lecture that would blister a fishwife's ears, then clasped me to his chest . . . and *cried*. My father, Angel! He cried." He shook his head. "I'll never forget it."

Prudence patted his hand, wishing her own problems could be solved so easily, following the same logic she had impressed on the viscount. "See, Leslie? All you had to do was be truly sorry, tell the truth, and all your problems were solved. Of course, you will also have to behave yourself in future. No more bedding of other men's wives, no more impromptu races through the Park during the Promenade with a monkey wrapped around your shoulders, no more attempting to foist a Cyprian on the patronesses of Almack's just for the sport of it."

He nodded, his handsome features sober. "All behind me now, Angel. All of it. Especially since I saw a certain young lady the other night at the theater."

Prudence leaned forward, delighting in the man's

uncharacteristic blush. "Leslie, you sly dog! You're in love, aren't you?"

"I think so, and with all thanks to you, Angel," the viscount said, taking her hand in his and raising it to his lips, a move that had Miss Prentice once more clearing her throat. "You're a wonderful young hellion, Angel, really, but you made me realize that—no matter how much fun we've had together, could still have together—what I really want, what I *need* is a sweet, innocent, unworldly young miss. Imagine! The world's greatest rake bowled down in a matter of seconds by a pair of melting blue eyes. Mother has invited her to dine with us this evening, just to show that I now have her approval."

Prudence could barely keep from grinning. "I think I'm insulted, Leslie. Are you saying that I am not a sweet, innocent, unworldly young miss?"

"In spades, darling," the viscount countered, leaning over to kiss her cheek, which caused the lizard to break into a near paroxysm of coughing. "Between us, we could lay waste to half of England within a week. I am hoping that Beatrice will save me from myself. When I look at her, I see myself riding the Ramsden estates, taking up the reins of my inheritance, and then coming home to her quiet comfort in the evening. It boggles the mind, I know, but I'm ready for some quiet comfort. More than ready. This past year, being cut off from all I knew, has not been a joy to me, but it has proved educational. And I owe it to you that my banishment is now over."

"Family ties are still the strongest, aren't they?" Prudence said, avoiding his eyes as a pain invaded her heart, to lie there like the weight of a thousand deceits.

"The thought of never seeing your mother and father again, never being welcome in their house, brings almost an unbearable sorrow. Please, tell me truthfully, Leslie—if you were forced to choose between your mother and Beatrice, whom would you choose?"

"I don't know, Angel," Ramsden said, "and, frankly, I'm not going to think about it, because that day will never come. It's much too lovely an afternoon to hurt my brain, thinking of things that could only depress me. I only came here to thank you —even if I'm still marveling at the way you got me to tell you my troubles in the first place."

"You tried to seduce me in the garden at that party we attended," she reminded him, laughing. "Once I'd boxed your ears, stomped on your toes, and cursed you for a bounder, I asked you why you were acting the complete fool when anyone with two good eyes in their head could see you were unhappy and that getting into mischief was the only way you could think of to keep people from guessing how sad you were."

"And I told you," Ramsden ended for her, shaking his head once more. "How simple everything becomes once one tells the truth. Not that I hadn't enjoyed my ramshackle ways, but it was beginning to wear on me, constantly playing the role of rake. I'd grown tired of it even before that fool pushed me into that damned duel. Daventry was smarter than I, and did his growing up a few years ago. Straight as an arrow, your guardian is; sober, upstanding, honest. You're lucky to have him, Angel. Imagine what would have happened if your brother had plunked you in *my* lap and then gone off to die in battle. You'd probably be singing at Covent Garden by now to earn your daily bread—or else I would have seduced you. Possibly both."

Prudence laughed at this because she felt she should, even as every word the viscount said made her see how terrible her own position was, and how hopeless it also was to harbor any notion of coming out of her predicament with a happy solution.

"Daventry is not the total sobersides you think him, Leslie, and you shouldn't be either, for even sweet young misses like Beatrice—and I will hear her last name from you at some point, I trust—enjoy an occasional flight of fancy," she said at last.

"In fact, as I believe you should perform at least one more naughty deed before settling down to raise babies with your Beatrice," she hesitated only a moment, looking to Miss Prentice to be sure she wasn't listening, "I believe I know just the naughty deed you could perform. Nothing that will get you into real trouble, I promise you. Just a small ride to Gracechurch Street, where you will deliver a private note to the gentleman residing in Room Three of the Spread Eagle Inn."

She removed the note from her pocket and slipped it to him as Miss Prentice turned to pick up her glass.

Ramsden frowned, pocketing the note. "Why didn't I notice at once? Your eyes are sad today, aren't they, Angel? Are you in some sort of trouble? If you are, God knows you can apply to me for any assistance— money—anything at all. I'll even break a head or two, if they need breaking. I'm reformed, if you'll remember your own warning to me, not dead."

Prudence sighed, shaking her head. The secret still wasn't hers to tell, not all of it anyway. Much as she longed to reveal everything to Ramsden—the only man she could think of who might understand her dilemma—she had to remain silent. "Just deliver the note, Leslie, and go have dinner with Beatrice. I'll be fine, honestly."

She pinned a bright smile on her face. "And if I'm wrong, and I'm *not* fine, well, perhaps you will be kind enough to toss a coin in my basket as I lower it from my cell in Newgate, angling for farthings. I understand that bribing the jailers improves the food."

CHAPTER 18

*For talk six times with the same single lady,
and you may get the wedding dresses ready.*

George Noel Gordon,
Lord Byron

Six o'clock. Hadn't it already gone six three hours ago? Had there ever been a day this long? Had ever an empty evening stretched out longer before him? Not even on the Peninsula, when waiting for dawn and another battle, had time dragged so slowly.

Banning eyed the brandy decanter almost longingly, but then dismissed the thought of drinking himself into a stupor, waking only in time for Rexford to dress him and point him in the direction of Park Lane, and the infuriating, maddening, delightful woman who had told him she loved him, and then sent him on his way.

Monday. Angel would have answers for him on Monday, not even at nine, but as soon after dawn as he could rouse her from her bed without alarming Freddie by breaking down the door and exploding into the house to demand to see her.

But how could she have answers for him, when she

257

hadn't sent any notes to this Enby person—and hadn't received any, if his friends could be trusted to keep their eyes open all day as they stood on the other side of the hedges lining the drive at Number 96 Park Lane, watching for Quimby's signal and then following Geranium or whoever carried Angel's message to the man.

Duke had returned to Chesterfield Street no less than five times since first taking up his assigned post that morning, Banning having chosen that man to keep him informed, knowing that the earl could not be trusted to remain in one place for more than a hour without finding some excuse to wander off in search of something to eat, something to see—anything that would keep him on the move.

Banning would have gone himself, feeling foolish as he hid behind the hedges, but he couldn't take the chance that Prudence might come to him while he was out. *Insane.* That's what he had thought last night, and it was what he still thought. Insane. Ridiculous. Juvenile.

And totally excusable for a man so deeply in love—or at least that's what he kept telling himself.

When he wasn't wondering who Enby was, that is.

"Viscount Ramsden to see you, my lord," Montgomery announced from the door to the study, shaking Banning out of his reverie. "Shall I show him in, sir?"

"Leslie? And at this hour?" Banning was instantly on his guard. He hadn't spoken to the viscount in years and had only nodded to the man in passing the other day in the park. There was only one reason the rakehell could have come to Chesterfield Street. One and one only—to petition Prudence MacAfee's guardian for her hand in marriage. Banning went instantly from cautiously curious to belligerent. "Tell him to go away. Tell him I'm sick. I've died. Anything you think might work to turn away a determined man, Montgomery. The last thing I need today is the viscount."

"My lord? Are you really ill? You barely picked at your luncheon today, as I recall, and Cook prepared many of your favorite dishes. Shall I send one of the footmen for the physician?" the butler inquired, and Banning knew he was beginning to fall apart, unraveling, as it were, right in front of the servants. If he didn't get himself together, and get himself together soon, Montgomery would be bringing him a toddy and a hot brick for his toes.

"Never mind, Montgomery," Banning told the man, at last giving in to the idea that a small snifter of brandy was just what he needed to calm his nerves, not that he'd—in all his four and thirty years of life—ever before been aware that he even *had* nerves. "Send him along in. God knows I'm certainly in the mood to say no to somebody. It might even improve my temper."

"In that case, my lord," Montgomery said with the familiarity of a long-time servant, and one who had been doing his best to placate his master's unaccustomedly vile disposition all the day long without marked success, "I shall have him in here before you can so much as blink." He turned sharply on his heels, muttering just a little too loudly as he strode out of the room, "I'll even tie a bleeding bell around the man's neck if it would help," a statement of exasperation that brought Banning his first smile in a very long day.

"Daventry, you old dog!" Viscount Ramsden called out heartily moments later as he strode into the study, his blond hair glistening like a halo, his finely sculpted, faintly wicked features making a mockery of his otherwise angelic appearance. "I was beginning to think you'd have your dragon deny me this privilege. I suppose it galls you to have to speak with me—not that you were always so starchy. Remember that night we met in the mews behind Portman Square? You shinning down one dashing matron's drainpipe, me just about to hoist myself up another one? Ah, those were the days. But we must all leave our hey-go-mad grasstime behind us at some point, eh?"

Banning smiled, caught up in the viscount's good humor in spite of himself. "We were devils, weren't we, Leslie? But you should have gone to war with the rest of us. It might have been the making of you."

Ramsden shook his head. "Couldn't, old fellow. Last of my line and all that, remember, although I was already so notorious even the most eager mama wouldn't let her little chick near me. Not that I was ready to get myself leg-shackled solely to provide another Ramsden heir. I think half the reason I cut up so shabbily was because I was ashamed I wasn't bleeding and dying with the rest of you." He grinned, shaking off any further mention of the past. "But that's not why I'm here, Banning."

"I hadn't thought so, Leslie," Banning said, pouring his old friend a drink. It was odd, he thought in a small corner of his mind. Some of us never grow up and others grow up entirely too much. Why couldn't he or Ramsden find some comfortable medium that would leave them both happy and solid? "You're here about Prudence, aren't you?"

"Nobody could ever say you're a slowtop, Banning," the viscount countered, accepting the wineglass, "but I'll be damned how you could know that. I didn't know myself that I'd be here until I saw Angel a few hours ago. How I adore that little minx, whether she's tempting me, encouraging me, or boxing my ears. What a great heart she has. A great, giving heart."

Now Banning was confused and beginning to feel angry again. A few hours ago? Ramsden had only made up his mind to ask for Prudence's hand a few hours ago? God! The viscount was right. She was a minx. Only someone like Prudence could make love with one man, try to get herself shed of another, and find time to flirt with a third—all within the same twenty-four hours!

He motioned the viscount to a chair, for they had both remained standing, their glasses in their hands, the space of ten feet, the memories of long-ago friendship, and the years of war and frivolity still between them. "I may be her guardian, Leslie, but Prudence will have her own way, no matter what I say. If she's turned you down and you've come to me so that I could intervene for you, plead your case, I'm afraid I have to disappoint you. The next time she obeys me will be the first, ashamed as I am to admit it."

"Turned me down? You think I want to marry Angel? Wait a minute! It's even better than that, isn't it? You've got that silver hair of yours all in a twist, just thinking she might have accepted me. You want her yourself, don't you? Of course you do! It's written all over your face. Oh, that is too good!" Ramsden threw back his head, laughing so hard and so long that Banning had to grip his snifter with both hands so as not to jump up, dash across the room, and throttle the man.

Banning waited for the viscount to sober himself, which took an unconscionably long time, to the marquess's way of thinking—time enough for him to accept the fact that he had somehow revealed to the man that he, Prudence's guardian, was top-over-tail in love with her.

This knowledge didn't embarrass Banning, but it did serve to make him realize that he should be paying closer attention to whatever it was the viscount was trying to say to him. Of course Ramsden and Prudence would never marry. They were too alike to suit each other, and between them they'd find themselves banished from society in a fortnight, having thoroughly ruined their reputations by coming to Almack's in riding clothes and a million other pranks two such high-spirited people could conceive of together.

So why was he here? What had happened in Park Lane to send Ramsden to him?

After pulling a large white handkerchief from his pocket to wipe at his streaming eyes, the viscount, obviously using all his powers of self-control, steeled his handsome features into a concerned frown and said, "I debated about coming here, but now I know I did the right thing. Loving her, you won't do anything too stupid, or at least you've never done anything too stupid in the past. Damned upstanding, Banning, that's what you are these days. Really do put me and my ramshackle ways to shame. You see, Angel put a mission before me today, and I thought—in my new role of responsible grown-up—her guardian should know about it. Can I have your promise that you'll not run to Angel, telling her how I've betrayed her trust in me?"

"Will you take my word that I will be discreet, or would you rather I took a blood oath? Using *your* blood, of course," Banning gritted out from between clenched teeth.

"Your word is sufficient, I suppose. Very well. I think Angel is in some trouble, Banning. Nothing too serious, or she would have never asked me for help, if that makes any sense to you. No murderers lurking in the shadows or anything like that, I'm sure, although she did mention something about possibly finding herself in jail. Still, it's something she thinks she can handle herself, I can feel it, even though she was distracted enough to have thought she needed to flirt with me in order to gain my help. She's an independent little puss, Angel is, and had to be, if half her stories of MacAfee Farm and that twit Shadwell are to be believed."

"They're all to be believed, Leslie, for I've both seen the farm and met the man," Banning told him, leaning forward on his chair. "What sort of help did she ask you for this afternoon? Did it have anything to do with delivering a note to a certain gentleman, probably one staying at a hotel here in London, but not one in anything closely resembling a fashionable area of the city?"

The viscount tipped his head and looked at Banning curiously. "Which is it, old fellow, a crystal ball—or have you taken up mind-reading? How did you know? Never mind, for you can't know the whole of it, now can you? Yes, it was a note, and I carried the thing to the Spread Eagle, in Gracechurch Street. Not a bad inn, really, and the carved eagle is handsome enough, if the gilt is chipping off its beak. Shall I say anything more, or do you want to tell me? I do admit to being curious."

Banning's mouth had gone dry, so that he downed the remainder of his brandy in a single gulp, shivering slightly as the liquid burned his throat. So much for setting his friends to watch Geranium's movements. He should have known that Prudence would choose another messenger. "Then you saw him. You saw Enby?"

"Enby? Is that the fellow's name?" The viscount shook his head. "No, didn't see him. All Angel told me was that I should deliver her note to Room Three. When the fellow didn't answer my knock I went looking in the common room, but the unnamed guest in Room Three wasn't there. A barmaid remembered him, though, although she didn't call him Enby. Called him 'sweetie,' if I recall correctly. Seems he's quite a lover, even if he's not too free with his money. She told me he'd gone out of the city for a few days. He might return yet today, but the barmaid couldn't be sure, although she misses him—'purely Oi does,'" he ended, imitating the barmaid.

"And the note?" Banning wanted to scream. To hit something. Break something. If Enby wasn't going to be back in town to get Prudence's note tonight, she wouldn't have an answer for him tomorrow. It was a good thing his hair had already turned silver, he thought wildly; otherwise he'd have been snow white by morning!

"Stuck it under his door. Dated it first, so that he'd know when it was delivered." The viscount downed the remainder of his wine, then stood, grinning from ear to ear. "Oh, and I read the note first, of course. I'm trying to reform myself, but I'm doing it by degrees. Wouldn't want to shock my system or anything, you understand. Would you like to know what it said?"

Banning wanted to strangle the man, but first he needed to learn the contents of Prudence's note. "If you wouldn't feel you were betraying a confidence," he said, doing his best to appear uninterested.

"Hang you for a lovesick fool, Banning," Ramsden replied, shaking his head. "You're dying inside, aren't you? But I won't prolong your torture. It was a single line and damned hard to decipher. Your ward's penmanship is execrable, in case you don't know that. Sit down, sit down—I'm getting to it! The note said, and I hereby quote: 'Need you. Midnight. Same place.'"

"That's all?"

"Yes. Hardly loverlike, wouldn't you say, although I can't imagine what this man is to her, can you? My money's on the rendezvous taking place in the mews behind Freddie's, as even Angel isn't daring enough to walk through London at midnight. I was going to go there myself—hide myself in the bushes just to be sure she doesn't come to any harm out there alone as she waits, most likely in vain—but now I'll allow you the pleasure."

He gave Banning a rakish salute. "And now I'll be off to continue my redemption by playing the gentleman for a certain young lady I plan to make my wife. I have Angel to thank for that, too, in a roundabout way. I do adore that girl. Don't hurt her, old friend, or else I'll feel obliged to put a hole in you, and Mama wouldn't like that."

Banning passed the remainder of the evening lost in thought, conjuring up varying scenarios and how they would play out in the mews behind Park Lane.

He would dress himself in a black cloak, stand with his face hidden in the darkness, and impersonate the absent Enby, listening silently while Prudence unburdened herself to the man—and learning her secret.

He would hide behind the stable door and wait for the man to approach. If this Enby fellow made a move to hurt Prudence, he, Banning, would kill him. If Prudence ran to the man and embraced him, kissed him, then he, Banning, would . . . he would . . .

"You know, Banning," Dewey Norton, who had been sitting in the Chesterfield Street study with Banning and Marmaduke, said as he puffed on one of his host's cigars, then held it out in front of him between his pinched fingers, visually examining the thing for flaws, "you really should apply to Farmington, ask him where he gets his cigars. Rolled beautifully, and no bite. No bite at all. Always avail m'self of two or three when I'm with him. Good man, Farmington. Generous."

"And he says you're a bleeding leech," the Earl of Preston said, frantically waving away the blue-tinged smoke Dewey blew in his direction. "Banning—tell me again. Why were we standing outside Freddie's all day? Not that I didn't enjoy my dinner, and I thank you for offering it in exchange for my help because your cook is one of the best, but I'll be damned if I understand what good Dewey and I did hanging around Park Lane, waiting for a maid who never stepped a foot outdoors all day long."

"Blockhead!" Dewey chided, reaching for the humidor and helping himself to a half dozen cigars, sticking them in his pocket. "I told you we weren't supposed to ask. Friends just do things for friends, that's all. Isn't that right, Banning?"

Grateful to both gentlemen for interrupting his depressing thoughts, Banning smiled, saying, "I appreciate your concern, Duke, as well as Dewey's unselfishness. However, as the hour grows late, I believe I'm going to have to leave you now for a space. Feel free to ring for anything you might desire. I should be back within the hour."

The earl jerked his head up at Banning. "You're going out? Where are you going out to? See, Dewey," he continued, glaring at his friend. "I don't know anything!"

"And never have," Dewey replied complacently, waving Banning on his way with a slightly condescending wink, although Banning knew the man hadn't the slightest idea where he was heading or why. "I'll explain it all to you someday, when I think you're ready," he continued, sighing as if he was weary with all the knowledge that sat on his head as he raised his feet to the leather ottoman and crossed his ankles. "Whistle for Montgomery, before you toddle off, won't you, Banning? I'm thinking another small slice of that torte we had earlier wouldn't come amiss. Do you think you've any cherries in the kitchens? Farmington always has the best cherries . . ."

Slightly buoyed by his friends' antics, Banning made short work of his journey to Park Lane, his black cloak covering his clothing, its hood pulled up to hide his face as he stepped into the narrow alley lit only by a few smoky torches burning low near the stables.

He still hadn't decided precisely what he would do, as he would feel foolish hiding either in the shrubbery or the stable, and pretending he was Enby was too farfetched a scheme, even for a man in love. After all, Enby could be taller, broader, smaller than he, and even in the darkness Banning knew he couldn't depend on carrying off such a deception for more than a few moments.

He just knew he had to be nearby, to protect Prudence if she needed protection. And, if Enby had returned in time to heed her note, he might just learn something as well. When dealing with Prudence, having a bit of extra knowledge on his side, no matter how deviously he went about gaining it, could only be seen as the action of a prudent man.

Keeping close to the shrubbery, he advanced down the narrow alleyway a good five minutes before midnight, heading for the rear of Number 96, only to be brought up short by Prudence's disembodied voice, coming to him from somewhere in the dark. "Is that you, Enby?"

His mind made up for him, Banning shrugged, believing he might as well be hung for a sheep as for a lamb, and replied gruffly, "Stay away, Angel. Sick." And then he coughed, just to drive home his point.

"Sick, is it? You ought to be dead, damn your hide," Prudence shot back in a very unlover-like voice, cheering Banning no end, although she couldn't know it. Then her tone softened. "Are you really ill, Enby? Do you have a fever? Here, let me feel your forehead."

She stepped out from behind a tree not ten feet from Banning, clad only in her night rail and dressing gown, which glowed ghostly white in the nearby torchlight. He pulled the hood of his cloak down to the top of his eyebrows.

"No!" Banning bit out, careful to keep his voice low. "No fuss. What'd'ya want?" He coughed again, sounding like a carriage wheel badly in need of grease.

She tipped her head to one side, as if trying to see better in the darkness. "What do *I* want? Well, now there's a question I never thought to hear you ask. All I get from you is, 'We'll do this, Angel . . . I've done this so we can do that, Angel . . . It will be above anything wonderful, Angel, you'll see.' Well, guess what, Enby—that's all over, do you hear me? We have to make a clean breast of everything, so that we can both get on with our lives. But," she hesitated a moment, then went on, more kindly, "I need your permission. I can't hurt you, dearest Enby, or take the chance of losing you, even when I want your liver and lights on a stick."

Banning's mind was racing. What to say? What to ask her next? What could he say that would boost the truth from her, without making her suspicious?

He didn't have to decide now any more than he had to a few moments earlier, however, for he suddenly became very aware that something hard and round and cold was poking straight into the small of his back.

"Angel," a voice from behind Banning said softly, even as the barrel of a pistol dug more firmly against his spine, "go inside now. I'll be happy to entertain our guest."

"Enby?" Angel's hands flew to her mouth as she

backed away a few steps, and he could imagine her eyes growing wider as she cudgeled her brain to remember everything she had said. "But then who . . . why . . . *Leslie!* Oh, how could you be such a sneak?"

"Leslie?" Enby repeated as Banning nodded and then quickly averted his head. "Angel, I thought I told you to get rid of this bounder. What in blazes is the matter with Daventry, anyway? He should know better than to allow you to within ten feet of Ramsden. And how did he know to be here tonight? Unless you told him? Angel, Angel, Angel," Enby lamented, sighing. "He talked to you, didn't he? You looked at him with those great golden eyes and the world's greatest rake bared his soul of every secret, so that you thought him harmless. You will pick up strays, won't you, love, never thinking you also end up with their fleas?"

"Never mind that now," Prudence retorted, belatedly drawing her dressing gown closer to her body. "I have to talk to you. Leslie, close your ears, or I'll cut them off next time I see you."

"Talk? Oh, I think not, love. Not now, at any rate, while we have such an interested audience, even if you still trust him," Enby told her, and Banning closed his eyes, deciding whether or not the man holding a pistol at his back would dare shoot him, with Prudence watching. He didn't think so. He could probably wheel about and grab the pistol, and have Enby on the ground in a heartbeat.

But he couldn't take the chance. Not if he wanted to keep his identity a secret from Prudence, who would never forgive him for spying on her, not trusting her.

"Why don't we meet again, tomorrow morning?" Enby suggested even as Banning gave up any notion of defending himself and prepared himself for a blistering headache. He only hoped Enby wouldn't stick around to examine his work, pulling back his hood to see that he had struck down not Viscount Ramsden, but the world's greatest idiot, the Marquess of Daventry. "You remember where. Now, go inside. I'll handle things from here."

"Enby? You aren't thinking about doing anything stupid, are you? Because I won't stand for it, you know. I really won't."

"Ah, hear that, Ramsden?" Enby said, chuckling low in his throat. "The little love is worried for you, or else she wouldn't even ask her beloved Enby such a silly question. I'm just going to *talk* to the man, Angel, that's all. Now, will you get the blazes out of here?"

So Enby wanted to "talk," did he? Good. At least the fellow was some sort of a gentleman. Banning, too, wanted Prudence out of the way so that he and the man could "talk," and a good fistfight was definitely preferable to being conked on the head with a pistol butt.

"Females!" Banning bit out gruffly as he spoke into the fabric of his hood in order to help mask his voice, dropping his pose as the mysterious, sickly Enby, and taking on that of the ne'er-do-well rake, Ramsden. "Pretty," he mumbled, "but thick as posts."

"Oh, is that right, Leslie? Well, to the devil with the both of you then!" Prudence exclaimed, turning on her heels and heading for the rear gate leading to the kitchen entrance of Number 96 Park Lane. "Go ahead, beat each other into flinders for all I care, if that's what you want, for I have too much on my mind now to worry about either of you. Just remember your mama, Leslie. No duels!"

Banning waited, as did Enby, for the sound of the kitchen door slamming shut—for Banning knew that Prudence wouldn't bother tiptoeing about when she was in a temper, and Enby must have known it too. He could feel his muscles tensing as he lifted his weight to the balls of his feet, ready to round on Enby and throw him down, getting answers to his questions once and for all, if he had to break the fellow's nose in the process.

The only thing Banning hadn't counted on was the fact that Enby wasn't about to play the proper English gentleman and fight fairly, obviously worrying more about having his identity revealed than he did any code of honor. Before Banning was able to move, he felt the impact of a pistol barrel against the back of his head, saw a flash of lightning behind his eyes, and dropped to his hands and knees in the alleyway, the sound of Enby's rapidly retreating footsteps the last sound he heard for several minutes.

When he awoke from his enforced slumber, he dragged himself back to Chesterfield Street—cursing himself for a fool with every painful step—and to Rexford, who spent the next hour alternately fussing over the nasty lump on his master's head, put there by the "horrible footpads" who had struck him down, and lamenting the loss of his lordship's cloak and nankeen trousers, which had been ruined through their contact with the dew-damp stones in the alleyway.

"Wake me no later than eight, Rexford," Banning said as he eased himself against the pillows. "It's important. Promise me, Rexford."

"I most certainly will not promise anything of the kind, my lord!" his loyal valet returned hotly, so that

Banning opened his mouth to repeat the order but fell asleep before he could say another word.

Banning's headache only got worse when he awoke at noon to hear Rexford pronounce heatedly, "I hereby resign from your employ, my lord! And may I say, sir, that you are without doubt the most block-headed gentleman in existence! I expect a reference, of course." With that, Rexford threw the morning paper in his former master's face before stomping out of the bedchamber, slamming the door behind him.

Fighting off his muzziness, Banning reached for the newspaper, attempting to focus his still slightly bleary eyes on the article Rexford had so graciously marked in a thick, angry circle of black ink:

The Honorable Frederick Broughton and his wife, of Broughton Hall, Surrey, and Grosvenor Square, are pleased to announce the betrothal of their daughter, Althea Grace, to Banning Talbot, Ninth Marquess of Daven—

"Bloody hell!" Banning shouted, flinging the newspaper to the floor even as he jumped from the bed. *"Bloody damn hell!"* he bellowed even louder when he looked at the mantel clock and saw the time. *"Rexford!"*

He was in Park Lane within the hour, his hair still damp, his cravat doing no credit to his once-again faithful valet, only to have his face slapped by his beloved sister, who then threw herself on his neck, crying, "She's gone, Banning. Angel's gone!"

BOOK THREE

COMMUNION

Man, proud man,
Drest in a little brief authority,
Most ignorant of what he's most assur'd,
His glass essence, like an angry ape,
Plays such fantastic tricks before high heaven,
As make the angels weep.

William Shakespeare

CHAPTER 19

Ay me! for aught that ever I could read,
Could ever hear by tale or history,
The course of true love never did run smooth.

William Shakespeare

Prudence sat inside the public coach, shrunk all in on herself, her straw hat jammed down tightly over her pinned up hair, her breeches smeared with grease from the meat pie she'd eaten half of, then stuck in her pocket to save for her dinner, her face set in a furious frown meant to keep the other five passengers from attempting to broach a conversation with her.

The old woman to her left was snoring as she rocked side to side with the movement of the coach, a single shining droplet of spittle hanging from the whiskers on her chin. To Prudence's right was another female, this one thin and haggard and probably suffering from the pox, for she had the look of a prostitute fallen on hard times.

Across from her, on the facing seat, were three out-at-the-cuffs fellows of indeterminate age and stunned-ox expressions, one of them digging a finger inside his nostrils, and then his ears, in search for truth, no doubt; the other two engaged in an animated debate over the merits of the fighters involved in the mill they were traveling to Epsom to see—and none of the three, in Prudence's opinion, would be missed if they were to disappear from the earth in the next five seconds.

Men! There wasn't a single one of them ever born worth a moment's thought, a moment's tears. Vile! Despicable! Two-faced, lying, arrogant, grasping, selfish, perfidious, ungrateful—and those were their good points!

Take, take, take!

What right did they have to be the takers, leaving women to be the givers, the ones who gave their loyalty, their kindness, their trust, their *love,* only to have it all thrown back in their faces when the men walked away?

Enby. Always doing what was "best" for her. Best for *him,* was more like it.

Leslie. Unburdening himself of his troubles, treating her as his friend, his equal, his confidante, and then butting in his aristocratic nose where it had no business being, probably in a typical male belief that women were incapable of handling their own decisions, solving their own problems without masculine interference.

And then there was Banning, the worst of the lot. He was beyond two-faced, for he lied even to himself, caught between behaving like the marquess he was and enjoying himself like the man he wanted to believe he could be—if only it weren't for the fact that he was the bloody marquess. Banning, the man, had fallen in love—or at least he'd said he'd fallen in

278

love—but Banning the marquess had chosen duty and honor and social consequence and all that rot over what his heart desired.

Well, Prudence was having none of it! She was going home, to MacAfee Farm. Back to yet another man—a man who saw her as no more than a cipher, a burden best ignored and hardly worth clothing or feeding.

Enby loved her, but he wanted something from her and had found her to be too much of a "burden."

Leslie liked her, but he didn't trust her, to the point of not only reading her private correspondence, but then skulking around in the dark, spying on her.

Banning—well, it was best not to think of that particular male "taker" at all.

So she was on her way to Shadwell. At least she knew where she stood with Shadwell.

And in less than three months she could consign all four men—all the useless, stupid men in the entire world—to the devil, and get on with her own life.

"'Ere, now, wipe yer face, ducks," the harlot whispered gruffly, poking Prudence in the ribs. "Yer gots tears big as a nabob's diamonds makin' tracks down yer cheeks. Wouldna want 'em buggers over there ta see yer wuz nothin' but a female. Lord knows how they'd try ta use yer, iffen they knowed."

Oh yes. Prudence was ready for a world without men. If she could only stop crying, that is . . .

Quimby had his hand on the latch when the front door of Number 96 Park Lane was thrown open and a worse-for-wear Earl of Preston exploded into the entrance hall, his cheeks puffing in and out from some recent exertion as he looked left, then right, before exclaiming, "Where's Banning? Montgomery said he was here. Damnit, man! Don't just stand there! Take me to him!"

"The Marquess is in with Lady Wendover, my lord," Quimby replied calmly, stepping forward to relieve Dewey Norton of his hat and cane, nodding understandingly as that gentleman told him not to crush the brim, for it was a new hat and had yet to be worn more than twice, let alone paid for. "Shall I announce you, sirs, or do you think you know the way?"

"He's gone, you know," the earl told Quimby, grabbing the butler's sleeve and giving the man's entire arm a shake. "Done a flit. Nothing left in his lodging at the Spread Eagle but an unpaid bill. Banning's going to think they've run off together, which is what Dewey here thought, but then Dewey's never had a straight thought in his life. You and I know Angel wouldn't do anything so shabby. But Banning's mad as fire that she left at all, and with this trouble with the Broughton muddying the waters, so he ain't thinking with more than half a brain either. What do you think, Quimby? Shall I lie?"

"I believe lying is your second best option, with keeping your voice to a whisper the best one, if you do plan to deceive me," Banning said, having come into the entrance hall in time to hear his friend's question of his sister's butler. "After all, incoherently angered as I am, I might leave my ungrateful ward to her own devices and take the coward's way out by simply marrying Althea or even committing suicide. Come to think of it, they're both much of the same thing, considering Althea's sister."

"Banning!" Marmaduke jiggled in place like a

blancmange, so that Quimby quickly supported the earl in case he should fall. "Deuce take it, man, don't sneak up on me like that. Gave me quite a turn, you know. We're back, as you can see, Dewey and me. But this Enby fellow is gone, left sometime during the night without paying his bill. But you heard that already, didn't you?"

"Duke introduced us as Enby's friend," Dewey told Banning, shaking his head like an old woman lamenting the lack of common sense in the younger generation. "Took me twenty minutes to talk the innkeeper out of taking my watch to settle the tab. M'father gave me this watch, you know. Would have done it for you, Banning, but not for this Enby fellow. As it is, it cost me two quid to get the innkeeper to show us Enby's rooms. Duke's right. They were picked cleaner than a marrow bone. The man's gone, leaving no trace."

Marmaduke nodded vigorously. "You must have scared him off last night, showing up the way you did. You really mucked that one up, didn't you? Even got yourself a good bump on the head for your troubles. But it's not to worry. If he's in the city, we'll find him. I got to talking with Ivy, the barmaid at the Spread Eagle—pretty little thing. She told me what Enby looks like, and even volunteered to go from inn to inn with me until we find him."

Dewey threw up his hands, shaking his head. "Tumble all over our Duke. Women, you understand. Fat ones, skinny ones, old ones, young ones—toothless hags and choice debutantes. Never understand the attraction. Never. So—are we going to stand here all day, or are you going to invite us in for a drink of something stronger than the watered wine at the Spread Eagle? This thief-chasing is thirsty work. Never appreciated Bow Street runners before now, but they don't have it easy. Not easy at all."

Banning waved his friends into the drawing room, where Freddie was lying down, a cool cloth on her forehead, for she had been mightily overset by Prudence's departure. The fact that Miss Prentice had also unexpectedly departed from Park Lane with all her luggage shortly before noon, Freddie had told him, could only be seen as the single ray of sunshine in an otherwise beastly Monday, but as this left his sister without a competent companion other than Quimby, Banning felt reluctant to leave her and get on with his search for Prudence.

"Angel left a note," Banning told his friends as Quimby, without being asked, went to the drinks table and poured four glasses of wine, one of which he allocated to himself before serving the other gentlemen and then, in a highly extraordinary move, sat himself down to become one of the party.

Marmaduke nodded again, looking like a professor giving approval to a student's dissertation. "Yes, yes. That's good. A note is quite customary in cases such as this. What does it say? Are there tear stains on the paper? All the best notes have tear stains. Shows the sensibility and heartache of the writer, you understand. You know, Banning, I keep wondering if I should call you out. I like Angel, truly I do, and I think this is all your fault. I don't know how, but you have the look of a guilty man. Dewey? Don't he look guilty?"

Dewey, who had been sitting forward in his chair, looking curiously at Quimby, who seemed very much at his ease in the drawing room chair, turned his head toward his friend. "Huh? Banning guilty? Oh yes.

Quite. Quite. I say, are there any scones or anything? I'm feeling peckish, having been torn from my breakfast by Banning's urgent summons. Um, Quimby?"

"I'll see to it, Mr. Norton," the butler said, then disappeared for a moment to confer with a footman before returning once more to his seat, and his glass of wine. "Perhaps you would wish to discuss the contents of Miss MacAfee's note with your friends, my lord?" he suggested calmly. "Rexford will arrive shortly with your traveling coach, and then you can be on your way."

Lady Wendover lifted the cloth from her forehead and smiled at her brother. "Yes, Banning, why don't you do that? Quimby will stay with me, turning away any well-wishers who might come to congratulate me on my brother's betrothal. Althea Broughton! Oh, is it any wonder my head feels fair to splitting?" She collapsed onto the cushions once more, removing herself from the conversation.

Banning reached into his pocket, drawing out the note Freddie had pressed in his hand before fainting into his arms. His own head was near to "splitting," the lump behind his ear near to the size of a pigeon's egg, but he still had things to do before he could take off after Prudence, who could not possibly outrun him in a public coach.

"I'll spare you the contents of the blistering note I sent to Althea's father, summarily ordering him to retract his asinine announcement within three days or I'd be forced to humiliate his daughter by buying a full page advertisement in all the papers, declaring the engagement to be at an end. Just allow me to say that it was rather *pithy*, wasn't it, Freddie?"

"You called him an encroaching mushroom, a toad-eating buffoon, and a desperate adventurer bent on ridding himself of a daughter while gaining a fortune, if I remember correctly, sir," Quimby offered quickly, so that Freddie had only to languidly wave one hand in agreement, then turn her face into the pillows. "It was in my opinion a sterling missive, sir, and I only wish I could have been a fly on the wall when Mr. Broughton called his wife and daughter into his study, and onto the carpet, as it were, to explain to him precisely how they had come to put him into such an untenable situation. Sir," Quimby ended, smiling as he lifted his wineglass in salute.

Banning felt himself begin to chuckle, in spite of himself. Quimby—the butler now sitting so familiarly and at his ease in his sister's drawing room—was right. Broughton was a proud man, and having to issue retractions to two betrothals within weeks of each other had to have a very lowering effect on his mood, not to mention his reputation in his clubs.

An early adjournment to Newmarket, that's the route Banning felt sure Broughton would take, hieing his wife and daughter off to the country until the gossip died. But then Althea might balk at leaving London and missing another season. A strange, thick-skinned, determined woman, Althea Broughton. She was also, Banning remembered with a grateful sigh, no longer his concern.

"The note, Banning," Marmaduke reminded him, rising. "I promised Ivy we'd take her up in less than an hour, so we might begin our investigating. Wouldn't do to keep a lady waiting."

"Lady? My God, man, that's a mighty stretch, even for a blockhead like you. Can't see as why I have to come along," Dewey protested, scooping up a handful of scones from the tray a maid had brought into the room and was now offering to each of its occupants in turn. "Not that I'm crying off, you understand. But I do have an appointment with my tailor at three. He made my new waistcoat too snug, although he won't own up to his mistake, going so far as to hint that I've put on some weight, as if that excuse will fadge. Well, he won't see a penny from me until the thing fits right, I can tell you, not one—"

"You're such a goose when it comes to tailors," Marmaduke interrupted.

Banning rubbed at his forehead, wishing his friends in the wilds of Scotland and his coach at the front door, ready to take him to Prudence, whom he owed several dozen apologies before he rang a mighty peal over her head for being so paperskulled as to leave London without even bothering to listen to his perfectly reasonable explanation about the notice in the newspapers.

Unless Enby had seen his face last night, returned to Park Lane to inform Prudence of his discovery, and the two of them had run off together before the newspaper had even been delivered. God knew her note didn't give him any answers as to the reason she had run away.

"Allow me to read to you all while I wait for my coach," Banning said wearily, interrupting the earl and Dewey, who had quickly fallen into a verbal dispute as to the merits of Stultz over Weston when it came to the cut of a waistcoat.

"Oh yes. The note," Marmaduke said, composing his long face into a considering frown. "Proceed, please, Banning. There may be a clue here, hmm?"

"Freddie found it in Angel's bedchamber. Seems

Angel swore the maid, Geranium, to secrecy, then stationed her inside to inform anyone who inquired that her mistress had the headache and couldn't be disturbed. As a result, Prudence was gone for more than three hours before Freddie became suspicious because the door was locked and got Quimby here to bodily break it down."

"Broke it down?" Marmaduke repeated, looking impressed. "And a locked door. Didn't it hurt—putting your shoulder to a locked door?"

"A very effective diversion, pleading a headache. That sounds just like Angel," Dewey slid in before taking another large bite of scone and ending, speaking around a mouthful of the stuff, "well up to snuff when it comes to using her brainbox."

"Yes," Banning agreed wryly. "Angel is rather accomplished in the less than admirable traits of duplicity and the like. Now, for the note." He held it up, although he did not have to look at Prudence's crab-fisted scribbling, for he had already memorized every word. "It is addressed to Freddie," he said, then quoted: "'It is impossible for me to remain in London, so I am returning to MacAfee Farm. Kindly use the enclosed funds to care for Lightning, whom I will send for in two months and sixteen days. I have enough money for the coach, so do not worry. I meant no harm. Angel.'"

Marmaduke, who was pacing the floor, stopped abruptly and sat himself down in the nearest chair. "No harm? What's that supposed to mean, Banning? Angel never harmed anyone, did she?"

"No, Duke, she never did," Banning answered, remembering the way Prudence had looked at him the last time he'd seen her, and remembering how she had told him that any decision concerning their future would be his.

Had she seen the announcement of his "engagement" as written proof of his decision? Or had she left London late Sunday night after that fiasco in the mews, departing on the arm of the mysterious Enby, who had some sort of hold over Prudence?

No matter what the answer—and he would have his answer by nightfall, if he had to shake it out of her and even beat Enby into a jelly in order to get to her—Banning felt certain that Prudence had not left London because she no longer had feelings for him. She had been forced into going, even shamed into returning to MacAfee Farm, because she could not bear facing him again.

Either that, or she hadn't taken the chance of seeing him again because she wouldn't have been able to stay in the same room with him without killing him, he decided, amazed to find himself grinning at the thought that she might love him that much.

The knocker banged, interrupting all conversation in the drawing room, and seconds later Rexford appeared, carrying a thick white document rolled up and tied with a ribbon. "You're all settled now, my lord. Your coach is waiting outside with your fastest horses in the traces, your bags are strapped inside the boot where they will shortly be joined by Miss MacAfee's portmanteau, and David and I wish for you to know that we wish you both happy."

"All right, all right, that's it!" Dewey exclaimed pushing the last of the scones into his mouth in a single bite as he stood up, then wiping his hands together to brush away any crumbs before yanking the paper from the valet's hand. "What's this, Banning?"

he asked, waving the paper in his friend's face. "Is this what I think it is? Because if it is, and you didn't tell us it is—well, it's damned shabby, Banning, damned shabby!"

"It's a special license to marry, Dewey," Banning told him, retrieving the official document he had been waiting for since sending Rexford to the Archbishop with both his entreaty and a generous donation for the Archbishop to "dispose of as you like."

"I've already sent notice of our marriage to the newspapers, for it will be fact by tomorrow morning, if I have to conk Angel on the head and give her responses for her. What do you think, my friends? Will the two notices run side by side? One retraction, one announcement? Save the newspapers for me, please, as I believe they might just be worth preserving in suitably gilt-edged frames."

"Marry?" Marmaduke was once more on his feet, seemingly propelled there by the application of a figurative hot poker to his hindquarters. "You and Angel? Well, if that don't beat the Dutch. Duke, you hear that? Banning's marrying Angel. I think he loves her."

Dewey merely sat down, yawned and crossed his legs, showing himself to be more composed than his friend, or less interested. "You are thick as a post, ain't you, Duke? I figured that one out dog's years ago. So, Banning, what are you standing here for? I'll handle things here, find this Enby fellow if he's to be found. And we'll keep an eye on Freddie here, too, in case you're worried."

"There will be no need for that, Dewey," Lady Wendover said, sitting up very sprightly and looking quite recovered. "Now that I know Angel is to be settled, I am feeling much more the thing. Why, with the lizard gone, I imagine Quimby and I will be just fine. Won't we, Quimby?"

"Exactly, my lady," Quimby said, then rose, bowing to the company before taking himself off to the entrance hall to retrieve Banning's hat and gloves, which he handed to the man once he had performed his farewells and was preparing to quit the house to begin the chase.

"You will take care of her, won't you Quimby?" Banning asked, once more fighting the niggling feeling that he should be paying more attention to his sister and her devoted butler. "I mean no insult—for you were the best of nurses during her illness and have likewise been a great help today—but Freddie is very precious to me."

"Lady Wendover holds a special place in all our hearts, my lord," Quimby answered smoothly, moving to open the door for the marquess. "By my reckoning, Angel will be most likely found in Epsom, where the mail stops for the night. The church of Saint Martin is particularly pleasant, I understand, and will most probably suit your needs admirably. God speed, my lord."

"Quimby," Banning asked, wondering why he should be asking such a question, and asking it now, of all times, "why would a soldier take on the position of butler in a small, female household? Especially a man as well-spoken, well-educated, and full of promise as yourself?"

"To indulge my love of polishing silver, my lord," Quimby answered, bowing, "nothing more. And now, my lord, if you wish to take advantage of the sunlight? . . ."

Banning shook his head, thinking he was beginning to see secrets and intrigue where none existed. "Goodbye, Quimby. I shall be out of the city for several days, I suppose, at which point Angel and I will return and reside in Chesterfield Street. The redoubtable Rexford has promised to transfer Angel's wardrobe there today, except for the gowns and other necessities he has most probably already packed and had placed in my coach. You might as well have Geranium come to Chesterfield Street with Rexford. I'll come by to see Freddie on Friday if not before. I think that's all."

"You've thought of everything, my lord," the butler said, holding open the door for Banning.

No, I haven't, Banning thought, some vague unease tickling at the back of his neck. *But I will. Once I settle this business of corralling my errant Angel, I going to have a small talk with my sister. And then I will have thought of everything.*

Prudence stood in the stable yard of the posting inn, counting out her coins and deciding if it would be worth it to her to ask for a private bedchamber and dining room. It wouldn't. Not that she was about to share a bed with one of the male travelers, which is where she would be put, thanks to her mannish attire.

No, she'd sleep behind the stables, borrowing a horse blanket when no one was looking. It would be safer than the inn and probably cleaner.

And it wasn't as if she planned to hide from Banning, who wouldn't bother looking for her anyway, not if he was busy allowing himself to be tied to Althea Broughton's apron strings. She knew no one was pursuing her, intent on dragging her back to London.

Enby would figure out where she was once she didn't meet him as he had requested—no, ordered—and even if he didn't, he was bound to come to MacAfee Farm in time for her birthday, just so he could watch from a distance as Shadwell choked and sputtered.

The duplicitous Viscount Ramsden was out of the picture, and she couldn't miss him, not after the way he had interrupted her meeting with Enby—although that had turned out to be a lucky interruption, as she had almost asked to be let out of a promise, expose Enby to danger, and all for nothing. Nothing.

Prudence knew she had probably upset Freddie, which was a shame, and she was very sorry for having to hurt the innocent woman. But she would see her again when she retrieved Lightning, and by then Freddie would have happier things on her mind than the memory of her brother's ward's short stay in Park Lane.

So she was back where she had started, alone and waiting, counting down the days until the day she would be free. Her fighting spirit was still intact, if bruised. Her future had not changed. She was still Angel MacAfee, and Angel MacAfee knew how to survive.

There was only one difference.

She no longer owned her own heart.

CHAPTER 20

*Women wear the breeches . . . in a word,
the world turned upside downward.*

Robert Burton

Banning alighted from his coach in the dusty stable yard of the Cross and Battle in Epsom a full hour past sundown, his mind full of the last time he had stayed the night at this particular inn. There were two other inns located in the village, The King's Head and, oddly, The Spread Eagle, but he had been told that the public coach stopped at The Cross and Battle, so he was fairly sure he would find Prudence here.

It had been here, in Epsom, that he had first seen Prudence in a gown—that totally unsuitable pink creation that still had not been able to conceal her unusual beauty. And it had been here that Prudence had joined him in his private dining room, alternately teasing him with her taunts and confusing him with her candor.

There were so many Prudence MacAfee's. The Angel. The devil's own daughter. The holder of other people's secrets. The impeccably behaved society miss. The warm and willing lover. The hurt child with all the misery and all the wisdom of the world visible in the depths of her beautiful golden eyes.

Which Prudence MacAfee would he find this time?

She would be clad in her breeches; that much he already knew, for Freddie had told him that Prudence hadn't taken a single stitch of her new clothing with her. Remembering how convincingly Prudence played the country-rough youth, he imagined she wouldn't bother parting with any of her money to rent a private dining room, although he was sure she possessed sufficient common sense to have gotten herself her own bedchamber for the night.

Not that he believed for a single moment that she would be tucked up in that bedchamber now, her door locked against intruders until she could safely board the public coach again in the morning. No, not Prudence—the most misnamed creature in creation. She was doubtless in the common room, sitting in a dark corner while filling her belly with mutton and ale, secure in her belief that she was invulnerable to discovery. And he didn't know if that knowledge made him angry or proud of the little minx.

Banning, taking a deep breath in order to control the temper that had been building inside him during the hours he had been on the road, pushed open the door to the inn, determined to behave like the gentleman he was when he entered the common room, discovered his errant love, and quietly—discreetly— removed her from danger.

The low-ceilinged room was thick with tobacco smoke and the smells of ale, manure-clogged boots, and honest sweat. Just the sort of place where Prudence would feel safe, he imagined with a sigh, his eyes scanning the crowded tables slowly, as the occupants seated closest to the doorway noticed his presence, and conversations trailed off, elbows were nudged into ribs, and he and his fine London clothes became the center of attention.

He inclined his head slightly, acknowledging that he was indeed the outsider in this particular scene, waved away a curious barmaid, and concentrated his gaze on a table in the far corner, a table crowded with men in the clothes of travelers, not laborers, bent over their cards, mugs of ale at their elbows, and a cloud of blue cigar smoke wreathing their heads.

"Me again," he heard one of the card players exclaim in a familiar, if ridiculously deeply pitched voice, and suddenly all Banning could see was the back of a ragged straw hat and a slim back covered by a bottle-green jacket he recognized at once. "Oi tells yer, boyos, it's a puir pleasure doin' business wit yer all. Barmaid—more ale here! Fleecin' these 'ere sheep is bloody thirsty work."

"I'll kill her," Banning whispered under his breath as he threaded his way between the tables, watching as Prudence tipped back her chair, plopped her booted feet on the table top, and took a deep puff from the cigar she held clamped between her teeth. "I'll damn well *kill* her!"

"Hoo! Look 'ere, mates, we's gots company, an' one o'the quality, no less," one of the men said as Banning pulled himself to a stop just to the left of and behind Prudence. "Care ta try yer luck fer a 'and or two, cove? 'Enry 'ere is havin' the devil's own luck, but yer welcome ta m'seat iffen yer game."

"Wot's that yer say, Jeffy?" Prudence asked, already tipping her chair back further, so that she could look up at the newcomer. "Oi've gots me another pigeon ta pluck? Let's 'ave a look at—"

The cigar nearly dropped from between her teeth thanks to her suddenly slack jaw even as her eyes widened into saucers, and Banning was hard-pressed not to laugh out loud at the sight of her dirty-angel face frozen into shocked surprise.

"Good evening, *Henry*," he said politely, tipping his hat to her. "How utterly delightful to discover you here, and still in one piece, too, although that could only be considered a stroke of dumb luck. Would it be possible for you to step outside with me for a moment? I believe we have some unfinished business?"

He had to say one thing for her—she recovered quickly. Her eyes never leaving his face, she slowly removed the cigar from between her teeth, said, "Take yerself off, bucko. Oi'm not goin' anywheres wit the loiks of yer." She slammed the chair onto all four legs and picked up the cards. "Wants me ta leave the table a winner, does 'e?" she asked the men around the table, winking broadly. "Yer wouldn't take kindly ta that, now would yer, boys?"

There was a general rumbling among the other players, all of them obviously having lost money to Prudence, and Banning knew himself to be friendless, not to mention greatly outnumbered. "Leave the money, Henry," he bit out from between clenched teeth. "I need to talk to you—now."

"The devil I will!" Prudence exclaimed, rounding on him. "I take nothing that isn't mine, but this money is mine. Every last groat of it earned fair and square!"

Banning bent down to whisper directly into her ear. "Careful, Angel, you're losing your low-bred accent. Leave with me now, or I'll pull off that hat and allow these gentlemen to see who they've been losing to. Shall I start counting, as you did to me not so very long ago in this same inn? Ten . . . nine . . . eight . . ."

Prudence sat very still for a moment—only her slim shoulders moving as she took several deep breaths—before lifting her mug, draining it, and then pushing all of her winnings to the center of the table, where it was pounced upon by the other players, who quickly descended into a loud argument over its division.

"Let's go get this over with," Prudence said, pushing back her chair and rising, giving Banning a shove as she brushed past him and toward the door, leaving him to follow after her, admiring the way she swaggered as she long-leggedly wove her way back through the tables with all the assurance of someone who knew who she was and didn't give a hoot in Hades what anyone thought of her. He had never forgotten how alluring she looked in breeches, even if her jacket now covered her to her knees, the memory haunting his dreams. Were all the men in this room blind, not to see what he saw? Or did the eyes of love simply see more clearly?

Behind him, he could hear the scrape and crash of chairs tipped over onto the floor as the card players decided to settle their argument over Prudence's winnings with their fists. Did chaos always follow where Prudence MacAfee led? Banning smiled, already knowing the answer to that question, and feeling oddly proud of her again, for if nothing else, she most certainly could never be called "ordinary."

He caught up to her in the hallway, taking hold of

her elbow and pulling her to a stop. "All hell is breaking loose back there, and I want you out of it. Me, too, come to think of it, as someone is bound to remember that the fight didn't start until the London gentry cove arrived. Now, quickly. Which is your room?" he asked, beginning to lead her toward the stairs.

"Oh no, Banning," she said, shaking her head even as a heavy metal mug flew past both their heads, smashing against the far wall and the noise coming from the common room threatened to drown out her words. "I agreed to talk, but I'm not so to-let-in-the-attic as to put myself in a room with you—even if I had a room, which I don't. I would have, though, if you hadn't made me give away all my winnings. We'll go outside. We'll even talk. And then you can just take yourself back to London, where you belong."

Banning closed the door to the inn just as he saw the innkeeper heading toward the common room, a large wooden club raised over his head. "You don't have a room? Christ on a crutch, Angel, where had you planned to sleep if you didn't win enough money for a room—in the stables? Where are your belongings? And where is Enby?"

"Go to hell, Banning, and look for him there, as he's not with me," she declared flatly, walking to the end of the building and reaching into the bushes, pulling out a large tapestry bag he recognized as the one she had brought with her from MacAfee Farm. "Better yet, go back to the Broughton and let her kiss your money while you make love to her social consequence. You bloody well deserve each other."

At least that question had been answered for him. Prudence had fled London because of the notice in the newspaper, not because of what had happened in the mews behind Park Lane. And she wouldn't have done that if she didn't love him. Love him but not trust him—any more than she had trusted him with the truth about Enby.

He would have taken hold of the tapestry bag, but he was in no mood to descend to a tug-of-war over the thing smack in the middle of the stable yard. Much easier, and worlds quicker, would be to simply toss Prudence up and over his shoulder, shove her stubborn carcass into his coach, and get the both of them out of Epsom.

Only his coach horses were already unhitched and eating their heads off inside the stables, leaving him with nothing else to do but pick Prudence up and put her over his shoulder, wrap both arms around her flailing legs, and chuckle to himself as she pounded her fists against his back and turned the air blue with her curses for the entirety of the time it took for him to carry her into the woods, then none too gently drop her onto the soft ground in a small clearing a good distance from the inn.

Having the wind knocked out of her kept her still long enough for Banning to drop to his knees beside her, place his hands on her shoulders, and press her back against the long grass. Breathing hard from his exertion and his sudden anger, he growled, "You don't trust anyone, do you? It never occurred to you to stay where you belonged, and wait for me to come to you and explain, did it? Oh, no! Not Prudence MacAfee. She only asks for others to trust *her*—never once thinking someone else might be deserving of the same consideration."

"And why should I?" she shot back at him, beginning to struggle beneath his grip. "You promised to come to me this morning but did you? No, you did not. I was up all night, counting the minutes until I saw you, ready to throw my life away, throw Enby's life away, on the chance that you'd understand, that you'd love me. But did you come? Promises, Banning. So many promises you've made. And kept them all—except your promise to me. Now let me up— your knee is in my stomach, and I can't breathe!"

"If I let you up, do you promise not to run away again?" he asked, immediately wincing as he heard what he'd just asked.

"You have my word, Banning," she answered, giving up her struggles, to lie quite still beneath him. "And my word is at least as good as yours."

Seconds later, as he lay sprawled on his back and Prudence was running away from him, deeper into the trees, he cursed himself for not listening more closely to what she had said and realizing that, not believing in his promises, she would not feel bound to holding to her own.

He was back on his feet in an instant, inexplicably picking up her straw hat and leaving his own curly brimmed beaver behind on the ground as he ran after her, following the sounds she made as she crashed through the underbrush in the darkness.

He knew he was close to her when the sounds stopped, when she had ceased her headlong dash into the night and hidden herself somewhere like a cornered fox doing its best to elude the pursuing hounds, out of sight but definitely within earshot.

Not knowing what else to do, and more than a little out of breath, he slipped off his jacket, spread it on the ground, and sat down. "Althea put that damned notice in the newspapers, Angel," he said quietly, knowing she could hear him. "She did it without my knowledge or permission, probably acting on her belief that a two-year-old proposal was still a proposal, even though she'd turned me down flat—a mercy for which I will be eternally grateful. Her father is issuing a retraction. If you don't believe me, I can take you to Freddie, and she can tell you."

He waited, hearing nothing but the sound of crickets, the scurrying of a small nocturnal animal, and the far-off hooting of an owl.

"I overslept this morning, Angel," he continued after a moment, deciding too much truth might not be prudent, at least not until he had her safely married, so that she wouldn't be tempted to shoot him for spying on her. "As excuses go, it's fairly shabby, I admit, but it's the truth. Rexford woke me by flinging the newspaper in my face and tendering his resignation. You have a myriad of extremely loyal friends, Angel, and I had to explain the error to all of them before they forgave me. Freddie hit me, as a matter of fact, and I doubt she's ever raised a hand to flick away a fly. Everyone loves you, Angel. But no one loves you the way I do. Madly. Passionately. With every breath I take, every new blunder I make, I love you."

He closed his eyes for a moment, then concluded, smiling to himself, "Please, Angel, come out where I can see you, as I'm feeling dashed silly sitting here, talking to the darkness. I doubt my behavior befits a man of my sober, dignified station in life."

"You do look fairly ridiculous, Banning," Prudence said from somewhere behind him as she emerged from the bushes and into the faint moonlight. "Your old-man's silver hair and your ramrod-straight posture, all that consequence plunked down in the middle of a forest like a love-charmed character in *A Midsummer-Night's Dream.*"

Banning remained quite still, so as not to frighten her away again, but only recited quietly, " 'Over hill, over dale, thorough bush, thorough brier, over park, over pale, thorough flood, thorough fire, I do wander everywhere, swifter than the moone's sphere; and I serve the fairy queen.' "

" 'My Oberon!' " Prudence said, coming to sit beside him, her smile a benediction." 'What visions I have seen! Methought I was enamored of an ass.' "

He reached out his hand to her, lifting her fingers to his smiling lips, both the Broughton and the false engagement announcement already only distant memories. "You probably were, Angel, for I have been an ass, the greatest in nature, I do believe. And you only know the half of it."

She pressed her fingertips against his mouth, shaking her head. "We both know only the half of it, Banning, so that it's probably better that neither of us apologizes to the other. We know the important half. We love each other. We want to give that love to each other, now, here in this totally outlandish place. For now, for tonight, isn't that enough?"

"It's more than enough, Angel, and entire worlds more than I deserve," he told her, tossing her hat into the bushes as he slipped a hand around her neck, pulling her over him even as he eased himself backwards, onto the night-damp grass. His mouth inches from hers, his gaze warm and wanting, he breathed softly, "A true gentleman wouldn't point this out, Angel, I'm sure, but as I'm practicing not to be such a true and perfect and boringly proper gentleman, I will ask—have you noticed that, no matter how I chase you, it is *you* who ends in seducing me?"

"Yes, I had noticed that, actually," she answered, her smile wide and unashamed, adding in outrageous accents as her hands were busy loosening his neck cloth, "Perishin' forward, ain't Oi, mate?"

"Perishin' forward," he agreed, pushing the bottle-green jacket from her shoulders even as he rolled her back against the sweet-smelling grass, at last giving in completely to the mood and the moment and the promise . . .

She was so small, so perfect, beneath his hands, her already familiar curves a landscape he knew he would never tire of in a thousand lifetimes. She was all the fire of heaven against the smoke of his building passion, his growing hunger, his determination to make her his, for now . . . for tonight . . . forever.

She was his personal angel as she gave herself up to him; his resident devil as she nipped at his ear with her small, sharp teeth; his personal torment and benediction as her untutored yet innocently seductive body was unveiled to him inch by tantalizing inch as he rid her of her ridiculous clothes.

He wanted all of her and she gave to him willingly, trading passion for passion, kiss for kiss, touch for touch. They were children of the night, innocents in their own Eden, exploring, tasting, feeling—their lovemaking as fierce as it was uninhibited, so that Banning had to remind himself of Angel's inexperience, temper his desire with concern for her initial pain.

Which was difficult to do as her small hand found him, and caressed him, touching off fires inside him that could only be quenched once he possessed her completely. He lay beside her, pressed close against her, his mouth on one exquisite breast, his fingers lost within the heat of her, the moist sweetness of her.

He worshiped her nipple with the rough side of his tongue, delighting in her soft moans, her quick breaths. And when he found the very center of her, and she raised her hips to him, opening herself to his every liberty, he had to lift his head and open his eyes in order to center himself, to keep from whirling off into the heavens.

Her body glowed white and gold in the moonlight, pale as sweet cream against the darkness of his own skin. She pressed his head against her ribcage, holding him tightly with both arms, cradling him as he marveled at the sight of his skin against hers. He held his breath even as he concentrated his gaze on the shadowy apex of her thighs, where his fingers were stroking and teasing, bringing her closer, ever closer, to ecstasy.

And then she stilled, her hips raised above the grass, one leg slung over his own bare hip, her other knee bent, her bare foot pressed hard into the ground. She took in a deep, shuddering breath and held it, her entire body rigid, only the sound of her heart beating strong and fast against his ear keeping him from believing she had been somehow rendered into marble.

He knew. He knew because he had brought her to this point once before.

She, too, must remember. She had to know he was going to shatter her now. The secret, intimate touch of his fingers would soon take her past all fear, beyond any shred of thought, and into a place that splintered with every color of the rainbow. The sensations he was bringing her would then drive her on and on and on, until her body took control of her mind, her reason, and the sweet, involuntary throbbing carried her beyond that rainbow and into a separate world.

And then it happened. He could feel her body begin its sweet convulsions, hear the hiss of her breath as she cried out his name, feel the hot, wet heat of her. She was all fire now, and all his, the perfect instrument come alive beneath his fingers, her entire body singing a siren's song of passion and fulfillment.

She would never be more ready for him, but even before he could move to take her she was pressed against him, her nails clawing at his back as she pulled him overtop her, her mouth hungry and eager, her near incoherence moaned against his hot skin, begging him to hold her, hold her tightly, or else she would die, she would simply die.

"Please, Banning . . . now . . . hold me now. You don't take. I was wrong. You don't, you don't. Stop all this giving. Always giving. Take me, Banning. Let me give to you. Oh, please . . . take me now!"

Her sheer abandon inflamed him, and when she put her hands between their two bodies, helping him, he braced his arms against the ground, throwing his head back as he felt himself against her, as his body met and then disposed of one last, slight resistance, so that he was free to plunge fully inside her, lose himself in the heat of her, find himself in her sweet, giving love.

Now it was he who was all sensation, reveling in her touch as she ran her hands over his chest, his shoulders, across his flat stomach, finally pulling him down against her breasts, locking him deep inside her by sliding her legs up and over his hips.

He could no longer tell where his body left off and hers began. His every thrust was met by her singing response; the deeper and faster he drove, the more she clung to him, taking his every new assault, giving back one of her own, until, together, their silent song of love swelled to a rhapsody. They were one, there, in the moonlight, floating above the trees, caught between heaven and earth . . . the angel and the mortal . . . the woman and the man.

In the morning, just after dawn, the rudely awakened but well-recompensed vicar of the church of Saint Martin performed a small ceremony in his private chambers.

The groom, slightly the worse for wear and a happy, if sleepless night, his grin ridiculously boyish, and sporting a slight stubble on his chin, remained blissfully unaware of the grass stains on his jacket.

The bride wore breeches.

CHAPTER 21

*O! the more angel she,
and you the blacker devil.*

William Shakespeare

Prudence snuggled against the soft pillows, a thin sheet her only covering in the comfortably warm room, and made a low, soft sound in her throat; a contented purr followed by a delicious giggle that caused Banning, who was standing in front of the mirror, tying his own cravat, to lift a single eyebrow in amused question.

"Was that an invitation, Angel? I'm more than willing, if possibly not able, not after our recent exertions, pleasurable as they were," he said, turning away from the mirror and seating himself on the edge of the bed located in Epsom's King's Head Inn. "Or have you forgotten this silver hair of mine?"

Prudence sat up, not caring that the sheet fell to her waist, and slipped her arms around her husband's sides, locking her hands over his stomach as she pressed her cheek against his strong back. "Are you trying to say that your bride is insatiable, Banning? That's rather poor-spirited of you, considering the fact that it was *you* who woke me before dawn this morning, insinuating your lascivious self against my innocent person, whispering all those naughty things into my virginal ear. Hmm, that was nice, wasn't it?"

"Nice?" Banning shook his head. "Innocent? *Virginal?* Pardon me, my dear, but have you seen my wife? She was here with me this morning, and for the past two—no, three days. Lovely girl, tasting of sweet cream and honey, and with the sexual appetite of a sailor who hasn't seen port in six months."

Prudence giggled again, even as she lowered one hand to the buttons of Banning's trousers, slipping them free of their moorings one, by one, by one. "No, sir, I haven't seen her. Would that be the same wife who told me the most shocking tale of how her randy husband had interrupted their wedding dinner, right in this room, by throwing her to the floor halfway through the meat course, ravishing her most pleasurably in front of the fire?"

"If you are referring to the woman who was creating an unbearable scene of seduction out of the formerly simple act of sucking on chicken bones as her sadly oppressed husband was forced to watch, then yes, that would be my wife," Banning answered, turning more fully onto the bed as Prudence slipped a hand inside his trousers, to discover to her delight that not only his spirit, but also his firm, warm flesh, was willing.

"No, sorry. Haven't seen her," Prudence told him, abruptly releasing her hold on him and throwing herself back against the pillows once more, pulling the sheet up to her chin. "You can be on your way now, making plans for your return to London. If she was to drop in, however, I'll tell her you were looking for her, if you want."

"If I *want?*" Banning repeated as he stood, taking hold of one bare ankle as he did so, and turning Prudence so that she was lying across the bed, her legs dangling over the edge, the sheet draped across her middle. "Oh, I *want,* all right, madam. I *want* very much."

Prudence looked up at her husband, at this man she loved more than she could have believed it possible to love any one. "And do you *love,* Banning?" she asked as he quickly divested himself of all clothing below his waist and stepped between her legs.

"I more than love, Angel," he said thickly, dropping to his knees, no longer teasing, but quite serious, quite solemn. "I adore. I worship."

"Banning?" His name, coming from her in an awed whisper, became a question, a hope, an answering prayer. She saw the love in his face, felt his passion as it quickly became hers, and melded into theirs.

Each time it was new, each time it was different. Sometimes slow, loving each other for hours and hours. Sometimes fast, urgent. This time . . . explosive. She gave herself up to the moment.

And then he was touching her . . . lifting her legs up and over his shoulders, drawing her closer . . . closer . . . until his mouth was against her . . . his fingers were spreading her . . . his tongue was inside her . . . and she was no longer the tease, no longer laughing, but only reaching down to him, pushing her hands into his thick silver mane, begging him to stop . . . praying he would never stop.

The small explosions she had come to expect, but knew she would never cease to marvel at, came so swiftly this time that she was caught off guard, her teeth clenched with the sweet agony of it, her neck arched back as Banning slid his hands beneath her, raising her more fully against him, his mouth sealed tightly all around her, his tongue a wild instrument of delight, of sweet torture.

Still lost in her reaction, she felt herself being lifted even higher, her legs levered against his shoulders as he stood and then entered her fully, in one swift movement, filling her more completely than she had ever thought possible.

She opened her eyes, looking up at him, seeing the tension in his face, the searing intensity of his gaze. It was hypnotic, watching him, and she was clearly able to gauge the climb of his passion, each thrust of his strong body matched by another slight flicker of his narrowed eyelids, another acceleration of his already rapid, shallow breathing.

She wanted all of him, all that she could take, all that he could give. Deliberately, she allowed her body to go slack, her legs held in place over his shoulders only by his strong arms, her fingers no longer digging into the mattress, but lying limp at her sides.

And all that time, as he took, and she gave, her eyes never left his, their love as unspoken as their passion, yet echoing loudly in the quiet room.

She was his vessel, and he filled her. Her body was his, and he took it . . . rocking her with his deep thrusts . . . moving into her faster and faster and faster . . . until at last . . . his head thrown back, his eyelids squeezed tightly closed, he gave himself over to sensation, calling out, "My Angel. Angel! Oh, sweet Christ—*Angel!*"

As the day slipped into evening, and Prudence lay curled against her sleeping husband, she gave way to silent tears. She had kept him with her for another day, safely away from London, safely away from the truth. Like Scheherazade, she was buying herself time, doing all that she could to delay the inevitable, and perhaps save herself from the almost certain disaster that awaited her back in the city.

And if the worst happened, at least she would have her memories, and perhaps, if the gods were kind, even a child to comfort her through all the dark, endless days she would be left to stumble through alone when Banning turned away from her in disgust.

As the coach rolled over the London cobblestones, Banning cradled the sleeping Prudence close against his shoulder, listening to the soft sounds of her breathing, cherishing these last few moments alone before they were once more thrust into the season and the loving, but for the moment, intrusive company of their friends.

They were coming home. Back to London. Back to reality. Back to Enby. Back to the secrets she wasn't going to tell him, the truths she was still too frightened to share, even now that they were married, and as intimate as two people could be.

She was still such a child, for all of her passion, all her astonishingly effective womanly wiles. And he had allowed her to divert him with her teasing seductions, drawing him close each time he tried to broach the subject she would do anything to avoid, luring him into her arms each time he so much as mentioned their return to London.

Allowed her? No, that wasn't true. He had aided and abetted her, more than willing to be caught up in her charms, just as greedily stealing another moment in Paradise as she was transparent in her desire to keep him safe in their own personal Eden.

But now was the time for truth, if they were ever to be truly at ease with each other. Passion such as they had shared could never die, but Banning had lived long enough to know that passion, even love, was not enough. Not enough for a lifetime. There had to be truth and trust and an end to secrets.

And knowing this, knowing that it was time that he, older and more mature, sat Prudence down and demanded the truth from her, he had still allowed himself to be talked into first stopping in Park Lane to visit his sister, thus delaying the inevitable for another few, precious hours of deliberate ignorance.

The coach halted, and Banning heard the driver jump down from the box even as Prudence awoke from her nap, smiling up at him as she stretched like a cat, saying, "Hello, darling, have I been ignoring you? Back at Freddie's already? Good, as I'm starving. Do you think she will have the fatted calf ready for us?"

Banning kissed the tip of her nose, then helped straighten her bonnet as the coachman opened the door and let down the steps. "As she probably isn't expecting us, we'll most likely have to make do with whatever is in the kitchens. Have I mentioned that it's not fashionable to have the appetite of a horse? I can see how keeping you fed is going to be a mighty drain on my fortune."

"Excuse me, your lordship," the coachman said as Banning alit from the coach, then turned to assist Prudence to the ground. "There's lights inside, all right, but the knocker's gone from the door. Do yer suppose somethin's wrong?"

Banning and Prudence exchanged quick, anxious looks, before he took her hand and the two of them fairly raced up the short flight of steps to the door. "Quimby?" Banning called out as he knocked loudly, suddenly afraid that his sister had taken ill once more and the butler had removed the knocker to keep away unwanted visitors.

Why had he left her behind to clean up after him, fending off questions about his short "engagement" to Althea Broughton and his bound-to-be-surprising marriage to his ward? He knew she had a delicate constitution, knew she had barely begun to go back into society—even with Prudence living in her house —preferring to remain in Park Lane, reading her novels and taking naps each day. Dear God, if anything had happened to her! "Quimby!"

"Banning, don't upset yourself for no reason," Prudence told him, squeezing his hand. "There could be a perfectly reasonable explanation for—"

The door was opened wide by a footman who quickly stepped back as Dewey Norton came forward, saying, "Not like you to bellow, Banning. Come in, come in. May I be one of the first to congratulate you and kiss the new Marchioness? Hullo, Angel."

"Dewey, how good to see you," Prudence said as she stepped into the entrance hall, lifting her cheek for his kiss. "And Duke? Is he here as well?"

Dewey shook his head. "Got him stationed in Chesterfield Street, in case you went there first. Took your sweet time coming home, didn't you, Banning? But you're here now, aren't you? Hungry? Freddie's cook is excellent. Excellent! Served me a brisket tonight that would make you weep. Sometimes there's fat on a brisket, you know. Stringy. Tastes well enough, but hard to swallow, so that you're sitting at table, smiling and nodding at everyone as you chew and chew and chew, wondering how you're ever going to be able to swallow the damn thing without—"

"Where is Freddie?" Banning asked as the footman walked off with their hats and cloaks, knowing Dewey could go on for a full ten minutes, describing every piece of tough meat he had ever been so unfortunate as to encounter. "Why is the knocker off the door? Why are you here? Why is Duke waiting for us at my house?"

Dewey looked to Prudence and rolled his eyes. "I imagine you can kiss that brisket goodbye, Angel, if Banning here is going to play the Grand Inquisitor. Sorry." He turned to Banning, who felt near to strangling the man. "Freddie's fine, probably better than you at the moment; she just ain't here, Banning, to answer one of your questions. May we get ourselves comfortable in the drawing room, old friend, before I tell you the rest of it, or would you rather set up the rack and thumbscrews right here in the entrance hall?"

Banning felt his tensed muscles begin to relax. Freddie wasn't here, but she was all right. He allowed himself to be led into the drawing room, sitting on one of the couches, Prudence close beside him, still holding his hand but not saying anything, which wasn't at all like her, he thought distractedly before glaring at Dewey, who was strutting back and forth across the carpet, full of self importance because he knew something his friends did not know.

"Banning," Dewey began at last, stopping his infernal pacing and turning toward the couch, his hands clasped behind his back as he began what Banning feared might be a lengthy presentation.

"There comes a time in every man's life," Dewey began, his first words telling Banning that he had been right to expect a long-winded speech, "when he has to bow to events. Readjust his thinking, as it were. Realize that what may seem, from the outside, to be a horrendous breach of the rules of society you have so recently and boringly clasped to your bosom, may be in fact, in this one particular case, a true miracle of serendipity, a coming together of lives, of hopes, of dreams not normally believed to be compatible, a curious but mutually beneficial blending of—"

Banning leapt to his feet. "Where's Quimby? At least I'll get a straight answer from him!"

Dewey winced, scratching at his balding head. "Quimby? Well, now, Banning, that's part of what I'm trying to tell you. This ain't easy, you know, and I've never done it before, even though I've been rehearsing what I'd say for days now, ever since coming here to report on another matter and finding . . . well, Duke and I found it, actually. Between us, we figured the best thing to do was to install ourselves here and in Chesterfield Street, so as we could cushion the shock a little, keep you from flying off into the treetops, as it were, maybe stop you from . . ."

His voice trailed off and he waved his right hand about in small circles, as if trying to physically "whip up" the correct words to explain what he meant, before pronouncing sternly, his eyes narrowed, "You know, Banning, come to think of it, you've been a prodigious lot of trouble to Duke and me lately."

"Really?" Banning answered, as Prudence began to giggle. "In what way?"

Dewey, nodding his head over and over, as if agreeing with something he was saying to himself, sat down in the chair across from the couch, slid an arm along the back of the chair, and crossed his legs—taking up the slightly superior, moderately condescending posture of one who was about to expound on a private theory. "Where do I begin?" he asked, sighing in a long-suffering way. "Where, oh where, do I begin?"

"Pick the transgression of your choice, Dewey, and get on with it!" Banning exploded, which only served to double the giggles emanating from his unsympathetic wife.

"Very well, Banning. No need to get your fur up," Dewey said, uncrossing his legs and sitting forward, his elbows on his knees. "First of all, you left Duke and me in the lurch when you decided being a marquess was like taking some Methodist pledge of sobriety, becoming the dullest stick in nature and making us feel like the most reprehensible of rackety infants for being happy while the whole world rested on your shoulders."

"Well, that's true enough, Banning," Prudence told him, patting his forearm. "You are extremely offputting when you're being sober and responsible and so terribly grown-up. Not to me, of course, as I could always see your heart wasn't really in it. Go on, please, Dewey. What else has my husband done to you?"

"He got married, of course," Dewey said in the accents of one stating the obvious. "Just when it seemed we had the old Banning back, he upped and bracketed himself, leaving Duke to ponder whether he should do the same. Even m'mother is holding Banning up to me, saying it's time I showed the same good sense and settled down. Lowering, that's what it is. Lowering."

Banning chuckled softly, allowing himself to be amused, even if he still hadn't learned the whereabouts of his sister. "You asked, Angel, remember? If my friends are crushed, you are a large part of the reason. Don't you think you should apologize to Dewey here?"

"Yes! That's the ticket. That's what I want. An apology! Pulling Duke and me back into intrigues even before Ramsden brought you Angel's note, and chasing about hunting up secrets, having the best of good fun—just to go and marry, and probably already planning on setting up your nursery, and retiring to your estates, and . . . and mucking stables or some such folly."

"Hunting up secrets? And Ramsden as well?" Prudence turned to Banning, who suddenly wished he had shut Dewey up when he'd had the chance. "What's our friend talking about, Banning?"

"Why, Enby, of course," Dewey supplied quickly, and Banning pressed his fist against his mouth, knowing he was in deep trouble. "Banning had us hanging around here all the day long last Sunday, watching for your maid to take a note to the man, which she never did, and then he wouldn't even let us come along when he visited the mews at midnight, to trip up the fellow. He showed you the lump on his head, didn't he, where that Enby fellow clipped him with his pistol?"

The silence in the drawing room was deep and long,

seeming years longer than the few seconds it took for Dewey to clear his throat nervously and ask, "Banning did tell you about all that, didn't he, Angel? I mean, you're married now, so everything's all right. Settled, as it were?"

Banning could feel the heat emanating from Prudence even as her slim body turned to rigid ice beside him. "Oh, yes, of course, Dewey," she said brightly. "Banning and I laughed and laughed at the silliness of it all. Leslie, dear Leslie, wishing the course of love to run true, brought my note to Banning, who read it before it was delivered to Enby, so that they ended up meeting in the mews. Served him right, getting that lump on his head, don't you think? Banning?" she inquired sweetly, turning her head toward him stiffly, while the rest of her body held taut as a bow string, immobile on the couch. "Why don't you tell Dewey how we laughed and laughed?"

"Another time, love," Banning told her quietly, knowing that when that time came, he was going to have to take his punishment like a man, because he should have immediately confessed what he'd done, and not held back the truth, hoping for the right moment, a decidedly more private moment, when all their secrets could be revealed. "Dewey, as I imagine that my final insult to your loyal friendship has something to do with my sister, do you suppose you could tell me where she is now, so that Angel and I can breathe easier?"

"Freddie and Robert have eloped, you stupid ass!" Prudence exclaimed, rising from the couch and glaring down at him angrily. "They probably left for Gretna Green the moment you took off after me, hot to marry me, figuring that if you bedded me you could hide your duplicity. They're gone, Banning. Freddie and Robert—both gone! They've been in love for months and months, not that Freddie dared to tell you about it, not with the way you were playing the starchy, dreary marquess. She probably thought you had turned human once more, telling her you were going to marry me, and took her chance when she saw it. How thick can you be, Banning, if you can't see what's right in front of your eyes?"

She rounded on Dewey, her fists clenched at her sides. "And you! Pretending to be my friend, when all you were doing was helping *him!* Sneaking around behind my back, spying on me because Banning told you to, watching my every move, knowing about Enby—or so you all thought—when none of you knows the smallest thing about him, or me, for that matter. I've seen alley cats with more loyalty. Now, give over Freddie's note, as I'm sure there is one, and let us get on with it!"

She was crying, huge tears chasing one another down her cheeks, tears she impatiently swiped away with the backs of her hands, so that Banning felt helpless and guilty and, yes, *stupid.* More stupid, and bumbling, and blind, than an elephant caught in a maze on a moonless midnight. "Robert?" was all he could say. "Quimby's name is Robert?"

"No, it's Ignatius," Prudence spit out sarcastically as Dewey, never one to insinuate himself in a situation that was proving sticky, removed the requested note from his pocket, placed it on a table, and tiptoed out of the room, probably on his way to Chesterfield Street to remove Duke from danger as well. "Of course his name is Robert! Or did you think your sister has run off with the local rat catcher?"

She snatched up the note, reading it quickly, then held it out to Banning, a small, watery smile momentarily lighting her features. "And he did it just as he told me he'd dreamed he would. Look—Freddie still didn't know everything when she wrote this, although he's probably told her by now. Some secrets are good, Banning—not like ours!"

Banning took the note, reading quickly: "'Dearest Brother, forgive me, but Robert and I are in love and have been for ever so long. Seeing you as you were today, so anxious for Angel, I knew you would understand. We fly now to Gretna—so irresistible a notion for such an aged and fragile widow who at last has found her true happiness!—and then to a place Robert refuses to name. Between us, Brother, we will set all London on its ear with our romantic exploits! Be happy for me, darling Banning, as I am happy for you and Angel. Freddie."

He looked to his angry wife, who refused to meet his eyes. "My sister has run off with her butler," he said, unable to understand how he could feel like laughing in the midst of all that had just gone wrong between Prudence and himself. "Well, good for her!"

Prudence's head snapped round as she looked at him in obvious surprise. "You're not livid? You aren't embarrassed by what she did? You aren't going to throw things and shout and blame me for not telling you, even though both Robert and Freddie swore me to secrecy? It isn't my fault that they confided in me, you know. I—I have this *trusting* face."

"A feature that I, obviously, lack," Banning said, balling the note in his fist and tossing it in the general direction of the fireplace. "However, if you could overlook that shortcoming for just a moment, perhaps you will tell me what Freddie doesn't know—or didn't know when she threw her cap over the windmill and headed for Gretna?"

Prudence wet her lips, eying him suspiciously, as if expecting him to lose his rein on his temper, then shrugged. "Very well, as it's too late to do anything about it now anyway, even if you are only pretending to be happy for Freddie. Robert told me all about it one night, when his wound pained him and he was drinking fairly deep to ease the hurt."

"And you shared a glass or two with him, I imagine, and listened to him ramble," Banning inserted, surprised at how difficult it was becoming to be surprised by anything his wife did.

"One or two," she admitted, playing with the strings on her gown. "Robert was on his way home from the war when he stopped here, to offer his condolences on Freddie's loss—the earl had been his immediate superior, you understand—and then promptly passed out on her doorstep, as he was far from recovered from his own wounds. Freddie, being Freddie, had him hauled into the house, to stay until he was recovered . . ."

"At which point Freddie became ill, and remained so for months," Banning added, already knowing that part of the story. "Quimby—I mean, Robert— volunteered himself as butler and nurse, for which I will be forever grateful. And they fell in love?"

Prudence nodded. "Robert did. Freddie, bless her, was too weak to be anything but grateful, at the time. The love grew slowly, long past the point where Robert felt comfortable in telling her more about himself than she already knew. He wanted her to love him for himself, or some such masculine drivel." Her smile was genuine as she ended, "And she did, she does. Isn't that wonderful?"

"Perceive me as overjoyed," Banning said, still somewhat lost. "So, what is Robert's great revelation? Will Freddie be pleased?"

She shrugged again, telling him without words that such things were not really important to her, no matter how much they mattered to people who, in her opinion, cared entirely too much about all the wrong things. "Nothing too earthshaking. Robert is the second son of Baron James Quimby, whose holdings are in Scotland, I think. Robert was the black sheep, and probably still is, so that he ran away and enlisted in the army. He was a very good soldier and finally bought himself a colonelship, just before he was injured. I knew at once that he was a gentleman's son. Didn't you?"

Banning took her arm and led her into the entrance hall, where a rather nervous-looking footman was already waiting. "First you learn about Rexford and his David, and now Freddie and her devoted butler. I really must learn to pay more attention to those around me, mustn't I?"

"As must I," Prudence replied tightly, avoiding his hand as he attempted to take her arm. "For instance, I had believed Leslie to be my friend, yet he ran straight to you with my note, didn't he? I was right in assuming that, wasn't I?"

"Enby wasn't at the Spread Eagle, Angel," Banning explained as they reentered the coach, Prudence taking up her seat across from him, directly in the middle of the seat, wordlessly telling him not to so much as attempt to sit beside her. "Leslie felt one of us should be in the mews, in case Enby didn't return in time to come to you. We couldn't be comfortable with the notion that you'd be alone out there at midnight. That's all."

He could see her nod her head in the darkness. "Oh yes, I can well imagine. With the number of bears and wolves and fire-breathing dragons one can be confronted by in Mayfair, not ten steps from her own back door, I'm only amazed that you didn't bring the earl and Dewey along as well—perhaps even an entire regiment of concerned souls, all out to protect me. Oh, cut line, Banning! This fish won't bite!"

"She won't trust, either, will she, Angel?" Banning asked quietly. "For all my bungling, I've somehow won your love—your heart and your body—although you're hating me mightily at the moment, aren't you? And yet I still haven't earned your trust. I love you, Angel, and if I've made mistakes it is because of that love. I love you enough to forgive—and forget—any secret you and this Enby might have. Please, Angel, let's get this behind us and get on with our lives."

"I want to, Banning," she said, her voice small in the darkness. "I really do, but it's not—"

"But it's not your secret to tell," he ended for her wearily, wanting to do as she had said he might do earlier—shout and throw something. "In the meantime, Angel, until you find this Enby and gain his permission to tell his secret—much as it pains me to say this—I believe we should separate, making it easier for Enby to contact you. I will see you settled in Chesterfield Street and then return to Park Lane, tonight, and for however long it takes you to settle the matter and tell me the truth."

"Is—is that what you really want, Banning?" she

asked, and he could hear the tears in her voice, replacing her earlier anger.

"No, damn it! It's not what I really want! But that's the way it has to be. I cannot live with a woman who can't trust me with a few home truths," he told her as the coach halted in Chesterfield Street.

He kicked open the door himself and pushed out the steps, not trusting himself to take her hand as she exited the coach. "Go inside now, where your maid is waiting," he bit out rapidly, before he looked into those maddening, appealing eyes and lost his resolve. "Tell Rexford, who is doubtless hanging over the bannister awaiting us, that he can come to Park Lane in the morning. I'll give you another day, Angel, and no more. Twenty-four hours. Then you will have forced me to find this Enby myself, at which time we will both have to deal with the consequences."

"Are we fighting, Banning? Because I can't—won't —tell you Enby's secret?" Prudence asked, avoiding his gaze. "Are you threatening me?"

"Call it what you will, Angel," Banning countered, staring at the top of her head. "I would have liked to think you now trust me sufficiently to confide in me, but you don't. I just know we can't go on this way much longer."

"Very well. I think I know how to contact Enby, if he is in London at all. But don't hold me to a single day and night, Banning. That isn't fair, no matter how angry you are at the moment."

"Twenty-four hours, Angel," he repeated, doggedly sticking to his spur-of-the-moment ultimatum.

"Will—will you kiss me before you leave?"

"I don't think that would be wise," he said softly,

hating himself, but unable to relent, or else he would never be able to walk away from her.

She looked up at him for a long time, as if memorizing a face she believed she would never see again, then left him, without another word, and ran inside the house.

CHAPTER 22

One was never married, and that's his hell;
another is, and that's his plague.

Robert Burton

The sun shone down brightly, too brightly for eyes that were still sore from weeping half the night, as Prudence and Geranium entered the Park on foot, the former dressed all in palest apricot, a matching, twirling, lace-edged parasol over her shoulder, looking quite fetching, but doing nothing to keep the sunlight at bay as she put on a determined smiling face, the latter walking a careful two steps behind and constantly complaining that her new shoes were "playing the devil with m'corns."

The Park was the last place Prudence wanted to be—and she would have much preferred to be back in Chesterfield Street, hiding her sorry self beneath the covers—but if Enby was to find her, and come to her within the time limit Banning had so arrogantly demanded, she had no choice but to make herself conspicuous.

And conspicuous she was! Newly married, most mysteriously married, the ward who had snagged her own wealthy, titled guardian—who himself had just been released from a one-day wonder of an engagement to the Broughton—she knew herself to be the cynosure of all eyes and the subject of all the whispers taking place behind the raised hands of other pedestrians, the reason for the occasional titters and amazed gasps of those passing by her in their carriages.

She fought down the urge to cross her eyes and poke out her tongue at Lady Jersey as that woman's horse-like laugh followed close after she had straightened her head, that had been bent close to her companion as they exchanged, none too discreetly, hushed comments concerning gentlemen who had to number their fiancees in order to be sure they wed the correct one.

Prudence felt herself to be as abandoned and friendless as poor Lord Byron must be feeling now that his Annabella had deserted him, his reputation hanging in shreds, and all of London falling over itself in its haste to turn its collective back on him.

And it was all Banning's fault, of course. He should be at her side, loving and attentive, introducing her to everyone as his "dear bride," and not leaving her on her own, so that she had no choice but to put a brave face on things and expose herself to gossip as she paraded herself around the Park, laying a trail for Enby to follow back to Chesterfield Street.

Not that she could blame Banning too much. She was keeping a secret from him, a secret concerning a man, of all things. As it was, she should be marveling at her husband's restraint, for she certainly owed him the truth. If she had told him sooner, he might even have been able to avert that messy business with the Broughton, her own flight into the country, and their new estrangement of last night.

But then there would have been no interlude in the woods of Epsom, no silly, romantic, dawn wedding, no unforgettable four days at the King's Head—for Banning would have, upon learning the truth, sworn off women forever and personally delivered her larcenous body back to Shadwell, wiping his hands of his guardianship before setting off to sea, or somewhere, any place where women were not allowed to be.

Which he could still do, if Prudence didn't believe that he loved her. And loving her, he was most probably doomed to a life of unhappiness and frustration, knowing that his perfidious wife had come into that life on false pretenses, bearing a guilt that should have kept her from so much as dreaming of his love.

"Good morning, my lady. Lady Angel—sounds almost heavenly, don't it?"

Prudence stiffened at the sound of Viscount Ramsden's silky, amused voice. She turned around slowly, moving her eyes in his direction first, before her head followed along, so that her withering stare was the first thing he would see. "Go throw yourself down a well, why don't you, you bloody traitor," she bit out tersely, wondering if it would amuse Lady Jersey if she were to repeatedly brain the viscount with her lovely parasol.

Ramsden grinned, showing his even white teeth as he fell into step beside her and they continued down the path. "Ah, so Daventry spilled the soup, did he? I thought he had a better head for intrigue than that. Pity, as I imagine I've blotted my copybook badly in your eyes, no matter that you and the leaky marquess are bracketed now. Where is the happy groom, may I ask?"

"Somewhere. Anywhere. Unwilling to be seen with

me—unlike you, who wouldn't know enough to go away if I suddenly stripped myself naked and broke into song. Haven't you noticed that I am being shunned?"

Ramsden nodded. "The Broughton is bruiting it about that you lured Daventry into a tawdry compromise, and he had no choice but to marry you. Naturally, for nothing is more fickle than the mentality of this herd we call the *ton,* all sympathy is with your husband and the Broughton, and you are this week's pariah, nearly on a par with our own Lord Byron. But not to worry. I heard some of the ladies are planning a party of sorts at Almack's next week, inviting poor George to attend, in hopes he can be brought back into good odor. Perhaps you might allow me to host a ball for you, for much the same reason?"

Prudence felt the corners of her mouth lift in reluctant amusement. "Oh yes. Yes, indeed. That ought to set me back in society's good graces. The deserted marchioness, guest of honor at the rake's ball. I imagine Banning and I both would then be in debt to you for all our lives."

"Point taken, Angel," the viscount said, pulling a cheroot from his pocket and sticking it, unlit, in the corner of his mouth. "So, is Enby watching us from the bushes, do you think?"

"What!"

"Enby," Ramsden repeated, taking her elbow as she had stopped dead on the path and had to be reminded to keep moving or else draw even more attention to herself. "Banning as well, I'd imagine, as only a dolt wouldn't realize that you wouldn't be within a mile of such a public place if you weren't trying to attract your mysterious correspondent's attention. You've a good mind, Angel, but lack experience in clandestine matters. Yes, it wouldn't surprise me a bit if this Enby fellow and your devoted but very worried husband bumped into each other in the bushes."

Prudence could feel the beginnings of what would doubtless prove to be a crushing headache building behind her eyes. "Banning gave me another day to locate Enby and gain his permission to tell his secret," she said wearily, "so I doubt that he is here, skulking in the bushes or otherwise, for he has learned his lesson on that head. I suppose you know I have a secret?"

"I know that you have a problem, little puss," the viscount told her as, without asking her permission, he stopped for a moment to put a flame to his cheroot. "I've been remembering our discussion of a few days ago, and your remarks about family and loyalty and the like. What is it? Is there a horse-thieving MacAfee hiding out in your family tree? A highwayman? A murderer? Someone you love, perhaps even support, but whose exposure might mean a cell—or a noose?"

Prudence shook her head. "No, nothing that simple, Leslie. Banning would forgive me a horse-thief or a murderer. This is worse. Much worse."

"Worse than a murderer? Well, I'm stumped!" Ramsden took a deep puff of his cheroot, blowing out a cloud of blue smoke just as Lady Hempstead and her mousy-looking maid walked by, heading in the opposite direction. Lady Hempstead avoided Prudence's gaze, pausing only long enough to cough as she was enveloped in the smoke and then give the viscount a sharp rap on the forearm with her reticule. "Ow!" he exclaimed as her ladyship lifted her chin and walked on. "Bloody fat sow," he whispered under his breath, looking thoroughly shocked, so that Prudence laughed out loud.

"So, Leslie, now that I've forgiven you, for I have, you know," she said, deliberately meeting the eyes of the next society matron to pass by them on the path and refusing to look away, "tell me about Beatrice. I've yet to learn her entire name, let alone know if I will be invited to the nuptials."

The viscount's handsome face darkened. "It doesn't matter what her name is, Angel, for she won't have me. I'm ramshackle, you know, and hardly steady. I have, to quote the lady, a 'certain reputation.' "

"You mean the one of knowing half the matrons in London by the moles on parts of their anatomy only their maids and husbands have seen?" Prudence asked, sensing that the viscount was not quite so brokenhearted as he would have her wish to believe.

His boyish grin proved her right. "Heard that, did you? It's a lie, you know. I know less than a quarter of our *ton* matrons, um, by sight. I'm a rake, but I'm a particular rake. It has always been quality and not quantity that appealed to me. But now that I am back in my family's good graces—with all thanks to you—I shall be even more particular, and even deliberate, in my choosing of a bride. Next time, I shall go for one with a brain, as well as melting blue eyes."

"But quiet and well-mannered and free of hoydenish ways," Prudence pronounced solemnly. "You can't have a hoyden, Leslie, or none of London will be safe. That is why Banning and I suit so well. We balance each other out, with just enough excitement in him and barely enough refinement in me to keep us both happy." Her smile slid away from her face. "Or at least that's how it would be, if I could only flush out Enby, so that I could talk to him."

"So you believe this Enby—this worse than a murderer—will be willing to allow you to expose his secret to Banning? And Banning will forgive you for whatever part you play in that secret?"

"Not at once, and possibly not for a long time, but yes, eventually I think he'll forgive me. If I didn't believe in at least the hope of that happening, Leslie," she answered honestly, "I would lay down right here on this path, curl myself up into a very small ball, and wait to die. Oh God!" she exclaimed, lowering her head so that the brim of her straw bonnet hid her face. "Quickly, Leslie—in that open carriage—is that the Broughton coming this way?"

"The Broughton? Why, I do believe it is," the viscount remarked, sounding amused as he stepped forward to shield her from view of the carriage path. "And there is a woman riding in the facing seat, a woman with a faintly familiar, if scrawny back. Wait, as they drive past. Yes, yes, it is. It's your lizard, Angel. Now what do you suppose dear Althea is doing with your lizard?"

Honoria Prentice riding with the Broughton? Honoria Prentice, who had been to MacAfee Farm, had seen Shadwell MacAfee, and could amuse the *ton* for months on the stories of Prudence's bizarre background? Make Banning a laughingstock with her tales of Shadwell's eccentricities and Prudence's uncouth behavior?

Prudence had never been able—or particularly eager—to bring the lizard round her thumb. It was enough to keep the vicious, mean-spirited woman beneath that thumb. She had an enemy in Honoria Prentice, an enemy who held the power to hurt her, even beyond the current gossip over her marriage, which would have been no more than a nine days' wonder once some other piece of gossip had come along to supplant it. But not now. Not with Banning living in Park Lane, and with Honoria Prentice hissing her little bits of bile into Althea Broughton's ear.

Damn Banning for not being with her, for playing the hurt husband, the proud gentleman, and staying away until she was ready to come to him with Enby's secret tied up in a bow for his edification!

Prudence's headache was now very real. "Walk me home to Chesterfield Street, please, Leslie," she said quietly, knowing that Enby, if he was indeed in the Park, would follow at a safe distance, so that he knew where to find her. "Unlike Lord Byron, who may be silly enough to lay his neck on society's chopping block, I believe I shall prudently hide myself away and continue my fight another day."

"She could hurt you?" the viscount asked, peering back over his shoulder at the carriage that was now stopped beside that of Lady Jersey's. "Shouldn't you tell Banning? After all, puss, you are married to the man."

Her laugh sounded hollow, even to her own ears. "Yes, Leslie, we're married, but we're not speaking at the moment, remember? Of course, if we had been speaking before we got married we wouldn't have gotten married at all, but as that's neither here nor there, and if I talk about it any more I'll probably start crying again, and since I refuse to cry any more, we'll simply drop the subject, won't we?"

* * *

"I win again, sir," Rexford announced smugly, laying down his cards one by one on the table before scooping his winnings toward him. "Knowing that your mind is otherwise occupied, your lordship, might I be so bold as to suggest we discontinue playing? I do not wish for you to think that I am taking unfair advantage."

Banning sat back in his chair, stretching his arms high over his head as he looked at his valet. "I've seen the bills your David has sent for my wife's new wardrobe. Unfair advantage does not begin to cover what, between the two of you, you have taken from me." He turned his head, looking at the pianoforte. "You don't play, do you? Pity. It's somber as a tomb in here, and the mantel clock is ticking louder and slower than a death knell. I knew Park Lane to be quiet, with the houses sitting back from the street, but this is beyond quiet; it's oppressive."

Rexford gathered up the cards, placing them in the drawer fashioned for that purpose, and began neatly piling up the chips in their wooden holder. "You could be in Chesterfield Street, with her ladyship, if you were to unbend a little, and I doubt that any place in which her ladyship resides could be quiet for long. That's ten quid you owe me, your lordship."

Banning looked up at the valet, shaking his head. "When did I lose control of our association, Rexford, do you know? Can you place a finger upon the precise moment you began believing that you had the right to counsel me, the authority to meddle in my affairs?"

"It was at the moment you began bungling those affairs, of course, my lord," Rexford replied calmly. "After all, as I may have mentioned previously, I do have my reputation to consider. Now, if you'll excuse me, I believe you might have a visitor, and I do have some ironing awaiting me. I've sent a footman round to Chesterfield Street for my pressing irons, as Lady Wendover's stock is sadly inadequate. The ruffle iron —ah! Good only for propping open a door."

"Don't allow me to detain you, Rexford," Banning said wryly, picking up the glass of claret he had been nursing for the past half hour and turning toward the door of the music room, hoping his visitor had news for him. This sitting and waiting, having made the totally brainless demand that Prudence bring him news of her "secret" within twenty-four hours, was beginning to wear on his nerves.

Pride and marriage. Marriage and pride. The two simply did not go together, and if he had learned anything in the past night and half a day, he had learned that particular lesson very well.

And if Prudence had no answers for him by tonight? What would he do then? Would he really search the man out on his own—against Angel's wishes? Having run out of ideas, he felt sadly in need of a common-sense solution—although crawling back to his wife over broken glass seemed one viable option.

"There you are, Banning! Never thought to see so much of you, or to want so badly to bash some sense into your head. You almost make me look brilliant, simply by comparison. I'll pour myself a drink, if you don't mind, and then we can discuss Angel, and how much you're hurting her."

Banning stood up then watched as Viscount Ramsden, always too handsome for Banning's liking and never known for his reticence, pulled the stopper out of the crystal decanter and filled a glass, swiftly draining half of it before filling it again.

"You've been to Chesterfield Street?" Banning asked.

"Just came from there, as a matter of fact, delivering your wife, who I found braving the *ton* gossips in the Park," Ramsden said, seating himself in the most comfortable chair in the room, crossing his legs at the knee as he smiled up at Banning. "Shabby, old fellow, leaving her to fend for herself like that, an innocent goldfish, forced to swim among the sharks."

"The Park?" Banning ran a hand through his hair, a mental image of the gauntlet Prudence must have run that morning forcing him to close his eyes. "Christ, Leslie, what in blue blazes was she doing in the Park?"

"Allowing this Enby fellow to see her and then follow her back to Chesterfield Street, of course," Ramsden answered calmly. "I thought you'd have picked up on that and been hiding in the bushes, hoping to discover the bounder. Oh, and by the bye—I don't appreciate you telling Angel that I ran hotfoot to you with the contents of her note. She's my friend, you know."

"I know," Banning said, sitting down, and feeling several levels lower than weary. "It's a pity she's not mine—or at least we're not friends enough for her to trust me."

"Yes, well, that's between the two of you, and I harbor no qualms that you won't work it out, one way or another. However, besotted and blind as you are, may I—in a clumsy attempt to be a friend to both of you—extend to you some of my own thoughts in the matter, gained both by experience and observation?"

Banning spread his hands wide, momentarily giving himself over to silliness. "Be my guest, Leslie, please. You see before you a man who has somehow found himself placed in the position of taking husbandly hints from his valet—a valet thoroughly in love with his wife's dressmaker, whose name is David, in case you're in the least curious—so accepting marital advice from a self-confessed rake shouldn't be too much of a stretch of my former, and fairly happily abandoned, code of behavior."

Leslie laughed, clearly liking the feeling of acting as mentor to a man so thoroughly in love he could see no farther than the tip of his nose. "Angel and I talked all the way back to Chesterfield Street, so I believe I am now quite conversant with all aspects of your dilemma. In other words, Banning, old fellow—I am aware of what a clod you have been, no matter how well-intentioned you believed yourself to be, although the dawn marriage was a nice touch, if shadowed by your behavior last night."

"Angel says we're *fighting,* although I don't agree. Shall I go over to the fireplace and hand you the poker, so that you can beat me soundly about the head and shoulders," Banning asked sourly, "or are you about done telling me what an ass I am?"

"I'm done—I think," the viscount answered, shrugging. "Now to get down to cases, and with the gloves off, all right? Angel has a secret—only it is not *her* secret, but hers and this fellow's, this Enby. A secret worse than murder, if we can believe her, and I for one don't. Women are so prone to melodrama. Strange name, Enby, don't you think? Anyway, she is under pressure from you to deliver this secret to you by tonight—the twenty-four hours you so graciously allowed her before storming here to Park Lane to perform a mightily disgusting impression of a bear with a sore paw."

"So, you weren't quite done insulting me after all, were you, Leslie?" Banning remarked, surprised that he wasn't feeling insulted, but only curious as to what else the viscount might say.

"Sorry. I'll try to control myself," the viscount said, smiling. "Now to continue. This ultimatum you delivered, obviously without considering what it would mean to Angel, sent her to the Park this morning, where she was dealt the cut direct by anyone the Broughton—thanks to the lizard, who is now in her employ—could fill with tales of your dear bride's rather, um, *varied* background. I myself was hard-pressed not to take off my gloves and slap silly one young buck who was bending my ear with stories of Shadwell MacAfee and his dirt baths."

"The lizard," Banning repeated, sighing. "She hates Angel. How did she handle it?"

"Better than most, I'd say," Ramsden told him. "But she can't be left alone much longer without everyone and his great aunt Harriet knowing that the two of you are living in separate domiciles—and my felicitations to Freddie and her baron's son, by the way; at least one of you knows how to marry without scandal. Go home, Banning. Forget your fight with Angel. Forget this Enby. Forget there ever was a secret. Take your bride into the country for a few months, until the furor can die down, and make babies. That's my advice."

"Advice? Leslie's giving advice? Pity I missed it," Dewey Norton exclaimed, for once leading the way into a room, as the Earl of Preston brought up the rear, reaching behind him as he walked, doing his best to adjust his new, too-tight breeches. "We found him, Banning. Found Enby."

Banning's heart stilled for a moment then began to pound hard in his chest. "Where?"

Duke stepped in front of his friend, pushing the shorter man behind him. "It's my story, if you please, and I'll tell it."

Viscount Ramsden very pointedly cleared his throat, looking at Banning, who sighed, then held up a hand to stop Duke from speaking.

"I don't want to hear it, Duke," Banning said, knowing it was a lie, but unable to go behind Prudence's back yet again. "Enby is Angel's secret, and I'll wait for her to come to me. I won't like it, but I'll do it."

"What!" Duke shook himself all over, throwing back his shoulders and then vigorously rubbing at his nose, as if he had just run into an invisible door. "Dewey—did you hear that? He don't want to know. Has us chasing our tails all over London—and there's many a place in this city a sane man doesn't go unless he's trying to help a bosom chum, let me tell you— and now he *doesn't want to know?* Well, that's gratitude, I tell you!"

Dewey tipped his head to one side, looking at Banning intensely, from head to foot and back to his head again, as if to measure him for a new suit of clothes. "You know what it is, Duke?" he then asked, nodding his head in the manner of a sage about to utter something profound. "Banning's a married man now. Married men are different. Apply to my father, if you don't believe me. Says he's done things, apologized for things, bought a ton of expensive presents to make up for things—things he'd never even known he'd done wrong. A wife will whirl your brains around inside your head, turn you inside-out like a sack, spin you about in circles—until you're so dizzy you don't know what's trumps. It's a curse that comes with the ceremony. Remember that, my friends, next time you start thinking of getting yourself bracketed."

The earl, faintly bug-eyed, looked to each of the other men in the room in turn, so that Dewey nodded yet again, Leslie winked, and Banning—who wished them all to the devil so he could go to Prudence—shrugged apologetically. He then blurted out: "He went back to the Spread Eagle—probably figuring it was the last place we'd look. Paid his bill and moved Ivy into his room this morning. Room Three, right back where he'd started. There!" he ended, puffing out his chest and lifting his chin. "Do what you want, Banning—I wash my hands of the whole tawdry business!"

In the silence that followed Duke's pronouncement, Rexford entered the music room, walked up to Banning, and whispered to him that his bags were once more packed and in the coach, ready for an immediate return to Chesterfield Street.

Without another word, Banning quit the room, leaving behind three men who rapidly fell into a heated argument, all three of them on the side of remaining permanently, blissfully, single.

CHAPTER 23

*Do not ask for what you will wish
you had not got.*

Lucius Annaeus Seneca

Banning's Chesterfield Street house was lovely, its
rooms light and airy, its furnishings a mix of cherry
woods and comfortable, overstuffed couches a man
could sit in without feeling he was in danger of
splintering a centuries-old antique.

It was a male residence, with softening touches
most probably put there by Lady Wendover, whose
love for blue was shown in many of the accent pieces
in the large drawing room Prudence sat in now,
unable to appreciate anything save that she was a new
bride, in her husband's house—in *their* house—and
she was alone.

She had dined alone in the smaller dining room last
night, had slept alone in the master bedchamber, and
had choked down a solitary breakfast in the morning
room only a few hours ago. She was surrounded by
everything she had ever dreamed of, ever wanted, and
she could appreciate none of it. Would have traded it
all gladly for another moment with Banning in the

stand of trees behind the Cross and Battle Inn in Epsom.

Her bonnet sat beside her on the couch, her parasol lay on the carpet—in pieces—after Prudence had vented her spleen over Enby's note by whacking the thing against the fireplace bricks until its ivory sticks splintered.

She had wanted to hear from Enby, and she had— his note telling her exactly what she didn't want to know. He had refused her permission to tell Banning the truth—flatly, baldly, and with not a single apology. He had congratulated her on her marriage, asked for money, reminded her of her coming birthday, and sworn her yet again to secrecy concerning him.

She hadn't had to contact him first, hadn't needed to send him the desperate, pleading note she had carried with her to the Park then carried home again, for his own note had been waiting for her upon her return to Chesterfield Street, brought there only the good Lord knew how—not that Prudence cared.

He hadn't even told her where he was. It had been left to Viscount Ramsden to inform her as to where he wasn't—and he was no longer at the Spread Eagle, according to that man, who had checked there only two days previously.

Enby didn't trust her anymore. He hadn't said that, but she knew. He would contact her from now on, and meet her at MacAfee Farm on her birthday—not that he'd given her a single hint as to how she was supposed to slip away from Banning long enough to travel into the country so that Enby could laugh in Shadwell's face.

She wasn't ever going to see Enby again after that

long anticipated day finally came and went, even if he hadn't told her so. She couldn't. It was too dangerous. The secret had to be kept, not just from Banning, but from the world. She'd known that all along, deep inside her heart she had both known it and feared it, but she had wanted everything to be different. She had wanted a happy ending, a reasonable solution—a miracle.

But there were no miracles for her. Not after what Enby had done, what she had allowed him to do, helped him to do.

For the blame wasn't all Enby's, much as she'd like to blame him for everything, angry as she knew herself to be at him this moment. She had held the power to, if not stop this madness, at least refuse to become such a willing participant in it.

But Banning had been so insistent, and then they had buried Molly in Shadwell's pit, so that he'd be even more impossible to live with, and already she'd heard the news that Shadwell had been keeping her allowance from her. And *then* there had been the promise of gowns instead of breeches, and a season in London to take the place of another spring spent watching weeds grow in the Shadwell Farm fields, and ample food on the table for every meal, and a roof over her head that didn't leak each time there was even a faint mist in the air.

Was what she had done so very bad? So completely unforgivable? After all, she hadn't known she would fall in love, that Banning would return that love, and that a plan begun with such levity, such a sense of having tweaked Shadwell's nose while making her own life more comfortable, could end so badly, become so very complicated.

America. That's where Enby would go, and she'd never see him again. That's where they had planned to settle, after traveling together and seeing all the capitals of the world—spitting in the Seine, seeing a living, breathing Cossack, and drinking wine in Paris.

But now he would go alone, as he had been alone, and she would stay in London, loving her husband, who would have to spend his life knowing there was one, unforgivable secret between them.

"I won't accept that!" Prudence exclaimed aloud in the empty room, balling her small hands into fists and pounding them on her knees. "Either I'll have them both or I'll have neither of them. There has to be a way to make this all right. There has to be!"

So saying, and with her eyes dry, Prudence stood, gave the ruined parasol a kick, and went off upstairs to take a bath. She always did her best thinking in the tub.

Banning, with the memory of Dewey's father's marital experience as his guide, returned to Chesterfield Street after directing his coachman to make a slight detour to Bond Street and the shop of a jeweler he had done business with in the past, purchasing pearls for his sister, and diamonds for one or two young fillies he'd had occasion to stable and ride during his salad days.

His guilty, expensive purchase neatly boxed and beribboned, and carried in his hand (in case he had to wave the peace offering inside the room before he'd be allowed admittance to Prudence's presence), he entered his own house with the nervousness of a first-time visitor, and inquired as to the whereabouts of his lady wife.

He ascended the gently curving staircase to the second floor as soundlessly as possible, for the house was unusually quiet for the middle of the day, and lifted one eyebrow a fraction as he saw a pair of footmen leaving his bedchamber with empty water pails in their hands.

Had his Angel attempted to burn down the house, angered enough by his desertion to set fire to what was to be their marital bed? Banning didn't think so, but what he did think served to put a rather wide smile on his face.

He waited outside the door for several minutes, deciding just how to approach his wife, when Geranium, her fiery red hair topped by a ridiculously large mobcap, exited through the dressing room door behind him and pronounced with the faintly haughty air of one whose mistress has just been elevated to a higher social status and now thinks better of herself as well, "My lady mistress is takin' herself a bath, and wants ta be left alone. Yer lordship," she ended, belatedly bobbing a curtsy to the man she may have just remembered was now also her employer.

"Thank you, Geranium," Banning said, lifting his hand so that the maid could see the package. "I think I can handle things from here."

"Cried all night, yer know, fair ta break a person's heart. Then got herself all but spit on in the Park." Geranium eyed the package. "Wot's in it, yer lordship, iffen I can be so bold as ta ask?"

"A topaz the size of a robin's egg," Banning told her, already anticipating how the stone, on its thin, golden chain, would look once nestled between Prudence's breasts. "Surrounded by diamonds. And with earrings that match its design, of course, and a bracelet I'd prefer to see making its home around a certain slim ankle. Now, will that buy me a few hours alone with my wife, or am I going to have to raise your quarterly wages?"

The maid curtsied again, her face as red as her hair, lifted her skirts high above her own beefy ankles, and ran off down the hallway, never looking back, as Banning, considering his options, turned toward the door to his dressing room, and slipped inside.

Once the door was locked behind him, and with the door to his bedchamber only slightly ajar, so that he could move about unnoticed if he could just be quiet about the thing, he hastily stripped out of his clothing —every last stitch of his clothing—and slipped into his dressing gown before picking up the jeweler's box once more.

After all, it was his tub his wife was bathing in, and it was a particularly large tub, certainly large enough for two, if the people in it pressed themselves very close together . . .

Nervous as a bridegroom, repentant as the worst sinner facing Saint Peter, and—he realized, grinning —randy as a billy goat, he headed for the chamber where his wife, his bride, his love, reclined in his own deep tub, beside a small, warming fire, her back to him, her body shrouded in bubbles up to her adorable, determined chin.

She was oblivious to his presence; her eyes closed, her head lying against the raised back edge of the tub, a small towel folded beneath her neck, her soft, honey-colored curls upswept and tied with a soft yellow bow. Her bubble-flecked, silkily wet arms were raised above the water, resting on either side of the tub, her exposed skin glowing faintly golden in the light from the fire and the candles someone had lit, even though it was still the middle of the day.

She was beautiful in her repose, her image reflected back to him at varying angles from the half dozen mirrors in the room, her stillness so unusual in the woman who never seemed to be still. Even in her sleep, she was always moving, snuggling against him like a kitten seeking warmth, her hand moving over his bare chest in a rhythmic, stroking motion, her legs always finding new ways to insinuate themselves between his.

Awake, she was perpetually animated; making comic faces, employing her hands as well as her mouth to make her point when speaking, using those marvelous golden-brown eyes of hers to entice, to implore, to tease, to anger, to incite, to seduce, and—when she cried—to break his heart.

She was so many things, so many different women, and all of them the woman he loved.

Even with her secret.

He would have her painted this way, in all her serene, womanly loveliness, if he wouldn't have to shoot the artist once the painting was done—for no one would ever see his wife this way save him.

Banning didn't know how long he stood there, silently watching his wife, but at last the spell was broken when Prudence lifted one hand to scratch at her face, leaving a trail of bubbles from cheekbone to chin before allowing her arm to drop to the tub brim once more, and inspiring her husband to action.

He walked across the room, his stealthy footfalls effectively smothered by the deep carpet, and approached the tub from the rear, going down on his knees on the stone hearth before reaching forward and lightly tickling the soft, heat-flushed skin of her cheek.

Her response mimicked her earlier one, and she reached up her hand to rub away the tickle, only to encounter the jeweler's box Banning slid into her hand.

Prudence's eyes opened wide and she looked up at the beribboned box in surprise, then twisted her head around to look at Banning, who knew he was grinning like a particularly vacant-faced village idiot who'd just won first prize at a village idiot's fair. "What's this, Banning?" she asked, poking the box backwards, nearly jabbing him in the eye with the thing.

"It's a present, my love," he told her, inhaling the perfume rising from the mountain of bubbles, a perfume that was so uniquely Prudence's and which was beginning to play havoc with his senses. "A peace offering, a token of my devotion, an apology for my behavior—a bribe. Anything you want it to be, just as long as you forgive me."

She looked at him for a long time, at him, and then to the unopened box, that once again rested in his hand, before—totally without warning, and to his complete and utter astonishment—he felt himself being brained with a very large, very wet sponge.

"You idiot!" Prudence exclaimed angrily, hitting him again, even as he squeezed his lids tightly shut, his eyes closed against the bubbles that had made them burn and sting. "Is this all you think of me? That I can be bought? That I would love you any more if you hung a bloody raft of diamonds around my neck?"

Banning came halfway to his feet, reached out blindly, taking hold of the sponge and tossing it aside before grabbing Prudence's forearm. This proved to be the second wrong move he had made in the course of half a day, for she immediately tried to wrest herself free, ending in pulling him headfirst into the tub with her—which was where he had wanted to be in the first place, only not quite in that way.

The impact of his body upon the water served to overflow the tub onto the floor, so that he slipped on the bubbles as he attempted to right himself, at last removing his upper trunk from the water, only to land ignominiously on his rump beside the tub.

He was covered in bubbles: bubbles in his hair, bubbles on his dripping wet dressing gown, small iridescent stalactites of bubbles growing down from his ears, his eyebrows, his nose, so that he shook himself like a spaniel coming out of a stream.

"Oh, Banning!" Prudence protested, laughing as she held up her hands, shielding herself from the spraying water and bubbles. "Stop! Stop! Oh Lord, but you look ridiculous!"

He heard her laughter and reacted to the softening of her mood. "Ridiculous, is it?" he exclaimed, rising to his feet and peeling away the sopping dressing gown. "First I'm an idiot and now I'm ridiculous. Is that any way for a loving wife to talk about her husband?"

"It is if he's a ridiculous idiot," she said, her eyes widening as he stepped into the tub, then lowered himself into the water. "And just what do you think you're doing now? I didn't give you permission to join me in my bath."

He wiped his face clear of the last of the clinging bubbles, saying, "Oh, so the marchioness has not given her permission? Well, that's just too bad, darling, for the marquess is about to exercise his husbandly rights, and the devil with asking your permission."

Prudence looked at him, looked down at the rapidly disappearing bubbles, and then grinned—an unholy grin, the sort of grin Prudence MacAfee of MacAfee Farm might have given before she locked the door on Shadwell MacAfee as he was caught in the rain—and then moved so that most of her upper body became exposed above the water.

"Coo, ducks, but yer a rare treat, ain't yer?" she teased, trailing her crossed arms down over her shoulders before cupping and lifting her slickly wet breasts in her hands. Breasts faintly pink from the warmth of the water, now appeared softly golden in the light from the fire, the glow of the candles. She ran the tip of a single finger over each of her nipples, so that they grew hard and tight even as he watched. "But Oi'm jist a simple country miss, what ain't never bin tumbled, an' don't ken wot ta do."

"You're as simple as a Gordian knot, you little minx," Banning said, his throat tight, his mouth suddenly dry, his body growing taut and hard and very, very ready. "And I'm going to delight in untying you."

He reached for her, only to have her slap his hand away. "No, no, your lordship," she warned, now the stern mistress, wagging a finger in his face. "It's my turn now, you see. A gift for a gift." She raised herself to her knees, bending over to retrieve the box that had fallen to the floor, forgotten, her movements sending even more water sloshing onto the carpet. "Let's see what you brought me first, shall we?"

She pulled on one end of the ribbons, slowly, so that

the bow took a long time to disappear into a single thread of ribbon, a ribbon she then draped around his neck, holding it at both ends with her free hand as she brought him close for her kiss—a kiss she broke off with yet another playful laugh as she pushed him away.

"I'll have my revenge, you know," Banning said thickly, watching as she opened the box. "Not that I'm not enjoying your little game."

"Oh, it gets better, darling. You want to buy me? I'm only trying my best to give you good value for your money," Angel told him as she lifted the necklace from its velvet bed and slipped the long chain over her head, so that the large topaz slid low, resting between her breasts, just as he had imagined it would. A moment later, the earbobs were in her ears, swinging tantalizing close to the clean sweep of her chin as she softly shook her head from side to side, delighting in the sensation.

"I saw that as belonging on your ankle," Banning, finding it difficult to swallow, told her thickly as she went to fasten the bracelet around her wrist.

"Really? Oh, Banning, I knew you had a world of adventure in you, once you loosened up sufficiently to let it see the light of day. Here, you do it." She leaned back and lifted her leg out of the water, pointing her toe as he reached for the bracelet, then fastened it around her ankle, pressing a single kiss to her damp flesh before the leg disappeared once more beneath the bubbles.

"Now what, Angel?" Banning asked, grinning as he succumbed completely to her game. "And I use that word loosely, for you are a very strange *angel*. Or do you think I've been punished enough? Personally, considering that I've been quite incorrigible and stubborn and even thickheaded, I believe I deserve the full measure of your retribution. *Please,"* he added, winking.

Angel was sitting back at her ease once more, her face screwed up almost comically in her concentration. "Hush, Banning, I'm thinking. I'm new to all this, you understand, and it's damned difficult playing the seductress when you're yapping in my ear. Now, where was I?"

"Well on your way to driving me crazy, if I might be allowed to speak," Banning offered, reaching below the water and giving her ankle a quick tug, so that she slid down the slippery wall of the tub, the top of her head disappearing under the surface of the water for a moment before she shot up, spluttering, and launched herself at him.

An hour later, the carpet around the tub soaked through to the floorboards, and the satin bedspread lying damp and discarded in front of the fireplace, Banning lay on the bed, feeling Prudence's warm, even breaths against his chest as she snuggled close, completely and—he thought rather smugly— *blissfully* asleep.

Nothing had been settled, not really. Enby's role in his wife's life was still a puzzle. Prudence's secret— Enby's secret—had yet to be discussed.

He should probably wake her in a few minutes, tell her he knew where Enby was, and the two of them could go to the man together; together find a way to work out the single remaining bar to their complete happiness. Because Prudence wasn't entirely happy.

He had seen the shadows in her eyes in the rare moments she sat quietly, and he needed to have those shadows removed.

Only the truth would do that; complete truth, total trust.

But just as Banning closed his eyes, putting off the inevitable with the notion that a small nap couldn't come amiss, he felt Prudence's hand begin its rhythmic stroking across his bare chest. He smiled, believing she was still asleep, until her hand moved lower, skimming down across his stomach, and then even lower.

He felt her begin to slide her body down the length of him, until she raised herself to her bent knees, her head bowed low and in line with the top of his thighs; then held his breath as she lifted him with both hands, deftly stroking him into immediate arousal before beginning to tease at him with her tongue, moving that tongue in small, tight circles around him.

Christ, but he had married himself a minx!

Involuntarily, he moaned low in his throat as she covered him fully, mimicking his own gentle assault on her most intimate places, her untutored loving shaking him to his core.

Tomorrow, he thought, carefully levering himself slightly sideways on the bed, so that he could take hold of her leg, gently draw her lower torso up and around, toward the pillows. He kissed her stomach, her hip, then moved her even closer, giving himself over to loving Prudence even while reveling in her mind-numbing, resolve-shattering ministrations. *We'll settle this tomorrow . . .*

CHAPTER 24

Birds of a feather will gather together.

Robert Burton

Banning exited his dressing room, Rexford still trailing behind him with the brush, flicking away invisible hairs and nonexistent strings from the shoulders of his master's midnight blue jacket, only to be waved to a halt by his wife, who raised a finger to her smiling lips and then pointed to Geranium, who was on her hands and knees on the carpet, sopping up water with a large white towel.

"Hoppin' 'round like a coupla bleedin' ducks," the maid was complaining, her country accent thickening in her agitation, and obviously believing she was speaking only for her own benefit, and not for the amusement of her employers. "M'mam woulda had a word or three ta say ta such goin's on, an' that's a fact! An' not a thought as ta who was goin' ta clean up after 'em either. Oh, no—jist bumpin' an' jumpin' an' playin' the beastie with two backs . . . an' thinkin' none o'us could see fer lookin' at all the water drippin' down on that lovely table in the dinin' room . . ."

"Um . . . Geranium?" Prudence interrupted, a

hand raised to her face to hide her smile as the maid raised up on her knees to squeeze the dripping towel over the bucket that sat beside her. "His lordship and I will be going out for a morning drive now, and as I'd hate to disturb you, could you please point me in the direction of the cabinet housing my straw bonnet with the peach-colored ribbons?"

"It be in that one, over there," Geranium answered, employing her bent elbow to point toward a tall satinwood wardrobe in the corner, and never even bothering to turn around as she shook out the towel, threw it onto the carpet, and began blotting at the soggy wool once more. "Got that purty satin thingy hangin' out the window like a bleedin' flag, blowin' dry . . . had ta strip the whole bleedin' bed . . . an' wot they was doin' with every candle in the room marchin' 'round the bed an' burnin' down ta nubs all the night long . . . well, there's jist some thin's a simple lass shouldna ask about, that's all . . ."

Prudence didn't bother putting on her bonnet before pushing Banning back the way he had entered the chamber, past a slack-jawed Rexford and out into the hallway, where the pair of them collapsed against each other, laughing like children caught out in a bit of mischief.

"Now I will have to raise her quarterly wages," Banning said when he had at last recovered from his mirth. "Of course, as I probably will never be able to look the woman in the eye again, it might be better if I just buy her a cottage in Kent and give her an independent income."

"If you're going to do that, darling," Prudence answered, wiping at her eyes before tying the strings of her bonnet at a jaunty angle beneath her left ear, "I suggest you send Rexford with her. I believe he thinks we're debauched. And we are, aren't we? Isn't it delicious?"

Banning bent to kiss the tip of her nose. "Decidedly delicious." He held out his arm and, when she placed her hand on his sleeve, led her to the stairway. "Now, madam wife, I think it is time the Marquess and Marchioness of Daventry introduced themselves to society. Once or twice around the Park, do you think?"

"Oh, twice. Definitely twice," Prudence answered, smiling up at him. "But isn't it rather early to parade ourselves through the Park? If we're going to stare down our noses at the gossips, I would rather have as many of them gathered in the same spot at once as possible. Especially the Broughton and her resident lizard, although dear Miss Prentice is probably otherwise occupied, on the hunt for a new employer."

Banning looked at her inquiringly. "Do I want to hear this, puss?" he asked, believing his wife never looked quite so lovely as when she was pretending a sophistication he knew to be a wonderful, outrageous fraud.

"Probably, Banning, as you're as bad as I am. You only hide it better. Anyway, and I hope you don't mind, but yesterday I enlisted Leslie's assistance in purchasing six dozen bottles of gin, which he had sent round to Grosvenor Square, listing the purchaser as one Miss Honoria Prentice. I doubt the Broughton was amused."

"Remind me to think long and hard before I attempt anything that might put me in your black books, minx," Banning said, chuckling as he handed her up into the open carriage and climbed in after her.

He looked to the driver, who only nodded and then gave the horses the office to be off.

He was taking a terrible chance, and he knew it, but he wanted this Enby business settled once and for all, and he had done with listening to either his friends' advice or his wife's pleas to let her solve her problems without his assistance. They were on their way to Gracechurch Street, and the Spread Eagle, and if Prudence objected he would just have to deal with her anger.

They passed by the Park and the coachman kept on driving, each turn of the wheels bringing them closer to the already visible dome of St. Paul's Cathedral. Enby had told her he could see the dome from his inn window, not an extraordinary feat considering the sheer size of the thing, but Prudence nevertheless began to feel uneasy, sitting beside her husband as he entertained her with an unending stream of information about this part of London she had not previously visited.

"We will be passing by St. Paul's in a few minutes, love," Banning told her as she began twisting her hands together in her lap, wishing she knew how he could be so calm when she knew—she just *knew*—that he was about to destroy her, destroy both of them. "I had to learn its history by rote in my younger years but will spare you a recitation, as I have another destination in mind, one you might recognize by name, if not by sight. The Spread Eagle Inn, just a few blocks away, in Gracechurch Street."

"Don't do this, Banning," Prudence said quietly. "I know it is past time for telling you on my own, but—"

"It's not your secret. Yes, I would find it difficult to

keep repeating that, if I were you," Banning said, slipping an arm around her shoulders and pulling her close to his side. "However, as your husband and a man who would continue to love you if you were to tell me that you and Enby had planned to blow up Parliament, I think it's time I made a few decisions, and you, in your role of meek and loving wife, just stood back and let me have at it."

"Enby's not at the Spread Eagle any more, Banning," Prudence told him, looking straight ahead and refusing to cry or become angry or even to react at all, except with the truth. She was tired of the intrigue, the pretense, the single lie that had grown into a lie as large and as heavy as the dome of St. Paul's. "Leslie told me so yesterday morning."

"And, after I had expressly requested he keep the information to himself, Duke told me yesterday afternoon that Enby is once more installed in his original room."

Prudence turned sideways on the seat, to look up at her husband. "And you knew that yesterday? You knew, and you came to me, rather than running hotfoot to Gracechurch Street and confronting Enby? When you've been near to bursting, wanting to know who he is and why I . . . why I . . . oh, Banning! *Why?*"

Her bottom lip began to quiver as he pulled her close once more, saying, "Because I love you, demented as I am. Ah, here we are, the Spread Eagle. Lovely isn't it, in a ramshackle, once glorious, but now fading sort of way? Shall we?"

"Wait!" Prudence put a restraining hand on his arm as he moved to open the low door to the carriage.

He turned his back toward her, his expression

solemn. "No more waiting, Angel. Let's get this behind us."

"I—I just thought maybe you should know something before we meet Enby," she said quietly, then smiled—a sad, faintly damp smile. "And I thought you might kiss me. Just once."

"First the kiss," he said, so that the groom, who had just hopped down from the rear of the carriage to assist his master, prudently turned his back.

Prudence clung to Banning for long moments, holding him tightly at the shoulders as they kissed, willing him to understand, giving him one last expression of her love for him. "My birthday, Banning," she whispered as he leaned back, his hands still at her waist. "On my birthday, just a few weeks from now, I will be twenty-three, not nineteen. I thought you should know that. Your infant bride isn't quite the infant you believed her to be."

"Twenty—twenty-*three?*" Banning looked puzzled for a moment, then threw back his head and laughed aloud. "That's it? That's your *secret?* No! This Enby is blackmailing you because you were well on your way to being an old maid until I married you? Ready to put on your caps, preparing to lead apes in hell, growing long in the tooth, and kneeling down for your last prayers? That's *it?*"

"I could hit you, you know," Prudence told him tightly, feeling hot color running into her cheeks. "Of course that's not *it*. My advanced age is only a part of the secret. Besides, you ought to be happy to know you haven't snatched a babe from her cradle. That had bothered you, hadn't it?"

"I had considered your age a—but wait a moment!

Henry led me to believe you were a child." Banning lifted his curly brimmed beaver and ran a hand through his hair, obviously in an attempt to remember a long-ago conversation, a conversation held when he was three parts drunk and trying to sober himself for a battle in the morning. "I went to MacAfee Farm expecting to find a child of ten or twelve at the most."

Prudence nodded, sensing that Banning's sharp mind was already racing in the direction she had wished, hoped, it never would. "Henry hadn't thought you'd come and check, I suppose, but only make sure I had an allowance until I passed this next birthday, and not be so dependent on our grandfather's whims," she said, knowing full well that her brother had counted on that fact. Banning had surprised her with his arrival on the scene the day Molly had died, and she had done her best to lie, even to the point of telling him she had been waiting nearly a year for him to arrive, but even in her agitation she had known she couldn't have adjusted her age by more than a few years. It had been the allowance she had missed all those months, not his presence.

Banning replaced his hat, his thoughtful frown still in place. "But I would have eventually learned the truth, Angel," he said, turning around to peer up at the second floor balcony, where the doors to the inn's rented rooms were located. "I will admit that I would have most happily allowed my solicitor to handle everything for a few more years, if it hadn't been that Freddie fancied having a young girl in her household."

"But I wouldn't have been there in a few more years, Banning. I wouldn't have been at MacAfee

Farm if you had held off your visit for another three months. I would have been in Vienna or Paris or maybe even Philadelphia. Enby and I both."

"Ah yes. Enby. We're back to the gentleman in Room Three again, aren't we?" Banning looked angry and sounded even angrier. "I may be only a gray-headed old fool—and a dupe, as well, I'm beginning to believe—but could I suppose that you are to inherit some money on your next birthday, Angel? Money you and this Enby planned to spend in Vienna or Philadelphia or maybe even Paris?"

"Philadelphia last. But yes, you've got it just about right. It's an inheritance from my grandmother. Even she didn't trust Shadwell to care for me if I didn't marry."

"Pardon me my mistake, and I stand corrected on that single point. May I also suppose that Henry, worried about his possible demise in battle, and knowing you were to come into this money—money Shadwell doubtless can't touch—wanted to make the time between Waterloo and your birthday more pleasant for his beloved 'Angel,' courtesy of your carefully chosen guardian?

"He did pick you especially," Prudence agreed, feeling herself dying by inches as Banning looked at her—looked through her. "He wrote me from Brussels, saying you would be a perfect guardian. I—I had no say in the matter. Henry's letter didn't arrive until Waterloo was long over, you understand. Not until a week after I had already read Henry's name on a list of casualties published in the newspaper. I cried for days and days, while Shadwell drank his purges and took his dirt baths and told me Henry had always been a dreamer and wasn't worth my tears."

"I'm sorry, Angel," Banning said, squeezing her hand. "I can imagine how alone you felt, with none but Shadwell to call as relative and your guardian's money nowhere to be found."

"You couldn't have known Shadwell would steal my allowance. I'm just angry with myself—and Enby— for not having thought of that myself."

"No, but I'm not guiltless in this. No matter what, Henry did pick me, singled me out, worked his way close to me, and trapped me the night of the Duchess of Richmond's ball. He got his sister a guardian he considered to be sober and responsible—and unlikely to make a personal visit to MacAfee Farm. Well, at least the man died happy, I suppose. But, as Henry underestimated your grandfather's greed, and you never saw any of the allowance I sent you, you— taking a chance for escape when it landed in your lap—decided to wait out the remainder of the time between my arrival at MacAfee Farm and your birth-day swimming in one of the deepest gravy boats in London. Could a reasonably intelligent man assume all of that?"

Prudence nodded, feeling slightly sick. "A reasona-bly intelligent man could assume that, Banning, yes. And I did like you—when you weren't making me angry with all your talk of promises, that is. I didn't want you to go away without me before I understood why I liked you so much. Although," she added, trying to smile, "leaving the lizard behind in a ditch did occur to me."

"Thank you." Banning looked to the balcony once more. "But Henry didn't know about your little friend upstairs, did he? Henry didn't know that you and this same little friend upstairs were planning to use your inheritance to run off together in some infantile plan to see the world. And when I arrived on the scene— and what an unpleasant surprise that must have been!—and you turned your back on Enby, he responded by following you to London. He's blackmailing you, isn't he, Angel? Threatening to tell your guardian that you have attained your majority years ago and had no need of a guardian or your guardian's money? Taking money under false pretenses is a crime, you know. Yes, I can see by your face that you do know that. And you actually once believed yourself in love with this bastard?"

"But I do love him—*and* you!" Prudence exploded, then subsided against the seat cushions, closing her eyes. "Oh, Banning, I'm so confused!"

She opened her eyes wide as she felt a slight shifting of the carriage and Banning jumped down onto the flagway, obviously preparing to go up the outside stairs of the Spread Eagle, break down the door to room three, and beat the perfidious Enby into a jelly.

"Banning, wait!" she cried, oblivious to the small audience of interested travelers who, while awaiting their coaches, had been watching the two exquisitely dressed Mayfair creatures alternately kissing and arguing in this most unusual setting for such goings-on. "Oh, Banning, wait, damn you! Don't go up there!"

"She swore, George," a rather plump matron said, poking her stick-thin husband. "Did you hear that? She said 'damn.' I heard her quite clearly. I thought the Quality were above such things."

"Turn away, Clarice. You don't want to look," her husband said sternly, as he watched Prudence lift her skirts nearly to her knees as she bounded out of the carriage without the groom's assistance and headed for the stairs.

"Banning!" Prudence called out again, following where her angry husband led, knowing she couldn't catch up with him in time to explain.

And she was right.

She had just reached the top of the steps when Banning kicked in the door to Room Three. And she was only skidding to a halt, breathing heavily, in front of that opened door as Banning was picking up the occupant of that room, holding him a full three inches off the ground by the simple expedient of grabbing the man's neck cloth in one hand, while he drew back his fist, ready to plow it into the man's face.

"Banning!" she cried. "Don't!"

"Daventry? Oh God—I'm a dead man."

"MacAfee? Christ on a crutch! *MacAfee!*"

Prudence winced and turned away as Banning's right fist collided with her brother's heavily whiskered face, not looking back until she heard the crash of his body as it made rude contact with the wooden floor.

"Good," she said succinctly, turning for the stairs. "I think he deserved that, actually. Banning—I'll be waiting in the carriage. Take me to Newgate or take me home. It's entirely your decision."

Banning was still rubbing at his sore right hand as the carriage rolled through the streets of London, his widely grinning wife beside him, humming a little tune easily recognized as one of the more bawdy ditties spawned by Wellington's defeat of Napoleon.

"Happy, puss?"

"In alt, my lord," Prudence responded, reaching up

to kiss his cheek. "You are, as Enby said, a most reasonable gentleman. At least that's what I think he said. Do you think he looks dashing, minus his front tooth?"

"I think he looks lucky—lucky I didn't kill him, or turn him over to—" He hesitated, frowning. "You know, with the war over nearly a year, and half the survivors of Waterloo already mustered out of the army, I'm not quite sure who I would have turned him over to, or if anyone would really care to have him."

"He didn't desert, you know," Prudence reminded him, for Henry was her brother, and no matter how he had complicated her life, she did love him. "He fought like a demon, only leaving the field when he ran out of Frenchmen to kill."

"And then went off to see the world, using the money he'd saved, leaving his sister safe, or so he thought, in the hands of the guardian he had picked for her. He had enough money for one, but not for two, and couldn't face another return to MacAfee Farm. I don't know why I didn't guess, didn't figure it all out earlier."

"You didn't know how old I was, for one thing," Prudence reminded him, feeling sure that the day would come, years and years from now, as he dandled his grandchildren on his knee, when her beloved husband would tell the story of this day in a vastly different way, taking all credit for his brilliant deductions. "And you couldn't know that Enby was my pet name for Henry, when I was too young to get my tongue around *Henry.* Otherwise, you would have known at once."

"You have all the cunning ways of a first rate bootlicker, my darling, but you can't lie worth a damn. Neither knowing that you were old as Methuselah or that Enby was nothing but a childish garbling of Henry would have told me a thing. But he's your brother and you love him," Banning said, lifting her hand to his lips and placing a kiss in her palm. "Which is the only reason I didn't knock *all* his teeth out of his head. If it hadn't been for your brother's mad scheme, I would never have met you."

"And now, thanks to your promise of a generous allowance, Henry is off on his adventures again, to India of all places. He does have the wanderlust, doesn't he? Do you think he'll ever be back?" Prudence blinked rapidly, fighting the tears she thought she had left behind her, at the Spread Eagle, as she had kissed her brother goodbye.

"Oh, never worry your head about that, Angel," Banning told her. "Bad pennies always find their way home again. As a matter of fact, while you were sulking in the carriage, and I was helping your brother locate his tooth, he mentioned something about a tale of amnesia, and local peasants, and a year spent traveling through Europe, trying to locate himself. More than a few slates off your beloved brother's roof, I believe, but I also believe it's part of his charm. Oh yes, Angel, Henry will be back."

Prudence laughed, her heart lighter than it had been in many a long day. "Banning? Do you suppose we could take a drive through the Park anyway, just a single loop for the Promenade? David says this is his absolute favorite of all my day gowns, and that all the ladies of the *ton* weep millstones when they see me in it, which brings him all sorts of new custom."

Banning leaned forward, giving instructions to the coachman, then sat back, lifting his chin as he said,

"We will stare all of London into insignificance, my love, and next week we shall give a ball, introducing my wife to all those fortunate enough to receive an invitation. Those excluded—the Broughton among them—will stand outside our door, weeping and gnashing their teeth. Now, how does that sound?"

"It sounds a quite reasonable course of action, my lord," Prudence told him as she cast her gaze over the crowded Park, "for a sober, responsible, upstanding gentleman as your—*oh Lord! Shadwell!*"

Prudence could feel her face paling as the open carriage approached from the opposite direction, the lizard conspicuous only by her absence and already replaced by a mousy-looking woman of indeterminate years who sat beside the Broughton—and Shadwell MacAfee, dressed in a rusty-looking suit of clothes twenty-five years past their highest fashion, gaily waving to his granddaughter from the facing seat.

"Look-ee, look-ee, Miss Brown-town," Shadwell was crying out loudly, his mouth opened wide in his maggoty face. "It's m'son's smallest grub—Prudence. You said we'd see her, and here she is, right and tight. And I've just claimed her as belonging to me, right here, in public, for everyone to see and hear. That's two hundred quid you owe me."

The two carriages halted abreast of each other, so that Prudence could see the Broughton clearly, and she smiled slightly as she noticed that the young lady was looking almost green as she held a scented handkerchief to her nostrils, as if such a paltry thing could keep away the scent of Prudence's dirt-bathing grandfather.

The lizard might be gone, but she had spread her poison well, and Althea Broughton had used the information garnered from Miss Prentice in order to humiliate Banning and his new bride. It was amazing, the lengths a jilted woman could travel to get a little of her own back.

Prudence looked to Shadwell again, shivering slightly as he smiled widely, exposing the fact that he now numbered his remaining teeth at two. "Not dead yet, Shadwell?" she asked pleasantly. "Did you bring Hatcher with you, or is he too busy digging you a new dirt bath? I'm going to see you buried in that damn bath, you know, standing upside down—and with your toes sticking out—seeing as how the hole is already there."

"Miss Broughton? Do you suppose we could move on?" the mousy little companion asked quietly. "The breeze is blowing toward us as we are situated, you understand, and I believe I might be unwell if we do not move on in the next few moments, which I most assuredly do not wish to be."

"Silence, Mrs. Geddings," the Broughton ordered, leaning forward and to her left, the better to see her one-time fiancé, Prudence supposed. "You've been so silent, Banning. Aren't you going to thank me for bringing Mr. MacAfee to town to help celebrate your nuptials? I've been driving him about all the day long, introducing him to everyone, simply *everyone*. He's causing quite a stir here in Mayfair, aren't you, Mr. MacAfee?"

"It's been all right, I suppose," Shadwell said, scratching at an itch dangerously close to his crotch. "But I'll be wanting my purge in an hour or so, so you'd better take me back to Grosvenor Square. I fancy a spot in your papa's gardens, just below my bedchamber window. Spied it out this morning, and it should suit just fine. Like to purge in the out-of-doors, you know."

Prudence looked to Banning, realizing that he hadn't spoken because he was entirely occupied in trying not to laugh out loud, which pleased her mightily, for another man might have been upset. No, another man might have been livid! But not her Banning. Oh no. She had married a sober, responsible man—with just enough of the devil in him to keep things interesting.

"So, MacAfee," he said at last, his voice sounding only faintly choked as tears of hilarity shone in his eyes, "you're enjoying yourself, then? Good, good. Have yourself a nice long stay in Grosvenor Square, why don't you? Pity we won't be here to squire you about, but Miss 'Brown-town' will see to your entertainment, won't you, Althea? And you'll be mightily entertained in return, I have no doubt."

"Payin' me for two weeks—a whole fortnight," Shadwell crowed, coughing and then spitting into his hand, examining what had been deposited there, and then wiping his palm on his already grimy neck cloth. "Couldn't budge me from Grosvenor Square with a pitchfork, not for the blunt she's paying."

Now Prudence was giggling, her active imagination conjuring up the unlikely vision of her grandfather and the Broughton being joined at the hip for a fortnight. Shadwell would most probably be "pitchforked" out of Grosvenor Square by sundown —his pockets considerably heavier than when he came to London.

"Won't—won't be here?" Althea asked, momentarily lowering the handkerchief, then quickly raising it into place once more. "Why, Banning, whatever do you mean?"

"Well," he answered, winking at Prudence, "we were going to host a ball next week but now that I've had a chance to think on it, I believe we'll take ourselves off on a trip. Yes, a trip. To Vienna. Or to Paris. Lovely to see you, Althea, and thank you again for playing hostess to Shadwell. You deserve each other. Coachman! Drive on!"

"Paris, Banning?" Prudence asked as her husband, defying all of Society, began to draw her into his embrace, his smiling mouth already only a few scandalous inches from hers. "Really?"

"Hmm, I suppose, Angel. Or Philadelphia," he answered, closing the gap.

HEAVEN-SENT

No cord nor cable can so forcibly draw,
or hold so fast, as love
can do with a twined thread.

Robert Burton

*To enlarge or illustrate this power and effect
of love is to set a candle in the sun.*

Robert Burton

"Do you like it?" Prudence asked, playfully twirling around in a full circle, holding the sheer fabric of the sari's skirt away from her long legs with one hand as she drew a transparent scarf over the lower half of her face, only her dancing, seductive eyes visible as Banning lay on the bed, admiring the "scenery."

"As gifts go, minx, I believe Henry has made a sterling choice," he said, marveling at the way the soft, light-green material covered as well as exposed his wife's considerable charms. "Now, if you were to kill me with pleasure tonight, would you then throw yourself on my funeral pyre in the morning?"

"Happily, my love," Prudence replied, moving to the bed so that she could take hold of one of the sturdy posts with both hands, her body swaying back and forth seductively as she leaned back, her gaze intent on her husband. "Although I shouldn't. Jared would need one of us about, to teach him how to climb trees, change signposts to trick unwary travelers, and filch the occasional chicken from the neighboring estate—all the finer accomplishments of a young lord."

Banning motioned for Prudence to join him on the wide bed, one of his wife's many improvements to Daventry Manor, and the one in which he took the most personal delight. "Then that settles it. You can delight me, but not mortally. We do have an obligation to Jared not to allow his ramshackle godfathers to be the ones in charge of his upbringing. Can you imagine what Dewey would teach him?"

"Yes, as a matter of fact, I believe I can," Prudence answered, becoming slightly tangled in the winding fabric of the sari even as she attempted to wriggle herself free of it. "How to squeeze a penny until it yelped, how to leap to conclusions and make them all sound as if he had tripped up a mountainside and brought them back on stone tablets, and," she ended, laughing, "how to get himself bracketed to a sweet young woman with a gap between her front teeth."

"He's already worried about popping off their as yet nonexistent daughters," Banning said, picking up the end of one length of the sari and, thanks to the imp of mischief that now invaded his brain with pleasing regularity, idly wondering if his beloved wife would spin like a top if he gave it a tug. "And then there's Duke, who could scarcely be counted upon to give Jared lessons in steadiness."

Prudence slipped her hand inside her husband's dressing gown, to begin lightly stroking his bare chest. "We'd have to put all our dependence on Leslie, wouldn't we? Or Henry. Egods, Banning, what an odd assortment of godfathers we have chosen for your heir. Well, that settles it. We will both simply have to live forever."

Banning drew her close, reveling in the sweet air of jasmine coming from her hair. "I believe Freddie and Robert would appreciate it, puss, seeing as how they're fairly well occupied with their own child."

"I do miss them," she said, sighing, "but I agree that Freddie is worlds healthier now that she's living almost exclusively in the country. And, of course, Robert fairly dotes on both her and Emily."

They lay silent for some time, Prudence still stroking Banning's chest, he lost in thoughts of how his world had changed so dramatically, and so much for the better, in the past two years. A wife he adored, a son he treasured, a life of contentment—and just enough excitement—to keep him a happy, happy man.

"Banning?" Prudence asked at last, breaking their mutual silence. "Would it upset you overmuch if we were to have another child? David has written me from London that he has come up with an inspiration—a new design for gowns specially made for 'increasing ladies,' as he so delicately puts it. He believes it would be a great help to his business if I, in my position of one of the 'shining lights of the fashionable world'—again, love, these were his words —were to enter the new season wearing . . ."

"Angel! Are you telling me—?"

"No, my sweet love," she answered, deftly untying the sash of his dressing gown. "I'm asking you. And it would be a delightful way to spend these long winter evenings in the country, don't you think?"

"Delightful," Banning agreed, reaching for her. "Simply delightful . . ."

DEAR READER:

After dealing for so many years with the Regency period and the elegant gentlemen and ladies of the *ton*, I've been asked by many why I've decided to uproot a few similarly sophisticated English creatures and plunk them down in 1763 Pennsylvania. I want to tell you why.

Have you ever ridden along a rural highway and looked deep into a stand of old trees, and thought—just for a moment—that you may have glimpsed a proud Native American silently running through those woods?

I have. Living in Eastern Pennsylvania, once the home of the Lenni Lenape, I probably couldn't avoid it. I grew up playing in the small woods behind my house, digging for arrowheads and imagining myself to be an Indian chief.

Eventually, I grew up, but around me the physical reminders—except for those that were bulldozed to make way for shopping malls—remained, and the memories lingered.

Then, several years ago, I was asked to compile a history of my township, Whitehall, Pennsylvania. That history began with the Lenni Lenape, or Original People, and they fascinated me. The colonists fascinated me. I began to see the Lenape, as well as the *shawanuk*, or White Fathers, who had settled in the area. They wouldn't leave me alone.

Over the years, I began to play the "what if" game all writers play. Slowly, that game became my ruling passion. What if there was this wise Lenape brave . . . and what if he befriended a wealthy, mysterious English gentleman who had not so much emigrated to Pennsylvania as he had fled there . . . and what if that gentleman suddenly found himself saddled with this fiery Irish wife . . .

Thus were born Lokwelend, Dominick Crown, and one Miss Bryna Cassidy . . . and, with them, THIS RULING PASSION.

I hope you enjoy the story.

Kasey Michaels, the award-winning author who has long regaled us with her dazzling portraits of Regency England, now takes us on a journey across the sea—to rugged frontier Pennsylvania in the late 1700s. Kasey Michaels delights us anew when English civility meets early American ardor, and fireworks explode in an unforgettable mix of unbridled emotions.

New Egypt,
Pennsylvania
1763

"Where is she?"

Dominick Crown had addressed this question to Alice Rudolph. She had entered the inn close on his heels, still slightly starry-eyed because Mr. Crown had actually helped her down from the wagon—treating her like a lady, and not just Truda Rudolph's unwanted cripple. Quick as she could, Alice pointed toward the corner, and a small table occupied by the lone female who had arrived at the inn last night.

Not that she had been dressed like a female when she'd arrived. Oh, no. As Alice had told Mr. Crown when her mama sent her to fetch him this morning, the female had shown up on the mail coach, dressed all in breeches and a heavy redingote, and with a muffler tied high round her mouth like it was still the dead of winter. She had been masquerading as a young lad, that's what she'd been doing —and carrying out her playacting fairly well until she'd heard all Alice's pa, Benjamin, had to tell her.

Then she had screamed, like a mad thing, calling Benjamin a "damned liar" and a few other things Truda Rudolph routinely called her husband but nobody else in New Egypt had ever dared.

The female had cursed Benjamin Rudolph a blue streak, she had—until, of course, he'd cuffed her a good one on the ear with one of his hamlike hands. Then she hadn't said anything at all; not even after Alice's pa had picked her up from the floor, thrown her over his shoulder, and carried her upstairs. He'd dumped her on a bed and then left it to Alice to undress the female's limp body and see that lovely white skin, those perfect legs—so unlike Alice's own—the lush beauty of the long, vibrant copper curls that had tumbled out from beneath the tricorne hat and bag wig that had previously concealed them.

No, Alice had not told Dominick Crown about any of that. And it wasn't as if she had to tell him, either, not now that the female was sitting right in front of him in the prettiest gown Alice had ever seen, her long fiery hair piled all in curls, her back as stiff and straight as a poker as she sipped tea and dared, with those strange, colorless eyes of hers, for any of the men in the common room to so much as blink at her.

"A rose among thorns, wouldn't you say, Alice? I can see that a rescue is very much in order, and I thank you again for apprising me of the situation," Dominick Crown said quietly. Alice nodded furiously, not understanding the half of what the Englishman said, then disappeared into the kitchens before her ma could spy her out and send her there anyway.

Dominick motioned to Benjamin Rudolph, who was in his usual position behind the small wooden bar, wordlessly commanding the man to bring him a pint, then nodded to the half-dozen men who sat all on one side of the tables jammed into the low-ceilinged room, their backs to the fire, having obviously positioned their chairs the better to goggle at the strange female.

"Good morning to you, gentlemen," he said as he removed his dusty hat, uncaring that his one-sided smile told them he had employed the title in jest, and aware that at least two of the men, the Austrians, Traxell and Miller, spoke little English.

"Newton," he then added coldly, giving one particular man, Jonah Newton, a more personal reminder that he knew the tannery owner was only sitting in his chair, watching, rather than pursuing some greater vulgarity because he had been warned that the damnable Dominick Crown was on his way to the inn, and would have the liver and lights of any man who dared approach the young woman.

Then, aware he had put off the inevitable as long as he could, Dominick started across the dirty wood floor. He halted, he sincerely hoped, a good fear-reducing four feet from the table where the young woman waited, her slim white hand holding the chipped handleless cup poised halfway between saucer and mouth.

Good Christ, but she was beautiful! How long had it been since he'd been in the presence of a woman half so refined, one quarter so lovely? It seemed like a lifetime and, in many ways, it was.

"Madam? Dominick Crown, at your service." Flourishing his worn, dusty hat in his right hand, and feeling more than slightly ludicrous, he made the young woman an elegant leg, the sort he had mastered in his youth but not had reason to practice in over six years, since his arrival in this fairly benighted community. "And you are Miss Cassidy, I presume?" he asked as he straightened once more, aware of both his rough clothing and her unsmiling refusal to extend her hand or in any other way return his greeting.

He didn't actually blame her. After all, Alice had found him already out in the fields, and he had pulled on his deerskin jacket, mounted his horse, and headed straightaway for the inn, choosing speed over respectability when told of the Cassidy woman's predicament. Leaving a gently bred female alone in Benjamin Rudolph's common room for any length of time was nothing short of an invitation to disaster, and he hadn't been of a mind to fatigue himself with having to bare-handedly beat anybody into flinders this morning.

The young woman's chin lifted a notch at his greeting, which was quite a remarkable feat, as she already held herself as high as a queen, for all that she was a mere scrap of a thing. When she finally spoke, her voice was cool, and cultured, and entirely devoid of either maidenly awe or mannerly respect. "Yes, Mister Crown. I am Miss Cassidy. Miss Bryna Cassidy. The only question, sir, is how you presumed to know my name, as we have not been formally introduced."

Dominick motioned to the empty chair across from her and, at her slight nod, sat himself down just as Rudolph slammed a mug of ale on the table.

"Pardon my informality, Miss Cassidy. But, as I doubt there is anyone save you and I in this small community who is actually aware of the niceties of social convention, we would have had a long wait for anyone to step forward and do the pretty. But, by way of explanation, Alice Rudolph informed me that you had introduced yourself here yesterday evening as being one Mister Sean Cassidy. I merely took the chance that although you are quite obviously an audacious fibber, you are not an extraordinarily inventive one. Although I would have paid down a goodly sum to have seen you in breeches."

The cup hit the saucer with an audible crack; if it had been constructed of anything less than the most crude pottery it would have shattered into a thousand pieces. Bryna Cassidy leaned forward, her eyes narrowed in fury. "You insufferable dolt! Give me at least a modicum of credit, if you will. Or would you have had me travel here from Philadelphia, alone, without disguising myself in some way? I had thought to fashion a false wart for the end of my nose, but a score of warts and even a rash of running sores wouldn't be enough to dissuade animals like those leering hyenas over there."

Dominick smiled, spreading his hands wide to show that he, at least, was harmless. "I see your point. However, I wouldn't have condoned your traveling unaccompanied at all, Miss Cassidy, especially since you are aware of the less-than-desirable element running rampant here in the colonies. But then I am not in charge of your comings and goings. Now, had I been your father, I would have—"

He frowned, seeing the sudden sorrow in her oddly intriguing eyes, darkly lashed, yet curiously colorless in a way that had first seemed gray, then had flashed a clear light green when she had defended her descent into breeches. "Yes, well, we'll leave that for the moment, shall we? I gather from Alice that you've already learned about the raid?"

She sat back against the rude wood of the chair, her posture still that of a gently bred female, but suddenly appearing so young, so small, so utterly vulnerable, that he gave a slight cough and quickly took a drink of ale, wishing himself out of this conversation, out of this inn, and miles from what looked to be a further complication of his already complicated existence.

"Yes, Mister Crown, I've heard. And in the bluntest of terms. My aunt and uncle, Daniel and Eileen Cassidy, were brutally murdered by savages not three months ago," she said quietly. "My young cousins, Joseph and Michael, are also dead. Hacked to death the same as Uncle Daniel and Aunt Eileen, I believe Mr. Rudolph said."

Her gaze was still steady, although he could see tears shining in her once more pale gray eyes, and her small, firm chin had begun to quiver. He felt instantly protective of her, which immediately made him angry, with her or with himself, he wasn't sure.

"Cousin Bridget," she continued doggedly, "just seventeen, and my dearest friend in all the world, has been taken by those savages, to be raped and abused, yet not you, nor any one of those *gentlemen* over there has so much as lifted a finger to try to rescue her in all these three months. And little Mary Catherine . . ." she hesitated, drawing in a long, shuddering breath. ". . . only five years old—who the innkeeper laughingly called the *dummy*—is with you. You, Mister Crown, the grasping, greedy Englishman who barely hesitated an instant before taking claim to my uncle's beloved farm. History has ever been so, hasn't it? The English seeing anything Irish and assuming it their God-given right to steal it."

"I'm sorry." Dominick winced even as he heard himself mouth those two woefully inadequate words. "Rudolph is an ass, if you'll excuse me for being frank. I wish you could have learned about your family some other way."

Her humorless smile blighted him. "Why? Would it have hurt less then, Mister Crown? I think not. Quick and clean. That's the way to sever an arm; to break a heart. The captain of the *Eagle* took an unconscionable amount of time dithering about with meaningless sympathies and maddening inanities before at last informing me that my father had gotten himself roaring drunk and fallen overboard two nights before we docked in Philadelphia harbor. It took Captain Bishop nearly ten minutes to tell me what I knew in an instant, that I was about to disembark in a strange country, alone, with my only chance for sanity residing in the hope of somehow getting myself to the comfort of my father's brother Daniel."

She picked up her teacup once more, lifting it to her lips and taking a sip before closing her eyes for a moment, then opening them again, to look at him levelly. All the misery in the world was visible in those two eyes, and she seemed to be holding herself so tightly, reining in her emotions with such determination, that if someone were to touch her, Dominick imagined she would shatter into a thousand small, pain-lashed pieces. "Thanks to Mister Rudolph's bluntness," she ended quietly as she put down the teacup, "it took less than an instant to know that, with Uncle Daniel also gone, I am now even more alone than before. And I can assure you, sir, I hurt none the more or the less for Mister Rudolph's quick telling."

"Christ," Dominick swore quietly, turning in his chair to glance over at Jonah Newton and the others, all of them still sitting there, grinning and staring, like bettors waiting for the cockfight to commence.

"Look, Miss Cassidy," he said, rising and holding out a hand to her. "If you don't mind, I think it might be best to continue this conversation at my estate. I give you my pledge as an English gentleman that you will be safe there. I'll see that Rudolph loads your luggage into the wagon, and I can tie my horse to the back. One of my staff will return the wagon later, not that I'm overly concerned on that head. At least then you can see Mary Catherine, and she can see you. Who knows, she might even talk to you."

Bryna looked at his hand for long moments, then placed hers in it and stood up, proving that his assessment of her size was correct, for she measured no taller than his shoulder. "My bags are already packed, Mister Crown, and waiting, as I should like above all things to go to my baby cousin, Mary Catherine. And then, Mister Crown, we will discuss mounting a rescue. Or did you think I would leave the baby and Bridget here with these barbarians when I return to England?"

Dominick Crown wasn't all *that* huge. Tall, yes. Obviously strong. But not the total savage he had appeared to be when first he had entered the inn, raised his head after navigating his way beneath the low lintel, and skewered her with a single look.

He had still reminded her of an all-powerful giant as he'd crossed the room toward her, dressed so outlandishly, almost barbarously, in tan ankle-length leggings gartered just below the knee. A ridiculous double-collared and fringed jacket, which looked as if it had been fashioned with a knife, was cinched at his waist by a multicolored sash, thus nearly concealing the pale blue and quite dirty homespun shirt that showed dark with sweat. He wasn't even wearing boots, but a sort of slipper made of some soft leather.

She had seen drawings of such attire in books she had read about the colonies before ever leaving Ireland, and knew Mister Crown's ensemble to be constructed from the hides of some animal or other. Perhaps that of a deer? Yes. His clothing *was* barbarous.

But not nearly so barbarous as the man himself. His long midnight black unpowdered hair was tied at his nape with a thin strip of leather, a crude device that had not proved sufficient to keep several locks from escaping to hang down straight on either side of his deeply tanned, rather hand-somely chiseled face. His eyes were just as black beneath straight, slashing brows, and although they seemed to laugh as he spoke, they revealed nothing of the man she now sat beside on the rough plank seat of the Rudolph wagon.

A man who seemed infinitely well suited physically to play the savage, that was Mister Dominick Crown, for all his courtly bows and cultured English speech.

And if it hadn't been for that cultured English speech, and his promise to take her to Mary Catherine, Bryna would have declined his invitation, not that the idea of remaining at the inn seemed any less dangerous than making her way, alone, through an endless forest that was probably knee-deep in bloodthirsty Indians.

Why had Uncle Daniel come here? Yes, life had been hard in Ireland, but surely not so terrible that he could have considered this desolate wilderness a near "paradise," as he had written in his letters to her father. And now this "paradise" had taken not only Uncle Daniel's dreams, but his very life—and the lives of his beloved family.

And for what? *For what?*

If this primitive wilderness was the "freedom" Uncle Daniel had spoken of, the "opportunity" he had chased with as much enthusiasm as her father pursued a winning streak at cards—well, she was having none of it! Her malleable English mother had followed wherever Bryna's loving but feckless father had led. Aunt Eileen and the children had followed where Uncle Daniel led.

But Bryna Cassidy had suffered enough at the whim of men and their dreams. From this day forward, she would direct her own steps, follow her own path—from the very moment she had Bridget and Mary Catherine safely in hand and they could board ship in Philadelphia, leaving this tragic land and its horrible memories behind them forever!

"I abhor this country," Bryna said feelingly as one of the wagon's wheels found an unusually deep rut in the dirt road and she was nearly pitched from the seat.

Dominick Crown turned his head and smiled at her, showing her both his straight white teeth and the small lines that appeared next to his eyes, making him look less a savage and more approachable—if she were idiot enough to be taken in by straight white teeth and laughing eyes. She might be her mother's daughter in many ways, but she was not the sort to trust her destiny in a handsome face.

"Abhor it, do you? Which, of course, Miss Cassidy, entirely explains your presence in it," he responded after a long moment in which she glared at him in what she knew to be real hatred directed toward both him in particular and at the male of the species in general. Either unaware or unimpressed by her purposeful disdain, he then once more turned his attention to the horses, who were showing a marked tendency to drift toward the side of the roadway, where clumps of tender spring grass seemed to wave an invitation to them.

"I was never to reside anywhere save the relatively civilized confines of Philadelphia, Mister Crown," Bryna informed him flatly, wishing she didn't feel compelled to explain herself, her chin quivering only slightly as she remembered her father's promises, her father's unrealistic dreams and schemes, all of which centered on either the throw of the dice or the turn of a card.

"Papa had suffered a few slight reverses of fortune in London during the past years, since my mother's death," she continued, not believing it a sin to lie in order to protect her father's memory. "Business reversals—unwise investments—you understand. In the end, we were forced to accept Uncle Daniel's kind offer that we reside in his home in Ireland, both before and after Uncle Daniel's family departed for the colonies last year. We remained in residence there until such time as we could sell the property and bring the proceeds here, where my uncle was to use them to patent the land he had claimed under warrant from . . . from—"

"From Thomas Penn, no doubt," Dominick said, "son of William, and the most rascally, pernicious piece of mischief to have ever mastered the bending of laws to the benefit of his own deep pockets. He has a long legacy of deceit and dishonor in dealing with the Lenni Lenape, the Indians native to this land, and the Lenni Lenape, sadly, have equally long memories."

"The savages who murdered my family, you mean? You will, of course, excuse me if I do not find it necessary to demonstrate any sympathy toward them," Bryna said, looking off into the forest to both her right and left, once more nervously aware that the trees were so dense, the underbrush so thick, that it would be impossible to see a band of attacking Indians until they were on top of the wagon. "You see, I doubt anything this Mister Thomas Penn could have done warrants the slaughter of innocent women and children."

Dominick smiled again, the action carving slashing lines into his thin, chiseled cheeks. She really did loathe his smile, which said without words that his knowledge of the history of this area was far superior to her own. "Remind me to tell you of a little ruse of more than five and twenty years ago called the Walking Purchase, Miss Cassidy, the consequences of which, in large part, led to the massacre of your family. Then you will be more able to judge the depth of Thomas Penn's perfidious nature."

"Yet you are also a landowner, so obviously you deigned to deal with the man?"

He shrugged. "I wanted land, and the Penns were selling.

Thomas is back in England these many years, old and fat and happy, I presume, and counting his money. I dealt with John Penn, a thankfully fairer man than Thomas, when I patented my own land five years ago, and again when I patented your uncle's land. Your uncle's, and that of two other properties adjoining mine and, as a result of the recent raids, suddenly without tenants."

"I see." Bryna's heart was pounding hurtfully in her chest, and her lips were stiff, so that she could barely force out her words. "How fortuitous for you, sir, that so many should die."

He was no longer smiling, and Bryna knew she had gone too far. "Yes, indeed, Miss Cassidy," he said shortly. "I took advantage of what could only be called a tragedy, knowing that my own property was spared an attack because I'd had the foresight to build myself a nearly impenetrable fortress, extending the hand of friendship to the natives here while prudently arming myself as well."

"And prudent as well, you say? I vow, sir, I grow more impressed by the moment." Bryna shivered, so intense was her hatred for this man that her blood ran cold.

"Please, Miss Cassidy. I suggest we cry friends for now, as what's done is done, and there is no recourse save to accept it. Now, as to what we have been discussing—well, I have developed an attachment to my scalp, nothing more. I am a colonist like all the others who have come here, perhaps better off financially, with the desire to grow an estate, a dynasty, here in this country. And the land in New Egypt is good, the whole of it. Your uncle's in particular. Daniel was a hard worker, and more than half the acreage is already clear and ready for planting. He'd hadn't had time to build a house, but the barn they built and lived in with their animals is still standing much as it was, if you want to see it."

"You'd agree to take me there?" Bryna asked, wondering why she was still sitting so still in the wagon, her hands folded in her lap, when all she really wanted to do was turn on this arrogant, boastful man and draw her fingernails down his cheeks, scarring him for life with the evidence of her disgust.

Perhaps she was simply too hungry to marshal the energy to do more than snipe at him. She had been conserving her small store of funds as best she could, and that had meant her meals for the past few days had been both scanty and rare. The cup of tea she'd had at Rudolph's was all the nourishment she'd allowed herself in the past four and twenty hours. Her head pounded as a result of weeping most of the night, and it was all she could do not to lean against Dominick Crown's deerskin-clad shoulder and beg him for a hot meal and a soft bed.

"Mister Crown? You haven't answered me. Will you take me to visit the graves?"

"All right. Tomorrow, perhaps. The Indians would have set fire to the barn, you know, but the troops stationed at Fort Deshler had rallied the local militia. They came out in force after seeing the smoke from the O'Reilly homestead, and probably frightened them off, thank God, or else Mary would have perished in the fire. As it was, I didn't discover her until the following day—tucked up under her parents' bed, where Eileen must have placed her—wide-eyed and silent as a mummy. Which, unfortunately, she remains. I don't take pleasure in telling you any of this, but as you said it would be no easier for you to hear bad news slowly, I thought it best we get the worst of it over quickly, and before you meet with your cousin."

Oh, God, oh, God! Oh, sweet Jesus! Would he never shut up? With her gentle English mother four years in her grave, with her father's hot-blooded Irish temper springing to the forefront, and with her stomach crying out to be fed, Bryna at last turned to the man, knowing her sharp tongue remained her most dangerous weapon, and dropped into an obviously deliberate, broad Irish brogue. "Ack, sich a tale of wild wonder ye tell, sir, with yourself cast as saint and savior and the smartest of men! And is it proud of yourself you are then, Dominick Crown—crowing of your brilliance like a cock on his own dunghill, then hopping so swiftly into a dead man's boots?"

His grin was maddening. "Well, hello! And who would you be, ma'am? I was just now speaking with a most imperious young society miss who learned her prunes and prisms in her cradle, and who fairly reeked of respectability. Would you have any notion where's she flitted off to—leaving in her place a fiery-haired Irish termagant who drips sarcasm and vile accusations exactly as if she weren't alone in a strange land, at the mercy of the man who did nothing more than look to increase his estate? While taking in that proud woman's young cousin, by the bye, which wasn't all that easy a trick, considering the fact that I first had to teach her to keep from biting me each time I came within a yard of her. Would you perhaps care to see my scars?"

"I'd prefer to see the back of you as you walk out of my life," Bryna told him, hating herself for having been so stupid as to show him a side of herself her mother had striven for many a long year to eradicate. She had nothing in this life, nothing save her pride, her dignity. Now she had sacrificed even that for the sake of getting some of her own back on the one man in this terrible country who had offered her anything more than a leering grin or the back of his hand. "However, as I am grateful to you—after a fashion—I hereby apologize for my outburst. It was uncalled-for." Swallowing her pride and anger made for a bitter, unsatisfying meal. Dear Christ, how she hated this man!

Dominick laughed out loud, and she swallowed hard on another sharp retort. "God's teeth, but I'll bet that hurt!" he remarked, still laughing. "Very well, your apology is accepted. And welcome back, Miss Cassidy—although I do believe you'd be wise to keep the fiery Bryna close at hand. She might be useful to frighten off the hyenas whenever you are in the village."

He gave the reins a quick flick, rousing the horses to a trot as he turned them off the dirt track and onto one that was not quite so narrow, and showed the effect of being carefully constructed rather than just carelessly hacked out of the forest. "We'll be at Pleasant Hill in a few minutes, in case you're interested."

"I care only to see my cousin, Mister Crown. Other than that, we could be heading straight into blazes for all I will be impressed by anything you may have had a hand in building."

"Do you wish to know something interesting, Miss Cassidy?" Dominick prompted, just as the horses moved out of the overhanging trees, and she espied a clear sweep of lawn and a softly rising hill topped by a large three-storied Georgian mansion fit for London's finest neighborhood. "I'm beginning to think the wrong Cassidy is mute. Mary Catherine, as I remember her from my visits to Daniel's homestead, had a most melodious voice. You, however, put me in mind of a carping fishwife, and I believe the world could only be improved by your vow of silence."

"Go to hell, Dominick Crown!" Bryna exploded, trying not to show any hint of admiration for the glorious house set here, in the midst of a wilderness.

"I already reside there, Miss Cassidy," he answered smoothly, pointing to his home. "Dubbing it Pleasant Hill is only my faint notion of a joke. And, Miss Bryna Cassidy, if you meant your vow to remain until your cousin Bridget is rescued from the savages who kidnapped her, and unless you harbor a wish to return to the Inn, *you* will be residing here as well. Now, that's a thought to give a person pause, don't you agree?"

Bryna lifted her chin imperiously, not answering, for Dominick Crown had said it all, damn him, and there was nothing else to be said.